Fire Heart

ALSO BY EMMA HAMM

The Otherworld
Heart of the Fae
Veins of Magic
The Faceless Woman
The Raven's Ballad
Bride of the Sea
Curse of the Troll

Of Goblin Kings
Of Goblins and Gold
Of Shadows and Elves
Of Pixies and Spells
Of Werewolves and Curses
Of Fairytales and Magic

Once Upon a Monster
Bleeding Hearts
Binding Moon
Ragged Lungs

and many more...

Fire Heart

Copyright © Emma Hamm 2021

All rights reserved. This book or parts thereof may not be reproduced in any form, stored in any retrieval system, or transmitted in any form by any means—electronic, mechanical, photocopy, recording, or otherwise—without prior written permission of the publisher, except as provided by United States of America copyright law. For permission requests, write to the publisher, at "Attention: Permissions Coordinator," at the address below.

Visit author online at www.emmahamm.com

Cover Design by Trif Book Designs

Interior Design by MIBL Art

This book is a work of fiction. Any references to historical events, real people, or real places are used fictitiously. Other names, characters, places, and events are products of the author's imagination, and any resemblance to actual events or places or persons, living or dead, is entirely coincidental.

For every little girl who was born a Fire Heart. Your difference is your power, and one day, you'll see just how important that power is.

One day at a time, my queen.

HALL OF HER

LU

DRACOMAQUIA

CASTLE OF THE LOST

UMBRAL KE

THE GLOAMIN

SOLIS OCCASUM

Kingdom of Umbra

MALIS

STYGIAN PEAKS

FIELD OF SOMBER

CITY OF TENEBROUS

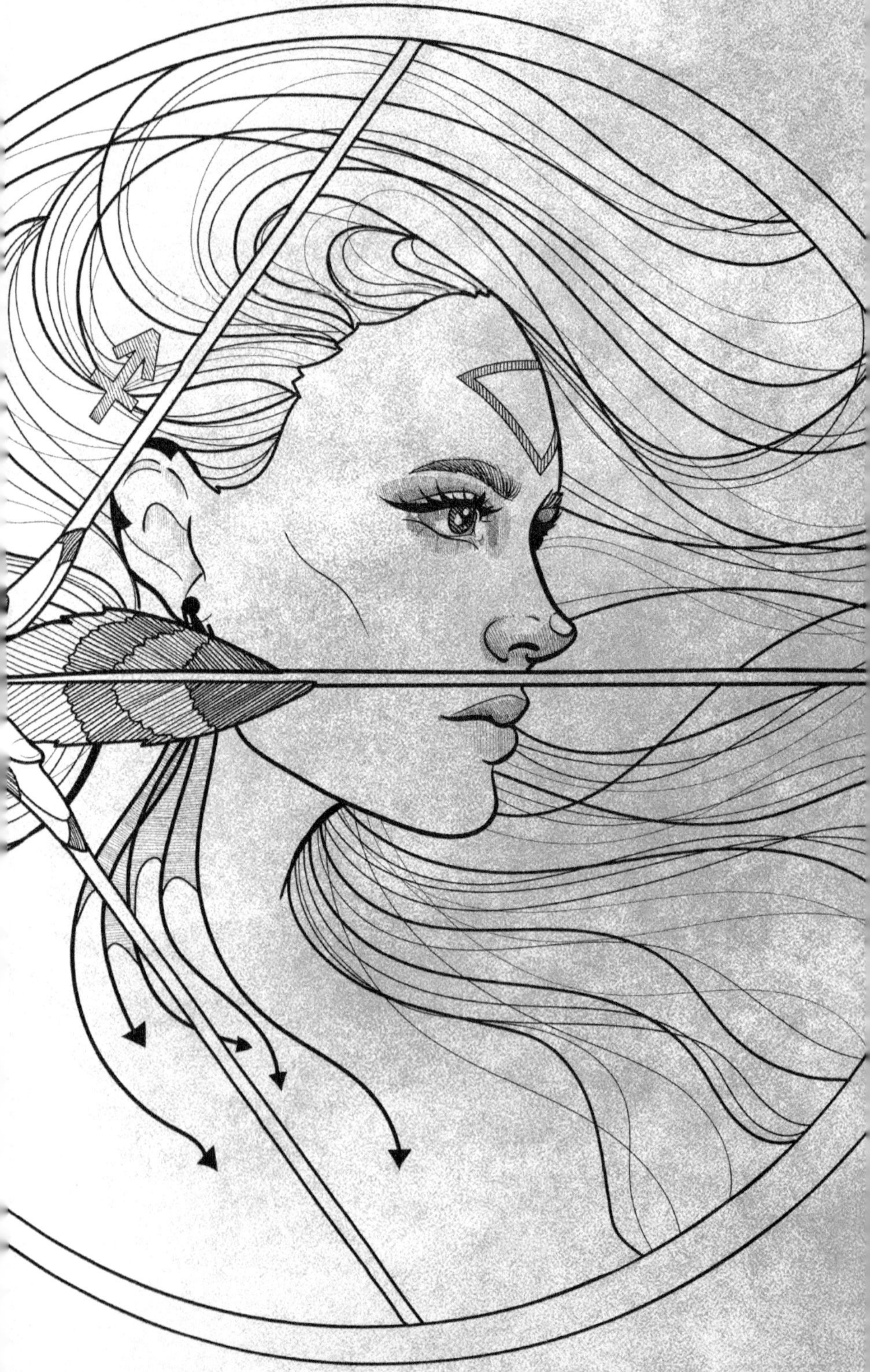

CHAPTER 1

The silhouette of the dragon blotted out the moon. Lorelei's hair shifted in the breeze made by its wings.

She took another heavy drag off the pipe in her hand and watched from the rooftops. If the sun were out, she might fear that the beast would see her. The dragon had little care for who it killed. Innocent or not, the beast would find anyone it could with its breath of fire.

But the moonlight made it hard for the creature to see. It would drift back toward the Umbral Castle, over the countless shingled rooftops where people snuggled in the safety of their beds. Children would whisper at the shadow passing by their windows and pray the creature didn't visit their nightmares.

If they behaved, they would never meet the dragon.

One last buffet of wind pushed down on her shoulders, tangling her pale locks on the sharp points of her ears. Lore reached up to ensure her secret remained hidden. Even in the middle of the night, there were eyes that saw every detail. The last thing she needed was to end up like her mother.

Her leather leggings stuck to her legs after a hard day of work. The billowing white peasant's shirt helped cool her down, though soon it would be too cold. Tapping her boots on the clay shingles, Lore watched as a small shard slipped free and tumbled down to the street below. The shattering sound was the only one at this time of night. No person in their right mind risked being out at night.

"You're crazy, you know that?" The voice flirted with the shadows, emerging from a window across the street.

Lore blew a few smoke rings at the dwarf, who hid in the attic of the house across from her. She could barely see his features this far away, with no light to illuminate his expression. Not that she needed the help.

When she first came to this horrible city, he'd been the first person to greet her. A dwarf about the height of her waist, with a smattering of red throughout his beard and wild hair that tangled in his eyebrows. He was a walking hairball, as she affectionately called him. And if that didn't call enough attention to his presence, then people would always stare at the man who preferred bright colored clothing.

Goliath, the name aptly humorous, had dogged her steps for weeks now. Always it was the same question. She always gave the same answer.

"I don't know why I can't be on my own roof at night," she replied. Lore blew another smoke ring that floated inside the other. "The dragon doesn't care if I want to absorb a little moonlight."

"But the Umbral Knights do." He shivered at the thought of those terrible creatures at the King's beck and call.

FIRE HEART

The City of Tenebrous was far from the Umbral Castle. The personal knights of the King kept everyone here under the King's thumb, though they weren't actual people. Tin soldiers with nothing inside them but a teeming mass of shadows that followed the whims of the King.

Lore knew the icy touch of those Knights. First hand experience, and all that.

Suddenly her elfweed wasn't hitting the right way anymore.

Disappointed, she put her pipe down on the shingles and leaned back on her hands. "Well, if that's the way I go, then that's the way I go."

"You know, you could join me and the others."

"The others and I," she corrected. Her training whispered in her mind that she was giving too much away. She should be like the others in Tenebrous. No schooling, no book learning to speak of, but talented when it came to keeping herself alive on the streets.

"Right." Goliath leaned out his window so she could see his face. "We've got a better way to go about it all, you know. We want to see the King dead but we don't want to lose anyone else in the process."

We. It was always we with him. "You're talking about a war."

"We're talking about a rebellion. A rising against the tyrant and taking our kingdom back." He thumped his fist against the window frame. "Considering all that your mother gave up, I thought you'd be more interested in helping."

Anger flared bright and hot in her chest. "Don't talk about my mother."

"And your father?"

Still working with the rebellion, she'd imagine. Or perhaps he'd gone back to the country they came from. Those elven lands where so many had given up their lives just so they could keep the Umbral King from their borders.

Too many people had given up everything they held dear so their descendents could cling to normalcy. So many deaths. And here she was, in the poorest city, trying to make ends meet by growing and selling elfweed in her basement.

They'd really given up their lives for a winner, obviously. Just look at her. Hiding her ears like she was ashamed of being an elf. Wearing scratchy wool clothing because the mist in Tenebrous never cleared to show the sun.

Lore shook her head. "I have no interest in making the same mistakes as my family, Goliath. I know my place."

"And that's at the bottom of the food chain, begging for scraps?" He spat, the wad of liquid hurtling down to the street four stories below them. "You are an elf. You hold all the magic of the moon at your fingertips and you want me to believe that the humans are stronger than us? I refuse."

"It's not about power or strength, it's about numbers." And there were too many of them. She had once thought her mother was right, all those years ago. She'd thought the rebellion could actually do something about this horrible life they all led. Once upon a time.

Then Lorelei grew up. She'd seen the world for herself and realized that while her mother had heart, she was nothing but a dreamer. Dreams didn't put food on the table, and they sure didn't raise a daughter after one's death.

Goliath sighed. "You don't want to even listen to what I have to say?"

"Not really." She already knew what he was going to say.

The rebellion always claimed the same things. The King wasn't an immortal, and he wasn't even magical. If they banded together, put their magic together, then they stood a chance.

FIRE HEART

What they forgot was that there was an army filled with soldier's the King could infinitely create. An army of creatures that weren't human underneath all that steel and iron. Not to mention there was a giant dragon that flew above the city every single day, reminding them all who controlled the kingdom.

She might be an elf. And yes, there might be a little moon magic left inside her. But that didn't mean she was equipped to battle a damn dragon. There was a reason those creatures used to have their own kingdom.

"Your mother wouldn't want you to sit on the sidelines," Goliath said. The wind brushed through the tangled red locks of his hair. "She would want you to fight, just like she did. She'd want you to prove yourself to be the daughter she raised."

"She'd want me to give my life for a cause that sees me as a pawn, not a person. That's what she would want." Lore didn't like to think of her mother, though.

Frantically, she grabbed at the elfweed and inhaled the smoke that should clear her mind from the memories that threatened to swallow her up. But she wasn't fast enough. She was never fast enough to battle back the memory of her mother's death.

She remembered the pyre the Umbral Knights had built. Larger than a building, they strapped all the offending rebellion leaders to large logs and laid them around the bonfire as if they were nothing more than kindling. She remembered her mother's eyes, wide with fear, as she screamed for Lorelei to run.

A Knight held Lore's shoulder with a grip that she couldn't wiggle out of. The steel bit into her shoulders until she felt blood run down her chest. She'd cried, but of course she had. She had only been eight years old.

And then the dragon. She remembered the damned beast that roared and made the very air shake with its hunger.

The dragon had landed on the ground so hard that she swore he made the earth wobble with his weight. He was larger than three buildings, too big for her little mind to fathom. He'd looked at her, his eye almost as large as a horse. She would never forget the membrane that slicked over the yellow orb of his eye before he turned his attention to her mother.

Heat literally glowed through the barrel of the dragon's chest. He had reared back and Lore watched as fire burned up his throat all the way to his mouth. It tore through his neck and the dragon let it all out in one massive eruption.

The flames had devoured her mother too quickly. One moment, the beautiful elf had glared defiantly at the creature who was her doom. And the next, her mother was nothing more than ash. Her body had mixed with that of the bonfire and the wood behind her. Nothing remained for Lore to collect.

A memory like that couldn't float away on the smoke of elfweed.

She let the vapor trail from her lips to her nostrils. Perhaps the haunted memories showed in her expression, or maybe Goliath could see the thoughts in her eyes. Either way, when she looked back at the dwarf, all his anger had leaked out of him. A crack in the armor.

"Lore," he said, quiet this time. So quiet she could barely hear his words. "You can't give up like this."

"I'm not giving up. I'm living my life." She refilled her lungs with the smog of the city rather than the elfweed, though. "I don't want to die like she did, Goliath. And if that means I have to keep my head down and pretend the past doesn't exist, then that's exactly what I'm going to do."

"All I'm asking for is an afternoon of your time." He braced his forearm on the windowsill and his beard split in half to reveal a bright grin. "There's free food and drink for you if you come."

No. She wouldn't be tempted by a full belly, no matter how bad her entire body clenched at the thought. When was the last time she'd stuffed herself?

Too long. Food was scarce in Tenebrous during a good year, considering most of the farmers outside of the city were entrenched in the swamp. It wasn't like Lore had a lot of money. She did what she could for people who were willing to pay for forbidden charms. Most of the time, her money came from odd jobs here and there.

But a full belly...

"Ah," Goliath said, pointing at her with a stubby finger. "You're thinking about it! I can tell."

"I will not meet with your people and shout 'Let the sun rise'." She sighed, remembering the words that had filled her little head with so many happy dreams. Her mother had promised the phrase would bring about a new age. That Lore would see a new sun on the horizon and that would be the day when she knew the magical creatures were free.

She shook her head. That was the worst kind of gift her mother had given her. Hope. Hope for a time that would never come to pass.

Goliath shrugged. "I don't care if you shout it. I just care that you believe it. Come and see all of us, Lore. We miss you."

The word 'no' pressed against her teeth, but at that moment, the dragon wheeled back around. She saw his wings shift and move. He glided through the air, so far away that his movements were silent. But apparently the beast wanted the entire city of Tenebrous to remember he'd be back in the morning.

A long, drawn out roar clapped like thunder in the distance. It rolled through the air, slamming windows shut and blasting over Lore with such force that the sound snuffed out the faint glow at the end of her pipe.

That sound. It haunted her dreams and every waking moment. The beast knew he held them all underneath his claws, but still he tormented them.

Somewhere down the street, a child started crying. Lore heard the poor thing's mother hush at it, trying so hard to not let the Umbral Knights think they were disturbing the peace. A child like that shouldn't fear a monster that flew over its city every night. Children feared imagined monsters underneath the bed that their fathers could battle. Not actual beasts that could kill them.

Or had killed some of their family while the children watched.

Another tap came from across the street. Goliath pointed toward the sound when she looked at him. "You won't come and meet with us just in hopes we might get rid of that thing?"

Lore reached into her pocket for a match. "You and the rebellion have really lost your mind if you think you can kill a dragon."

"Maybe we have." Goliath nodded, then grinned brightly in the shadows. "But you still want to hear what we have to say."

She lit the match, and the flare illuminated her small hideaway on the roof. Lore took her time setting the elfweed ablaze once more, even puffing at the pipe until the smoke surrounded her like a cloud. "Maybe," she replied. "Promising revenge on the scaly bastard certainly has its appeal."

"So we'll see you tomorrow night, then?"

"Don't get your hopes up." She blew a ring of smoke out of her screen of white cloud. The ring danced through the air and struck Goliath square in the face. "Sleep well, little man."

"Good night, Lorelei."

He shut the window with a solid thud, and that was when Lore saw the painting. A bright yellow sun rising through a bank of clouds, the sunset red as blood.

She snorted. The dwarf had better run if he left that painting on the window. The Umbral Knights would take one look at it and ransack the entire place, thinking they'd found a rebellion leader.

Goliath was smart, though. He hadn't survived this long without having a few tricks up his sleeve. He'd run off into the shadows and give the Knights something to do while he and his people plotted.

Schemed.

She blew another ring of smoke into the air. But for the first time in a long time, she couldn't get the image of the sun out of her head.

"Let the sun rise," she muttered.

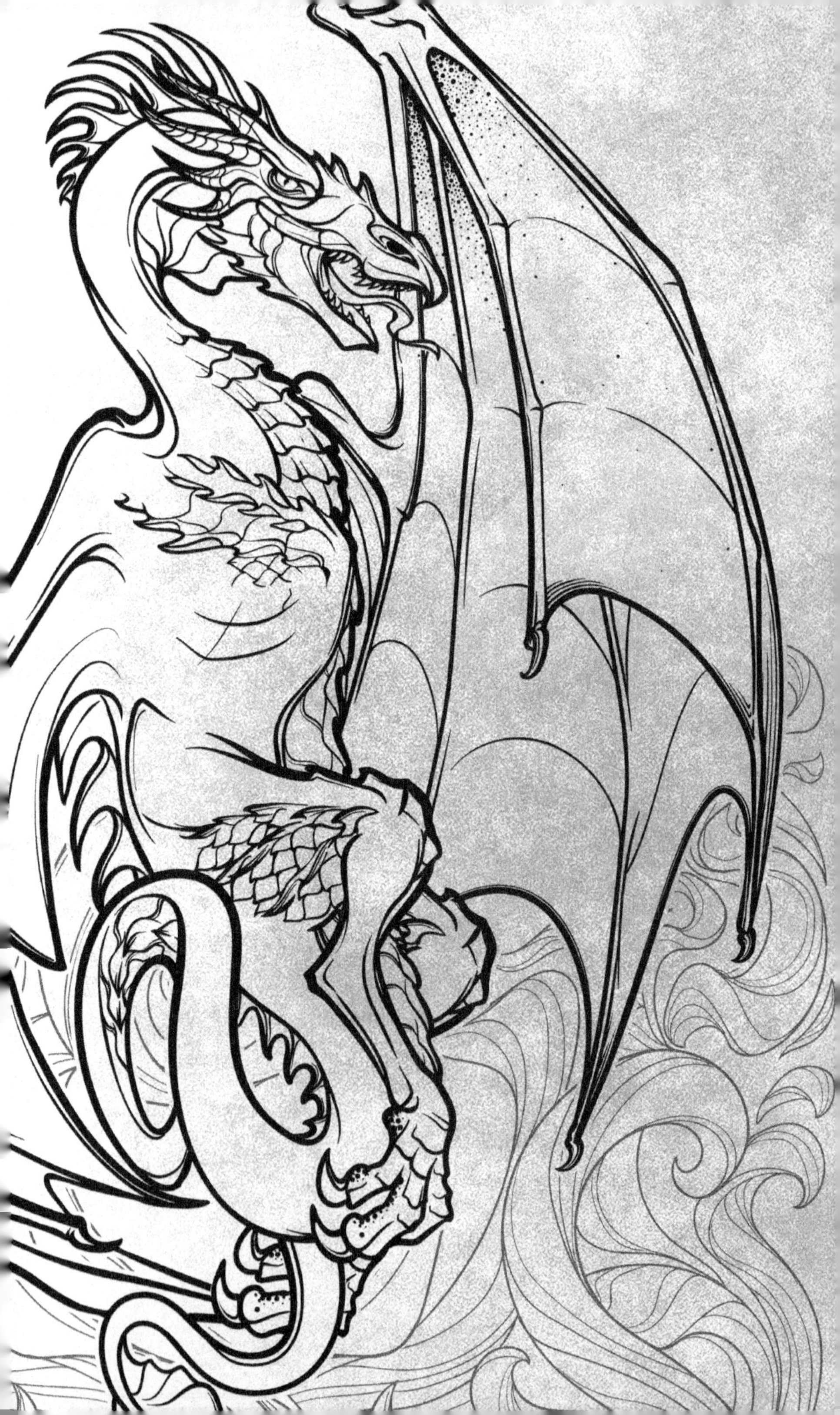

CHAPTER 2

The carriage swayed from side to side until it almost felt like he was at sea. He hated being at sea.

Gaze slanting to the right, he tried to focus on the mountains moving past the carriage, but that didn't help. He couldn't focus on anything other than the rolling of his stomach. Was that his breakfast pressing against the back of his throat? Had he eaten something poisonous, and it was just now coming to light?

"Abraxas?"

Yes, that was his name, but he didn't have the energy to listen to anyone right now. What had he done last night? He couldn't quite remember, and maybe that was the alcohol. He had gotten drunker than he'd thought he could. That was definitely part of the problem right now.

"Abraxas!" The voice whipped through the air, cracking against his skull until he moaned.

"What?" he asked. "What is it now?"

"You're supposed to be listening to me. Are you incapable of doing your job today, or are you going to pay attention to your king?"

Right. The King. The duty. All that ridiculous nonsense that he'd drowned in for years.

Abraxas rolled his head on the plush cushion and focused on the interior of the carriage. The entire inside was drenched in gold, just like the outside. He knew for a fact that the carriage itself was not dipped in metal, nor was it made of the precious ore. He'd broken one and seen the wooden frame within. But the villagers outside would think their king rode past in a solid gold carriage. And their opinion of the King's wealth was what mattered.

The brightly colored cushions made his head ache. The color was too much, really. And the tiny chandelier hanging right above their heads? If Abraxas straightened in his seat, he'd get bonked in the eye with a small crystal every time the carriage shifted.

Like it currently swayed in tune with his heartbeat, and that was going to make him vomit all over the King if he wasn't careful.

"I am listening," he grumbled. "But you might as well say it again. Just to make sure I got it right."

The King pursed his lips and looked every inch the disappointed noble. Fine. Abraxas didn't care.

After all, they had a strange relationship. The King would not kill him any time soon, and he would not do what the King wanted any time soon. They would both have to suffer in this strange battle for a while longer.

But it wasn't fair that the King looked so healthy this morning. They had drank together last night, and Abraxas was certain the man had put away the same amount of alcohol.

The Umbral King, known as Zander to his closest friends, never had a single hair out of place. His handsome features were perhaps a little too symmetrical, but striking. His sharp jaw and slightly upturned nose were disarming to most women. And the female kind thought the wings of grey hair at each temple were swoon worthy. They frequently fell in front of the King, hoping they would capture his attention.

They did. Anyone who wanted a night with the King would have one, and they were usually brought to the King's private rooms by Abraxas himself. But no woman should assume they would be the only woman in the King's bed that night.

Today, Zander wore his brightest red suit with gold trim. Why? Abraxas couldn't remember.

"We're going to Tenebrous. Apparently the council there has found more information on the rebellion, and we both need to look the part." Zander straightened his shoulders and made a face. "Do I look like I'm appropriately disappointed in the people who should protect my kingdom?"

The narrowed eyes and pursed lips looked more like Zander was trying to woo a woman. Or maybe like he was constipated?

Abraxas wrinkled his forehead and took a deep, steadying breath. "I'm not sure what you want me to say."

"Well, damn it, you're my personal guard! The only person standing between me and certain death at all times!" Zander threw his hands in the air. "Do I look intimidating or not, man?"

"Not." Abraxas normally would have schooled his tone at the very least, but he felt unwell.

He hated riding in carriages. He needed to be out in the fresh air, otherwise he always got sick like this and he could only blame the King for putting him in this situation.

Because, yes, he was the King's right-hand man. Abraxas was the shadow of the King that so many forgot existed, but he was the one who protected their leader. And he would be the man who jumped in front of any sword, ate any poison, and killed any man who tried to touch the ruler of Umbra.

And yet, he was laid low by the sway of a carriage.

Groaning, he put his forehead back to the cold glass of the window. "If you want to be intimidating, then at least stop with the fuck me eyes."

"I wasn't looking at you with those eyes." Zander paused, the silence between them stretching thin until he added, "I didn't think, at least. Did you feel anything?"

"I have never and will never. I'm not interested in you like that, Zander. Stop asking." Even though Abraxas should be flattered, the comment never failed to force a shiver down his spine.

"You could at least admit it would be a wild night if you would join the ladies and I for an evening." The soft hush of fabric suggested the King had leaned back on his cushioned seat and crossed his arms over his chest. Like a child.

Most of the time, Zander was childish. Abraxas had gotten used to the temper tantrums and the hilarious attempts at being more manly than he actually was. Zander had been raised as a boy king who then turned into a man. And that man had never had a single person deny him anything.

As such, the King had become spoiled. Brattish. Pampered.

But he still made Abraxas smile sometimes. Sure, most of the time he was laughing *at* the King rather than with him, but that had to count for something. It wasn't like Abraxas could get out of this binding contract any time soon.

The cool glass had already worked some of its magic on his rolling stomach. At least with his eyes shut, he didn't have to think about how quickly the land moved on the other side of the door. "Why do you want to be intimidating, anyway? The only people you'll talk to are the Umbral Knights and conversations with them aren't exactly stimulating."

When Zander didn't respond, he glanced over at the King, who was taking an unbelievable amount of time to straighten his sleeves.

Still nothing. What was the man doing?

Abraxas sighed and put his head back on the window. Maybe the conversation was over and he could get some peace while he tried to keep his breakfast in his stomach.

"I think it's interesting that you don't like the Knights."

There it was. Like the King had been told his work wasn't good enough, Zander wanted to know what Abraxas thought of his precious Knights.

"Putting an entire battalion of soldiers made of smoke in charge of a city isn't the best idea." Abraxas swallowed hard, then opened his eyes. "In my opinion, that is. The City of Tenebrous has always been unstable. Too many people here are not fond of your ruling, nor were they fond of your father. They require a firm hand, but not one that is incapable of seeing reason."

"The magician who made them confirmed that the Knights were more than capable of seeing reason." Zander sniffed hard and waved a bejeweled hand at the door. "If you're only going to insult me, then why don't you just join us in the city? You can make your own way."

Abraxas didn't want that. He was the only one who kept the King in line on his better days, and if he wasn't in the carriage with Zander, then the King would likely stop and terrorize some poor family along the way. He didn't want that to happen.

For all that he worked for the corrupt king, he still had a bit of a soul left in him. Zander was horrible if he was left to his own devices. It wasn't like the carriage driver would say no to the King.

"Zander," he scolded, keeping his voice and tone low. "You shouldn't have to make the journey on your own. I understand that I've been in a terrible mood, and that's not the companion you wished to travel with. But I promise you, I'll get over whatever stomach problem is plaguing me and we'll work on your intimidating face."

Like the child he was, Zander lit up. "You mean it?"

"I do."

"Well, why don't you show me your intimidating face, then? I can practice by mirroring you."

That wasn't fair. Abraxas was everything that Zander wasn't.

Where the King was naturally handsome, Abraxas was terrifying. His raven locks were constantly falling in front of his face, which was too aggressive. The word "sharp" had frequently been used to describe what he looked like. Angular. Jagged.

His face was too long, his nose too broken, his brow too strong. And it didn't help that he stood over six and a half feet tall, with broad shoulders that tapered into too lean hips. He didn't look like he belonged at court, and maybe that was because he didn't. Nobles were soft things, like feathers. He was a weapon.

Still, if the King wanted him to make an intimidating expression, then he didn't have a leg to stand on. He couldn't deny the King something so simple.

He bared his teeth in a snarl, brows drawn down and eyes heating with an inner power the King could never have. No matter how many magicians he hired, the King would always be nothing more than a human man.

"Tsk," the King muttered, waving his hand at the window again. "Off with you. I have no patience for your antics today."

Ah well, at least he tried.

Abraxas threw the door open and tossed himself out of the carriage. The change rippled through his body almost immediately. Magic caught at the edges of his frame, tearing flesh from bone while making room for scales and leathery wings. Some people had described his transformation as an explosion. The sound crackled through the field as the carriage rode past, and then a dragon stepped onto the ground as though he had meant to leap from the carriage.

He reared up and spread his wings wide, feeling the last lingering effect of sickness disappear. With a great heave, he tossed his head back and let out a roar that thundered through the air.

Free.

Like this, he was always free.

The wind slid along his wings as though the very element had missed him. He had missed feeling it touch the leathery membranes. Lifting an arm, he looked down at his wing to make sure everything was in place. His overly large hands became claws that held out his front wings, and his back legs stretched as though he'd been cramped for too long.

He hated being in that mortal form. That limiting form. Everyone wanted him to look like that, particularly the King, but he wanted to be free.

Abraxas was meant to fly through the air and take over kingdoms with the merest breath. He was meant to be feared by all who saw him, and mortals should drop to their knees in worship.

That wouldn't happen, of course. No mortal would ever fall to their knees again, even for the last dragon.

With great beats of his wings, he threw his significant weight into the air. He soared through the sky and into the clouds above. Sure, he still had to watch over the King and the caravan that traveled towards Tenebrous. But now he could see the moors for miles. The whisperpines that gave way into the sodden hills, then the swamp lands surrounding the city. He'd notice if anyone approached the King's carriage. He saw everything.

Some thought that a dragon couldn't see when they were that high in the sky, but it wasn't true. Their eyes in this form were like those of an eagle. Abraxas noticed every tiny detail on the land below.

He saw the farmer and his wife, who both ran for cover the moment his shadow darkened their land. He saw the deer that sprinted toward the trees, heard their hearts beating faster as they realized a predator hunted above them. Drool fountained from his mouth and down the large teeth that split his mouth open. He wouldn't go hunting tonight, not yet at least, but he wouldn't mind a fresh deer soon.

He had to focus on keeping the King safe for now, however, and that meant he didn't have time to sneak a meal. Even though he wanted to.

The wind whistled over his scales and the City of Tenebrous bloomed before his eyes. First, it was the sight of the swamps. Emerald green pools and grey water filled with dancing will-o'-the-wisps. The scent of decay always came after. Then the city itself, all those hundreds of broken homes, pieced together in layers upon layers of rotting wood in the hopes that the buildings wouldn't fall over.

Too many people. Too many smells. Tenebrous was always too much and yet never enough for those who struggled to live there.

Abraxas pitched his body low, soaring over the tops of the buildings while keeping a watchful eye on the ground. The streets were filled with Umbral Knights, ready to protect their king should anyone be foolish enough to attack the caravan. Abraxas was only there to intimidate if need be. Though rarely was it necessary. Everyone already knew he was here.

For a heartbeat, he thought he saw someone on a rooftop. A pale figure who laid out on the charcoal shingles, one knee propped up and an arm over her head. But then he blinked, and the vision disappeared. Like he'd imagined it.

Strange. He'd never been one to hallucinate women, and yet...

A commotion on the street caught his attention. Abraxas turned away, eyes watching two boys scrabble with each other over a fresh piece of bread that the King had tossed out of his carriage window.

Sighing, he beat his wings until he rose higher in the air. He'd land just outside the city and join the King in his human form. Tenebrous was too tightly packed for his liking.

A dragon had no place in a city like this.

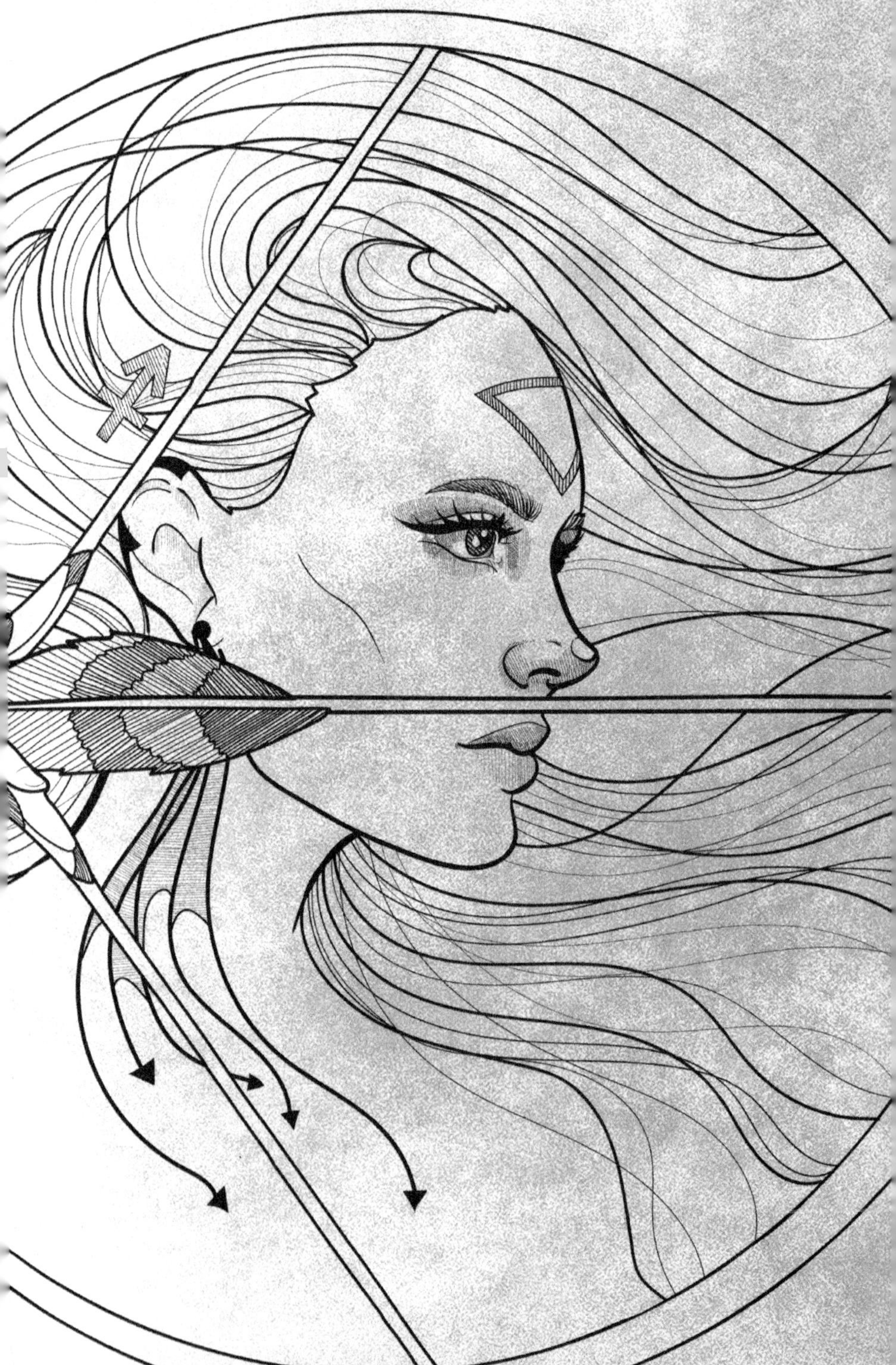

CHAPTER 3

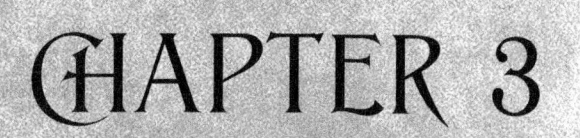

Lore stood outside the tavern and told herself she could do this. She could walk into an establishment, and it meant nothing. She didn't have to join the rebellion if she was in the same room as them. Right?

The problem lay in the fact that the dragon had flown over Tenebrous early this morning.

Again.

Two days in a row, he'd been so close to the city that she could have thrown a stone and hit him. That wasn't a good sign. She could only assume that meant the King was here, probably visiting his horrible creations, and somehow that made this situation all the more terrifying.

If the Umbral Knights found them, then every single person inside this tavern was dead. They would be dragged out into the town square and beheaded. It didn't matter if anyone witnessed magic or a creature.

Everyone in Tenebrous knew what happened if you got caught.

Lore clutched the edges of her jacket a little tighter and looked back down the street. She could go home if she wanted to. She could walk right back the way she'd come and dive headfirst into a fresh pile of elfweed. All her thoughts would leak out of her head. No one would ever know she'd stood outside the tavern.

The door opened, and a couple spilled out. They were both well on their way to drunk, and the man had his arm over the young woman's shoulders.

"I love you," he kept muttering.

"I love you, too," she replied. "So much my sweet man, my light, my muse."

Yuck.

But if the two of them could be in the tavern, then the rebellion was actually being sneaky for once. She stared up at the moon and sighed. "Fine," she muttered. "Fine, let's do this."

She pushed open the door and ignored the bell that jangled over her head. Lore's senses were assaulted by too much of everything. The room smelled heavily of body odor and beer. Her feet stuck to the floor. Somehow, the air was sticky and wet. Too many people talked all at once until she couldn't tell who was saying what.

Peeling posters covered the walls. Most of them were some sort of advertisement for a fix for mortal ailments. She noted the one for fairywater that had a little green woman with brightly colored wings. Someone had written "Fake advert" over her face in bright red paint. Not surprising. Fairywater was more addictive than it was helpful. She'd seen people lose their entire lives over getting another drop of the stuff.

Sighing, she weaved through the crowd of people who should hide themselves better. The King didn't like it when magical creatures were overtly easy to see. He hated knowing that there were beings out there who were more powerful than him.

The Umbral Knights looked for those differences when they walked the streets. Even though they were also made of magic, they could sense when someone was different. Ears. Horns. Strange eyes. All of those were a warning sign to those beasts that they needed to take someone in for questioning.

Lore rubbed a spot just over her hip where a tiny starburst scar still pained her. The Knights did whatever they wanted when they caught a magical creature of Tenebrous. That was the dangerous part.

Her feet carried her to the back corner of the tavern where it was quietest. Fewer people congregated in the shadows of this place, but she should have known this was where the rebellion would hide. After all, they thrived in the shadows.

The group was smaller than she remembered from the days with her mother. Goliath stood with a tankard the size of his head in his hands. He lifted it in her direction, the grin on his face a little too bright. Too excited that she was here. A couple of satyrs stood beside him, elaborate scarves covering the horns atop their heads.

A deer woman sat with her feet unbound. Lore hadn't seen a woman with hooves so blatant in such a long time that it almost took her breath away.

How lovely it was to see a magical creature free like that. Centuries had passed since the time it was safe to show off hooves with a mortal body. And yet, she flaunted what made her different. The feral grin on her face dared anyone to tell her to put her fake shoes back on.

Lore's heart swelled with pride at the same time her stomach turned with fear. She forced herself to look back at Goliath, ready to wipe the smile off his face once and for all. "Well? Are you going to get me a drink?"

"I didn't actually think you'd come."

"You made a good argument. And I suppose it's all right if I just listen."

Another voice interrupted them, threading through the shadows as though a siren called out for her attention. "My dear, my darling, you are not going to just listen. A daughter of Silverfell can't help herself."

Lore froze. She knew that voice. She'd heard that voice a thousand times in her early years, but she hadn't thought to hear it again. After all, how many rebellion leaders lived more than a couple of years?

"Margaret," she murmured. "I'm surprised you're still alive."

"I don't take risks like the others." The shadows parted and revealed an elf sitting at the single table in the dark corner. "You know how risks like that usually end up."

All too well.

Lorelei let her eyes feast on the sight of another elf. Margaret was an intimidating woman before she had joined the rebellion, but now she showed the signs of a silent war. Her leather outfit was plastered to her from the top of her shoulders to the bottom of her feet. More black leather straps surrounded her thighs and arms, holding knives to every part of her body. Thirty of them, each sharper than the last.

But it was her face that made Lore's heart twist in her chest. Margaret had her white hair bound in a bun at the top of her head, tiny tendrils of curls framing her long, pointed ears. Her skin was darkened by the sun, dusky and deep. Her pale eyes were nearly as white as her hair and saw everything.

She knew. Of course, Margaret knew how it would affect Lore to see another elf.

Their kind was all but gone now. They were all fighters in the early days. No one could convince an elf to not draw their bow to protect a loved one. Elves were known for their prowess on the battlefield and so they had fought until the very last of them took a dying breath.

Even Lore was only half elf. Only half of what she could have been if her mother had been able to find another like herself.

She sighed. "I'm not my mother."

"No one is asking you to be her." Margaret pointed to the only other chair at the table. "Have a seat, Silverfell. There's a lot I need to tell you."

No one was foolish enough to argue with Margaret when she wanted something. However, Lore felt a bit frustrated when those damned tendrils of shadows touched her legs. "Don't yank me into the gloom, Darkveil."

Margaret's right ear twitched. "So you do remember the old ways, then. I'm surprised. Here I was thinking that you'd taken on the persona of a human so well that you had wiped all memory of us from your mind."

"It's hard to forget," she muttered.

Lore shouldered past a satyr, her hands still empty. She desperately wanted something for her hands to do. Whether that was lifting a tankard of ale or bringing elfweed to her mouth. It didn't matter. She didn't know what to do with the hands that laid limp at her sides.

She sat down hard and watched as Margaret swung her feet up onto the table. Mud clung to the edges of her leather boots and rained down on the empty plates. Where had the rebellion leader been?

"You realize the King was here today?" Margaret asked.

"I could have guessed. The Umbral Knights were out in full force, and no one missed the shadow of the dragon." A shiver traveled down her spine. "No one ever misses the dragon."

"Well, a little birdie told me that there's been an interesting development."

She was going to make her ask. Margaret liked to make people think her plans were actually their plans. The more she got them involved, the more she could guide their thoughts in a direction she wanted.

Lore hated that kind of manipulation.

If she were going to make her own mind up about the whole plan, then she didn't want someone putting ideas in her head. Biting her lip, she eyed Margaret's boots one more time. "Obviously you were involved in that interesting development in some way."

"I wasn't, surprisingly. I was watching from the rafters. This is too big for me to not see for myself, and I worried that my informant wouldn't tell me the entire truth." Margaret slid her feet off the table and leaned forward.

The movement happened so quickly that Lore didn't have time to back away. She got a face full of mad elf before she had time to react.

"You're excited," Lore muttered. "What's got you all riled up, Margaret?"

"The King is looking for a bride," she whispered. "He's going to have women from all over Tenebrous flocking to his castle hoping they can capture his attention. He's not even looking at the other cities."

So?

Lore didn't care if the King wanted a wife. He'd need one, eventually. No king wanted to pass the crown to someone other than his own child, and a legitimate one at that. And their king hadn't exactly been trying very hard as of late.

Maybe he'd waited too long. He was getting a little older than his court was probably comfortable with. She wouldn't be surprised to hear they had urged him to have this bride show so they could look over all the breeding stock."

"Why does that involve the rebellion?" she asked.

"Because this is the perfect opportunity to do the one thing we've all desired for years. Ever since this line of kings came into power, they have taken from us. Time and time again." Margaret's eyes burned and her cheeks darkened with an angry blush. "This one is the worst of them all. He wants to wipe us from this kingdom for good. He and his Umbral Knights have ruled this place for too long, and now we have the opportunity to end all of that."

"Do we?" Lore wasn't following. "You need to be crystal clear with your words."

"We're going to put a bride into the race. A bride he simply cannot resist. And then, when the time is right, she's going to put a dagger through his black heart." Margaret leaned back in her chair, putting one of her feet back on the table.

Lore tried to make sense of the plan. Obviously, Margaret thought it was their best idea yet, considering the wicked grin on her face. But there were too many things that could go wrong.

"You're sending a young woman to her death," she said. "I don't know why you ever thought this would work, but you have to know that the King will sniff out any magical creature in his court. He's going to find her, and then he's going to kill her in front of the entire kingdom. All you're going to do is murder an innocent person and get everyone's hopes up."

"Ah," Margaret held up a single finger. All the other creatures surrounding them went silent. "But we won't send someone he can sniff out. Even a magician can't tell if someone is half elf."

Oh.

Oh.

"No," Lore replied, standing up so quickly that her chair screamed across the stone floor. "If you think I'm going to fall for the same treatment that my mother did, then you don't know me at all. I will not give my life for a cause that I don't even believe in."

"Don't believe in? You're an elf! You have seen what this king has done to all of us. If we aren't the ones to stop him, then who will?"

They were all staring at her. She could feel the weight of their gazes like a physical touch on her back. Not a single person in this tavern thought she would deny Margaret this request. But they weren't the ones being asked to risk their necks for a cause that was ridiculous. Foolish. The King would see right through her. She would die trying to live up to their hopes and dreams.

She shook her head again. "No. Margaret, this king is more powerful. Every generation that passes watches our people get weaker and this line of kings gets stronger. He has the last dragon on his side! Do you really think we can defeat that?"

"I do."

Damn it. The woman had gone mad in her old age.

"I don't," Lore replied. "I know you think that this is the only plan that will work. My mother would have fought alongside you, and she probably would urge me to do my duty as an elf. I'm not so blind that I don't recognize that. But I also know when the timing is wrong."

Goliath stepped into the conversation. He set his tankard of ale on the table. And that's how Lore knew he was serious. He never put down his drink.

The dwarf straightened his shoulders, swallowed hard, and said, "Lorelei Silverfell, we need you. I know you're afraid of what might happen and I think we all share that same fear. The King will be distracted by all the women trying to win his heart. The dragon will have his attention divided with all the opportunities for each of those women to kill the King. The Umbral Knights won't be involved because they would terrify the potential new queen. Everything is exactly where it needs to be. You just need to trust us."

Lore choked. "Trust you? Trust the people who got my mother killed?"

She'd said that too loud. Now everyone in the entire tavern was quiet and staring at her.

Too many eyes. She didn't do well with so many eyes on her, it made her skin itchy. Lore scratched at her arms, wishing she had some of that elfweed in her pocket. She needed it.

Margaret watched her with an all too knowing gaze. "Your mother would want you to do this, Lore. She knew how important it was to save this kingdom and our people. You could make her memory proud."

"No," she replied.

"Then you give us no choice," Margaret said with a heavy sigh. "We'll call the Umbral Knights. We'll inform them of your name, what you have been selling, using, and destroying your body with. We'll tell them that you're a half elf, but that doesn't matter to them, really. They will string you up for everyone to see."

"You wouldn't," she hissed.

"I would. The future of the kingdom hangs on your shoulders, little girl. I will do whatever it takes to make sure you do your job."

Her job? Lorelei had nothing to do with any of this. She didn't want to kill the King. She didn't want to get involved with any of this whatsoever.

"Right," she muttered. "Well, you do all that and let me know how it works out for you. I'll take my chances with the Umbral Knights."

She was calling Margaret's bluff, really. The dangerous elf had been best friends with Lore's mother. She wouldn't kill a dear friend's only child, would she?

Lore started walking away from the shadows and thought for a second that she was free. Margaret wouldn't do anything. The others were watching her go, eyes wide with surprise. But they weren't trying to stop her.

Good. They should see someone leave with their head on their shoulders, at the very least.

The door to the tavern opened and two Umbral Knights walked in. One of them had dented armor and bright splashes of blood on his chest plate. The other was pristine as the day he was made, but the dark holes in his helmet swirled with a smoke that stared at her with rage. Her blood turned cold.

"We were alerted there was a half elf in this tavern," the clean knight announced. "Everyone stop where you are, and we will inspect each and every one of you."

Shadows reached for her ankles again, stroking her skin and cajoling her to turn back. "I can still save you." Margaret's voice caressed her ear. "All you have to do is agree to my terms."

Lorelei's heart raced. Did she take her chances? The Umbral Knights couldn't prove she was half elf, could they? Pointed ears weren't definitive proof. And if they could, was the King really killing people for being half a magical creature? She still had mortal blood in her.

Staring into those dark eyes, she knew this Knight would kill her on the spot. It wanted to. The dark mist inside that armor wanted to tear apart something magical, as though it were punishing the creature who had made it.

Margaret had trapped her. Lore didn't have a choice at all.

She never should have come here.

"Fine," she snarled. "I'll do what you want."

The shadows wrapped around her body and drew her back into the waiting arms of Margaret Darkveil.

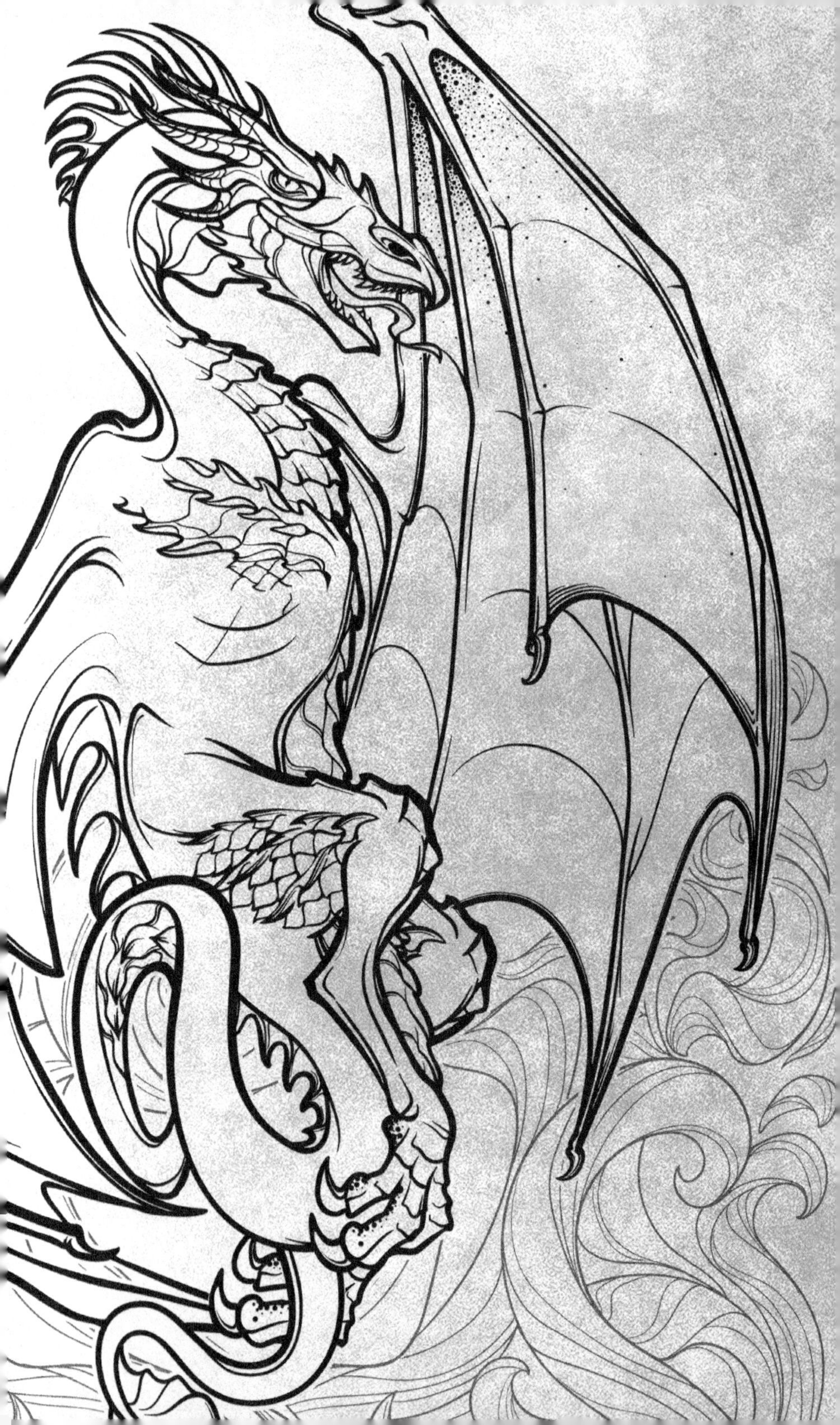

Chapter 4

Abraxas returned to his lair with no small amount of disgust. He landed hard outside the cave that connected to the castle, higher on the mountain peak. The cave was his only sanctuary, the one place the King had allowed him to build so that he could remain himself.

Even the King knew how much Abraxas hated being a mortal. And with good reason.

But now the King wanted to take a bride.

Why hadn't Zander told him of this plan? Usually the King wouldn't keep his mouth shut about women or his newest plaything. He always tried to invite Abraxas to join in on the fun, but that had never once happened. Besides, the King was constantly comparing himself to others. He didn't need to compare himself to a dragon in human form.

Shouldering past the long tendrils of greenery that hid his cave, Abraxas folded his wings tight to his body and wiggled through the stonework. Someone, long ago, had carved stone dragons into the sides of the entrance. He followed their long, serpentine bodies all the way to his coveted hoard.

Or, he supposed, the King's hoard. Considering Zander owned Abraxas, he likely owned all the gold and wealth that Abraxas had amassed over the years.

Even Zander's father had come down here and enjoyed the sight of the wealth. After all, what human got to see a mountain of gold coins?

Abraxas picked his way over the mound, slowly coiling his crimson body around the coins that shifted in a clinking shower as he settled. Only then did he open up his wings and let them rest upon twin mounds on either side of him.

Gold coins. Gemstones. Crowns, necklaces, and jewels. A thousand items gathered here, all sacrificed to the dragon in hopes that he would spare their life. Sometimes it worked. Like in the old days, when he was allowed free rein to do what he had wanted. Back when there had been other dragons to keep the mortal rulers busy.

But now, it was only him. The wealth of gold and glimmering power had started to trickle away. He wasn't sure if it was the King stealing from him, or if the movement of his giant body had caused some coins to leak out of the cave and into mortal hands. Perhaps he'd never know.

Abraxas sighed and rested his massive head on the gold. Flying was wonderful and the best part of being a dragon, but it was so damned tiring sometimes.

He wanted to sleep. He wanted to think about the poor woman who would be bound to the King for the rest of her life.

Some of the King's people said he was evil. They claimed his soul was marked by all the dead that had fallen in his father's wars. A war the son had finished. Maybe that was the truth, Abraxas didn't know. He didn't see the same person the villagers and residents of the Umbral Kingdom saw.

Zander was a child. He would make a poor husband, and perhaps an even worse king when he really looked at the boy's choices, but what immortal didn't think a human was young? The King would learn or he would die.

Most of them did.

Footsteps clattered down the stairwell that led to the castle, and Abraxas lazily lifted his head. Had the King sent a servant to him? He didn't want food, but he was more than ready to roast someone for interrupting his sleep.

It wasn't a servant who emerged from the stairwell, however. The King himself waltzed onto the small cliff that overlooked Abraxas's hoard as though every gold coin had been placed there by his own hands.

"Abraxas!" Zander called out. "I want to know your thoughts after the meeting. I thought the leaders of Tenebrous looked quite excited, didn't you?"

They hadn't. The men had worn pinched expressions of disbelief, anger, and then sadness. They were all likely thinking about the many young women they were going to sacrifice to this king's whims. And they were probably wondering if any of those women would return to them.

Still, he couldn't tell the King any of that or he'd send his Knights to cut down every leader who had looked at him with a cross expression.

"They were all very busy trying to figure out how to find the best women in their provinces, Your Highness." Talking in this form was sometimes a little uncomfortable for humans, but thankfully Zander was very used to it.

Abraxas wasn't even sure how he talked. The voice built in his chest like someone else was speaking through his throat. Or perhaps that was simply his mortal form. Either way, all he had to do was open his mouth, and the voice came out. Though sometimes it sounded a bit like a hiss rather than a voice. He hadn't quite gotten used to the sensation himself, even after all these years.

His deep voice rumbled throughout the cavern, but the sound didn't phase Zander one bit.

"Do you think they will find the prettiest ones, though?" Zander held out his hand as though he were reaching for a young woman. "That's what is most important, after all. I want to make sure that my children are the most beautiful royals this family has ever seen."

"More beautiful than yourself?" he asked wryly.

"Of course not." With a flourish, the King propped his hands on his hips and glared at the dragon. "I wanted to make sure you and I were on the same page with this one. I need a bride, and I need her to be an impressive queen or none of them will take me seriously."

"Yes, sire. You are ever so intelligent."

Ah, he was too sarcastic with that phrase. Zander would notice, and the King absolutely did.

The pretense of a foolish boy dropped from Zander's shoulders and the glare on his face warned that Abraxas had gone too far. "You do realize that you have to support me on this?"

"Have to?" Abraxas didn't like the boy's tone. He was the dragon in the room, not the King. And though his life was bound by the boy's father, that didn't mean he respected this boy king in the slightest. "You want a bride, boy, and I will watch you get married. I will ensure none of them tries to kill you. None of that means I have to agree with your scheme to get Tenebrous back under your thumb."

Zander's eyes grew bigger with every word. If he were a more intelligent man, he would have taken the threat for what it was and left it. A mere mortal couldn't conquer a dragon.

The King was not that intelligent.

He narrowed his eyes and a muscle on his neck jumped with his too fast pulse. "You want to challenge me on this? You think I shouldn't get married?"

"I think you should leave the poor girls alone for a little while. They are trying to live their lives as well, Zander. You don't need to pluck them from their homes while you decide if one of them suits your taste."

He'd gone too far. Abraxas knew he'd gone too far and yet the words wouldn't stop coming out of his mouth.

This king took so much from his people. Abraxas had seen enough of Zander's greed to know these women wouldn't be welcomed with open arms. They would be played with. Toyed with. Made to think that they were the only person in the King's life, when they were really agreeing to a life of mistresses and misery.

Some days, the guilt of working for the King threatened to overwhelm him. Today was one of those days.

Zander watched him with a calculating look on his face. "You seem to have everything under control, don't you? The great dragon of old. The last of your kind. And yet, here you are, working for me."

"Your father," he corrected. "Your father was the one who trapped me."

"And given the chance, you wouldn't leave this place. Is that what you want me to believe?" Zander laughed, but the sound was filled with dark intent. "You are only here for one reason. We both know that."

Of course he was. Abraxas was the last dragon. Why would he ever subject himself to servitude if he didn't have to?

A growl rumbled through his chest and he knew the base of his throat glowed with flames that wanted to erupt from his mouth and spew out onto this little boy who had stepped too close to the dragon.

"Ah, ah, ah." Zander waved a finger in the air. "Don't try me, Abraxas. You have gotten far too confident, I think. Every move you believe is orchestrated by yourself! Or perhaps you think that I am a lesser king than my father. Is that what it is?"

Yes.

He thought Zander was so much less than his father. The previous king had brought countless magical creatures to their knees. He'd trapped a dragon and then he'd razed Umbra to ash and dust just because an uprising had begun. That was a man to fear.

Zander gestured with his fingers, two unfurling and his thumb wide, and a chest rose out of the gold. The large metal box was the only treasure that Abraxas didn't control. He couldn't summon it out of the depths, no matter how many times he'd tried.

Every muscle in his body tensed. He stared at the jewels encrusted on the side. Ruby, emerald, and sapphire. Three colors that made his entire soul scream in pain.

The King watched him with a fanatic gaze. "There it is. The fear I wanted to see from you. You know exactly what this box is, don't you?"

"Of course I do."

"I've only seen it twice myself, you know. Father always talked about it, and he made sure I knew how to summon it should you ever step out of line." He smoothed his hands over the top, lovingly stroking the chest as though it meant everything to him. "Just a peek. Shall we?"

No. Abraxas didn't want this foolish man to look inside that box. He didn't want Zander to see what was hidden inside the only thing that mattered to Abraxas.

The King was the only person who could open the chest. The spell had been woven by a magician long dead, and only the King could flip those two latches and reveal the contents within. The treasure that haunted Abraxas every morning and every night.

Zander pulled the lid open and sighed. "Would you look at that? They really are more beautiful than my father had described. I see now why they mean so much to you."

Abraxas didn't have to look. He knew what was nestled safely inside that chest. Three perfect eggs, each one crystalized like the gems on the outside of the chest. Three perfect symbols of hope that someday he wouldn't be alone anymore.

They were the last dragon eggs in the realm. Long before the King had caught him, he had searched for their existence. The last sister of his kind had passed in the mountains of the far west. Her dying words were of the last hope that another female dragon had told her about.

Unfortunately, the human king got to them before Abraxas. And then he'd placed a curse on the chest that only a king of Umbra could open the box. All others would be killed, magic lashing out at them and tearing into their very being if they tried to open it.

Abraxas still had the scars from when he'd tried to open it himself.

"It's rather sad," Zander murmured. "These are your only hope of ever seeing another creature like yourself. Isn't that right? The last chance for anyone to see another dragon after you're gone."

"Be careful with them," he snarled.

"Oh. With this?" The King reached into the box and picked up the ruby egg. It glimmered in the torchlight.

Abraxas could barely think. The King was touching the egg, and no one should be allowed to do that. But also it was so beautiful. The egg would hatch to become the same kind of dragon that he was. Rubies were rare, and they were always fiery. Their flames burned hotter than any other, but their loyalty was something to be admired.

"Don't touch what isn't yours, little king."

"Or what?" Zander palmed the egg and shut the chest. "You'll burn me to a crisp? Abraxas, I need you to listen to me right now because what I'm going to say is very important. And I'm going to hold on to this egg so that you take me very seriously. Do you hear me?"

He ground his teeth, gnashing them at the King. "I'm listening."

"I am the most powerful king you have ever seen. The most powerful king Umbra has ever had before. And if you don't believe that, then no one else will." Zander's eyes widened as if the words terrified him. "You are the great dragon of Umbra. The shadow of the king. You have to believe it. Do you understand?"

Abraxas lied. "I do. You are more powerful and greater than your father or any king before. I would know, because I was there."

"Good." Zander nodded, reaching a hand behind him and scratching his back. "That's good. I'm glad you understand. I wish it didn't have to come to this. You know I don't enjoy threatening you."

"That is because you are a just king as well." He swallowed hard, wanting nothing more than to scream at the King to put the egg down.

Zander didn't put the egg down. Instead, he lifted it into the light and the faint outline of a draconic body could be seen through the clear layer of gem. "I wish I believed you. But someday soon, you will see that

I am all that you lied about."

With a swift movement, Zander pulled a knife from behind his back and plunged it into the egg.

A shriek echoed through the cavern, so loud and piercing that Abraxas opened his mouth in a silent roar. It was the soul of a dragon. The soul of an innocent who had never seen the light of day. And he could do nothing to stop this horrible monster from taking that life.

The sound died down. He finally opened his eyes, peering through the splitting pain in his head. The tiny dragon in the egg twitched, its tail wiggling one last time, and then all the light died out.

"A shame," Zander said. He dropped the egg and the knife onto the ground, releasing the spell so the chest sank back into the gold. "I didn't want to do that, my friend. You see, I need you to be on your best behavior when all these brides and their fathers arrive. I need you to remember who I really am."

As the King left, Abraxas knew exactly who Zander really was.

A monster.

He should have known. He should have predicted that this child would take what wasn't his. But, as he coiled himself around the deflating egg to mourn his loss, he reminded himself of one thing.

There were still two more eggs.

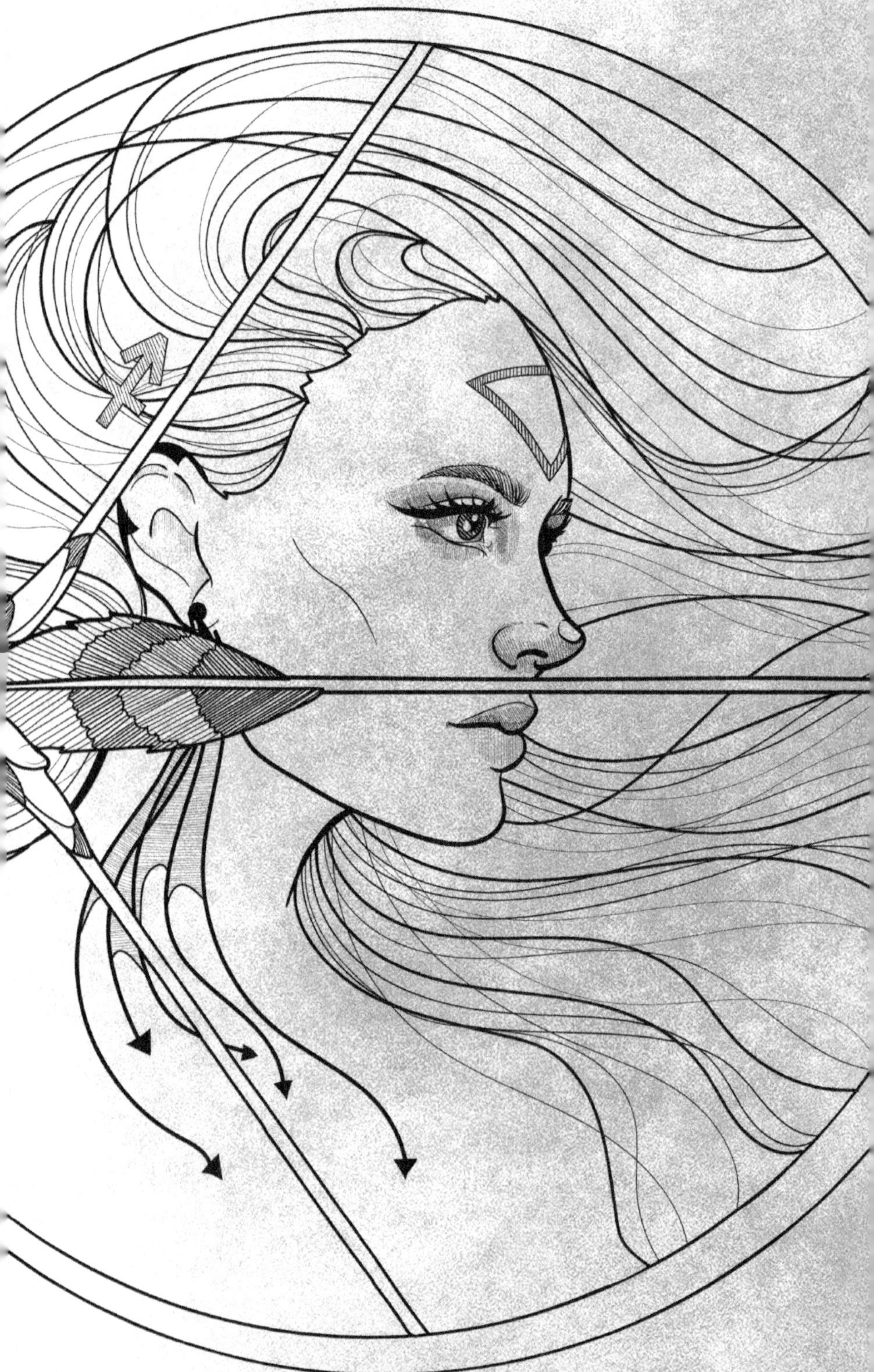

Chapter 5

"So you see, he is the best person for the job." Goliath grabbed her arm and jerked her to a halt in front of a house that was far, far too nice.

Lore didn't even know houses existed like this in Tenebrous. She was used to ragged homes. Ones that were falling down around the edges and that desperately needed someone to put another board over that hole in the roof. Not... this.

The white marble of the house still gleamed in the sunlight. The walls were built to be sturdy and had ten columns holding up a giant roof. Ivy tangled around the silvery columns and spread out onto a yard that might have grass underneath the ivy, but she couldn't be sure. The swells of greenery were hard to peer underneath.

She frowned at the bright red door and glanced around them at all the other houses that were in complete and utter ruin. "Did he build a portal or something? There's no way this man lives here. Right?"

"Oh, he does." Goliath patted her back and shoved her forward. "I can't go in with you, though. He's very private."

"Then why would he want me in his house? He could have met me at mine." Lorelei glanced over her shoulder at the retreating dwarf. "Why do you look like you're running away?"

"Because he is."

She sighed, preparing herself for whatever stood behind her. Considering the look on Goliath's face, she could only assume the creature who was supposed to make her irresistible to the King was also one to fear.

Lore turned and looked at the man who stood in front of the red door. His silhouette was strangely stretched, like he was a shadow late in the day.

He stepped into the sunlight, revealing lank brown hair that hung in his face. Moss grew on his shoulders and broad chest, and a butterfly sunned its wings on his right shoulder. His fingers were aged with bark, and his pinky finger grew a small dual leafed plant. Dark eyes stared back at her with no whites at all to tame the wild nature of his soul.

"Leshy," she breathed, trying hard not to look him in the eyes. "I thought your kind was long gone."

"I could say the same about you, elf." His voice was ragged, like stones grinding against each other. "And yet, here you are. Still standing even though the King has done his best to remove your kind from the light."

She felt something in her soul spark. A shifting of silver and moonlight that glimmered to the surface of her skin. "I prefer the darkness."

"Ah, a Silverfell. How rare." He shook his head. "I should be surprised, but your tribe always had a talent for trouble. Come inside, child. You're here for a reason and that's not to darken my doorstep. The neighbors will talk."

And then he walked back into his house as though the neighbors weren't already talking about the man made of trees and the glowing elf in his yard.

She'd been right originally. This entire plan was going to get them all killed, and now she had a leshy's death on her shoulders. Probably the last of his kind, although she knew very little about them.

Still, the least she could do was be respectful.

Lore followed him into his house, tripping over the threshold into a room that looked like the depths of the forest. Thick moss covered the floor and squished beneath her feet. Sunlight speared through the windows and the open ceiling, catching on tiny golden dust motes that danced before her eyes. The walls had been hand painted so realistically she could almost sense the ancient trees of old. A single actual tree grew in the center of his home. Butterflies in every color swayed around the branches.

A trickle of warmth trailed down her cheek. Confused, she touched a finger to the liquid, only to realize she'd started crying.

"Don't look so surprised," the leshy grumbled. "You might have forgotten about the forest, but your soul hasn't. This is our home, little elf. Or was. Before the fires."

Flashing red lights danced beneath her eyes every time she blinked. Like she remembered that fire, though she hadn't lived through it.

"I don't... That is, I don't think..." Did she remember?

"Keep struggling like that, and you'll hurt yourself." He chuckled, then tapped a gnarled hand on his chest. "My name is Borovoi. Margaret said she had a plan and sent you to deliver the message."

"She didn't even tell you herself?" Of course not. If Lore was the one to tell this creature, then it sounded like it was all her idea. "She wants to send me to the King's bridal games. If I'm tempting enough, it's her opinion that I will get close enough to kill the man."

"Ah." He nodded, then turned his attention to the tree. "And you are so mad that you agreed to this plan?"

"I am not. She threatened to turn me into the Umbral Knights for..." No, she wasn't going to admit to anything. The fewer people who knew about her little side business, the better. "Doesn't matter. She threatened, and that was enough."

"She does have a way about her." Borovoi took the butterfly off his shoulder and held it up to the branches of the tree. The tiny thing didn't fly, or apparently couldn't. It crawled onto the nearest branch and waved its wings again. "You will have to be very careful if you are to tempt a king."

"I can't look like a magical creature, that's for sure." Lore touched her ears, making sure they were hidden. "If he gets even a whiff of magic, then I'm done for."

"Are you so sure of that?"

"Yes. Everyone says the King hates our kind. I think he's proven that, considering we're hunted like animals." She still didn't want to know what the Umbral Knights would do if they found either her or the leshy. The fact that this man waved what he was around and lived like this? It was dangerous.

"The King doesn't hate our kind. He envies us. He wants to become like us, and that's why he's killed so many. It's frustration, little elf. Not hatred." Borovoi returned his attention to her, and those black eyes saw too much. "You want to get his attention? Hint at what you might be. Leave little clues but never give any admission. Let him assume what you are."

"You're asking me to risk giving myself up?" She shook her head. "Now I know you're mad."

"Not mad. I know the King better than most." A slash of sunlight caught in his hair. Tiny caterpillars stretched their bodies on every strand, giving him a faintly fluffy appearance. "He comes to visit me when he wants to see magic. Tame magic, you see, not wild like we once were."

Her heart squeezed in her chest. Tame magic? What did that even mean?

"It means he wants to see us as less than him. Magic he can control or advise where it goes. That's what he wants. A pet. Entertainment. But never something dangerous." Borovoi gestured for her to follow him. "Come here. Let me show you something."

He shambled behind the tree, but she was tired of all this. He might be one of the most ancient creatures she'd ever met, but that didn't mean he could waste her time.

"Look, Margaret said you would prepare me for the King. Whatever that means. If you aren't capable of doing that, then I can find someone else to help." She hoped, at least. It wasn't like she had anyone else guiding her on what the King might want.

"And you should be a little more grateful to the only person who's willing to help you. Get over here, elf."

"Lorelei," she grumbled as she trudged after him. "My name is Lorelei."

The other side of the tree was much the same as the rest of the room. The only difference was a small table he'd set up with all manner of magical objects. Skulls, crystals, bones, and shards of glass decorated the top.

Borovoi looked rather pleased with himself. He pointed to a deer skull on the table and said, "Well, then, Lorelei, what do you think that is?"

"A skull."

"Indeed. And where do you think it came from?"

"Probably outside somewhere. Or a forest." She shrugged. "There aren't a lot of deer around here. They don't like the dragon visiting as often as he does."

A skull was a skull. Why did he want her to see it so badly?

"Pick it up," he said. "Then tell me if you believe the same."

She sighed, but did as he said. "I don't have time for these ridiculous games, Borovoi. I don't even know when the King is going to have his first bridal... whatever he's calling it. But if I miss that, then the plan really doesn't work."

The moment she touched the skull, visions flashed in front of her eyes. She saw a woman laying on the ground. Seven arrows pierced through her chest, and her eyes stared blankly up at the sky. Blood soaked the ground around her. A keening sound could be heard, like twin voices calling out for their mother only to be silenced with a quick slice through wind.

A stag walked over to the woman, lowering itself down onto its front legs. It lay beside her and a faint breeze ruffled her hair. Pointed ears were revealed in the setting sun. The dying light that burst into flames until she realized it wasn't the sky at all.

Fire consumed the land. Rolling toward the woman and the deer like a wave that could not be avoided. It poured over the ground, lava coiling toward them until it devoured the elf and the deer.

Lore flinched, raising her arm over her eyes and half expecting to feel the heat on her own body. But the light died down and when she looked again, all that remained was a skull in her hands.

"What was that?" she hissed.

"A small portion of your history, little girl. Those memories live inside you. Why do you think you cried when you walked in here?" Borovoi pointed to the tree behind them. "That is the last great being from an age when you and I would have lived free. An age your soul remembers, even if your mind refuses to believe it happened."

She touched her fingers to her soaked cheeks again. "Why are you showing me this?"

"Because Margaret said you weren't entirely convinced this was necessary. You don't care that the King wants to destroy more, or that he wants to unleash that hellish beast upon us again." Borovoi strode forward so quickly she didn't see him move.

His outstretched hand grasped her skull, squeezing her forehead too tight. And then she saw it.

Memories. Visions. Whatever anyone wanted to call them. Flashes of the past that she hadn't remembered.

She saw a dryad woman in a black dress, hugging her own arms as her horns caught fire. A fairy laughed and danced in the flames as her wings disintegrated in bright embers. A dwarf staggered by her, clutching a bundle of coals in her arms.

"Enough," she sobbed, wrenching herself out of his grip. "Enough. I don't want to see it."

"You have to see it." Borovoi lurched forward. He tried to catch her even as she rushed away from him. "You have to see all that they have done so you can understand how important this is. You have to do this, Lorelei. For all of our sakes."

"I'm afraid," she choked. The sound of her own fear made her freeze. She'd promised herself that she would never feel so afraid. Her mother had shown how little that emotion helped. Hands shaking, Lore pressed them to her cheeks and exhaled. Long, low, counting to ten as she pulled herself back together.

Once her armor was back in place, she met Borovoi's dark gaze head on. "I will do this because I will die if I don't. No other reason. You cannot change my mind."

His haunted eyes darkened, and she swore she saw smoke in those orbs. "When you have seen what Margaret and I have seen, it's hard to hold that armor up any longer. We are laid bare by our memories, Silverfell. I hope you can keep that shield up for as long as possible."

Every breath was drawn ragged and roughly into her lungs. She fought with every ounce of her soul not to cry.

What had that bundle of coals been?

"I am only doing this to save myself," she muttered. But she couldn't look him in the eye any longer. "Whatever happened in the past? I'm sorry for it. Those aren't my memories and I hate that you went through that. The best I can offer is that the King will die by my hand if I can get close enough. I think that's where you come in."

"Ah, yes. It is. I am on the Tenebrous Council and we're already talking about how to get him the prettiest girls. The King doesn't care at all for intelligent women, I'll warn you of that." Borovoi stroked his chin, looking her up and down. "You have enough beauty to tempt him, I suppose. But there are more beautiful girls throughout this realm. What you need is a miracle."

"Thanks for that," Lore grumbled. She might not be the most beautiful, but at least being an elf had to get her somewhere. Didn't it?

"I'm going to help you. I'll prepare the meeting for him. Any king would be pleased with a party that I host. And then we will get to work on making all this..." He waved a hand up and down her body. "More presentable."

"That's it? That's your help?"

"And I'll train you on everything I know about the King." Borovoi nodded firmly. "Only in exchange that you let that armor down a bit more, Silverfell."

"No deal. I'll figure it out on my own." Lore moved to leave, already done with these ridiculous rules.

"Fine!" Borovoi called out. "Fine. I'll prepare you and nothing else. Is that what you wanted?"

It was. She hardened herself, grinding her teeth and watching the butterflies float above their heads. "Just teach me how to tempt the King, Borovoi. I already know how to kill a man."

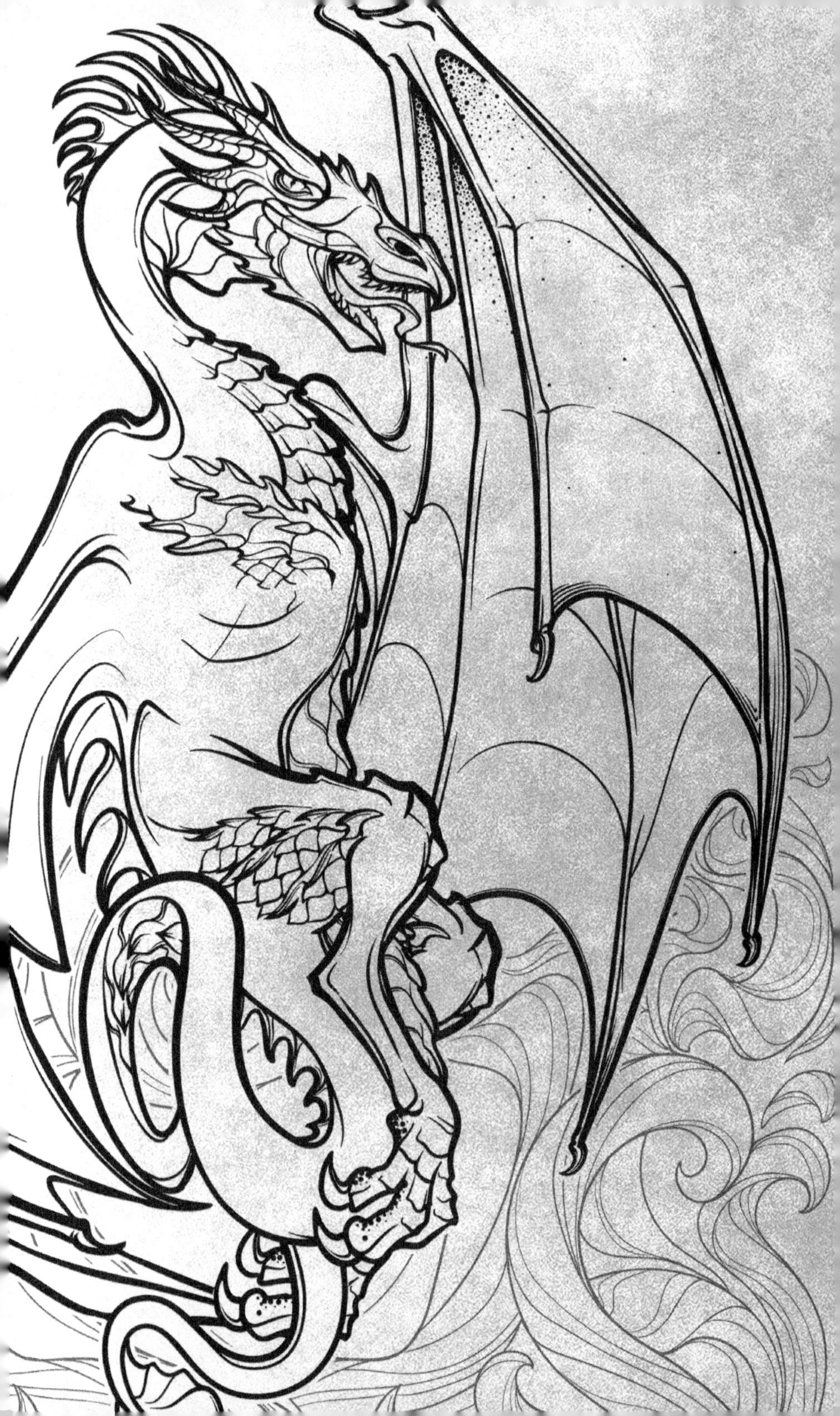

CHAPTER 6

"Are you ready for the party, Abraxas?" Zander strode into the cavern with all the confidence of a man who never had to worry about a single thing in his life.

His clothing was pressed into points, the royal amethyst fabric plastered to his faintly muscular body. His hair slicked back and coiffed to ensure that his grey colored wings were on display. Jewelry dripped from every limb that could have it, and he wore four necklaces around his neck.

In contrast, Abraxas had been told to be more careful with how he dressed. No one wanted to look at the dragon for very long. Especially not longer than the King.

Zander had sent his servants to make sure Abraxas was ready. So he wasn't sure why the King would waste his time asking if his dragon had prepared himself for the party. Of course he had. The plain black suit was too starched, and it rose up to his very chin, almost as though it were strangling him.

Or maybe that was the memory of the King plunging that knife into his future. Like he'd done since he had inherited the throne from his father.

Either way, he didn't really know how to reply to the King. "I suppose I am."

"Come now, old chap! You should at least be a little excited about this endeavor. The ladies do love to see you when you're in this garb." Zander waved a hand up and down, gesturing to his form. "Although I'll be honest, I can't see what they see in you."

The King rarely understood women being interested in anyone other than him, so Abraxas wasn't all that surprised. The King especially didn't like it when a woman was interested in Abraxas. It was unnatural for a beautiful mortal to find herself in the arms of a dragon, he'd once said. That was the only reason why. The only reason. Of course.

Abraxas wasn't so sure that was the truth. Zander hated anything magical, and he definitely didn't want a dragon getting anything that the King himself couldn't have. And a woman who had eyes only for the dragon?

That would never happen.

Sighing, Abraxas stuck a finger underneath the neck of his suit and shook his head. "I don't understand the point of this, Zander. You've said yourself, many times I might add, that you want nothing to do with anything magical. And yet, here we are, going to a party hosted by one of the oldest creatures in the book."

"Borovoi is not old," Zander corrected him. "He's a young buck with a hope for getting into nobility someday. I don't know why you'd even think to call him magical!"

Had the leshy cast a spell on the King so he thought the creature was mortal? No, the King was protected by more than just the Umbral Knights. Abraxas thought it more likely that the King was disregarding the fact that the leshy was one of the creatures he wanted to kill. And that was because Borovoi made the most intricate, beautiful parties there were. The nobility loved it, therefore, the creature was useful.

How many mortals could fill the air with stars that twinkled within reach and butterflies that landed on the hands of maidens the King wished to woo? No one. Not a single person could do all that.

Now, he wondered what the leshy had up his sleeve for tonight. The party seemed a little... odd. It had been announced out of the blue, and though Zander was certain it was because Tenebrous wanted to ensure that his brides were offered in the most glorious of settings, Abraxas had seen their faces.

No one wanted to give their daughter to the King. He feared tonight could turn bloody.

Zander caught a glimpse of his expression and rolled his eyes. "Are you going to be so sullen all night? If that's your plan, then you should stay far away from me. You'll scare all the lovely ladies of Tenebrous away and then where would we be?"

"Exactly where we are now." Abraxas blinked at his king. "There are no lovely ladies in Tenebrous, or have you forgotten? They are where we send everyone who doesn't deserve to live in the Umbral Castle or the surrounding areas."

"Oh, that's right," the King waved a hand. "Well, it's been a long time since some of them have been there. They are bound to have made some beauties. But you bring up a very good point, my dragon. I should inform all the other nobles that their daughters should be added to this whole affair. It doesn't matter if I've tasted my wife before!"

Abraxas wanted to hit him. He wanted to change into a dragon and devour the King whole, but then where would he be? His eggs would forever be locked in that damned box, and he would be alone for the rest of his life.

Best to wait until the King had a child. Then he could kill this one, raise the boy or girl on his own somewhere in the wilds. That would give him enough time to convince them to open the box and release the last two dragons into the world.

Three dragons left. Slim pickings for the growth of his kind. Maybe he would bring those babes into a world where they would eventually suffer the same fate that he fought against. They might become the last of their kind, knowing that their children would only make the pool of their magic even smaller.

But he had to try. If there were three of them, three minds searching for others, then he was more likely to find dragons who were still out there. Or, at the very least, more forgotten nests that had solidified into stone. Buried under the water, perhaps? Someone had to have hidden their children in the hopes that another would find them someday.

"Abraxas!" the King shouted.

His name echoed throughout the chamber. Bouncing back at him as though he had been summoned by a god.

And in the eyes of the last dragon, this King unfortunately was exactly that.

He focused on the tiny man before him and forced his lips into something that resembled a smile. "Yes, my king?"

"What has gotten into you today?" Zander tossed his hands in the air, and the jewelry hanging off his wrists clanked. "Is this all still about the egg? That was a week ago, my friend. Let the past stay in the past."

Easy for the King to say. He hadn't had someone kill his children in front of him, nor did he then have to work with the murderer and keep him alive for a night of drunken foolishness.

Abraxas knew he was letting all this get to him a little more than he should. He'd never had this issue before. He'd always been able to separate the man from the monster when he worked for Zander's father. The previous king had been no less devious or cruel. And yet, there was something about this king that wiggled underneath his guard no matter how many times he tried to still his emotions.

Maybe he had simply gotten tired of being underneath the royal thumbs.

Zander watched every expression on his face before rolling his eyes and making his way out of the cavern. "Is that how tonight is going to go? You're worse than a wife, Abraxas. I have only a few more months of freedom before I have to look at someone wearing that exact expression for the rest of my life. Would you give me at least a slight break?"

No. He wouldn't.

With the King's back turned, he let a snarl cross his features. If he had been in his true form, then the King would have trembled in fear. But this mortal form only allowed him a small amount of intimidation, though still it was impressive, or so he'd been told.

His dark hair swaying in front of his face, he marched up the stairs behind the King. With every step, he reminded himself of all the terrible things he could do to a man like that. He could devour him whole, of course. But he could burn him to death like the King had bid him to do to countless others. He could pull all his limbs off, one by one, forcing him to stay awake by burning the bloody stumps so he wouldn't bleed out too quickly and die.

A thousand ways to kill a man all rested in his ancient mind, and he could do none of them to this mortal child who apparently thought it was fun to torment a dragon.

Someday.

Someday.

They strode out of the castle, likely a strange pair. Even the carriage man eyed Abraxas as though the dragon was about to reveal himself at any moment.

Zander stepped up onto the carriage, held onto the door, and leaned back to grin at Abraxas. "Ah, I forgot. Listen, after the whole jumping out of the carriage and then turning into a dragon episode, the servants would prefer it if you didn't scare the horses like that."

"We had planned for me to remain a human, anyway," he grumbled.

"Yes, but..." Zander shrugged. "The servants are frightened of you as well, my dragon. They'd prefer it if you stayed a safe distance away while we travel. You know how it is."

"So you want me to arrive at the party where your potential new brides will be as a dragon?" He crossed his arms over his chest. "That sounds like a fantastic way to scare all of them off. Their fathers aren't going to send them away with you if they think their daughters will end up with me. You remember the old legends."

Part of the reason everyone feared dragons was that they used to steal "brides". They weren't actually marrying the women, of course, but there was a time when the dragons wondered if they could mix their own lineage with that of mortals. Unfortunately, it never worked out the way anyone planned and the women were eventually released into a village where they could live their own lives.

The dragons had never treated their captives poorly, but explaining that to a father who missed his child was difficult. Especially when that child didn't want to return home because living in a kingdom of dragons on her own was easier than going back to the mortal kingdoms.

Zander made a face, but then waved his hand in the air. "Yes, yes. I see your point. Traveling with you gets more and more difficult, you know that? Just land in the woods outside the area somewhere and walk, will you?"

And with that, he shut the door to the carriage. A faint pounding could be heard from the interior and the carriage man winced before he snapped the reins on the horses.

Right. Abraxas would have to find his own way to Borovoi's party and then make sure no one saw him arrive. After all, it would be rather suspicious to see a dragon fly over the woods, disappear, and then have a man walk out.

The first King was the one to ask Abraxas to remain a secret. Separate from his draconic form. And the King had been smart for it.

Now, all the royals of that line had two men working for them. A personal guard with powers stronger than the average man. And a dragon who burned anyone who stood in the King's way.

He sighed and walked to the central courtyard, where he was allowed to turn into a dragon.

A little boy wandered past him, a footman in training if the uniform revealed anything about the boy's job. He staggered to a stop in front of Abraxas with his mouth wide open, then forgot to move as the dragon walked right into him.

"Sorry, sir!" The boy stumbled, almost falling onto his behind. "I didn't mean to get in your way, you see. I just... well... I thought to see the King first, and then I realized that I was going to be late and..." His eyes widened in fear. "Please don't eat me."

They all did this when they were young. He'd seen so many servants come and go as their lives ended or began. At this point, he barely even remembered their faces, let alone their names. Some of them were kind. Others were downright frightened. But none of them had ever taken the time to talk to him.

Of course, there were always the odd ducks. The random children who weren't afraid to talk to a monster rumored to eat mortals in one bite. And it was always the children who were willing to give him a chance.

He didn't have it in him to be the terrifying monster right now. Abraxas might feel a little sentimental considering the loss of his own child. But he had the time to bend down on his knee in front of the little boy and brace a forearm on his leg. "I don't eat children. You're all bones and not enough meat."

The boy's eyes widened even further. "What about when I'm all growned up then?"

"Grown up," he corrected. "And that all depends on how good you are. If you don't make the King angry, or you don't get in trouble, then I probably won't look at you."

"My father says all dragons eat humans as snacks, and that the King feeds you people he doesn't like in that cavern." A tremble shook through the child's shoulders. "I said that seemed horribly scary, but I don't know. People don't seem like they would taste all that good."

"And they're quite small," Abraxas added. "I much prefer cows or deer."

"So you don't eat people?" The hope in the boy's voice was infectious.

He hated to burst the child's bubble when he was already so excited that the dragon might be a hero in the story.

Dragons were never heroes.

"I've eaten my fair share of people. Some of them are legends in your stories that came to my home to kill my family. Some of them were wanderers on a path they didn't know." He clapped a hand to the child's shoulder and then stood. "I'll be honest about my failings, boy. I've killed more people than you've met in your life, but you have less to fear from me than your king."

The boy's forehead wrinkled as he thought about what the dragon said. Seeds of doubt took root in his mind about the King his father claimed was perfect.

Perhaps the boy would become a martyr. Maybe he would join the rebellion against the King and try to overthrow this reign of torment and terror. Abraxas didn't care. Some part of him hoped that the mortals would eventually see their rulers for who they were.

For now, he had a party to attend.

In the future, he hoped it would be a pyre with a crown atop it.

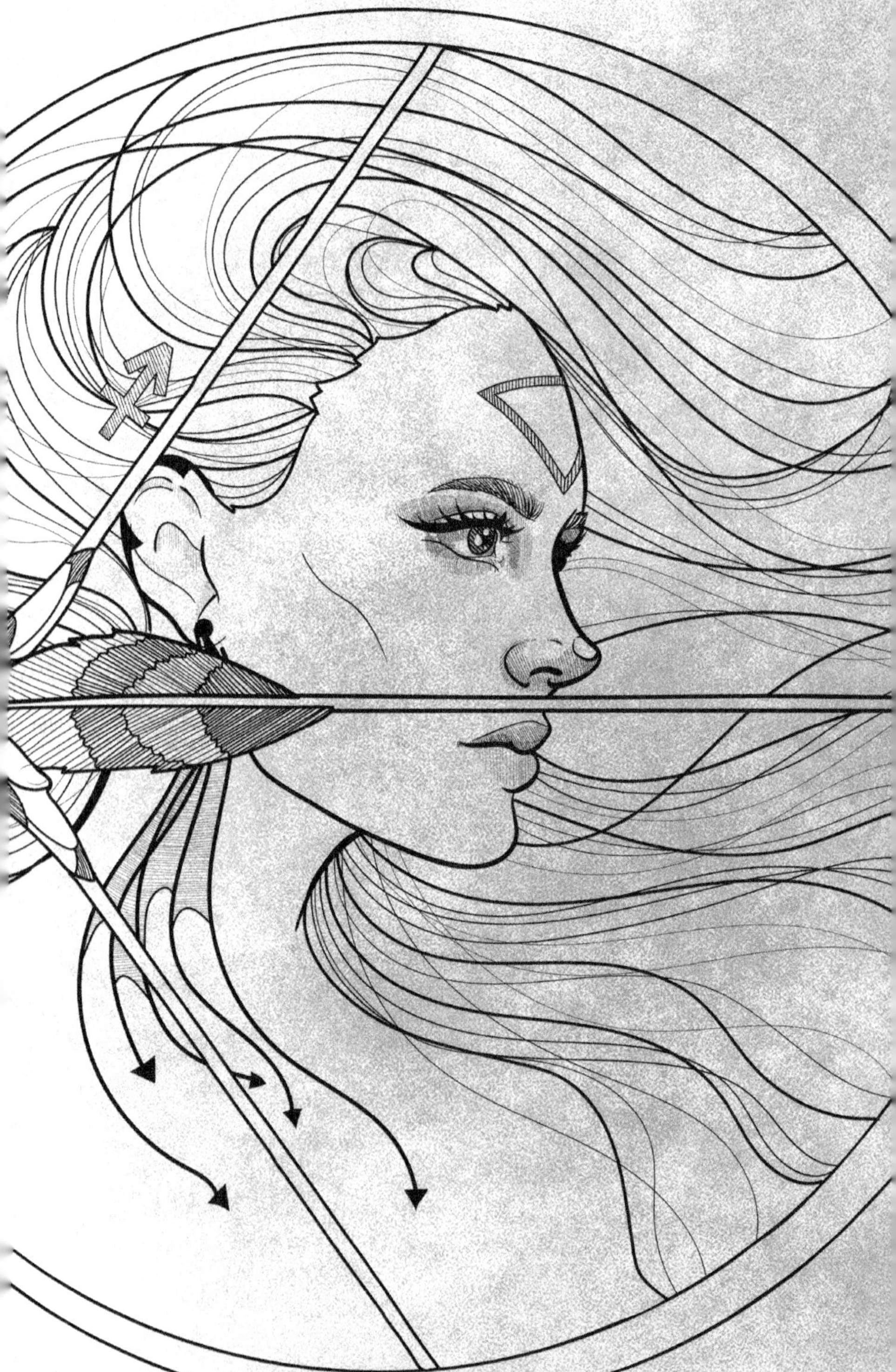

Chapter 7

I know you're nervous, but you shouldn't be," Borovoi said. He stepped back with a pin in his mouth, looking her over as though she were his newest art piece rather than a person standing in front of him. "After all, you're only meeting the King today."

"That doesn't make me feel any better," she grumbled.

Lore knew she didn't look like herself. She could feel it. The dress the leshy had chosen covered so little of her skin that it made her want to scratch it off. All this gossamer and spider silk was wasted on a person like her.

He'd spent the better part of four hours pinning cherry blossoms and pink dahlias to the dress, starting at her right shoulder and tumbling down her chest, her stomach, all the way to her hips where they barely covered her skin at all. The rest was a gauzy fabric that would look better on a window than it did on a person. And the butterflies. So many pale pink butterflies that opened and closed their wings, covering the parts of her that no one should see without permission.

Yet, the King was coming. And the King was sorely tempted by those hidden parts of women.

She couldn't be any less surprised.

He'd always had a way with women, at least in the rumors that went around Tenebrous. Lore had caught the tail end of a few conversations where women claimed they'd spent a night in the King's bed. They always bragged about it, but she'd never heard them say they actually enjoyed their heated moments with the King. In fact, the conversations were always that they had bedded a royal. And that was it.

"Do you think the King is horrible in bed?" she asked.

Borovoi spluttered, all the pins falling from his mouth as he coughed. "Excuse me?"

"I've heard women talk about him before. It's not like he hasn't gotten around a bit. But they never say they had a good time with him." She lifted a brow. "So I'm asking you, because you seem to know the King more than most in this city. And I want to know if he's horrible in bed."

"I don't think you'll have a reason to find out."

"If bedding him is what it takes to put that man in a compromising position, then that's exactly what I'll do. I don't care what it takes to kill him." She'd killed a man before. A couple, in fact. They always cried and screamed when they realized their death came at the hands of an elf.

She wondered if the King would cry. For all the things he'd done to her people, she'd liked to see a few tears before she plunged a knife into his heart.

Speaking of... "Are you going to put a knife in here somewhere?"

"A knife?" He parroted her as though she were speaking in tongues.

"Yes, a knife. I'm supposed to kill the King. How am I going to do that without a weapon of some sort?" She pointed to the table. "There are a few items on there that would do. I could always strap one to my thigh. A dagger is better, but if you want to give me a shard of bone, that'll do."

He stared at her like she'd suggested that they burn down the tree in the middle of his house. "Why would we do that?"

"So I can kill the King and get this over with. If there's going to be so many people there, it should be rather easy to get him alone. Everyone will be distracted." She wiggled her leg, her thigh muscle jiggling. "Go ahead. You know you want to add a weapon here. And you're a leshy, so you should have some magical weapons that will really make an impact."

"You aren't killing anyone tonight," he snapped.

"Isn't that the entire point of this whole thing?" Lore wasn't going to wander around the entire kingdom waiting for the perfect moment when the King was alone. He had a dragon to look after him! She wasn't ever going to get a perfect moment, and this was as good as any.

"Yes, that's the point, but if you kill him now, then everyone will think that I was the one who made all this happen. The Umbral Knights will be on my doorstep within minutes, and then I'm the one who takes the fall for all this." Borovoi hit her on the nose with a flower. It exploded, showering petals down her shoulders and making her sneeze. "Foolish girl. You are not allowed to do all this without thinking. If you want to kill a king, then you have to be mildly intelligent."

"Intelligence has nothing to do with killing people in my experience. Brute force gets you farther than thinking about the right plan." At least, that's how it had always been in Tenebrous. People wanted to think they could assassinate someone with poison, but that never worked. It always ended up being a heavy-browed man with a sledgehammer in an alleyway.

"Not in this world." Borovoi knocked her again with the butt end of the flower, then shook his head in disappointment. "You need to think more about where you are now, girl. You aren't in some brothel or tavern where people are more likely to brawl. You're entering a world where words can hurt far more than a sword."

"I don't think the King is going to die because I insulted him with fancy words."

He pinned one last flower to her shoulder, then stepped back to look over his handy work. "No, he probably won't die of that. But you could dethrone him with the right rumor or the wrong place to have caught him. The King knows this. Everyone knows this in the nobility. Play your cards right, Lorelei."

Why did it sound like he was warning her? As though he knew something about this entire process that he wasn't sharing?

"Borovoi," she asked. "Are you not telling me a very key detail about tonight?"

His response was a mere wink that didn't settle any of the nerves in her stomach, and then a wave of his hand. The tree spun in a small circle, its roots ripping from the ground and a massive groan filling the air. All the butterflies burst into flight, and then the trunk of the great oak split open.

Bark parted. Leaves rained down on their heads and suddenly, she realized that a door had opened. A door through the forest, through the very tree itself. Light sparkled from within.

She glanced over at Borovoi, who wore an outfit fit for a king. Lace sprayed from his wrists and around his throat. The cream-colored suit was carefully beaded with tiny pearls. His dark hair was swept back from his face, revealing a bone structure that she hadn't realized was there.

He looked... handsome. Expensive, even. And perhaps slightly passable as a mortal.

"Now I see why the King likes to keep you around," she muttered. "You're just as pretty as the rest of them."

"Ah, am I?" He winked. "Or do I just know how to look the part? You're stunning yourself, miss half elf. Now, don't let anyone know what you are and they might think you are a natural beauty."

Borovoi stepped through the tree and didn't wait for her to follow. Apparently, he was done with her. A single minced piece of advice, one that was hard to chew on, and she was on her own again.

"Not helpful," she snarled.

But there was no other option here. She had to follow him and continue this ruse that she was even interested in taking down the royalty of Umbra. Because if she worked for anyone, then she worked for herself. And Lore didn't want to die. Nor did she want to spend the rest of her life running from the King's men because she was a known half breed who had made a living selling an illegal weed.

Grumbling, she stepped through the tree while bracing herself for the feeling of magic. She hated the slick slide of power against her skin. It always felt so unnatural. Which, she could admit, was a little hypocritical.

Borovoi's magic felt like she'd stepped through a waterfall. Cold. Wet. Definitely not something she wanted to feel again any time soon. She gritted her teeth and made it through, however. And then she stepped out into a party that was unlike anything she could have imagined.

He wasn't kidding when he said his parties were better. The entire landscape of the field in front of her had changed. Even the grass, usually yellowed in this area or at least soggy with marshwater, was bright blue. The stars were much closer, or they appeared to be. The bright orbs in the sky twinkled as though Borovoi had summoned the heavens down for the King's amusement. A large white tent was set up, filled to the brim with more food than she could name.

And the people. She couldn't breathe with this many people around her. It seemed like all the key players in the Tenebrous leadership were here with their entire families. Women, children, young men, they all wandered through the field with nets in their hands.

Nets?

Borovoi wandered back to her side and handed her a small white net. "There will be butterflies released soon. Each one will give you a special power for the rest of the night. Only a few hours of magic, you see."

"Is that smart?" She took the offered net. "You're giving mortals a glimpse into what it would be like to be us?"

"They love magic. They love using it and seeing what we can do, but none of them wish to admit that they fear us for having it." He winked. "I'm not giving them anything too powerful for the night. There will be no turning into a dragon for the night."

Lore still thought it was foolish. She watched the leshy wander off and wondered what it must be like to know that he was in the King's favor and didn't have to worry about what others would say if he was his magical self. She watched a young woman run up to his side, clap her hands, and then squeal with delight when he pulled a live butterfly from behind her ear.

He could do whatever he wanted and no one would call the Umbral Knights on him. They laughed and smiled and cheered with glee when he walked by.

Now, what would happen if she mentioned she was half elf to anyone here? They would scream in terror, point her directly to the Knights, and then tell their friends they had such a fright.

What was the difference between her and Borovoi? Other than the fact that the King claimed he wasn't dangerous, but she was?

Maybe Margaret was right. This King had to go, and why shouldn't that assassin be the young half elf who had lost her mother to his cruelty?

"Hello." A young woman stood beside her, staring up at the large stars. "I've never seen you here before."

The newcomer was a lovely vision in bright green. The fabrics of her skirt were layered to look like she was walking on waves. And with that lovely golden hair and eyes the color of the earth's heart, she was a vision. Lorelei had no clue who this young woman was, but it was obvious her family had money. One of the few in Tenebrous.

"I'm not usually out very often," she replied. Lorelei gripped the net in her hands a little too hard, but she didn't really know what to do with them.

Now that she was in this society of beautiful people, her hands seemed a liability. She didn't know how to hold them, where to put them, or if someone would see the callouses on her knuckles. All she could do was clutch the net in her fists and hope no one noticed she didn't belong.

"I find it best to hold your skirts," the young woman said with a soft smile. "I remember my first party. It's awfully terrifying, but you'll get through it. And every one after that gets a little easier. Just keep out of the King's way, and you'll be just fine."

Had the young woman said the last bit with a hardened edge? She was certain there was a warning in those words.

Was the woman trying to warn her off the King? Oh, that wouldn't do. The competition hadn't even started yet, and these girls were trying to weed out the weak.

She hated women.

The more she looked around, the more she saw dirty looks being thrown left and right. All the women here were aware of the competition that had started already. They were all waiting for the King. For the chance to make an impression and if they didn't, then they were aware of what it would look like on their families.

Thankfully, Lore didn't have a family. It didn't matter what other people thought of her, or how she got the attention of the King at all.

Which meant she needed a plan.

These young women were not only beautiful, they were hungry. They wanted the King to look at them and only them. Lorelei wasn't that good of an actress. The King would see how little she wanted to be around him, and he'd know that from a league away.

She needed to think. She needed a breath away from all these perfumed lovely flowers and their poisonous thorns.

Weaving through the crowd, she made her way past the tent and into the forest beyond. Just a few steps. Just enough to get out of the bubble of Borovoi's magic so she could breathe easier again. The net suddenly jerked, as though it were tugging her back to the crowd. Maybe it was. Borovoi wouldn't let one of his sheep get lost in the woods when they were supposed to be seeing the King.

A faint cheer went up behind her, and Lore knew she'd missed the King's entrance. He'd notice that.

Breathing hard, she launched farther from Borovoi's magic and filled her lungs with the clean, cool air of the forest. All the sounds of the party were muffled here. Sure, she could still hear them all. The faint sound of laughter and happiness that she knew was fake.

But at least for the moment, she could take a deep breath and be alone. Too many people. Too much of a risk for them to see her ears, even though she'd carefully put her hair over the tiny points.

She had to get back there. She had to...

No. Lorelei had to think about how to capture the King's attention, and her best chance now was to arrive at the party late. Perhaps a little drunk.

She looked down at the net. "Magic for the night," she muttered.

Borovoi had said he hadn't given them anything too strong. So, had he thought of taking Silverfell's particular power? She hadn't used it in a while, but it was certain to cause a scene.

A twig cracked to her right. Lore froze, eyes still straight ahead, but her ears listened for the next movement. Apparently, she wasn't the only one in the forest tonight.

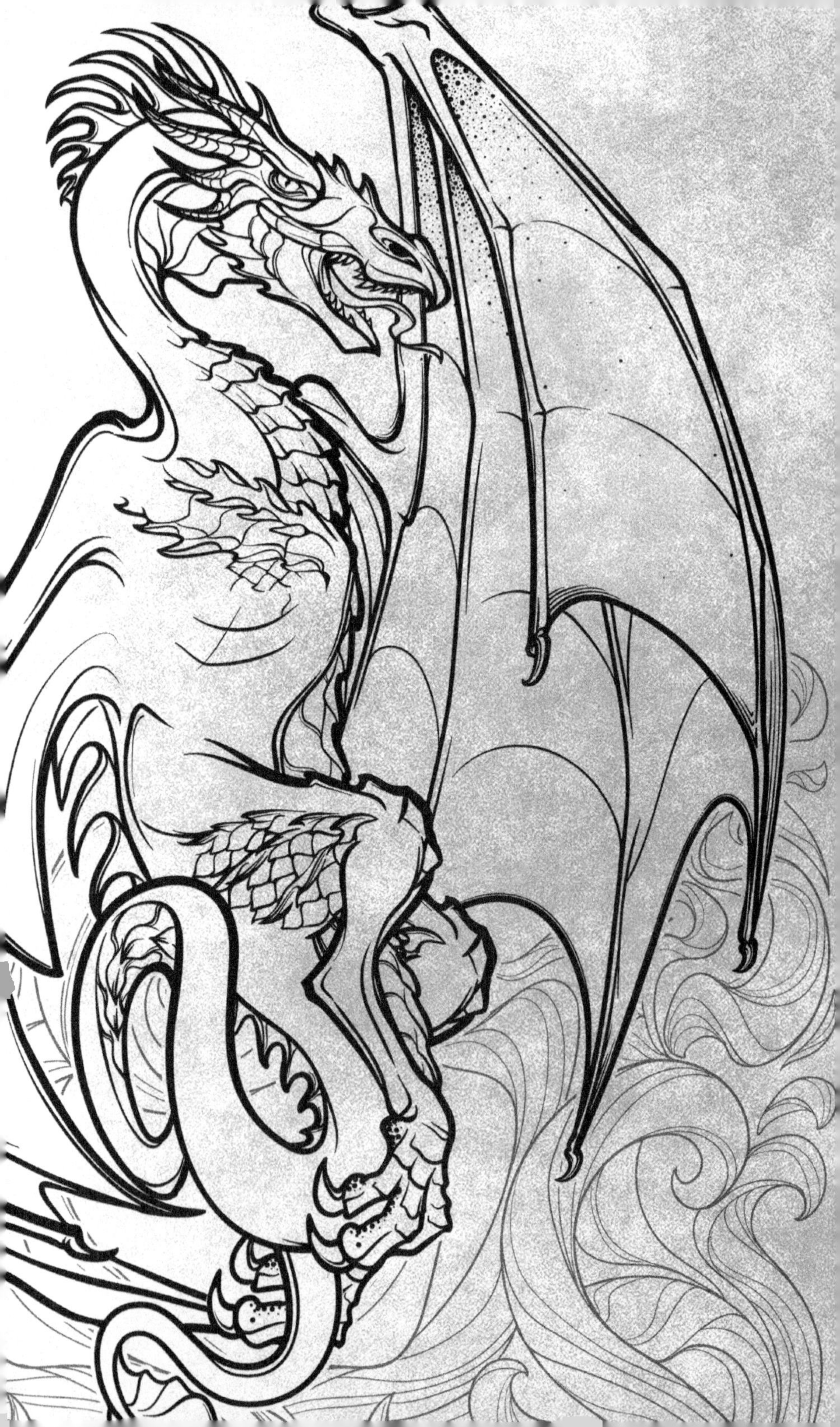

CHAPTER 8

"Walk through the forest," the King had said. It will be easy to find the party.

Of course it would be. Except Borovoi hated Abraxas, and that meant the damned leshy had made it almost impossible to find the location of his cursed party. He grunted and smacked another branch out of his way. It appeared even the forest worked against him tonight.

The King was completely incapable of protecting himself. The leshy knew that. And this all only made Abraxas think this whole bride contest was a way to get to the King.

The rebellion was smart like that. It sounded like a plan they would have cooked up, although he still had a hard time believing Borovoi would be involved. Too much of the King's coffers had gone into that devious creature's pockets.

And yet, here he was. Lost in the woods and hoping he stumbled upon the party he'd seen from the air but clearly couldn't find on foot. This was why he hated being in a mortal body. He had no way of knowing where he was, or where he was going.

"Damn it," he grumbled, smacking a tree with a little too much force.

At this rate, the entire gathering would be over by the time he found the hidden tents. Abraxas stepped into a smaller clearing in the woods, still cursing the leshy for all that he'd done. Except he stopped in his tracks almost immediately.

A figure stood in the clearing, a subtle breeze toying with the strands of her hair. And for some strange reason, his breath caught in his throat.

She didn't face him, but he could see her profile perfectly. The straight edge of her nose. The pale waves of her blonde hair. The faint scent of rainwater and the aftermath of lightning lingered in the air. It captivated him, zinging straight through his chest.

Abraxas felt as though he stood in the eye of a storm. And that certainly couldn't be the way of it. He didn't need the company of women, nor did he look to them for their attention. Women were a means to an end, unless they were of draconic blood, and then he supposed he had to focus on them a little more.

What was it about this strange woman that had struck such a nerve?

"My apologies," he rasped, then cleared his throat. "I didn't mean to startle you."

"You didn't." She continued not to look at him. "I heard you coming."

Had he been that loud? Abraxas was usually more aware of his surroundings. Being loud in any Umbral forest was bound to bring about creatures that most people didn't want to fight.

He scratched the back of his neck and tried to not sound embarrassed.

"I'm afraid I have a lot on my mind as of late. I'm glad you heard me, however. I would hate to have startled someone like... you."

Oh, that sounded horrible. Was he trying to flirt with her? No. He was the King's dragon and there was no room for women in his life. He'd only drag them into the depths of despair with him.

She snorted. "There's a lot of that going around tonight, I think."

And then she turned to look at him and he felt as though he'd captured a star. The flowers of her dress glimmered in the moonlight from tiny dewdrops hanging on the edges of every single petal. A few butterflies rested on her chest and hips. And those eyes. Those big, beautiful eyes that were as vivid and bright as the sea on a clear day.

The sea he so desperately missed.

One look at those eyes reminded him of when he'd soared over the waves. He'd thought that color of sapphire couldn't exist anywhere else and yet... Here she was. A woman made of the elements and just as heartrending.

Who was she? She obviously wasn't one of the villagers, or she would have recognized him. Or perhaps she was from Tenebrous, but she wasn't anyone of importance.

That made little sense, however. If she wasn't of any importance, why would she be here?

Abraxas knew she was meant for the King. Look at her. Her dress was made with the utmost care and beauty, not to mention that her hair was clearly done with magic. Those curls didn't make themselves, and he would not fool himself into thinking that she dressed like this often.

The days of meeting elven maidens in the woods were long past, even though he would have preferred their return. He'd always loved the elves. Their beauty. Their wit. And the deadly manner in which they eviscerated all of their opponents.

She swallowed hard, staring at him with obvious distrust. "Are you going to talk? Or were you planning on standing there silently staring at me?"

Had he said nothing since she'd spoken last? He was a dolt. And he knew better than to corner a poor woman in the woods and then stare at her like he'd never seen a woman before.

Sighing, Abraxas swept into a deep bow. "My apologies, Lady of Starlight. I did not expect to find someone in the woods while I searched for Borovoi's party. I'm afraid that surprise has stolen my tongue and turned me into the fool you see before you now. I must beg for your forgiveness and perhaps that you might forget what I have said."

She said nothing in response to that, and his belly churned in the silence. Had he done something wrong again? Women were Zander's forte, not his. And besides, the only women he'd ever tried to woo in his life had been the dragon females long ago.

They were easy to convince, considering the size of his draconic form and how hot his flames burned. Human women were much less interested in that side of him.

He looked up from his deep bow and saw she still watched him with a calculating expression. "Have I said too much again?" he asked.

"I'm trying to understand you," she replied. "You come out of the woods as though you are some hunter who happened upon my path. But you claim to seek Borovoi's party. Which means you are certainly someone of higher status than a mere hunter."

"I am more than a hunter," he agreed. Did he really look like some peasant?

"Then why are you walking in the woods in the middle of the night rather than already at the party?" She hooked a thumb over her back and the butterfly at her shoulder took flight. "That's where the rest of your kind are waiting. The King has already arrived, so I'm afraid you're rather late."

"As are you." He straightened, tucking his hands behind his back for good measure. But he couldn't stop himself from staring at the small patch of skin the butterfly had revealed. "If you're here, then I assume you're also meant to be at that same party."

"I needed some air."

"Ah." He nodded. "They are all rather intimidating, I know that for certain. You don't seem like the women I had expected to find here."

Apparently, that was not the right thing to say. Her eyebrows lifted in obvious anger and she snorted out an unladylike breath. "Just what did you expect to find?"

Oh, she would not trap him like that. Abraxas had lived a long time, and he didn't fall into the schemes of feminine wiles that easily. After all, he knew when a woman wanted a compliment and when she wanted a battle.

This woman wanted a battle and then some.

He stepped forward, too quickly for her eyes to track, and yet he was almost certain she saw him. He lifted a hand to her cheek. Impossibly, she caught his wrist with strong hands, their limbs suddenly frozen between them as though they were about to start an intricate dance.

Her fingers warmed against his skin. The flames inside him rose to the surface. The part of him that remained a dragon wanted to flick out its tongue and taste the air for her scent.

She'd seen him move. She'd tracked every moment of speed that was too fast for mortal eyes to see, and yet, she had.

"Who are you?" he whispered.

"I'm a woman here to see if the King has an interest in me. Nothing more, nothing less." But her words shook as though she was shocked to realize that he had noticed she was different.

She'd have to do better than that if she wanted to hide from the eyes of the Umbral King and his Knights. And there would be many Knights at the party tonight. The King went nowhere without his protection.

Even now, those Knights could be hiding in the woods, waiting for her to make one wrong step.

He feared he would cause that misstep.

Because he didn't think for a second that she was mortal. Not now that he was looking down into the depths of those seascape eyes and could see just how much she was willing to lie.

Leaning down so close that he could feel her breath on his face, he muttered, "I don't think you're entirely human, are you?"

She rotated her wrist around his, the jerking movement so sudden that he didn't have time to stop her. One moment, their hands were raised, the next, he'd slapped himself across the face.

Reeling, he spun away from her with a startled laugh.

"I don't take kindly to anyone claiming I'm something I am not," she snarled. But the wildness in her gaze already betrayed her. "You have a lot of nerve to walk through the woods on your own and then accost a woman who is meant for the King."

"You're meant for something far greater than that," he corrected. His cheek stung. She'd really made him slap himself so hard that he feared there might be a handprint on his face when he arrived at the party.

This woman... Who was she?

Mouth ajar, he couldn't help but look at her with no small measure of surprise. Abraxas hadn't met a woman like this in years. And if he didn't know any better, or hadn't been warned not to suggest she was something so dangerous, he would swear she was an elf.

Their kind was always fiery. There were days in both their kind's history when the elves and dragons had lived together. Some of them had even chosen to ride beasts like him, though that age was long ago. The King would be sure to kill anyone who dared to do that. Even he hadn't ridden the last mighty dragon.

Still. If she was an elf, he suddenly had a sense to protect her at all costs.

He cleared his throat, chuckled again, then rubbed his sore cheek. "I've been forewarned, Lady of Starlight."

"Stop calling me that," she growled.

For the first time, he noticed she held a net in her other hand. She'd tucked it against the gauzy fabric of her skirt, so close to the fabric that he hadn't noticed it before.

"Why do you have a butterfly net?" he asked, then pointed at the small object in her hands. "I've been to a lot of Borovoi's parties, but I cannot say that I've ever seen someone walking around with a weapon in their hands."

She looked down at the object as though she had entirely forgotten she was holding it. "Oh. We're supposed to catch butterflies for the evening and they'll give us all a special power. The magic is only supposed to last a couple of hours, you see. Borovoi thought it would give everyone something to talk about."

Dangerous choice, but the leshy knew how to play the King well enough.

"Ah, of course, he had some trick up his sleeve. It wouldn't be a Borovoi party if people weren't thrust into danger." He looked at the net, then back at her.

If this woman wanted to continue claiming that she wasn't part creature, or entirely a magical creature, then he was afraid he would have to challenge her. After all, what was a party without a little drama?

Abraxas told himself that he was just causing mischief, but in the end, he wanted her to leave. He wanted her to run from this place and give up the idea of being with a king. She was too beautiful. Too intriguing.

Zander would eat her alive.

He took another step toward her, chuckling when she raised her hand again. "I must ask that you not slap me again, lady."

"I didn't," she replied with a glint in her eyes. "You slapped yourself, sir."

He supposed she was right. No one could argue that he had done the slapping and that the mark on his face was the size of a man's hand. "I understand that. However, I'm arriving to the party quite late and I did not get my hands on a net."

With a swooping movement, he snagged the net from her hands and held it behind his back.

"Well, I still need to capture myself a butterfly," she stammered.

"So do I." He gestured at her dress, even daring so far as to touch one of the butterflies over her heart. His finger brushed briefly over smooth, velvet skin. "And it appears you have plenty of them to yourself, Lady of Starlight. You'll have to forgive me while I take this opportunity to look like I'm not as late as I was."

"Hey!" she shouted, but it was far too late for her to stop him.

Abraxas raced from the clearing, only pausing at the edge of the leshy's magic. Of course she'd followed him. The woman was a fighter, like him.

She stood at the very edge of the forest, butterflies floating around her in the air. Her hair glimmered in the moonlight, and the only thing that ruined the image of some goddess who had walked out of the trees was the angry expression on her face.

He grinned. "My name is Abraxas, if you're wondering."

"I wasn't."

"I would have your name, lady. If only so that I might think of it in the night while I dream." He waved the net in the air. "I plan to capture myself a power for the evening and then plan our wedding."

"As if I would ever fall for a man like you." She crossed her arms over her chest, and her jaw jumped. "My name is Lorelei."

He clutched his chest as though an arrow had pierced his heart. "A beautiful name. One I will surely never forget."

"It would be hard to forget the name of the woman who ruined you for all others." Though her words were sarcastic, he could see she had eased to his antics. Perhaps she saw something in him as well. Some part of her that was drawn to him like a moth to a flame. "You best run to the party and find your power, sir. Otherwise, the King will surely outshine you."

"Him?" He shrugged. "Never."

Abraxas plunged through Borovoi's magic and into the clearing beyond. He felt lighter than he had in years. As though she'd somehow given him a gift. He might be the last dragon and he might be in a contract with a horrible king who wanted to destroy the very realm they all lived in.

But a woman like that still existed. He could feel the power of her soul calling out to him. There was unfinished business between them.

He could only hope to see her again.

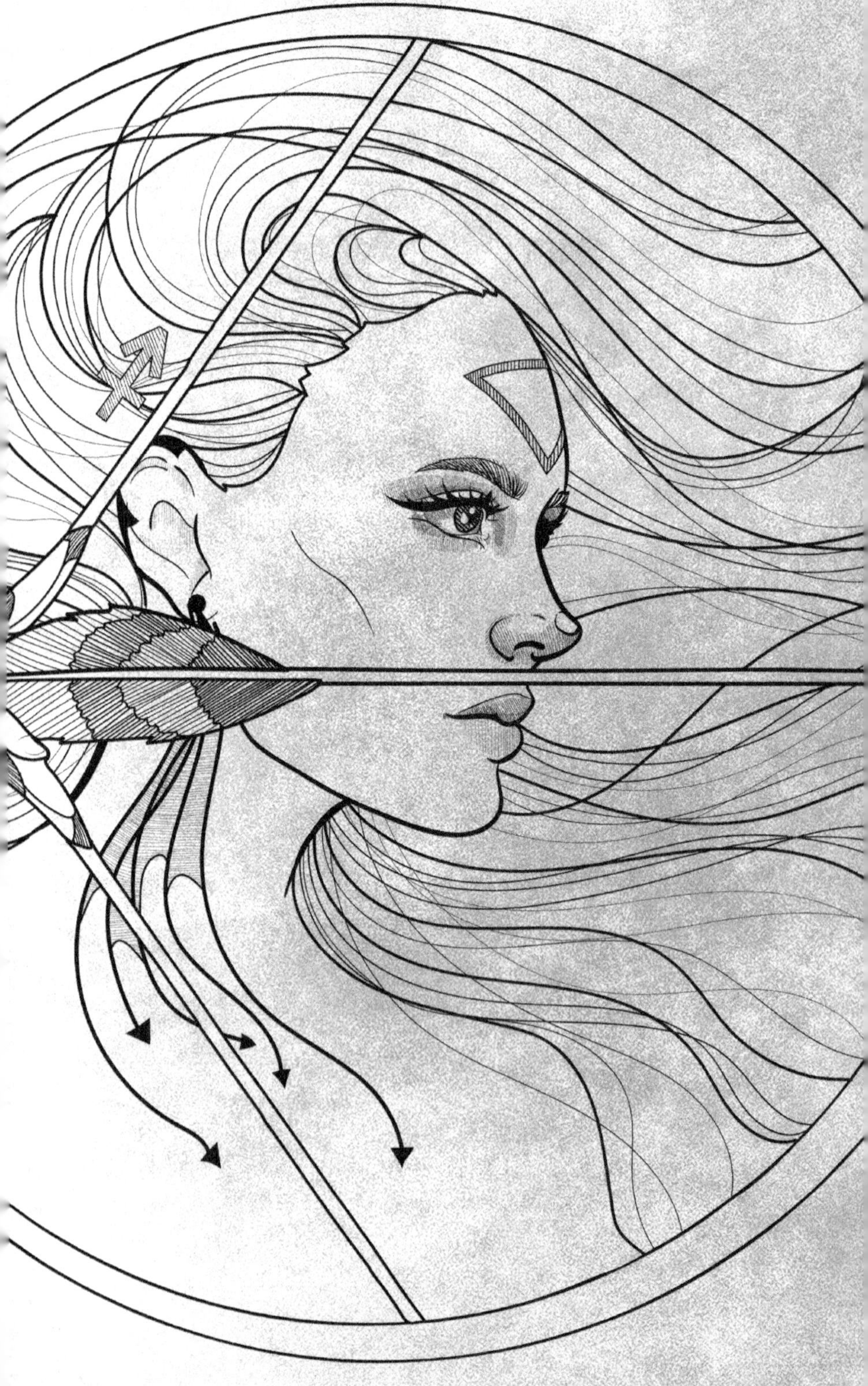

CHAPTER 9

Who was that man?

Lore watched him disappear into the party, but her heart refused to stop thundering in her chest. She'd never felt such an instant attraction to anyone in her life. And she'd seen handsome men in Tenebrous, although they were always dirty and covered with grime. Perhaps that was the difference. She'd never seen a man that was clean and dressed so well.

Whatever it was, it didn't matter. She couldn't go to the party looking for him. She had to find the King and impress him, but now she wouldn't have a power like the rest of the people there. Or at least, a fake power.

Would that look odd? She was quite certain it would. Even though everyone had become the magical version of themselves, she couldn't walk into that party as the only person without a power. Then she would be the odd woman out and the King wouldn't like that.

He'd gone through a lot of effort to make sure that Borovoi's party was different. Obviously he wanted everyone to fall in line and look the part, or unlike themselves, she supposed.

But she didn't have a butterfly.

The leshy's magic would likely be useless in changing her powers, anyway. She hadn't seen a lot of magic that could give more to a magical creature, and maybe that was the King's plan. If someone was magical in the audience, then he would be able to see that by the person who wasn't affected.

It was all a great trap; she realized. A trap that would weed out anyone in the rebellion if they weren't capable of showing their power in a way that was simplistic. Like Borovoi had meant for it to happen.

Tilting her head back, she stared up at the moon. "Why?" she asked the mother of all Silverfell elves. "Why did it have to be like this?"

The moon didn't respond, but when did she?

Lore had spent a lot of time collecting her power from the moon. It was slow going. Maybe that was why the Silverfell elves were rarely thought of as powerful creatures. They were deadly in battle, but only because they didn't rely on their magic. They relied on their own knowledge of how to fight.

Tonight, it seemed, she would have to use all the power that she'd gathered for months now.

Lore sighed and let her magic seep out into her skin. She hadn't used the moon's magic in a while. It took some time for all that power to come to the surface. But, by the time she was done letting it free, her skin glimmered like a thousand stars covered her from head to toe.

Would the man who had seen her know what she was? He'd already alluded that she wasn't human. How dare he! But obviously now she had become what he'd called her.

Lady of Starlight.

It had a nice ring to it, even if the words could get her killed.

Lore lifted her arm and stared down at all the stars embedded in her skin. It was beautiful, especially up close. Silverfell elves had always looked like gods and goddesses when they ran through the forest like this. She remembered the ceremonies where so many of them had worshiped the moon, then ran through birch groves with white stags at their sides.

Those were the good days. The days before the King.

She shouldn't fall into line with the rebellion this easily. They wanted what other people didn't. Freedom. A life where magical creatures were back in charge.

The King's rule suited the mortals, not the magical creatures. Another war was on the horizon and if she didn't choose a side, then she would be swept away by the tides of change.

Lore knew that.

She stepped into the party with these thoughts riding on her shoulders. Knowing without question that she had only a few more days before she had to throw herself into this assassination attempt. To pick a side.

And she already knew what side she'd choose. Even before she saw the King.

He stood at the front of a large crowd, gesturing with his hands as though he were a magician. A massive group of young women stood in front of him. They all swayed with his hand movements, as though they were part of the music he thought he was playing.

They'd all fallen under his spell already. Clearly. Each one of them watched him with rapt attention and hungry eyes. They wanted to be queen. They wanted the power only he could give them, even though they had to know that authority was minimal and weak.

She stood at the back of the crowd, unsure of what she should do next. Had he already called all the eligible ladies to the front? Was that where all the bridal candidates stood?

She really shouldn't have been late. Her own need to get her head on straight could cost her the entirety of this mission. She might as well walk into the arms of one of the Umbral Knights and give herself up now.

If Margaret didn't kill her first.

Damn it, she had already botched this job. How had she done that so quickly?

As she mused on a new way to get the King's attention, she didn't notice the quiet hush that fell over the crowd. She noticed once everyone fell into utter silence, however. Lorelei looked up and met the eyes of the King.

He'd stopped moving. Frozen, so to speak, in front of all those beautiful women who vied for an ounce of his attention. And yet, here he was. Staring at her.

Lore swallowed hard, lips parting in a deep breath as she stilled herself for the moment he remembered what she was. The King surely hadn't forgotten the power of the elves. There were legends that spoke of Silverfell and how all her people had glittered with starlight. He must remember. Any moment now, he would send the Umbral Knights to make an example of her for his party.

Instead, he lifted his hand and stretched it out to her. "My lady," he said, his voice shattering through the silence. "Where did you come from?"

Oh no.

Lore didn't like so many eyes on her, and suddenly her tongue wouldn't move. Her lips remained parted, as though she would speak at any moment, but then she never did.

This was the first time she'd ever seen the King. In her mind, she had conjured the image of a man made of nightmares and shadows. A disgusting individual with a horrible face who was too large to fit through doorways. A monster who devoured everything in his path. That had fit her thoughts of him.

But the man at the front of the crowd was handsome. He had a pleasing face with angular features and perfect symmetry. The wings of gray hair at his temple made him seem more approachable, and certainly added to his attractiveness. Yet there was something in his eyes. A darkness, perhaps, or a hunger that he had never satisfied.

A smile spread across his face, warming the cold edges of steel that made up his jaw and cheekbones. "Is that part of the magic? Borovoi, you outdid yourself with this one! Beauty and silence? You've created a mystery woman who, I must admit, I cannot look away from."

She glanced over at the leshy, who pressed a finger to his lips. So she would stay silent. That was probably for the better.

Then she noticed the man from the woods. He stood just behind the King, easy to miss amongst the shadows. His eyes burned as he met her gaze, his jaw clenched so hard she could see the outline of his muscles quaking. And as the King eyed her, the other man curled his hands into fists.

Borovoi strode to the King's side and proclaimed, "This is Lorelei, my king. Her beauty far surpasses any magic I could conjure, I'm afraid.

Whatever spell she has cast upon you, that is not my doing."

"Dangerous words," the King replied. "And yet, I am intrigued. Come here, my splendid."

Splendid? Ugh. The title put a foul taste in her mouth. It was like he already thought he owned her, and as the King of this realm, she had to assume he did.

Her feet dragged across the ground. She didn't want to look graceful, because that would only tempt the King more. By the look in his eyes, the hunger that heated with every one of her movements, Lore knew she had failed.

He watched her like a predator watched its prey, and the weight of his eyes made her skin itch.

The other women in the crowd were displeased. Even the girl who had tried to warn her away watched her with fire in her eyes. They didn't like it that someone else had stolen their moment with the King. Some of them had probably spoken with the King already. They thought they had gotten the upper hand over all the other women and then in she walked.

A woman with stars for skin. The power wasn't nearly as impressive as some of the others. One girl's hair moved on its own. Another had butterfly wings for lashes. Yet another had clothing that had turned to water and now everything was on complete display.

None of them had convinced the King to publically call out to them. Instead, it was her. Lorelei.

The elf.

Swallowing hard, she stopped in front of the King and sank to her knees. She meant it to look clumsy and forgetful, as though she didn't know how to curtsey. Borovoi's magical gown had other ideas, however.

The fabric billowed around her, falling with such grace that she looked like a flower laying to rest at the King's feet. Damn the leshy and his magic. He'd only made all of this more difficult for her.

The King reached down and tucked a finger underneath her chin. Slowly, he tilted her face up until he could see all of her. "Where have you been hiding?" he asked, with no small amount of awe. "I've never seen you in Tenebrous, before."

She should lie. She should keep her mouth shut.

Lorelei should make up some grand story about how she had fallen from grace, or that she was some elderman's daughter who had been forgotten in a closet somewhere. Anything but the truth.

And yet, she had no interest in remembering a lie. If she were going to kill the King, then she wanted him to know exactly who had done it.

"I have no family, my king." The words grated, and she had difficulty hiding a wince. "No father. No home. I have come in the hopes that you would see a poor woman like me, and find some use in my beauty."

"So you can speak, after all." He tilted her head with an easy flick of his wrist. "You mean to say that you're homeless?"

"Not quite. There are homes for people like me, and those who are willing to do what it takes to survive." There, that should disgust him. She'd all but alluded to being a lady of the night.

Instead, his eyes flashed with even more interest. His cheeks turned bright red, and she knew it wasn't with embarrassment. "My, my. I didn't think to find a woman like you in the crowd of Tenebrous's best women, and yet, here you are. The woman I've been searching for my entire life, it seems."

No.

No, please, she wasn't that woman. She wanted to live in the shadows, not to find the King's favor. Lorelei let her eyes drift shut lest he see the horror radiating through her entire body.

Apparently, the King didn't care. He took his finger away from her face and proclaimed, "Join the others! Tonight is one for revelry and dance. Soon I will choose the women I bring home with me to the castle, and you shall see the glory of your king."

For all the attention he'd brought upon her, he dismissed her rather easily.

Lorelei slunk back into the crowd of women, though she noticed how they all distanced themselves from her. Not a single girl wanted to be seen with the woman glittering like starlight. Perhaps they feared their own beauty would dim in the wake of someone who looked like her.

Perhaps they had a reason to fear.

"Bravo," a voice muttered in her ear. "If you wanted to get his attention, that was the perfect way to do it. How are you casting this spell, by the way?"

"What spell?" She didn't even look at the man standing behind her.

"The one that made you what I named," Abraxas said. He was too close, and he saw far too much. "Lady of Starlight."

She turned then, certain he was about to give her up. "It's the butterfly I caught. You can thank Borovoi and the fates for whatever you see before you."

He gave her a knowing glance. "Somehow I doubt that."

Lore swallowed hard. Was this it? Had he seen through every ounce of her hiding and knew that she was a magical creature? He'd give her up if he did. The Umbral Knights would descend upon her and throw her from the party.

His eyes said he wouldn't. The smile on his face was kind and thoughtful. It was not the expression of a man who knew he was going to harm someone. Somehow, she wondered if he had it in him to hurt anyone the way she had expected him to do.

He was a complete and utter mystery. Who was this man?

"You never said where you were from," she murmured. "I find it hard to believe that you are one of the Tenebrous crowd, considering your clothing and the way you hold yourself."

"Really?" He smiled a half smile that was so alluring. "What makes you say that?"

"You don't carry yourself like you've been wanting your entire life."

"Wanting what?"

Did he step closer to her? As though maybe he thought she meant that he had wanted her, but that wasn't how she wanted this conversation to go. And yet, now he was in her space and she could feel the heat radiating off him as though he housed a furnace in his chest.

"Food," she whispered. "Clean water. Clothing that hasn't been ripped off the back of the dead. Countless dreams and wants that other people seem to get but Tenebrous never has."

"Ah." He licked his lips, the movement so distracting that she almost didn't hear his reply. "I've had my fair share of wanting. Perhaps not in the most recent years. But I have wanted, Lady of Starlight. I have thirsted and desired much in my life."

"And how much of that did you not get?"

It was the right question to ask. Clearly, he didn't have an answer for her. He looked away, back toward the King, who was calling out names.

Lorelei didn't care. Let the King forget she existed while this man stood in front of her. This man of mystery and shadows with his dark hair and yellow eyes. She'd never thought to meet someone like him in her entire life.

He made a thousand questions burst to life in her chest. Questions that she knew would likely never have answers.

"He called your name," Abraxas said. He took a hefty step back from her. "You should go to the King. It's what you wanted, after all."

"I don't want the King," she corrected him. But she turned toward the villain who would now own her body and soul. "I don't want any of this. And yet, here I am."

A blast of heat struck her back, and for a moment, she thought she felt the slide of a hand over her stomach. Her muscles tensed, locking up tight as he whispered a single phrase in her ear.

"Arce Damnatorum."

City of the Lost.

And then he was gone.

Disappearing as though he'd never even stood in that crowd with her. She looked for him, but he had well and truly disappeared.

Had she dreamt it all? Conjured a man in her mind that would help her through this horrible situation with the King? Surely she hadn't already lost her mind.

"Lorelei!" Her name thundered through the crowd, said with impressive annoyance. "Where are you, woman? Here I was thinking that the most beautiful lady would be last on my list, and she disappears into the night once again!"

The crowd laughed, and she knew she had little time. The King called for her, and she needed to kill the King.

"Here!" she called out, still glimmering with starlight a little too brightly.

As the others stared at her in shock, she let the moonlight fall from her skin and pretended to be surprised when it disappeared. At least some of them would believe her charade that the magic had worn off of her before everyone else.

"Oh," she added. "I thought it would last longer than that."

The King had little patience for her antics. "Well, come on then! We all have to get going and you're holding us all up, now."

So much for being his favorite.

Lorelei fell into line with the other women and realized they were already leaving Tenebrous. The rest of the women had family members bringing their bags, promising that the rest of their clothing would be sent in trunks later on. The King's men gathered up those large bags and carried them to a caravan of carriages that appeared out of the forest.

She didn't have time to go get her things or gather up her weapons. This wouldn't work. There was too much on the line for her to not have a single weapon of her own.

"Here you are, my dear." Borovoi appeared at her side, holding out a bag that appeared light as a feather. "It's everything you'll need, I'm certain of it."

She took the bag. Enchanted, obviously. It weighed as though there wasn't a single thing inside it. "All my things? Or yours?"

"Your dwarf friend found everything in your apartment and gathered it up for you. He said to tell you that yes, he went through your things." Borovoi winked. "And I might have put a few outfits in among the rest, so you won't be the worst dressed woman in the castle. Who knows what's in there."

"It adds to the adventure, I suppose." She threw it over her shoulder and managed a weak smile. "To the carriages I go."

"Good luck, Lorelei." Borovoi bowed deep and low before muttering, "I think you're going to need it."

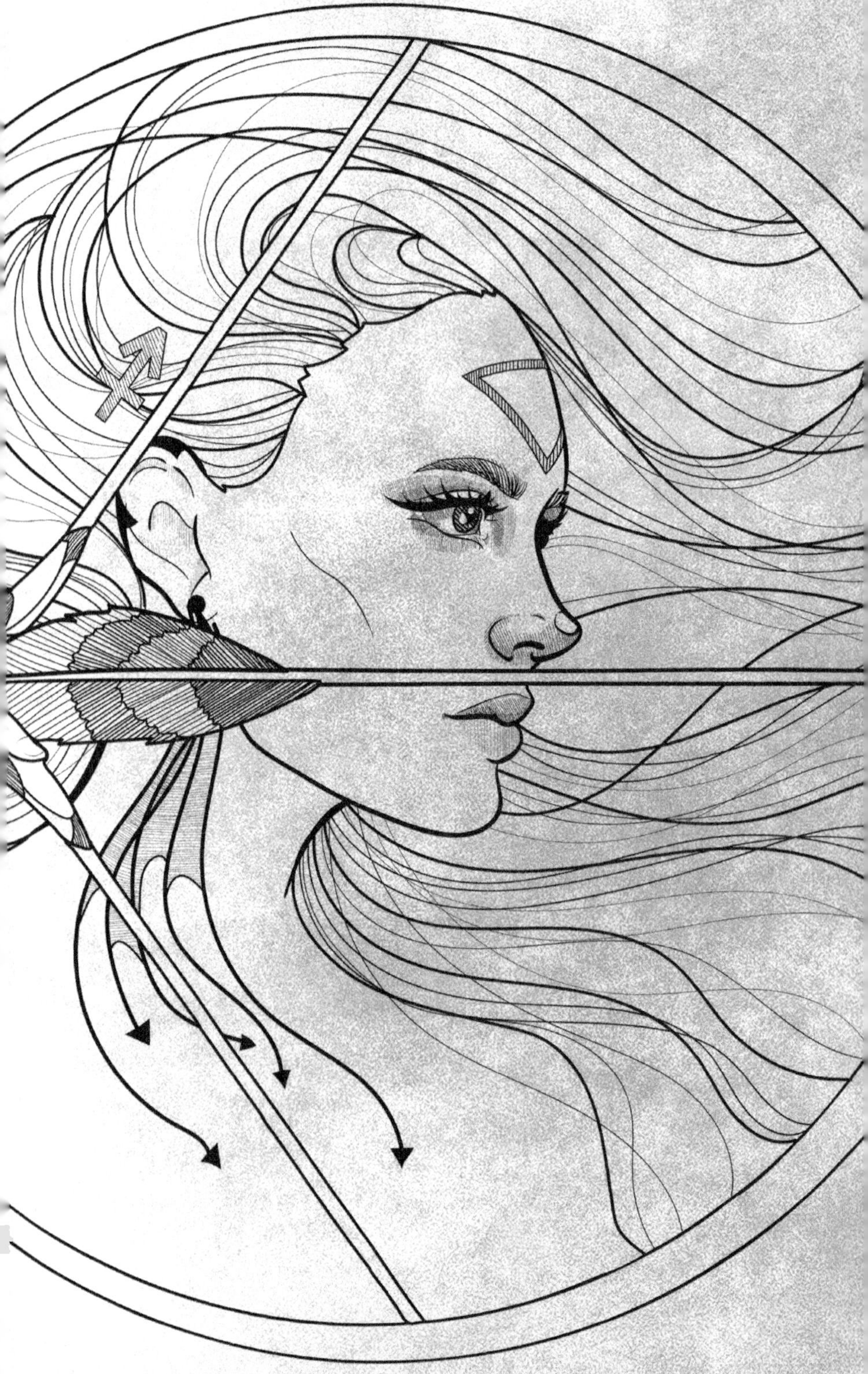

CHAPTER 10

The carriages the King had sent were beautiful. Lorelei stepped into the one that the Umbral Knight pointed her to, and didn't even clip her head on the ceiling. Already a rarity, considering she wasn't a short woman by any means.

Three other girls already waited for her. And she meant girls.

None of them looked a day over twenty, and every inch of their beings shifted with nerves. She supposed that was natural, considering they were heading to the castle for the first time in their life. And most of them were likely afraid of what the King had planned for them. He was a king with a dragon, after all.

She sat down next to the window, crossed her hands in her lap, and waited for someone to say something. The two girls across from her looked like they were sisters. Perfect cherubs, really. Their dark hair was neatly tied up on their heads in buns, while their dresses were exactly the same cut. Only one was pink and the other was green. They ducked their heads together and began whispering. Pointing out the window at things that Lore couldn't see.

There would be no talking to little girls like that. She had no interest in learning about their newest crush or whatever it was children talked about these days. Which meant the only potential ally she might have was the girl sitting beside her.

She turned and gave her seatmate a once over. She was pretty in a healthy kind of way. And Lore thought that with the utmost respect. It's just that the girl was plumper than the rest, and while that didn't make her any less beautiful, it certainly meant she had led an easier life than the others.

A nobleman's daughter, perhaps?

Her seatmate met her gaze and grinned. The smile lit up her entire face and made her glow with happiness. "Hello. My name is Beauty. What is yours?"

"Beauty?" Lore asked. "What a strange name. I've never heard it before."

Beauty tucked a strand of chestnut colored hair behind her ear and shrugged. "My father thought I would be the most beautiful girl in Tenebrous when I was little. He was the one to name me."

What father didn't want their daughter to be that? Lorelei was certain he hadn't intended to send this little girl into the lion's mouth of the King, however.

"My name is Lorelei," she replied. "Are you excited about going to the castle?"

"Oh, very much! I've heard it's the most beautiful building in all the land." She covered her mouth with her hand. "I'm sorry. I keep saying that word over and over again, lately. I don't know how to talk to people like him."

"The King?" Lore leaned back on the plush cushions and snorted. "I don't think he's all that interested in what women have to say, if we're being honest."

Beauty gasped. "You can't say things like that! A Knight will hear you!"

"Mm, maybe." She doubted it, though. All the Knights were off with the King, and if they were even thinking about the carriages with the women in them, then they were more likely guarding the outsides and they weren't going to overhear what the women were saying.

The King was vain, and he'd already proven himself to be controlling. Neither of those qualities translated into a man who cared about the opinions of women. He likely thought they were all bumbling dolts that he could control with a wave of his hand.

She supposed he could. He was, after all, the King.

The other two women in the carriage still hadn't looked up. They had eyes only for each other, and she wondered how young they were. They had to be at least eighteen, although they looked younger than that.

"How old are you?" she asked Beauty. "There appears to be quite a bit of age difference throughout all the women that were brought before the King."

"Eighteen," she blurted quickly. Too quickly.

Lore raised a brow and eyed the girl. Even she appeared younger than she said she was. Though that could easily be the soft roundness of her cheeks. "How old are you, really?"

She'd at least expected a bit of a fight from the child. More lies or arguments that twisted her words. But Beauty was not a liar, it seemed.

The girl's cheeks turned bright red, and she sighed. "Seventeen, technically. But I'm turning eighteen in a month, so my father said I should lie. How many opportunities does a girl get to marry a king?"

Lorelei supposed very few of them in their lifetime, but she didn't think that Beauty would end up as the queen. She was too kind. Too soft. And the King was a hard man who wanted someone next to him who was just as cruel.

She'd already seen that in his eyes.

Beauty twisted, facing Lorelei with her back to the window. "How old are you?"

Three hundred. Lorelei almost told her the truth. Her attention was on the battle ahead of her where she had to convince the King that she was worthy of his attention more than these young women who were in the prime of their lives.

"Thr..." She cleared her throat. "Thirty."

"Oh!" Beauty's eyes widened. "And you aren't married yet?"

Right, because at that age she should have been married with three children on her hip by now. Lorelei controlled her eye roll and glanced out the window. "Uh, no. I've never been all that interested in being married."

That apparently was the signal to summon the attention of the girls seated across from them. The twins stopped talking and glared at her with no small amount of hatred. "Then why are you here wasting the King's time?"

Lore hadn't expected them to be quite so aggressive about it. The girls glared like they had some personal connection with the man who had ruined so much of this country. Lore almost wanted to tell them exactly what this king had done to her and her people, but she had to check herself.

These children didn't care about the plight of the magical creatures. They didn't care about the future of Umbra or how much their world would change if people like Lore were eradicated from this realm.

All they cared about was a crown, a throne, and a future that was easier than living in Tenebrous. Lore couldn't blame them for wanting to claw their way out of the cesspit they all lived in.

She forced a smile and shook her head. "I suppose I shouldn't say it like that. I've never been interested in anyone I've met in Tenebrous, and I will not marry anyone that I don't want to marry."

The girls relaxed and whispered to each other again. Apparently, that was the right thing to say.

Lore glanced back at Beauty, who still wore a frown on her face. The girl was thinking, and that was good. She shouldn't stop herself from making her own opinions. The more she watched this girl, the more she liked her.

Beauty opened her mouth, closed it, and then blurted, "You aren't like anyone I've ever met."

She gave the child a little half smile. Perhaps there was no small amount of secrets in that look, because Lorelei hid more than Beauty could ever guess. "I take that as a compliment, dear girl."

"I meant it as a compliment. Tenebrous is filled with everything that I've come to expect from people. They all wander through life as though every day is going to be exactly the same as the last." She licked her lips. "I don't want every day to be the same. I want to live my life with adventures and excitement. That's why I want to marry the King. I don't think living a boring life is worth living."

Oh, she could easily love this little girl. Those words were right out of Lore's heart.

She reached forward and cupped Beauty's jaw. "You are a rare flower in a desert wasteland, Beauty. Your father was right when he said you would be more beautiful than any girl in Tenebrous. Your soul glows with a thousand suns."

Beauty's eyes widened with every word. She took in what Lore said and soaked it up as though she really were a flower. Somehow, Lore thought, no one had ever told Beauty that she lived up to her namesake.

The girls across from them snickered. The one in pink muttered, "Now if she could lose a few pounds, then maybe she actually would live up to her name."

Lore watched all the happiness drain out of Beauty. It was like all the energy that she'd brought into herself from kind words just... died. Lore had felt that before. She knew what it was like to have someone believe she was lesser because of how she looked. That horrible feeling should never be felt by such a rare and kind creature as Beauty.

"Listen here, little girl," she snarled, turning toward the girl in pink and ready to give the child the tongue lashing of her life.

She didn't have the chance.

A whistling sound pierced the air, then the glass window of the carriage shattered. Shards burst into their faces and the girls all screamed. Lore didn't move. She watched the arrow fly through the window and embed itself in the pink dressed girl's throat. Silencing her immediately.

All sounds stopped. The girl let out a horrible gurgle, pressing her hands to the arrow in her neck that had come out the other side. Lore had heard that sound before, long ago, when the war meant her people were still fighting.

"Save her!" the girl in green screamed. "Someone save her!"

Lore tilted her head to the side, expressionless and empty. "I'm afraid that's not possible. Your sister is going to drown in her own blood."

"What? No! You have to do something."

A small amount of pity filtered through the shock. Lore had to get them out of the carriage. Someone had attacked them and that was not good. She had to save herself.

"Fine," she snarled. Lore lunged forward and ripped the arrow out of the girl's throat. "She'll die faster now."

She wasted no time on the grieving sister. Planting her hand firmly on Beauty's back, she shoved the girl out of the carriage and landed in a crouch outside. Already the Umbral Knights were forming a protective barrier around the carriages that were all gathered together on the road. Other windows were broken, and considering she could hear a few other girls screaming, she had to assume more were dead.

None of the trees moved. She saw nothing in the bushes. With a quick glance, she noted the few arrows that hadn't found windows were pointed down slightly. Meaning they had been shot from above.

Smart. Their attackers were high in the trees somewhere. Harder to find for the Umbral Knights who used their swords rather than bows. She'd never seen them touch the crossbows on their backs.

More whistling. She grabbed Beauty and slammed the girl's back into the open door of the carriage, holding it in front of them while three thuds shook the frame.

"You're covered in blood," Beauty gasped. "Your dress."

Who cared?

Lore glanced down at her front to see a small amount of splatters. The dress was ruined, of course, but she wasn't covered.

"Stay here," she muttered.

The arrows weren't the rebellion's. She knew that much. They were crudely made with twisted wood. That's why they weren't flying correctly. Amateurs.

If Beauty moved, then it wasn't on her anymore. Lore had set the girl up as best she could, but they weren't able to run now. Keeping the door in front of her would help a little. At least she was crouched on the ground with solid wood in between her and the flying arrows. However, she couldn't stay there forever.

The Umbral Knights were doing nothing. They stood there like the empty headed soldiers they were, swords drawn, ready for their enemy to attack them. But their enemy was in the air.

Someone had to do something, or they were all going to die.

Grumbling under her breath, Lore ripped the skirts on either side of her legs so she could at least run freely. She spun around the door and grabbed the arrows still stuck to the wood. They hadn't gone too deep, thankfully, so she could rip them free with relative ease.

The next part she worried about. She sprinted toward an Umbral Knight, arms pumping with only three arrows in her hand. Lore leapt into the air, snagged the bow from the nearest Knight, and rolled over his back. She landed hard on her feet, but moved quickly so he couldn't catch her.

Only then did she spin on her heel, nock her arrow, and let it fly into the leaves beyond.

Her target fell from the trees with a loud cry, then landed on the ground in silence. One down. Now she had two more arrows and whatever others she could rip out of the carriages.

The Umbral Knights all turned as one toward her, as though she were the person attacking the brides.

Damn it. She was trying to help them, and no one could control the shadow soldiers once they set their eyes on someone. One of the nearest Knights drew his sword and the metal contraption that made up his body thundered toward her. Step by unforgiving step.

She didn't have a sword. She had a bow, and arrows would do nothing against the smoke inside that armor.

Some force slapped her in the back. Then a horrible sound wrenched through her body. She fell to her knees with her hands over her ears as the cry of a dragon ripped over their heads. The force had been wind, she realized.

The dragon had arrived.

One giant wing landed next to her. She stared in horror at the claw that was as long as she was tall. Dark red scales covered the flesh, while the membranes of his wings spread back with deep blue veins. He flexed his claw, and it left deep furrows in the ground. Through the thin membrane, she could see the dark outline of Umbral Knights that had frozen in place. Staring at her through the flimsy barrier.

Breath shaking, eyes wide, she looked up into the massive eye of the dragon. His elongated snout created a narrow structure for his face that led back to twin horns on either side of his head. Large tusks framed his mouth, while even more spikes trailed down his muscular neck.

He stared down at her with a tilted head, as though he were trying to figure out what she was. Some kind of little bug that had somehow gotten stuck between his claws. But then an arrow sliced through the air again and bounced off one of his scales.

With a rippling snarl, he turned toward the trees and let loose a mouthful of fire that spewed across the forest.

"No," she whispered, letting her hands drop into her lap. Limp.

She could hear them screaming. Those ancient, beautiful trees. They cried out in pain as the sap inside them boiled and the men in their branches fell, ripping and tearing until they hit the ground.

The entire grove died while she listened to their cries.

And when the dragon was done, he took off into the air without a second glance at the woman who knelt on the earth between his claw marks. Hands grabbed her shoulders and shoved her back toward the carriage. But she didn't care. All she could hear was the sound of death in her ears.

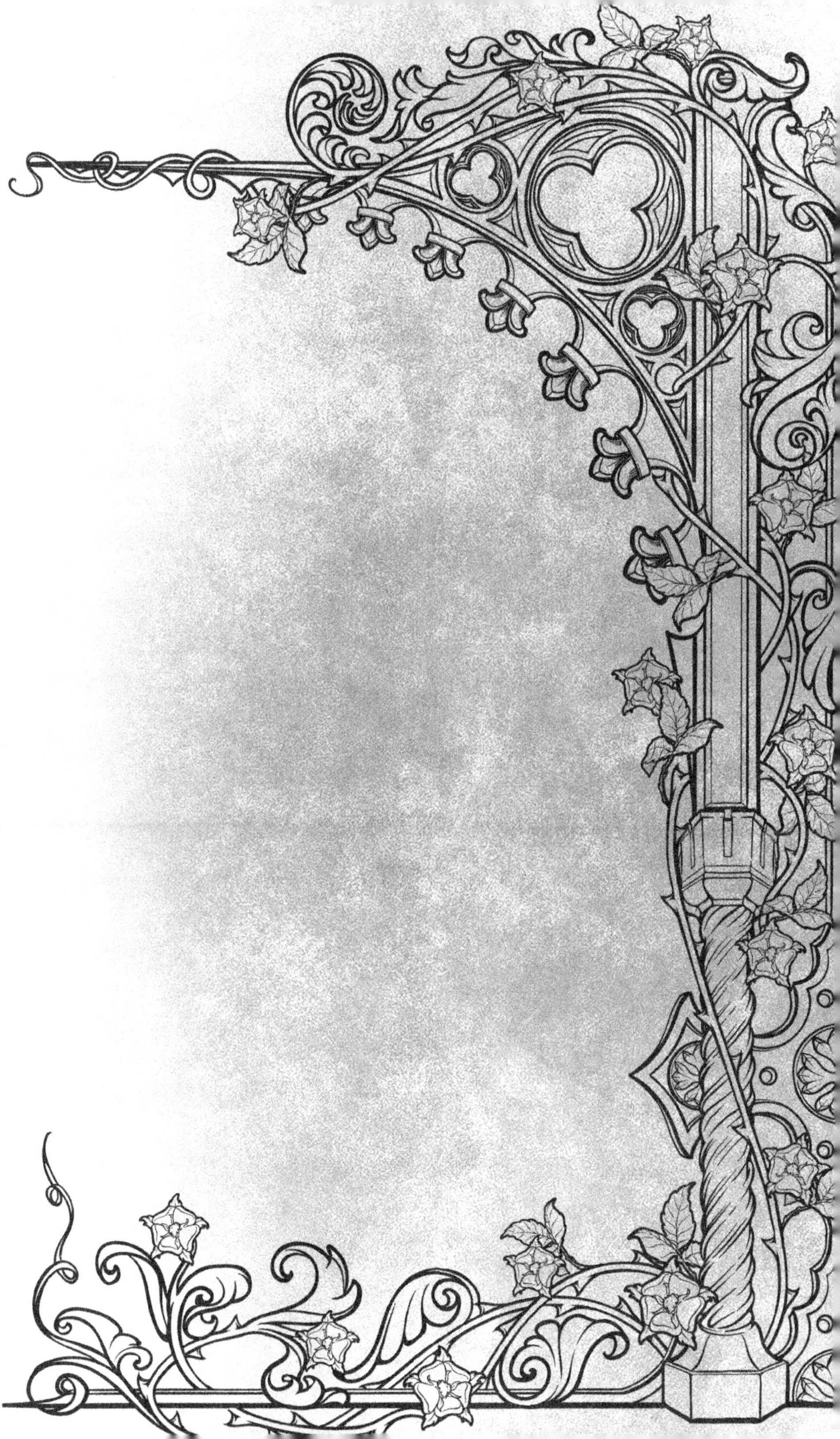

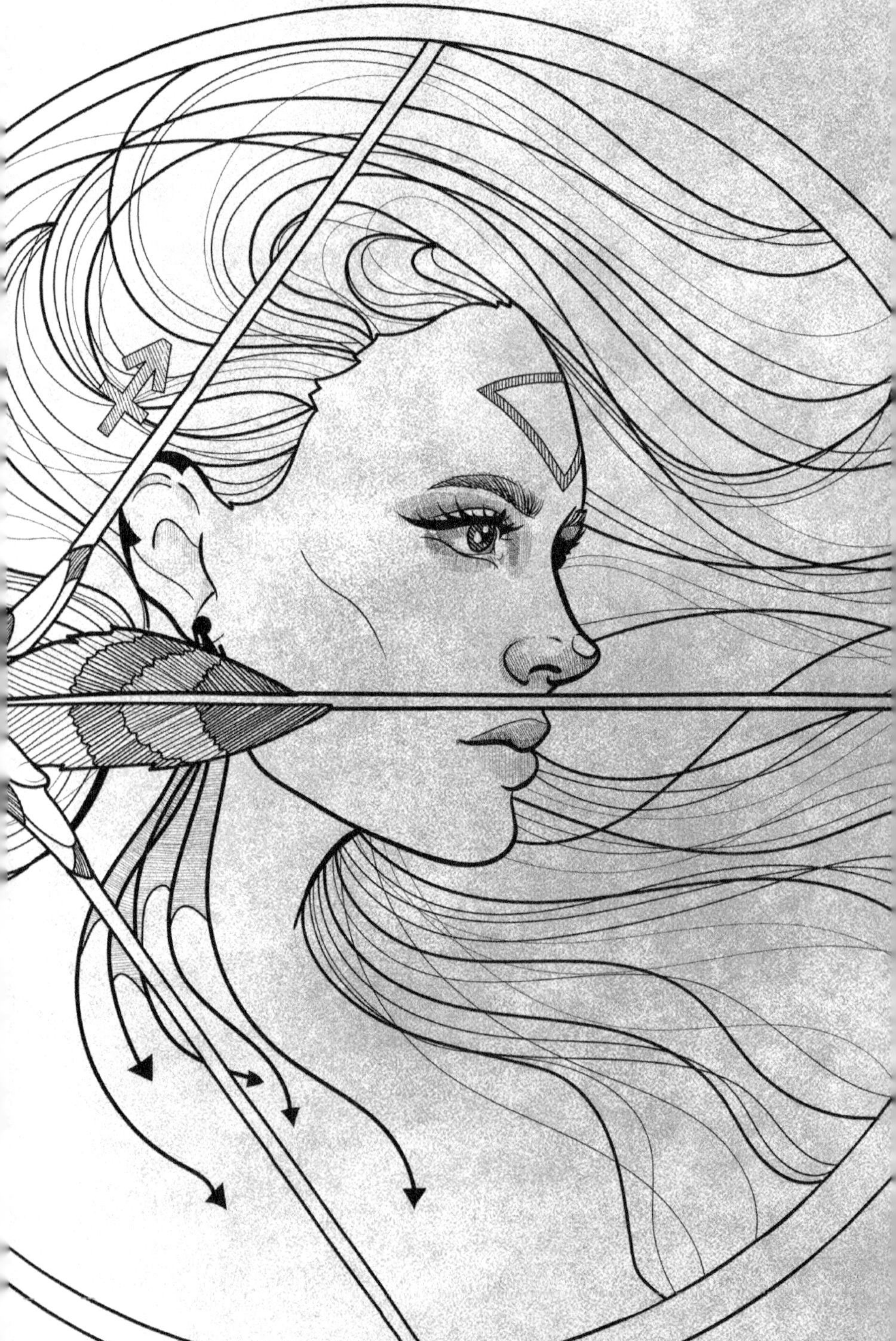

Chapter 11

By the time the carriages arrived back at the castle, Lore could have sworn most of the young women had forgotten anything happened at all. She stepped out of their transport, expecting to see tears and screams as the potential brides fell onto their knees in fear.

What she ended up finding in the castle courtyard was a handful of stoic fearful children, while the rest stared at the spiked towers in awe.

Lore could admit that the castle was intimidating. With its large, twisting spires built out of white marble, the gothic building was stunning. It captured the attention immediately, as no other building in Umbra looked like… well…this. But wasn't that the point?

The Umbral Kingdom was one of shadows and darkness. Most of its inhabitants knew only hardship and difficulties. The castle, however, was pristine and clean as the day it was first built. So many of the young women who had arrived here in the carriages had never seen a building like this before.

Lore didn't like it. The extravagant show of wealth was clearly driven by a man who cared little for the rest of his kingdom. Even the courtyard was perfectly swept, as though no horses or carriages ever drove on the square marble stones.

Beauty paused beside her, hands still shaking. "What do you think?" she whispered.

"About what?"

She eyed the young women who stood at the front of the crowd. Those were the ladies that she had to worry about the most. The blatant display of death hadn't phased them in the slightest. They all stood with bloody hems, some of them even had blood on their hands, but their hungry eyes were turned toward the castle.

They cared little for the loss of life. They hardly even cared that someone had died in front of them. All that mattered was that their future was within their grasp. The castle was right here. The King was beyond those doors waiting for them, and that's all they wanted.

Lore didn't question in the slightest that the King had gone ahead of the caravan. If he had been attacked, the Umbral Knights would have shown a lot more aggression. Instead, they had merely stood around, wondering what to do with themselves while the brides died.

With a soft sound, Beauty stepped closer to Lorelei. "About the other brides? Some of them don't even seem... Well..."

"They don't care that others have died," she said to the girl. "I think we have some competition here, dear girl. And that means that these women will stop at nothing to get the King."

She wanted to warn Beauty to keep her wits about her. The only way either of them was going to make it out of this alive was by watching each other's back. But could she trust the young woman? She really didn't know if she could trust anyone here.

The doors to the castle opened and a pinched-faced woman walked into the courtyard. Her white hair was swept back on her head, so tightly that it pulled the corners of her eyes back. A good thing, considering the wrinkles that gathered around the woman's eyes and lips. Permanent frown lines grooved her forehead, and Lore knew this was the person who actually ran the castle.

"Ladies!" the woman shouted, clapping her hands for silence. "You may call me Agatha. I am the head housekeeper of the castle. Anything you might desire or need should be sent through me first, and then I will give your request to the King. In the meantime, you are to be cleaned, washed, and clothed before supper. Is that clear?"

All the other young women nodded.

"Good." Agatha's eyes found Lore.

She knew what the other woman saw. A bride older than any of the others, holding herself strong and proud, as though she were above all this. Lore wouldn't hold herself like a child, nor would she try to hide her own confidence. And yet, her clothing was ripped, she was covered in blood, and the hard edge in her eyes likely gave her away as something other.

Agatha sniffed and then walked back to the castle, clearly dismissing the sight of such a horrid creature.

"Wow," Beauty whispered. "I don't think she likes you."

"No, I imagine she won't like me. Ever." Considering Lore would be the biggest thorn in her side. "Shall we follow them?"

"I don't think we have much of a choice, now do we?" Beauty held out her arm for Lore to take. "My lady."

Lorelei snorted, but linked her arm with Beauty's. "Lady? I don't think I have ever been called that before."

"Well, someone should. You saved my life back there, you know. I don't have a doubt about it. I think, maybe, you saved all our lives with that arrow you loosed. Killing that man gave all the others pause and the dragon enough time to arrive." Beauty shuddered as they walked up the steps to the giant wooden doors. "I don't want to think about what would have happened if you hadn't done that. They would have killed all of us."

Probably. Lore knew that the attackers had only one goal in mind. They wanted to ensure that the King never passed on his lineage. They wanted the line of the Umbral King to end here and then let the kingdom fade into chaos as they all tried to figure out who was more deserving of the throne.

That was the rebellion's work, but she didn't think Margaret sent those men. They had been too clumsy. Too green. Margaret wasn't so foolish as to send men who were clearly not warriors to do a job like that.

Was she?

Lorelei shook her head and tried to focus on the matter at hand. She needed to infiltrate the castle, and the easiest way to do that was by becoming friends with the servants. They were the ones who knew the real comings and goings of a building like this.

Now the question was how to find them. They ducked into the shadows, hiding behind Umbral Knights, as if they weren't even here. Other than Agatha, of course, and that woman wouldn't help her.

A slight tug on her arm turned her attention back to the girl hanging off her. "Look," Beauty pointed ahead of them. "Have you ever seen anything like it?"

Lorelei didn't want to know. She looked, though, and she wished she hadn't. The King had filled the grand foyer with paintings and trophies from his father's era. From the time when mortals had seen creatures like Lorelei and decided to tear apart what they saw.

Small stands held the trophies. Some of them were skulls of beasts the King's father had killed. Others were items from her kingdom like swords made by elf hands, wands made of an ent's favorite branch. But the thing that caught her attention the most was all the jars that hung from the ceiling and cast twinkling lights over the entire room. Like prisms hit by the sun.

Her breath caught in her throat. She released her hold on Beauty and nudged her forward to the other girls.

Her voice was only a little thick when she said, "Go on ahead. I don't like to be in crowds, but I think you should make some friends."

"I thought we were friends," Beauty replied.

She heard the hurt in the girl's voice. Lore couldn't forget that the only other brides Beauty had talked to only commented on her weight.

Fiercely protective, she bared a feral grin at the perfect young woman in front of her. "You have nothing to fear, my girl. The only people who would dare say anything mean to you already got what they deserved. A drowning in blood and a great loss. Now go into that crowd with your head held high because you are just as terrifying as the dragon who saved us. Remember that."

Beauty lifted her chin and made her way into the group of young women. She really was beautiful. Regardless of her shape, that young woman would become a force to be reckoned with. Lorelei knew it.

She waited until the brides had all but left the grand hall before she turned to the nearest hanging jar. Her heart clenched in her chest and tears gathered in her eyes.

"What are you doing here?" she asked as she gently unhooked the jar from the tie on the ceiling.

A tiny woman pressed her hands against the inside of the jar. Her wings glowed bright yellow, so brightly that it was almost painful to look at. Her entire form was light at the moment, but Lorelei remembered when the pixies had sat on large leaves next to her, at least ten of them to a leaf, while they watched the moon festival.

She'd been a child back then. But the pixies had always been her favorite. They were so hard to find other than at the festival, when they were happy to let everyone see their bright glow.

The pixie pounded a hand to the glass and let out a tiny squeak.

"I'm sorry," she whispered again. "I don't know what you're trying to say. But I'm going to let you out."

"I wouldn't do that if I were you." His warm voice was unexpected, although she should have guessed he'd be here. Abraxas always seemed to show up when she least expected him.

Lorelei turned and put the jar behind her back. "Do what?"

"Let that pixie out of the jar," he replied with a soft snort. "Or do you think I didn't notice you pull it down from the hanger?"

She had to figure out a way to distract him so he wouldn't notice that she was twisting off the lid of the jar. "I think it's strange that you're following me, sir. Unless you actually work for the King. In which case, I must say, I have a lesser opinion of you than I already did."

"I would imagine it would be hard for me to lower your opinion any further, and yet, I must." He swept into a low bow, though he watched her every movement. "I am part of the King's personal guard. The head of it, in fact."

"You are not." Just one more slow twist and the pixie would be released. "What a horrible job for such a handsome man."

"Handsome?" He looked up at her, mouth slightly ajar. It seemed like he struggled for a moment to find the words. Time suspended between them until he straightened with a laugh. "Now I know you're hiding something. You would never call me that unless you were up to mischief."

"I wouldn't know the first bit of it. Exactly what are you accusing me of, Head of the King's Guard?"

There it was. The lid of the jar popped out of her hand and the pixie attached itself to her back. She could feel the tiny creature's claws ripping into the fabric at her spine. A couple more tears and it would be able to slide into her dress and hide. Smart little thing.

"Lorelei," he growled. "I said don't let the pixie out of the jar."

She pulled her arms out from behind her back, the jar in one hand and the lid in the other. "Oh, this jar? I'm afraid you didn't tell me fast enough. If I had known it contained such a dangerous creature, I never would have put everyone at risk."

Sarcasm dripped from every word.

"Damn it, woman," he snarled. "Do you know how long it took for the King's servants to capture those? Gathering pixies is risky business, and he'll notice that one is missing. Then I have to make up a lie about why one is gone."

"Why would you have to make up a lie?" The pixie burrowed into the small of her back. It tucked itself into the hollow of her spine, pressed against the two hills of muscles. "You could always tell the King that you saw me do it. He would send me back to my boring old life in Tenebrous and no one would be the wiser."

"He'd kill you for touching anything that was his." His eyes flashed with anger, and for a moment, it almost looked as though they had turned an even brighter orange. But then he shook his head and took a step away from her. "No, I don't plan to tell him it was you."

"Why not?" she asked.

"I will not tell you why, just let no more out!" His hiss echoed through the room. It bounced off the ceiling and struck her again.

She refused to feel guilty for doing what was necessary. The pixie didn't deserve to live out its days in a jar. She didn't care what the King wanted with them.

Lorelei squared her shoulders and endured his anger. But she would not rise to the same folly. "They will die in jars like that. They have to be in nature. To feel the sun on their skin. Otherwise, all their light will die out and then they'll be pressed against the glass, begging for someone to help them. But none of you can hear their calls. Over and over, they will beg until they shrivel up into little husks of pixie skeletons. All alone."

He flinched with every word, backing away from her and shaking his head. "It's funny how you think I can't hear their screams."

Only magical creatures could.

She narrowed her eyes. "Just how would you be able to hear them, Abraxas?"

"There's more to this place than you know." He nodded at her, dismissing the conversation with far too much ease.

Abraxas tucked his hands behind his back and suddenly, he looked like a royal guard. That straight spine. The empty expression as he stared over her shoulder, not wanting to get involved in anything that his king would disapprove of. "You are requested to be with the other brides at all times. If you don't go now, then Agatha will report you to the King."

"For what? Meandering?" She gestured at the room. "This place is supposed to be mine one day, anyway. Why can't I explore it?"

"You can test your limits with me, Lorelei. But I cannot promise that Agatha will give you as much leeway." His brows furrowed and his gaze hardened yet again. "Now go find the other brides before someone notices you are missing."

"Yes, sir." She clacked her heels together and pressed a hand to her forehead in salute. For good measure, Lorelei dropped the jar onto the floor and had the satisfying moment of seeing him flinch at the sound of broken glass.

Let him try to order her around. Let him try to convince her that others in this castle were more dangerous than him. Whatever his reasoning, this guard seemed like he had a soft heart. He wouldn't give her up.

But as she left the room, he called out, "And do something with that creature in your dress! If someone sees you with it, your head will roll tomorrow morning."

Perhaps he had his limits, then.

Gulping, Lorelei sped up down the hall where she had seen the tail end of a fancy dress rounding a corner.

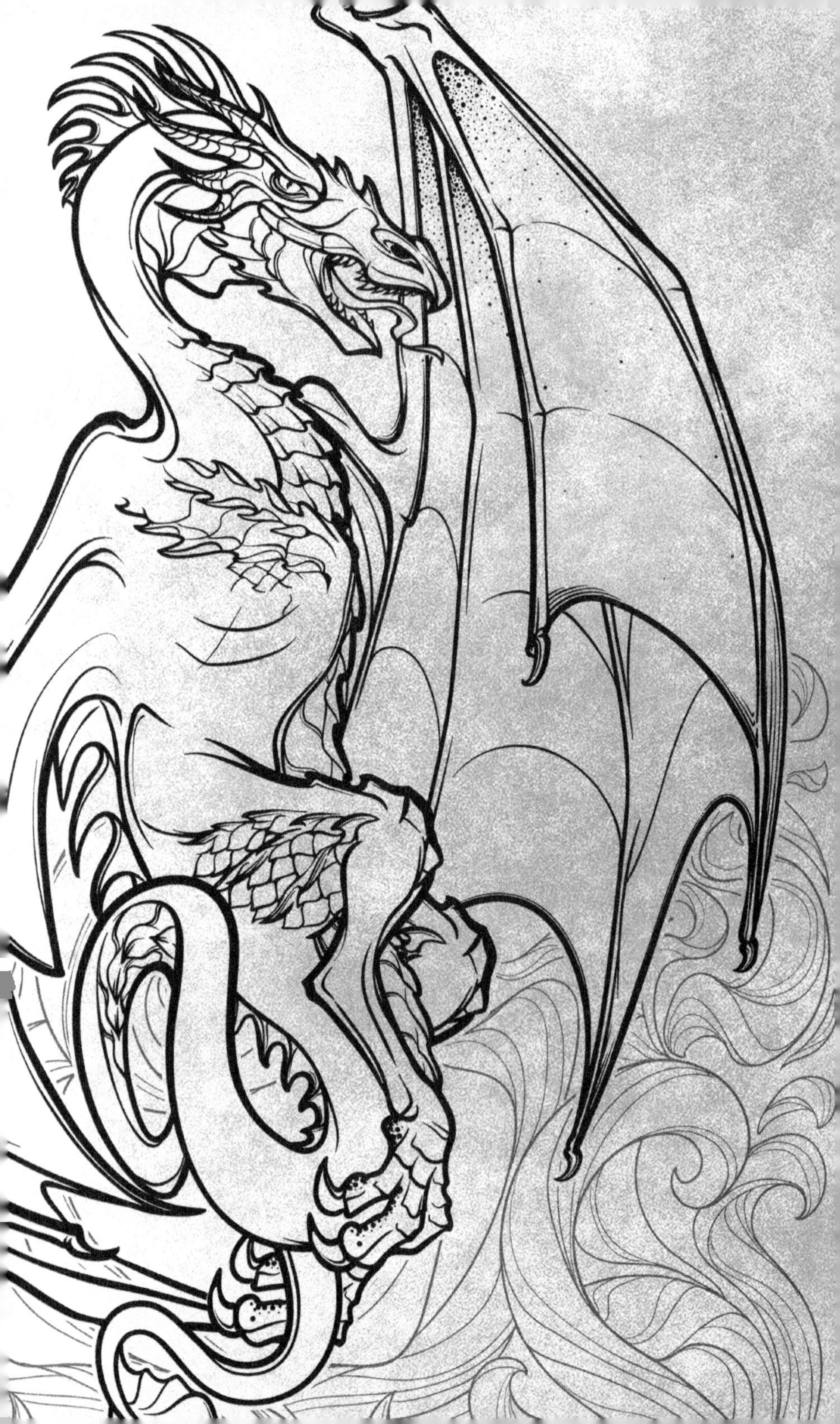

CHAPTER 12

He had to admit, the curious woman had him wrapped right around her finger. Anyone else, he would have sent to the dungeons for touching one of the King's captured magical creatures. And yet... He couldn't. Not with her.

The idea of her in those damp dungeons sent a chill down his spine. Or perhaps it was a pulse of red hot anger that made him want to punch something. Abraxas hated that he was under her spell.

She'd held the jar with such careful hands. The golden light of the pixie's body had spilled over her features, delicately highlighting the lovely bow of her lips. But it wasn't her beauty that had stopped him. It wasn't the stunning picture she painted that tugged at his heart.

It was the way she stroked the jar and how her heart had sped up when she looked at the pixie. She cared about the creature. And that kindness didn't match the woman he'd seen at the attack.

Her arrow had flown straight and true. Even with the warped wood and poorly fletched ends, she had sent that clumsily made weapon straight into the heart of the man who had fired it.

He had never seen a woman do that before. He'd never even thought that a mortal woman could be so deadly. She hadn't even hesitated.

Battle did not scare her. She didn't even care about the clothing that she'd ripped apart to move easier. Like a true warrior would.

This was not the kind of woman he'd expected to come to the bridal games. The Umbral Knights would tell the King what had happened. He was certain of that. The King would then want to meet her. This starlight woman who fought like a man.

And now she released his pixies.

Abraxas would have his hands full keeping this woman alive.

Shaking his head, he moved through the hallways toward the King's private quarters. As he walked, he wondered what the potential brides thought of this castle and all its luxuries. Magical pixie lights hung from every corner that someone could attach a string to. The walls were covered with the finest wallpaper, every hall a different color or pattern, so the servants knew where they were going. And the warm oak floors had been carefully crafted a hundred years ago from trees that no longer existed.

He should mourn those losses. He'd seen those trees when they had grown so tall, even the dragons had flown around the forest lest they fly too high and lose their breath in the clouds.

It had been so long since he'd been in the King's service, however, that he'd forgotten what it meant to be nostalgic. Those memories dulled in comparison to a hundred years of torment and suffering.

Abraxas pressed his hand to a giant blue flower on the wall, the symbol of the King, and the secret entrance opened. He didn't look to see if anyone was watching him. Abraxas would know. The hairs on his arms would stand on end, unless the person was a magical creature. And if they were, well... he almost hoped they'd find this secret entrance and save them all.

The rooms beyond were an entire wing of the castle that dripped with too much beauty. Just walking into these rooms always made his eyes burn.

The King preferred gold. His father had preferred crimson. Together, they had created a series of gilded rooms with wallpaper that looked like it were dripping blood onto the floor. He hated every second of this place. The King thought it made him a stronger man to live like he was always in a war. No matter that Zander had never even seen a war, nor had he ever seen a battle.

A cluster of maids stood around the King. Zander had apparently forgotten a shirt, or perhaps he thought it appropriate to be half naked with a group of women surrounding him. Each woman had her hands full of different fabric and material.

The King faced a floor to ceiling mirror with the edges wrapped in gold leaf, his reflection one of a handsome man who was ridiculously proud of himself. Zander touched a hand to his chest now and then, lovingly stroking the soft planes of his chest. As though the body he saw was the most perfect one anyone could ask for.

He snapped his fingers and one maid held up the fabric in her hands. Ah. This was a fitting.

Abraxas snagged a gilded chair from the corner and dragged it across the floor. The noise screamed through the room and a few of the maids flinched. Zander, to his credit, hardly reacted other than to glare at the dragon.

"Is that necessary?" the King snarled. "I'm trying to look my best for the brides."

"Potential brides," Abraxas corrected. He stopped dragging the chair once he reached the middle of the room, then sat down on the hard red cushion. "What are you doing, anyway? Your outfit was fine before."

"But now it will be the most magnificent they have ever seen. Don't you know anything about women, Abraxas? They want to be wooed with luxury and colors and pretty things." He waved his hand, and the next maid lifted her doublet so he could see it in the mirror. "They don't care about the castle or the food. They care about what I can give them."

That seemed like a horrible relationship to be setting himself up with, but what did Abraxas know about mortal women? He nodded sagely, as though the King had spoken only the truth. "Then I look forward to dinner."

"Why are you here, Abraxas?" Zander snarled.

"I'm the head of your personal guard. I'm supposed to be here at all times to ensure that no one has tried to take your head off." Not that he would mind it all that much. But he was bound to those eggs and to his people. He had to do whatever the King wanted.

"I hardly doubt any of my maids are going to do that. Not a single one of them is strong enough to do it, anyway." Zander snapped his fingers again.

But Abraxas noted the women's expressions behind the King's back. One of them couldn't hide the widening of her eyes, and another couldn't hide the blush that stained her cheeks. These were working women. Their arms were strong, their backs even stronger. They had taken life by the horns and dared to work for the King.

Maids weren't weak little creatures that the King could easily overwhelm. Abraxas would bet on any of the maids if a fight broke out in this room.

He winked at the girl with bright red cheeks. "I think I'll stick around, if it's all right with you. No offense to your fighting skill, my king, but these maids look terrifying indeed."

A few of the women giggled. At least he'd won them over. In his opinion, it was more important to be friends with the servants than the nobles. At least then he'd get an extra biscuit at dinner.

Zander sighed. "Would you stop flirting with the help? You're a dragon! Have a little dignity."

"I lost that a long time ago." He settled his ankle on the opposite knee, reclining in the chair without a care in the world. "Would you hurry up, though? I'm getting hungry."

"You will wait until I'm ready. And put something nicer on than that, would you? The women will think you're some vagabond who walked in from the street." The King sniffed and returned his attention to the clothing.

Abraxas settled in for a long night. He knew the King's moods could shift like the breeze, and the last thing he needed was to offend Zander before dinner. But he wouldn't change. There was nothing wrong with the clothing he wore currently, even if Zander thought his outfit was messy.

The entire process of dressing the King took longer than Abraxas had anticipated. The sun was already setting on the horizon before Zander had finally clothed himself and liked what he saw in the mirror.

"Well?" Zander asked, stepping in front of Abraxas and smoothing his hand down his sleeve one more time.

The King had chosen a bright purple outfit for dinner. The collar was too high around his neck. Gemstones had been painstakingly stitched down the shoulder and arms, perhaps to create a line for the eyes to follow. But the King didn't have the shoulders for that embellishment. And the pants... The pants were studded with amethyst chunks that Abraxas could not believe were comfortable to sit on.

However, he looked back up into the King's eyes and smiled. "You will stun the ladies with this fashion choice, my king."

"And you will terrify them with yours." Zander waved a hand in the air. "I pity the fool who tries to teach you how to dress. It certainly won't be me."

Abraxas pitied whoever tried to teach the dragon that as well. It wouldn't be a fruitful meeting, nor would he listen to the advice of mortals who put gemstones on their clothing instead of within a hoard.

He plastered a bright smile on his face and bowed. "Someday, you may have the satisfaction of seeing a person try, Zander. But for now, I do believe your ladies are waiting for us."

"Indeed. As they should be." The King straightened the arm of his jacket one last time, before leading the way through the castle to the grand dining hall.

Abraxas had always thought the dining hall was too ridiculous for anyone to take seriously. The chandelier on the ceiling dripped with diamonds, casting rainbows all over the walls and floor. The table itself had the legs of a lion and seated almost a hundred people. Each chair was crafted by the most talented of woodworkers in Umbra. Some of them had flowers crawling up and over the back. Others were carved with wings, birds, even other strange creatures that Abraxas couldn't name.

Those chairs were already filled with all the ladies who might one day become queen. They watched the King with hungry eyes. All of them dressed in the best gowns they had brought with them. It was overwhelming even looking at some of them who were covered in so much jewelry that Abraxas didn't know how anyone could see past the glittering stones.

The King didn't let his eyes linger on anyone in particular. He marched to the head of the table, sat down in his chair, and then opened his arms wide. "Welcome to the feast, ladies of my heart! Tonight there will be no tests. No talk of marriage. I wish only for you to enjoy your first night here. And perhaps for a few of us to speak."

Whispers billowed through the room, so suddenly that Abraxas could almost feel a slight breeze from their breath. The ladies were obviously unhappy with what Zander had said. As Abraxas stationed himself behind the King, he read the lips of each lady who had started to speak.

One in bright blue leaned over to the girl in yellow and whispered, "I just want to get this all over with. Why can't we get on with all this? I don't understand why he wants to wait."

The girl in yellow covered her mouth with her hand for part of what she said, but then said, "—with all the deaths, I can't imagine he wouldn't give some of the women time to grieve."

Ah, yes. The deaths. Even Abraxas had forgotten that there had been numerous young women lost on the way to the castle. The King apparently had forgotten as well. He doubted that Zander would be so kind as to allow these young women the time to heal. The King didn't want to play any games tonight. Perhaps he was tired, or perhaps he was hungry.

Whatever it was, he didn't do anything other than look at the women, smile, and have a few bantering conversations with the ladies who were seated directly next to him. Considering they were the ones who had the most jewelry on their bodies, he was sure the head housekeeper had something to do with that. Agatha always did like to meddle.

He was certain there were no dangers to the King at present, other than the young ladies who were certain they would steal his heart with their batting eyelashes. Abraxas let his eyes wander, looking down the table as though he had to find her. Unbidden, he stared at the young woman who had no right to be so pretty in such a plain dress.

Lorelei sat in between two hideously colored abominations. One girl wore a neon blue so bright that it hurt to look at, the other a putrid green. Perhaps that was a blessing, however, because it made her black dress look a little nicer, even though it wasn't.

She had no jewelry. No one had done her hair to look stunning, like the other girls. She had worn it in a low twist at the back of her head, clearly done by her own hand.

He could only assume she'd come here alone. Many of the other women had their siblings with them.

Her eyes missed nothing. She watched the other women with a calculating glance that saw far too much. Abraxas couldn't help but wonder what her past was. Her history. She didn't react to any situation like a normal woman.

Lorelei leaned forward and put her elbows on the table, only to flinch back as she noted none of the other women were doing that.

The other women here had come from the same place. They all had seen the poverty of Tenebrous, but none of them were so uncomfortable as her. She made her way through the meal in silence, watching to see which was the right fork to use or the right knife.

She really had no idea what she was doing.

Abraxas remained still as stone as he watched her. If anyone had cared to look behind the King at the head of his personal guard, they might have wondered why he was so invested in this single, unremarkable woman.

He didn't have an answer for that. He didn't know if he could put it into words why he wanted to see her every move and understand her every choice. She was so different, so unexpected, and perhaps that was the real reason why he was so curious.

The others were predictable. They moved in the same way as the others. They spoke the way he thought they would, and some of them even dressed the way he assumed they would. And yet, she defied all he knew about mortal women.

And that was curious.

He wanted to understand her. He hadn't wanted to do that in a very long time.

Lorelei lasted through most of the dinner before she cast a sideways glance and then slowly stood. No one else noticed. They all talked amongst each other and then, strangely, the two women she'd sat between talked with each other as though she had never sat in that chair.

He couldn't help himself.

He had to follow her.

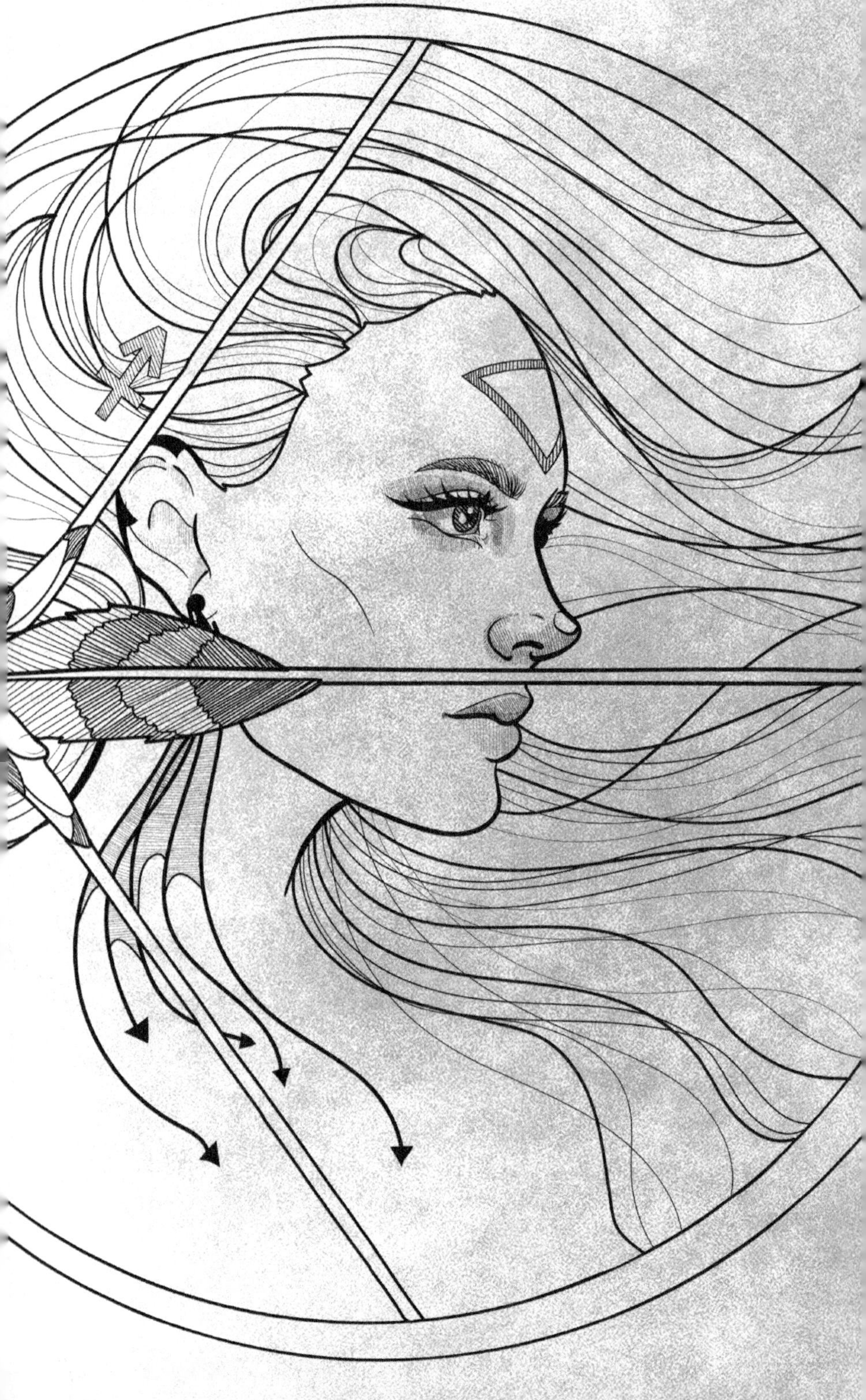

Chapter 13

She wanted to kick herself for not even making it through the first dinner. Lorelei knew better. If she wanted to capture the King's attention, then she had to actually be present in the room for him to look at her. Her best bet with a man like him was her looks, not that she had much looks in comparison to the other women.

But the girls next to her had started talking about the King. And that had naturally led to a conversation about magical creatures.

They had listed off the ones they'd seen in their lives, obviously adding pixies to that list now that they'd seen the jarred lights. Lorelei had gotten lost for a second, wondering about the pixie she'd left in her room. The little woman had promised it wouldn't wander off, but it was a pixie. They weren't exactly the most reliable.

Then she'd heard the words that turned the entire dinner into a waking nightmare.

"Have you ever seen an elf?" one of them had asked.

"No, but I heard they're hideous beasts. All the legends claim they're so beautiful, but my father said they were disgusting monsters. He said everyone who looked at them remembered why they hated magical creatures." The girl in the neon blue dress then lifted a snail to her lips and sucked the meat out of the shell. "What use were they, anyway? All they wanted to do was wander around in the woods. Heathens."

Then, of course, the conversation devolved into further speculations about her kind and why the elves didn't last. They were all wrong, of course. None of the elves had given up their place in this realm. They had been incredible fighters, warriors to the very core. Nothing the girls said was true and yet... The words still hurt.

Lorelei couldn't take it anymore. She couldn't sit at that table with all these people who wanted to laugh at her people's expense. Women who knew what fork and knife to use in a setting like this, but who also couldn't see past their own transgressions.

If she could have slapped the smug expression off every one of their faces, she would have. She'd have hit them so hard they might have felt something other than disdain for her kind.

But she couldn't. And that meant she needed to leave.

Lorelei quietly stood and made her way down the table. Perhaps it was the black gown she'd chosen to wear, or maybe she was using magic without knowing, but no one looked at her. No one even noticed that she'd left her seat and wandered out into the hall.

The door she opened didn't lead her into a hall, however. It led her into what appeared to be the servant's stairwell. At least it would give her a little privacy for what she was embarrassed that she was about to do.

Lorelei let all her fear and worry coil up in her chest. A wave of cold rolled down over her head, although she immediately started sweating even as goosebumps broke out over her arms. And her heart raced with the tears gathering in her eyes. A panic attack was the worst thing to happen right now but... but...

She was tired.

So damned tired.

All she wanted to do was retreat to her room, where she could curl up under the covers and pretend she wasn't here. Lorelei wasn't used to so many people wandering around, so many eyes on her at all times.

But most of all, she hated that everyone judged her. For what she was. What she might be. And finally, what they thought was impossible for her to be.

What would they do if they found out she was an elf? She had no idea. The women had no power here, that was for certain, but what if the King found out? Obviously, they all were in agreement that women or creatures like her shouldn't exist.

A knock resounded through the small corridor, and Lorelei curled in on herself. She wasn't proud of the movement. She'd survived worse than a startling sound in her life, and yet she cowered like a woman under attack.

"My apologies." His deep voice eased down her spine like a soft touch. "I didn't think you'd be surprised. I'm not sure I've ever seen you startled."

"Abraxas," she said with a long sigh. "I wasn't expecting anyone to find me in here."

Least of all him. Why wouldn't this guard leave her alone? She wasn't sure what had gotten into him, but he always seemed to be around when she didn't want him to be around.

Lorelei swiped her hands underneath her eyes and hoped it wasn't so obvious that she'd been crying. Turning slowly, she put a brave face on and tried her best to look like herself. "Can I help you?"

"Funny, I was thinking about asking the same question of you." He took another step into the room, gently closing the door behind him. "I hope you know that your absence will eventually be noticed."

"I'm not sure anyone in that room even noticed I got up and left," she replied.

That shouldn't sting. If they didn't notice her leaving, then that meant it would be that much easier to become the assassin that she was supposed to be. And yet, it made her feel thoroughly unwanted.

They had already made it very obvious that they thought her people were lesser. Maybe that was why it stung so much. Even not knowing that she was an elf, they still treated her like she wasn't worth their time or effort.

Lorelei needed to get some room to breathe, and she didn't have that opportunity while this man took up even more air.

He watched her a little too closely, as though he could read her mind while her thoughts played through her head. "I'm not sure what you're thinking, Miss Lorelei, but I think it's rather obvious that you are not enjoying your first dinner in the Umbral Court."

Wordlessly, she shook her head.

"Is there anything I can do to make this night easier for you?"

What lovely, meaningless words. She shook her head again and tried very hard not to look at him. She didn't want to know what he would do to make the night easier. An evening in his bed? Hardly worth it. An insider's look at the King's life? The last thing she needed was more opinions rattling around in her mind.

She supposed he could kill the King for her, but that also wouldn't end well. He was a personal guard to the man she'd been hired to kill! If he found out why she was here, or what she planned on doing, then he would likely serve her head on a platter to the man who paid him.

Lorelei was alone here. And she thought it would be easier than what it actually was.

Abraxas's eyes darkened and again, she swore there was a hint of gold in them, or perhaps fire that burned just slightly. "You are a very somber woman for one who wants to marry the King."

"I don't want to marry the King, and I realize I shouldn't tell you that," she replied. "I'm here to do my duty, and that is all. It feels as though everyone's eyes are on me all the time, and I'm unused to it."

His hands flexed at his sides, clenching in that confusing movement. A muscle in his jaw jumped. He looked past her for a few moments, his entire body stiff as though he were expecting a fight.

Then he blew out a long breath, obviously forcing himself to relax. "That is something I can help you with, Lady of Starlight. I am very used to having eyes on me."

She had a hard time believing that. He'd stood behind the King and not a single potential bride had mentioned him. They were all staring at the man in garish bright purple, as though nothing else existed other than him. But Lorelei had seen Abraxas.

She'd noticed he hadn't taken his eyes off her for most of the dinner. She had seen the intensity in his gaze as he analyzed every one of her movements. Strangely, knowing that he was watching had helped her try to fit in with the others.

Her attempts had failed, of course. The other young women wanted nothing to do with her, other than Beauty, and even that little darling had started making her own friends here.

Lorelei fisted her hands and propped them on her hips. "Just how are you going to help me with that? In case you didn't notice, you're the King's shadow. Not the King's right hand."

"Ah, but there are things you do not know and things you might not wish to know about my life." He grinned. "Regardless, I think it's important that you know how to handle the eyes of hundreds upon you. After all, you're here to marry the King. If you succeed..."

His lifted brow obviously suggested that he thought she might. But that wouldn't do. No one should even remember that she was ever here.

Lore tucked a strand of hair behind her ear and stared over his shoulder at the door that led out into the dining hall. "What's your trick, then?"

"I remember that I am not like the others. In your case, you are not some young woman who wandered into a castle and hopes to find herself a king. You're so much more than that." He lowered his head, staring up at her with meaning in his gaze. "You ripped arrows out of a carriage, attacked an Umbral soldier, and then killed a man all on your first day here. Those other women couldn't hold a candle to you, or what you are capable of doing."

His words made her go cold.

"Pretty words," she murmured. "And so interesting that you would remember what I did. Considering you weren't there."

She knew he wasn't there. He couldn't have been. If he was the King's personal guard, then he would have been with the King in the carriage that had gone ahead of all his brides.

Abraxas froze, and she knew she'd caught him in a lie. Somehow, he'd heard about what she had done. Or maybe he had been there, and she simply hadn't seen him. But whatever the reason was, she wanted to know how he knew about her actions at the attack.

"Abraxas," she said again. "How did you know any of that?"

He wouldn't look her in the eye, and that was enough of an answer. He was searching for something in his head, an explanation, a lie, a distraction so he could get out of this situation without her poking any harder.

She'd let him try to figure all that out. Lorelei leaned against the wall behind her, crossed her arms over her chest, and stared at him while he thought. Apparently, that made it much more difficult. He cleared his throat, tucked his hands behind his back, and looked anywhere but at her.

Perhaps he thought he could wait her out. That if he said nothing for long enough, that she'd at least attempt to fill the silence.

She wouldn't.

Lorelei waited until he broke.

Abraxas snarled out a long sound that was eerily animalistic. "I was curious if anyone knew anything about you, considering our conversation in the great hall. Another guard was in your caravan and saw what happened."

"The only guards in our caravan were the Umbral Knights. And if you're going to tell me those tin canisters can hold a real conversation, then I will definitely assume you are lying."

His eyes slid to the side again. "You are far more astute than I gave you credit for, Lorelei of Tenebrous."

The title hit her harder than if he'd thrust a knife between her ribs. Lorelei of Tenebrous? No one had ever called her that, but to be leveled down to a legacy of swamp and ash? She'd never been so insulted in her life.

She knew he had no way of knowing her correct title. No way of understanding why his words had made her straighten her back and clench her teeth. It wasn't fair to be angry at him for something he had no clue was so insulting.

But she was.

She was so angry that she couldn't even see straight. Lips pressed into a thin line, she snarled, "That will be all, Abraxas. Go back to standing behind your king like the good little guard dog you are."

He made a mistake. She walked by him and he grabbed her arm as though he had any right to touch her.

"I don't know what I said—"

He didn't get to finish those words.

Lorelei whipped around. She grabbed onto his fingers and pulled them in the wrong direction, pushing them back to his wrist until he let out a low sound of pain and dropped down onto one knee. He stared up at her with surprise in those strange, yellow eyes, but she refused to feel any kind of pity for him.

"I don't like being touched," she growled. "Particularly by someone who thinks they can grab me whenever they want. Do it again, and I will take these fingers for myself. Do you understand me?"

He should have been afraid. Instead, he grinned, and the expression was one of feral pleasure. "Lesson learned."

She threw his hand away and stomped out of the servant's corridor. Lorelei looked at the table with all those squabbling idiots, her stomach sinking. She couldn't sit by those foolish little girls who didn't understand what it meant to have a heart.

So instead, she found the single soul at the table who had given her the smallest bit of kindness. Beauty. She sat between two sticks of women who were barely touching their food at all. In fact, most women here weren't eating.

Good. They wouldn't mind having a change of scenery then.

She walked down the line of the table and not a single person looked at her. Maybe they all thought she was one of the servants. She certainly could have been with her dark clothing and ability to stay out of sight.

They were fools to not look at her, but she supposed it helped in the long run. She leaned over and muttered in the ear of the girl she'd sat next to, "You need to move down one."

"Excuse me?" the girl blinked up at her. "I can't. There's someone sitting next to me."

"There isn't." Lorelei pointed to the blank seat. "You're in the wrong seat."

The girl looked at Lorelei's vacant spot with a surprised stare. "Oh. I thought someone was sitting there earlier. I must have been wrong."

"I suppose you were."

She then moved her attention to the next person. And the next. Until she got to the spot beside Beauty, vacated it, and sat down with a satisfied smile. "How's your dinner going?"

Beauty set her fork down and cleared her throat. "How did you do that?"

"Do what, my dear?" Lorelei raised her brows comically high.

And this was why she liked the girl so much. Beauty didn't question why or how she'd gotten every single person to move. Instead, she burst out laughing. The snorts mixed with giggles reminded Lorelei why she was doing this. Taking on all this stress and the danger of killing the King.

For people like Beauty. For the kind-hearted lovers of Tenebrous, who deserved a better leader than this horrible man who only wanted what was best for him. Beauty deserved to live in a world where there was more for her. Where she could grow and help her family, or start her own business and impact the entire world at large.

Lorelei picked up her new fork and knife, then peered down at the food on the plate in front of her. "What was that stick eating? This looks like rabbit food."

"You're actually going to eat that?" Beauty asked. "I couldn't force myself to put it in my mouth. The servants brought me soup instead. I said I was sick."

She sighed and did her best to mimic puppy dog eyes. "If I say I'm sick too, do you think they'll cast pity on me?"

Beauty laughed again, and the sound was music. "Maybe, if you're a good enough liar."

Thankfully, Lore was very good at that.

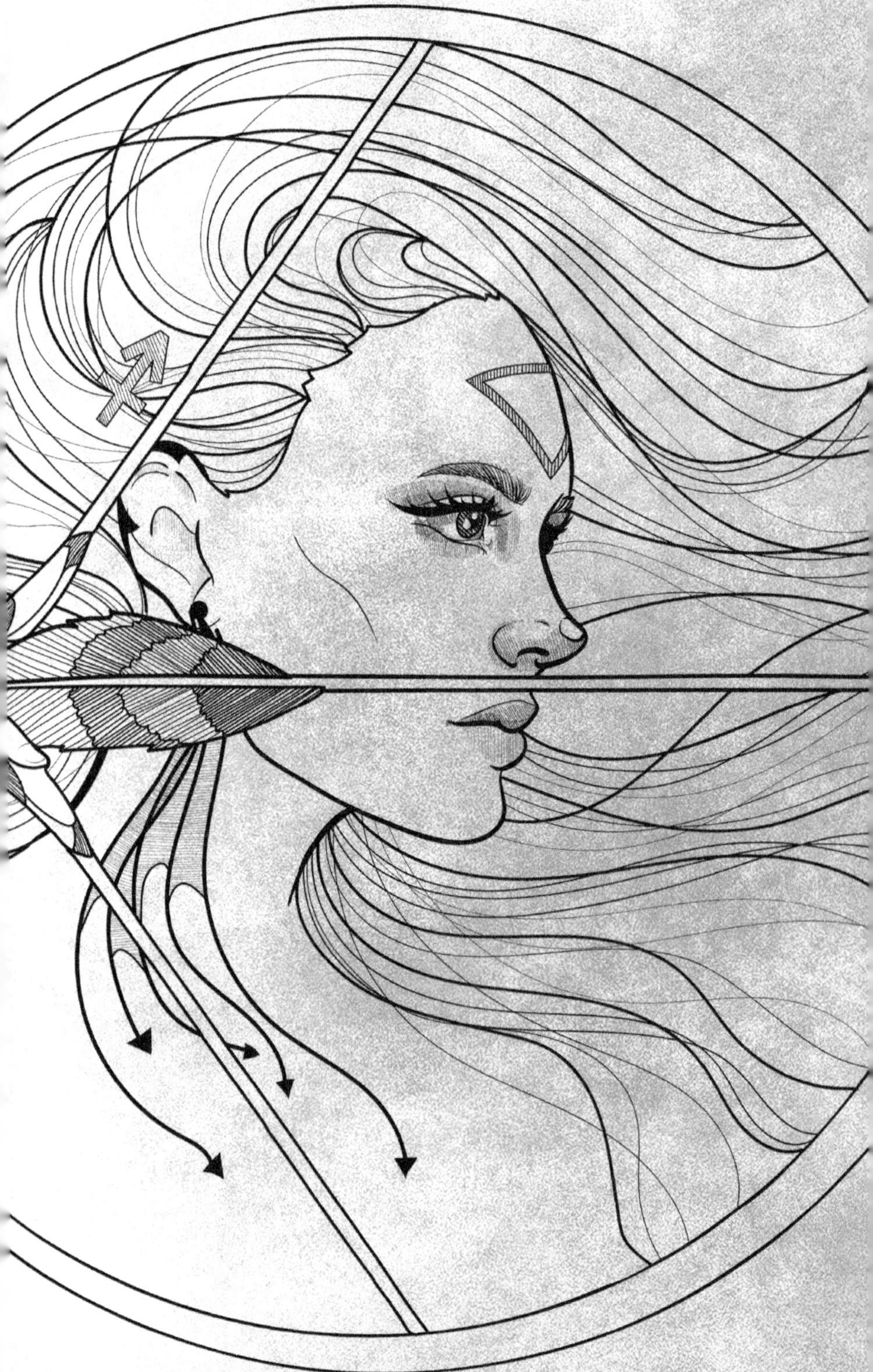

Chapter 14

Arm in arm, Lorelei walked with Beauty back to the long hallway of rooms where the brides were sequestered. Each door had been painted a different color, and she could only assume that was so Agatha could keep track of who was who. Why would she learn their names when she could just remember colors?

Beauty paused in front of her door that was painted a lovely shade of blush pink. "Well, this is me. I hope you have a pleasant night."

As if they were on a date.

Lorelei couldn't help herself. She swept into a low bow and held her arms out wide. "It was an honor to spend my evening with you."

"Lorelei," Beauty scolded. "Go back to your room before someone sees you!"

As if any of the Umbral Knights would care. They lined the halls like shadows, tucked behind the curtains of the windows between each room. Like they were nothing more than decorations or statues.

Lore didn't remove the grin from her face as she waltzed away from her new friend. Beauty had made the evening bearable, and here she had been thinking that wouldn't be possible in the slightest.

Who'd have thought? An elf could become friends with a mortal woman. Perhaps times were changing.

She tucked a dusky strand of blonde hair behind her ear and walked over to the rather disgusting bruised mauve that signified her room. Had Agatha picked this color because it was a fine shade of vomit? The head of housekeeping had something against Lorelei. Every time she walked by the old hag, the woman would glare at her as though she wished her stare could set a person on fire.

Lorelei stepped into the room and locked the door firmly behind her. The King had given them luxury, that much was certain. She was so used to her tiny room in the attic of a person who likely had no idea there was an elf living above their head. This room, however, made her reconsider how comfortable she'd been in the dust and cobwebs.

The four poster bed stretched to the ceiling. Real white lilies tangled in a canopy overhead, clearly enchanted so that they would never wilt. The ceiling was painted with fluffy white clouds, so real they looked like she could touch them. A giant wardrobe at the end stood ready to be filled with all her lovely gowns, if she'd had any. And floor to ceiling windows at the end opened up onto a lovely white marble balcony. Likely the King thought he could ride up to the castle and wave to all his prizes as they leaned out their windows to watch him.

He'd be lucky if one of the fools didn't fall off the balcony in their hope to reach him. But perhaps that was a rather morbid thought.

Lorelei stepped farther into the room, in case anyone was listening, before she called out, "Pixie? Are you still here?"

She wouldn't be surprised if the little thing had wiggled out underneath the balcony doors and headed home. If there was a home for her to return to. Lorelei knew most of their homelands had been destroyed when the mortals built their homes in the Solis Occasum region.

The bed skirt rippled and a tiny lady stuck her head out.

"Ah," she said with a soft smile. "There you are."

The pixie crawled out from under the bed with a tuft of dust on her head. She was clearly not happy about still being in the castle, but determination rode on her shoulders. The pixie put her hands on her hips and pointed to the wardrobe.

"What?" Lorelei asked. "I know I brought nothing that suited a woman trying to marry a king."

The pixie shook her head and then took off toward the wardrobe. Her wings fluttered like she was trying to fly, but she didn't manage to get into the air. If anything, she looked like a regular tiny woman running across the floor.

Lorelei frowned. Something had clearly happened in her room while she was gone, though she didn't have the faintest idea what could have made the pixie so upset.

She walked to the wardrobe and threw it open. If someone were hiding in her closet, then they would have a battle ready to greet them. But instead, all she saw were an infinite amount of gowns that were so beautiful, they made her eyes hurt.

These weren't just dresses. These were the works of Borovoi. Only a leshy could make twenty gowns that looked like the gods had stitched them.

The pixie made a chirping sound and glared up at her as though to say she had some explaining to do.

"I suppose I should tell you what's going on. Is that what you want?"

The pixie nodded firmly.

"Right. Well." Lorelei supposed the pixie was the only person she could trust with the truth. This little creature had every reason to want the King dead. After all, the man had captured her and her entire family to place in little glass jars. Specifically to light his castle because regular bulbs wouldn't do.

She leaned down, lifted the pixie into her hands, and then carried the other creature to the bed with her. Gently, Lorelei set her down on the goose down coverlet.

"I don't want to marry the King," she began.

And then she told the pixie everything.

Every tiny detail of the rebellion's plan and how she feared it wouldn't work. She held nothing back and purged all the lies and half truths from her soul. At least now she could feel better about herself. She could assume that her debts were wiped clean because someone else knew.

Although, if Lore had anything to do with it, the pixie wouldn't still be here when she finally killed the King. She wanted the pixie off in her homeland with the rest of her family. It was the least Lorelei could do.

When she finished purging her soul of all the things she knew she had to do, she paused and looked the pixie in the eye. The creature had crossed her arms firmly over her chest again.

Lorelei didn't know if that was a good or bad sign.

"Well?" she asked. "What do you think?"

The pixie shrugged.

FIRE HEART

"That's not exactly an answer. You've lived here for a long time, shouldn't you know the workings of the castle?" Having someone on her side who knew how to get through the hidden corridors would certainly make things easier. The question was if the pixie would even help her.

Considering the glare on the tiny creature's face, Lore wasn't so sure she would get an ally this easily. The pixie had her reasons, she was sure, but Lore would so love to not be alone.

Finally, the pixie nodded.

"You'll help?" Lore clarified.

Again, the pixie nodded.

"Good. Mostly, I want to know where the King spends his time alone. I understand that asking for that is probably more difficult than it sounds, but I think if I knew where he spends his evenings, then that might give me an opportunity to find the perfect time to kill him. Now, I know you might want to know how I plan on killing him. That's the part I haven't figured out yet."

The pixie flapped her wings, obviously telling Lore to stop talking.

"What is it?"

She had to lean down all the way to the bed to hear what the pixie was trying to say. Their voices were notoriously high pitched, and some of the magical creatures couldn't hear them at all. Elves had good hearing, better than most magical creatures. Lore could just barely make out what she was saying.

The pixie squeaked like a mouse trying to talk. "The Umbral Knights are with him always. Some of them outside of their armor. Killing him in his sleep would not be easy to do."

Damn it, she should have guessed that he would have the Umbral Knights involved. "That was the only option I could think of. He's always surrounded by people. It's not as if I could poison his food."

"You will need to get him in a more compromising position." The pixie gestured crudely with her fingers.

Lorelei refused to do that. Even though Borovoi had suggested the same thing, she refused to seduce the King so that she could have the perfect opportunity to kill him.

Leaning back, she shook her head. "No. I'm not doing that. There has to be another way."

The pixie shot into the air, her wings suddenly working just fine, and landed on her shoulder. She grabbed onto Lore's ear with both hands and shouted, "This is not about you!"

No, of course it wasn't. It was about all the other creatures the King had killed. The ones he'd enslaved in this castle of madness simply because he thought they were pretty. Or useful, like the pixie.

"But do I have to seduce him?" she whispered, staring at the balcony as though there might be something on the other side that could help her. "I can't stand to have him in my bed. After all he's done."

The soft sigh in her ear suggested the pixie understood. She knew the pixie had to do things in her life that she hadn't wanted to do. What woman hadn't? But this was the greatest of betrayals. To allow a man like this to look at her, to paw at her, perhaps even to put himself inside her…

Lorelei stood abruptly. The pixie held onto her hair desperately, and then tagged along for the ride as Lorelei raced to the balcony and threw the doors open.

If anything could help, it was the fresh air. She took a deep breath of the mountain air that swirled around her. A storm brewed on the horizon. Dark clouds gathered in thunderheads that would give them all quite a show tonight.

Perhaps the other women would seek each other out. Storms were terrifying. But Lorelei refused to be like them. She couldn't stand to be one of those cowering little girls who hoped the King would look at her.

She stood in silence, watching the storm approach and then arrive. Icy shards of rain dashed against her face, tore at her skin and threatened to throw her back into the room. Lightning illuminated the courtyard and a rumble of thunder crashed behind it.

Still, she stood with her face to the sky. The storm could threaten all it wanted, but it would not scare her. She would not return to her room like a good little girl. She would soak its energy into her skin and she would gather the storm's power to help her through the hardest battle of her life. The battle she did not want to fight.

The pixie squeaked in her ear, but Lorelei didn't want to look.

She wanted to stand there and let the thunderstorm fill her with something other than dread or fear. Her skirts plastered to her legs, the fabric suctioned to her skin. Her hair slicked back from her face, although a few wet strands still clung to her cheeks. She shivered in the stiff wind, but it felt good to be alive. And that was exactly what this moment was.

A reminder that she was still alive. That she could survive this no matter what the cost.

Again, the pixie squeaked and tugged on her hair.

Lorelei opened her eyes and stared down the long length of the tower. A gathering of shadows had stopped in the middle of the marble courtyard. She blinked, and a flash of lightning revealed the man who watched her every move.

"Who is he?" she asked, even though she already knew the man's name.

Abraxas.

The pixie squeaked again, but she couldn't make out what the little thing tried to tell her. Instead, all she could do was stare back at the man, who was soaked to the bone. Just like her.

Another flash of lightning revealed an image of dark, wet hair that clung to his face. He'd unbuttoned his shirt from the dinner, and the slice of chest that was revealed had a smattering of dark hair. But it was his eyes that haunted her. Those yellow chips of gold in the crags of his jagged features.

"Is he not afraid of the storm?" Her voice rippled with the power she'd gathered from the thunderheads. "He should fear it. All mortals fear what they cannot explain."

Another rumble of thunder broke their connection, and the cold settled deeper into her flesh. Lorelei left the balcony to seek the warmth of the castle, although she kept the doors open.

She peeled the wet layers off, but didn't dry herself as she clambered onto the too soft bed. No matter how hard she tried to sleep, she couldn't.

She stared out the open balcony doors and wondered why a mortal man would have been out in the rain like that.

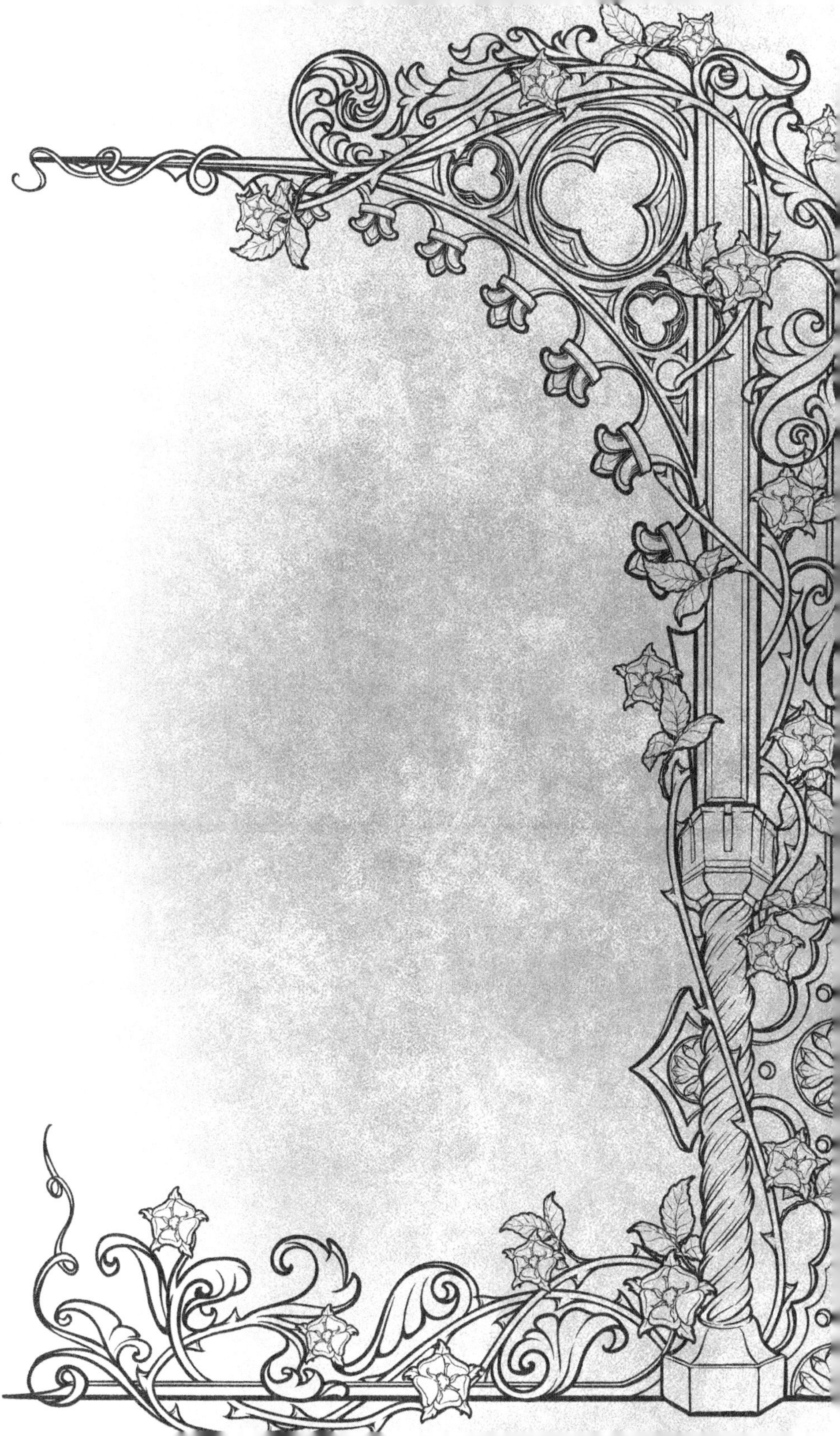

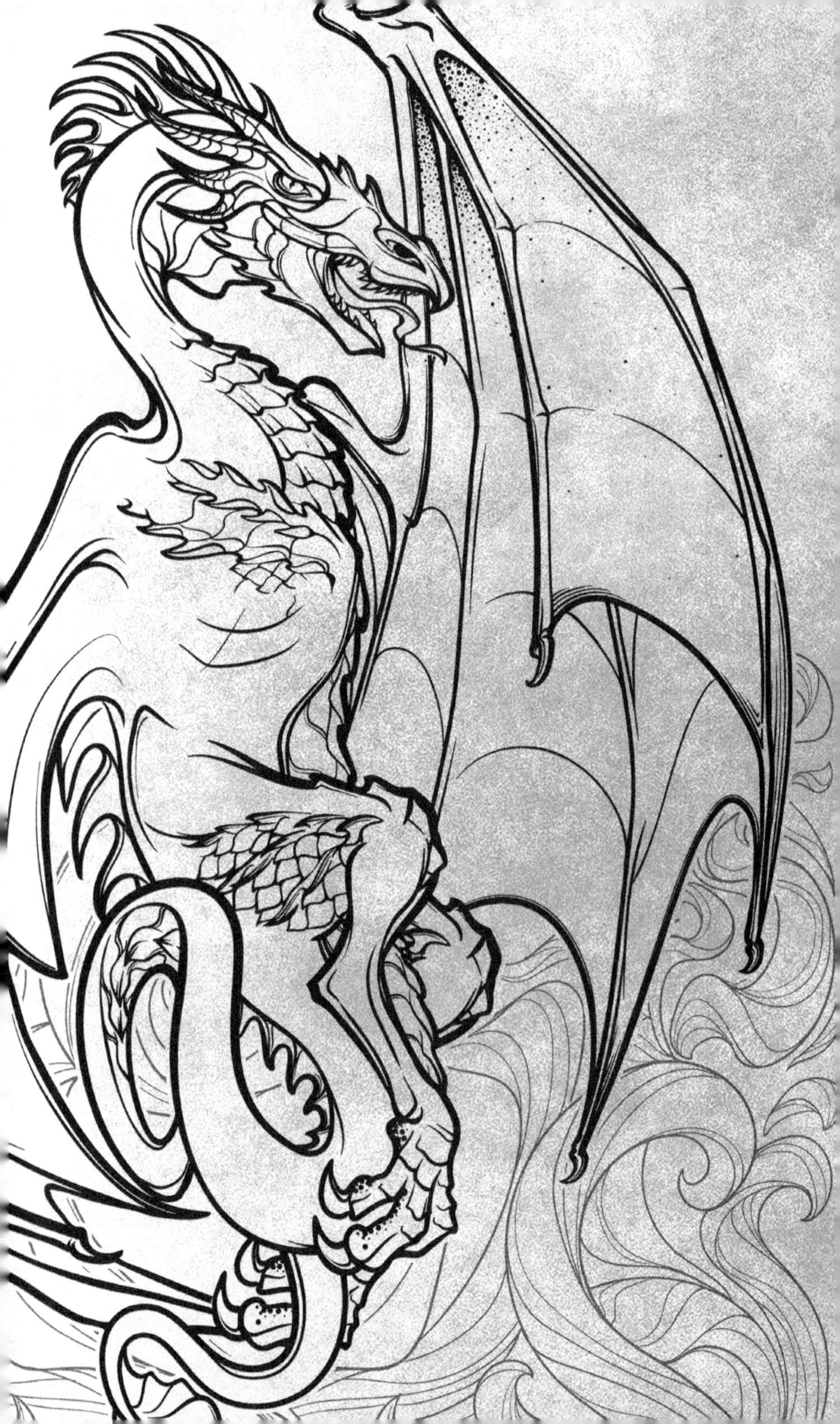

CHAPTER 15

"I want it known that I think this is a terrible idea," Abraxas snarled.

Obviously, the King no longer listened to him. And if he did, then Zander was doing a good job of pretending he'd suddenly gone deaf.

The King wandered through the garden as if in a dream. The long tails of his white and gold suit caught on a few of the rose bushes, but he just ripped the expensive fabric clear. Even the linen suit refused to risk angering Zander.

"Abraxas," the King called back. "Do you have any idea how to woo a woman?"

"I thought I did, but apparently you're going to teach me," he grumbled.

"A woman wants to think she's in charge. She doesn't want to be coddled. Nor does she want me to treat her like a child. She wants to be seen as an equal." Zander opened his arms wide and spun in a circle.

The day was beautiful after that massive storm front that shook the castle windows for three days straight. Abraxas still couldn't get the image out of his head of a woman in a black dress greeting the storm as though it were an old friend.

A shiver traveled through him. He ground his teeth, trying to keep his mind on the moment. But she'd been so otherworldly, standing up there. A creature from his memories of a time long ago.

Right, he was supposed to be paying attention to the King.

"That advice is the exact opposite of what you said when you first brought the brides here," Abraxas replied. "Your opinion of what a woman wants changes as quickly as the weather, my king."

"Ah, but isn't that the nature of a woman? They are fickle creatures with confusing intent, and even stranger minds. To understand them is to understand the ways of the moon, the stars, and all the planets in the sky. Do you see how mad an attempt that would be? Better to not understand them at all." He tilted his head back with a laugh. "Surely you know this. A dragon should see other magical creatures and know what they are thinking."

"Women are not inherently magical."

"Are they not?" The King lifted a brow. "My dear Abraxas, I do believe you have a lot to learn."

He supposed there was some truth to that. Women were rather difficult to understand, and they appeared to have connections to the world that men could only dream of. However, that didn't mean they were magical, like a dragon.

Zander moved too far ahead of him. The King had already reached the red roses while Abraxas was still stuck in the white ones.

"Zander!" he shouted as he caught up. "I still don't think this is a smart idea. You seem to think that one of them will at least try to save you from this mad assassination attempt, but what if none of them do? They aren't exactly warriors."

Except one. One of them was more than qualified to save the King, but Abraxas still hoped she wouldn't.

"One of them will give themselves up for me. That's how all the romantics say it works. She'll throw herself into the line of the arrow, and then I will nurse her back to health." Zander rolled his eyes. "Honestly, Abraxas, it's like you've never heard any of the famous ballads. There are very specific ways to woo a woman. Obviously, the other way I tried was unsuccessful."

If this actually worked, Abraxas would swallow his own tongue. "I'm going to take all this as you wanting me to be in the form of the dragon. Just in case one of your potential brides throws herself in front of the arrow, but isn't as quick as you think mortals are?"

"Precisely. If the arrow gets too close to me, you'll take care of it. I always knew you would."

The King walked to the large pavilion at the center of his garden without a care in the world hanging over his head. And what a lovely life it must be to never question that, even though he had set up a man firing an arrow at him, said weapon would never touch his skin.

If only Abraxas were so lucky. Now he had to make sure that he actually prevented the arrow from killing anyone, and that wasn't as easy as the King thought.

Sighing, he crossed his arms over his chest and watched the King approach a white pillared pagoda. The large columns were randomly framed by marble women who were sculpted with large urns in their hands. During the height of the summer, those urns would pour water into troughs that took the liquid throughout the garden. The irrigation system was as remarkable as it was expensive to create.

The brides who had already sought shade immediately called out to the King. Zander sauntered toward them with a skip in his step and a grin on his face as they all cheered at his entrance.

This was the environment that the King thrived in. He loved the attention these women gave him, but he also loved feeling as though he were more important than everyone else. And he was that all the time, considering he was the King. But Zander struggled to let that sink into his mind.

He needed constant approval. Constant reassurance that he was the most important person in the court and no one would ever surpass him.

Perhaps that was why he kept Abraxas so close.

"Your dedication to the King shows no mercy at all, does it?" Her voice flooded over his senses like a balm to the fire that brewed in his chest.

Abraxas looked beside him to see that the strange woman had snuck up on him. Lorelei was stunning today in a dress that looked like sea foam. It bubbled around her body, even making small bubbles that popped off her shoulders.

Did she smell like lavender today? Or was that part of the bubbling dress? He'd leaned down before he even noticed what he was doing, all to catch a whiff of her hair.

Abraxas straightened with an abrupt jerk. He needed to put space between them. Somehow. "I thought I was the one who startled you in this relationship."

"Relationship?" She arched her brow. "You're the head of his personal guard, and I'm supposed to be his wife. That would be a rather odd relationship, don't you think?"

Oh, that would dig underneath Zander's skin like a splinter he would never get out. Abraxas could steal the most beautiful bride out from underneath the King's nose, and they could fly off into the sunset together.

He wouldn't, of course. The remaining two eggs of his kind would bear the horrible fate of his choices, and he would never see another dragon again.

"It's a lovely dream," he said, making sure she read between the lines of his words. "And one I may entice during my evenings from here on out."

Did he imagine the way her face softened? How the wrinkles at the edges of her eyes deepened in disappointment for a few heartbeats?

Abraxas might not know a lot about mortal women, but he knew one thing that made everyone feel better. He reached for one of the red roses beside him, one that was fully in bloom and smelled divine. With a quick snap, he pulled it from the bush and twirled it in his hands.

The thorns tugged at his flesh, but even in this form, they couldn't break through his dragon skin. He took his time stripping all the thorns from the stalk.

She didn't say a word. Lorelei watched him with rapt attention, her eyes never leaving the rose in his hands.

And when he finished stripping away anything that might harm her, he held the rose out for her to take. "May I?" he asked.

"I don't know what you're asking to do," she replied.

"Do you trust me?"

Lorelei looked up at him with shadows in her eyes. Shadows he knew he hadn't caused, but that broke his heart all the same. "I don't think I do, if I'm being honest. I have no idea who you are, and you don't seem all that interested in answering my questions."

He sighed. "Right now, I'm trying to be nice."

"Ah." She swallowed hard. "Then I suppose I trust you enough for that."

Prickly woman. Maybe he should have left the thorns. She might have liked them in addition to a beautiful thing like the rose.

Abraxas threaded the stem of the rose through her hair, just behind her ear. He settled the fat bloom and released it carefully, making sure it didn't fall as he no longer held its weight. "There," he murmured. "Now there is something in this garden that might rival your beauty."

"Did you compare me to a rose?" she asked, eyes wide.

"Oh, no rose could compare to you. For a rose is beautiful, Lady of Starlight, but it has no secrets to uncover. No mysteries to unfold. You are a thousand questions and a million truths just out of my reach."

The King snapped his name from across the garden, and he realized he'd run out of time. He had a job to do. Protect the King from the errant arrow that was going to fly through the air very soon. He couldn't do that while he was in this form, and for some reason, he didn't want her to see him change.

Not yet. He didn't want to frighten her by having her realize too soon that he wasn't a mortal man. That he was a dragon.

Was it so shameful to want her to himself for a little while longer?

Abraxas dipped into a low bow. "I hope to see you again, Lorelei of Tenebrous."

Did she flinch when he said those words?

Lorelei forced a smile onto her face. "Just Lorelei, please. And I'm sure you will, Abraxas. We both live in the same building now."

She had a spine of steel to dare call the Umbral Castle a building. But he'd come to expect that from her. She was daring, and a little on the wild side. He supposed that wasn't a bad thing after all. Abraxas bowed one last time and then rushed out of the garden to a private place where he could turn into a dragon. It was time to put on a show, apparently, and the King was so certain this was a good idea.

Far outside of the garden, he passed by the young man who had been enlisted to shoot the arrow at the King. His hands shook as he plucked at his bow's strings, testing them to make sure they wouldn't fail him.

"Don't worry, boy," Abraxas growled as they passed each other. "The arrow won't touch the King."

"Can you be sure of that, dragon?"

Yes. Although he didn't feel the need to explain how or why to this child who had taken a job he feared.

Abraxas snorted. "I'm sure."

At least his confidence seemed to transfer to the young man. The bowman squared his shoulders and straightened his back, giving the dragon a nod before he disappeared into the hedges. If the plan went exactly as they anticipated, then no one would even see the attacker. Hopefully no one did, considering the archer still wore his Umbral uniform.

If a bride did see him, Abraxas feared the King would have him killed, just so they didn't find out that the entire assassination attempt was orchestrated for show.

He hated this.

With a swift surge of magic, the dragon clawed its way out of his skin. The blast of magic flattened a few of the tomato plants near him, but nothing that would make the King angry. Beating his great, leathery wings, he rose slowly straight up into the air.

Careful, he reminded himself. No one can know.

Once he was high in the clouds, high enough that he could see the gathering in the gardens, he let himself drift toward the clearing. The

King had chosen this giant space so that he could land right beside his self named master.

How impressed would the ladies be to see that their King controlled a creature like him? A man with a dragon was one thing. A man who could control a dragon was entirely different.

Abraxas landed behind Zander and ignored all the screams of fear. The women scattered before him like leaves in a fall storm. Except one. A single woman who stared up at him with a curious expression on her face.

Lorelei remembered him. How could she forget the moment when he'd landed above her? He had made certain not a single arrow had found its mark on the bride he couldn't have. And that no Umbral Knight would cleave her head from her shoulders.

Maybe he shouldn't have done that.

The King put his arms up and shouted, "Do not be afraid, my flowers! This dragon is completely under my control. I wanted you all to see him, so you knew you could trust him. If the dragon is ever near you, from now until the end of your days, you will know that you are safe."

That was a lie.

If the King ever wanted to kill any of these women, then it would be Abraxas who wielded the flame or fang. Every woman here was too high in station for anyone but the dragon to kill them. A few knew it. They gathered together as far away from his wings as they possibly could. They whispered in their small cluster of arms and limbs, praying that the dragon never came close to them again.

If they were lucky, he wouldn't. Abraxas prayed along with them that they would never see his shadow darken their doorstep.

"My father was the first to capture this great beast!" Zander brought his hands together as though he were carrying a sword. "Through might and power, he brought the beast to its knees."

Also a lie. No one had brought Abraxas to his knees. His father had snuck into the last dragon nursery and slaughtered all the eggs. He'd then had his armies slit the throats of his brethren in their sleep. He'd awoken to a massacre of blood and nightmarish screams as the souls of the dragons disappeared into nothing. All those ancient beings. Lost.

What else was he supposed to do? He'd been the largest. A crimson dragon whose only use was to protect. He had nowhere else to go, and the King had the last three eggs.

"And once the dragon submitted to my father, the man he knew would lead this kingdom into a new age..." Zander drew himself up tall and strong. "He gave my lineage the name of Dragon King."

That was the trigger. The archer rustled the bushes and poked the arrow out from them. The sunlight hit the tip perfectly, blinding a few of the women closest. And then the arrow was loosed.

It flew through the garden and sliced through the bow in one bride's hair. No one tried to stop it. No one but Abraxas, who readied his wing for yet another injury.

Except, the arrow never reached the King.

Lorelei, his mystery woman, stood with her arm outstretched. She had a dagger in her hand, although he had no idea where she'd gotten it from, and the arrow lay at her feet in two pieces.

She'd sliced it in half.

Mid air.

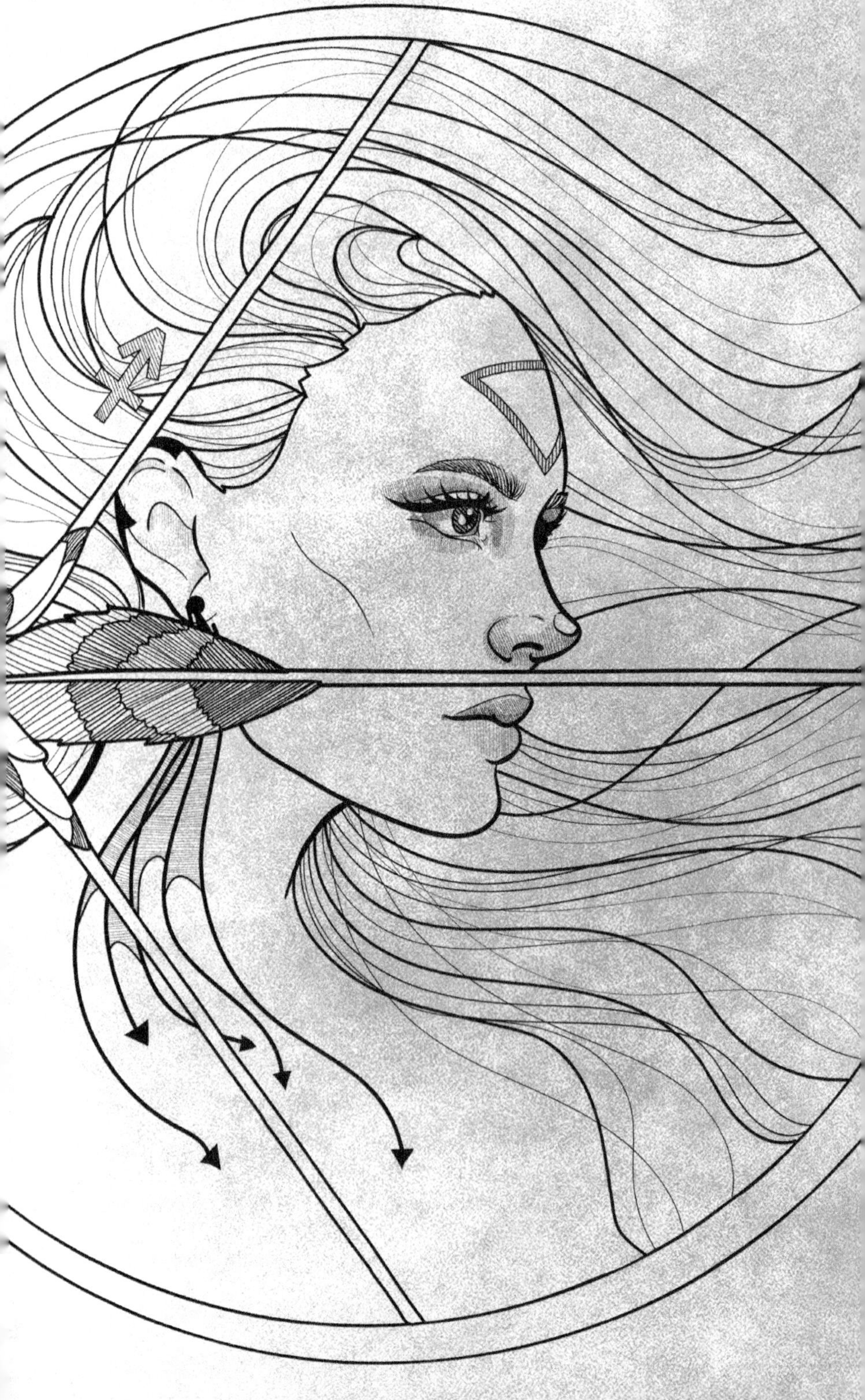

CHAPTER 16

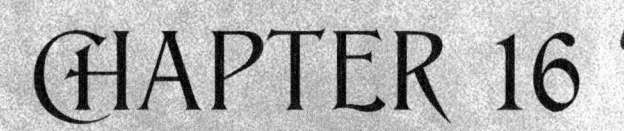

What had she done?

Lorelei looked at the pieces of arrow split right in half at her feet. She shouldn't even have a dagger on her person. Let alone use it to save the King. This could have been her moment to see him die in front of her without ever having to lift a finger.

But the dragon. She had known the dragon wouldn't let the arrow touch the King. So why had she tried to stop it?

She'd seen the glint in the bushes and recognized the shape of the weapon. An arrow head. She always knew what they looked like. As if time had slowed, she looked toward the King and the young woman who had moved in front of him.

Beauty.

That foolish girl had no idea what she'd done. She had put herself in front of the King, ready to let the arrow pierce her heart because that was the righteous thing to do. Her heart was too big for a castle like this and for the shadows that lingered, waiting to pull her apart.

Lorelei couldn't let the arrow hit her. She didn't know if the King would even save the girl who was simply too kind for this place.

In doing so, she had given herself up. What kind of woman carried a dagger with her? Not even one for dinner, but clearly a wicked blade with black metal and a curved handle, so she could use it with a backhanded motion.

An elven blade that was forged with the steel of her ancestors. She'd been there when it had been made by the blacksmith who'd drunk all the moon's power. He had imbued this weapon with every ounce of his devotion to the craft. And now the King knew it existed.

But she couldn't have let Beauty die.

Even the dragon stared at her, shocked. The beast shouldn't have been able to have that kind of emotion on his face, but there it was. Wide eyes. Sides heaving. Mouth slightly open to reveal all those wicked teeth.

Finally, Lore looked to the King. He stood with his arms limp at his sides, clearly surprised that anyone had tried to stop the arrow. Let alone her. He didn't even notice Beauty standing in front of him, ready to protect her king. He threw her to the side as he walked toward Lore, clapping his hands.

"Bravo. I didn't know there was a warrior in our midst," the King called out.

"I am no warrior," she replied. "Merely your servant, my king."

"Obviously you are the only one here who could protect me." That expression on his face was one of sly intelligence. "You were the only one who tried."

She let her arms drop, though pointed at Beauty with the blade in her hand. "I think you'll find there was another. I stopped the arrow. But she would have let it pierce her heart so that it didn't hit you."

He glanced over at Beauty with a dismissive look. She knew that look. The King wasn't attracted to the soft woman he saw next to him, and therefore, he ignored the fact that she could have died.

At least he let out a low grunt and gestured at Beauty. "Yes, well. Thank you, dear maiden. I'd like to meet with you later tonight, if it pleases you."

Beauty's cheeks turned a bright red. She dipped into a shaky curtsey and nodded her head. Apparently, the girl was at a loss for words.

Lore hadn't saved her so the girl could be thrown into the lion's den. She wanted to scream at the child to run, to get far away from this castle that would tear her apart. But she couldn't do that with everyone looking at her.

And suddenly she realized everyone was looking at her. They all stared with matching expressions of shock. Of course, they had never seen anyone do what she had done before. None of these ladies were warriors. They hadn't grown up fighting for every scrap of food that they ate.

Anger riding on her shoulders, she met the King's gaze once more. "I may have some training."

"Using the word 'some' seems to be a rather extravagant lie, wouldn't you agree?" The King stopped in front of her and crossed his arms over his chest. "You have more than a little training. What is your name?"

"Lorelei of Tenebrous." The words stung, but she'd suffer the insult if it meant she got out of this alive.

"Lorelei of Tenebrous." He repeated the words and circled her. "I know very few women who can do what you just did."

"I know quite a few who can," she corrected. "Tenebrous is full of women with surprising talents, my king."

"But so few women like you. I have been through my kingdom, although you might think I have not. Tenebrous is a beautiful place made of swamps and people who are better off forgotten." He paused in front of her again, looking her up and down. "I don't think I've ever seen you there. Only the night of the bridal greeting, in fact. Where did you say you were from again?"

She needed to come up with an excellent lie, or he was going to feed her to the dragon. "I don't think you would have seen me, my king. I am not among the nobility of Tenebrous, nor do I frequent those circles."

"A thief!" he exclaimed. "Or something similar, I suppose."

All the other potential brides started whispering. She already had such a long way to climb, and they hated her even more now. At least Beauty wasn't looking at her like she'd peeled off her skin and revealed herself to be a dragon like the beast with heaving sides.

"Not a thief," she whispered. "I never took anything that someone couldn't give."

"But you did steal," he corrected. The King reacted explosively. One moment he stood in front of her, ready to listen to what she had to say. And the next, he'd recoiled away from her as though she were a leper. "A thief! In my castle?"

"I am but a woman who was chosen to compete for your hand." Lore tried very hard not to snarl the words.

"There are very few thieves in Tenebrous, but most of them belong to a group I have heard called the rebellion." His entire face changed. One moment, he was handsome. And the next, his features drew down into a sneer that was downright ugly. "Have you ever heard of them?"

Oh, no. This was bad. This was very, very bad, and there was no way for her to get out of this situation.

Lorelei needed to lie better than she ever had in her life. She drew herself up straight and tall, tucked the knife back into her pockets, and faked a smile. "I'm afraid I've never heard of them, my king. I understand that such a group would be very dangerous to your reputation, and the mere idea of their existence is horrific."

"Is it?" His horrible expression never budged. "I think I need a little time with you, darling. Just to see how much you don't agree with these practices."

Metal hands clamped down on her shoulders. She flinched at the bitter cold touch and worry set in deep in her stomach. Anxiety churned through her, tearing up any and all rational thought.

She sought out Beauty and saw the young woman stood beside two others who were holding her back. At least they still had their wits about them. If she ran to Lorelei's aid, then she would end up wherever they were taking Lore. And that wasn't fair.

Lore gave her a sharp nod and ignored all the whispers that bloomed. Who was this woman that none of the others knew? Did Lorelei work for the rebellion? It would certainly make sense. She hadn't ever fit in with the others, nor had she ever tried.

The dragon lurched forward slightly, then remained next to the King. She swore its muscles were quivering. Perhaps it already sensed its next meal in Lorelei, and the thought sent shivers down her spine. She wouldn't die on a pyre like her mother. If she had to kill a hundred guards to make the King have the dragon eat her, then she would seek that fate with pleasure.

The Umbral Knights dragged her out of the garden and around the back of the castle. They didn't even walk through the regular doors. Instead, they took her to the servant's entrance that they kicked in. A few maids squeaked from inside the kitchen, scattering as soon as the shadowy Knights walked past them.

"Where are you taking me?" she snarled, even though she knew they would not respond to her question. They never spoke to the guilty.

She kicked out her feet, trying to catch the lip of a stone tile with her heels so she could at least fight back against them. But they dragged her ever forward, no matter how hard she fought against them.

They brought her to a set of double doors, stained black with age. The silver rivets on either side were perfectly polished to reflect the woman struggling not to go near them. Lore had heard of these doors.

The black opening into the dungeon of the Umbral Keep. The only doors that led into the dungeons that no one ever came out of.

"No," she shouted, struggling ever harder to get out of the Umbral Knight's arms. "Do not bring me down there! I saved the King, didn't I? I didn't try to kill him."

They didn't care at all. Of course they didn't. Tin soldiers didn't care for anything other than the whims of their master.

One of the Knights pushed the door open. Then they brought her, kicking and screaming, into the darkness. They dragged her down the long hallway framed by many cells. She continued to fight against them, but her movements grew weaker the farther away from those dark doors they dragged her.

She caught glimpses of the other prisoners. Some were men that had likely tried to kill the King. But most were creatures like her. Men with curled horns on their heads. Women with tails that turned their backs to her. Even a child with eyes too big for his head.

These were magical creatures. Every single one of them. And he'd locked them up because he didn't see the value in people who were different.

She should have let the arrow go. Maybe it would have sliced through Beauty and struck him in his black, evil heart.

The Umbral Knights tossed her into an open cell. She flew through the air and hit the ground hard on her hands and knees. The beautiful dress that Borovoi had crafted was no match for the dirt on the ground. It ripped at the knees. Her hands ached where tiny stones had dug into her flesh and drawn blood. Wincing, she leaned back on her haunches, holding her hands up to the dim light to see the damage.

The door clanked shut behind her. The harsh echo ringing through her head. Trapped.

"Even now, you don't react as a normal woman would." The King's voice came out of the darkness as if she were in a nightmare. "Most would cry, or perhaps beg for their freedom. But you? You assess the damage first."

Her spine was a steel bar from the top of her head to her hips. She would not bend or bow before a man like this. "I think you'll find I spend very little time on my knees."

"Ah. And so we have dropped the pretense."

"I make no apologies for who I am." She looked back at him and added, "But I am not part of this rebellion you speak of. I do not know what you're talking about, nor do I wish to go against my king like that. Working against you would be signing my own death warrant."

"Yes, it would," he replied. The King leaned against the bars of her cell, staring down at his fingernails.

Did he not care that he'd locked her up? As far as he knew, she was an innocent woman who he was terrifying for no reason at all.

"I don't know what you want from me," she muttered, remaining on her knees. "I know you think that my stopping an arrow is proof that I am someone other than I claim to be. But I am just a woman, like all the others here."

"I believe you are much more than that." The King pushed himself away from the bars. "But we'll see how truthful you are. It's difficult for most to lie to the one person who can terrify them into telling the truth."

She had no idea who he was talking about. "Who?"

The King walked away, whistling down the hall. The jaunty tune echoed, creating a haunting melody that mocked her sudden fear.

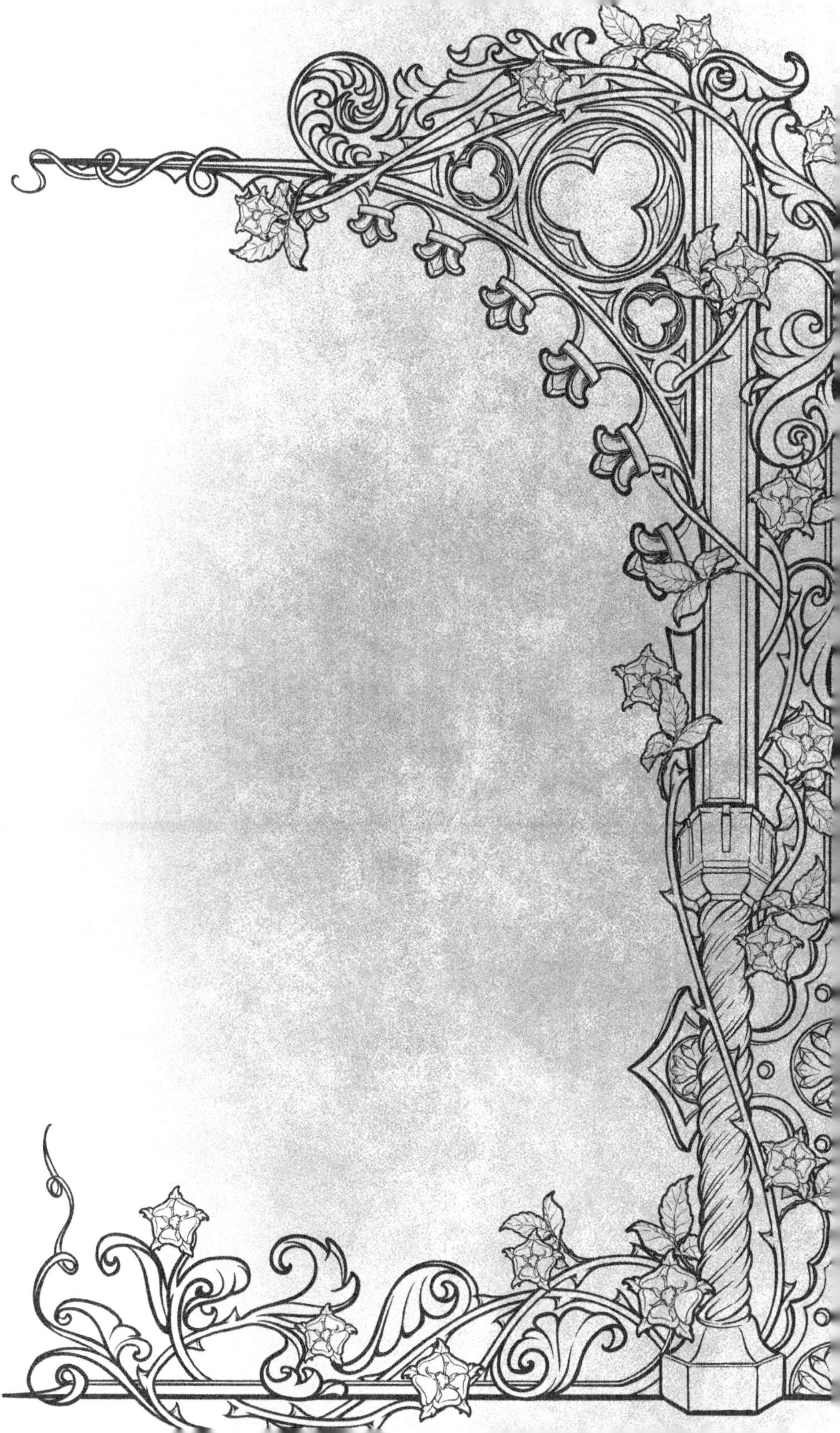

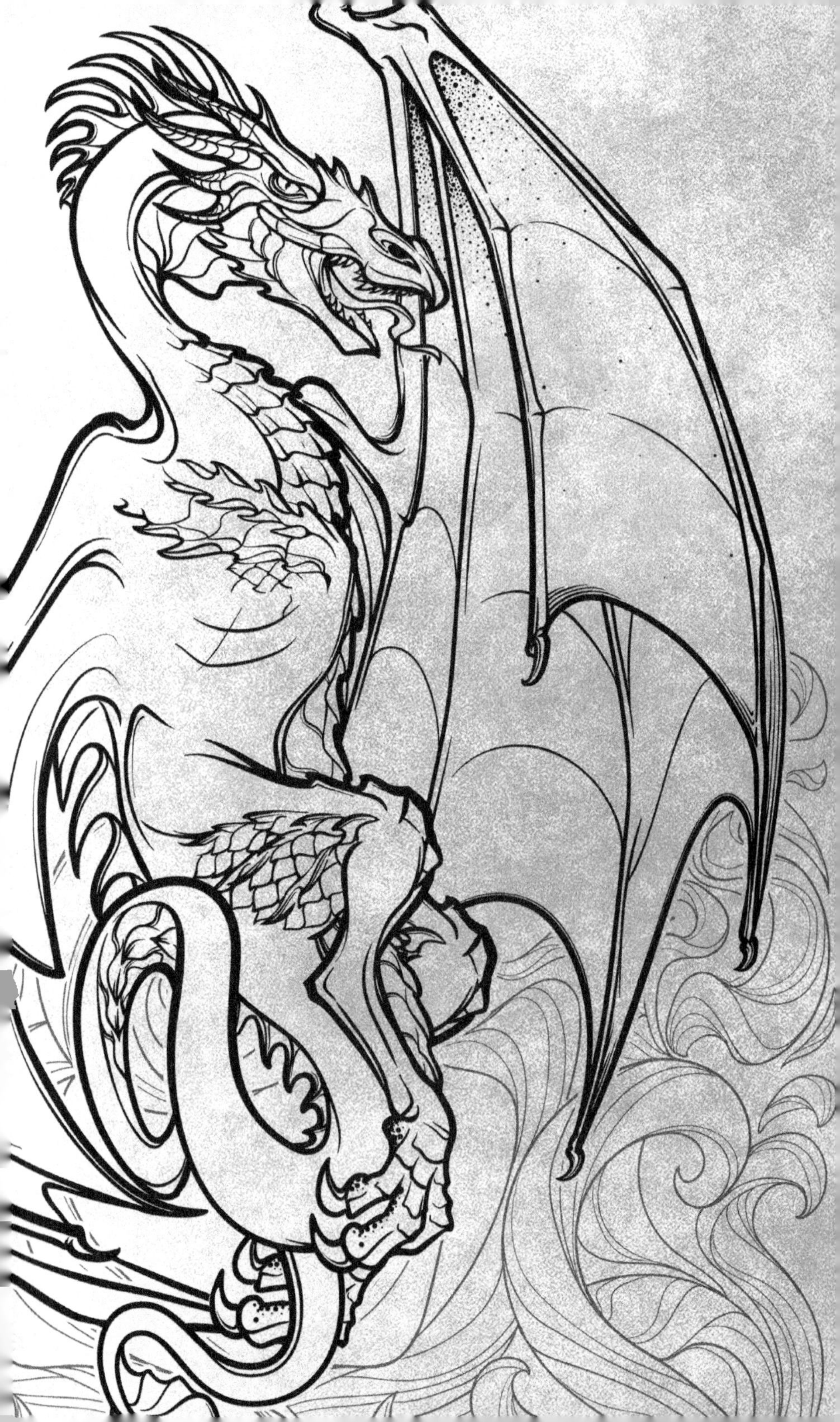

CHAPTER 17

Abraxas could do nothing as the King took Lorelei away. And though his heart screamed at him to do something, anything, he knew that would only end in sadness for him. He had to make the right choice for his people, no matter the cost.

But he could do something for her. He could be the one to interrogate her, even though he knew she must not be anyone more than a regular woman who had found herself in trouble. There were many women among the potential brides who didn't want to marry the King. They had already been sent home for failing him in the assassination attempt. Some of them were the ones that the King wasn't attracted to, but many had simply not tried to capture Zander's attention.

As soon as he'd seen the other women into their carriages, Abraxas caught up with the King as he made his way back to his chambers.

"My King," Abraxas called out. "A word."

"What is it, Abraxas?" Even Zander's voice was a little quieter than normal. "I'm exhausted. This has been a very long, trying day. The drama, you know."

"Of course. This won't take long. I thought perhaps I could interrogate the young woman?" He held his breath, hoping that the King wouldn't hear the desperation in his voice.

Zander blinked at him with a blank expression on his face. "What woman?"

Ah, this would be easier than Abraxas originally thought. "The young woman in your dungeon? The one you put there because you thought she was part of the rebellion."

"Right! That one." The King grinned and shook his head. "I've been so busy sending all those young women home. And it's so sad to see them go, don't you think? Forgot all about the one in my dungeon."

Sometimes Abraxas hated him more than normal. The King refused to focus on anything serious, and instead, mourned the loss of adoring women who cheered when he walked into the gardens.

Abraxas didn't find saying goodbye to any of those young women sad at all. He found it sad that Lorelei was sitting with criminals and thieves, wondering if the King was going to kill her for saving his life.

"Because I'm head of your personal guard, I thought you would want me to take care of the situation for you." Abraxas had to throw every ounce of his concentration into not snarling the words like an animal. "If anyone can get the truth out of her, then you can be assured I will."

Like he'd lit a fire in the King, Zander's eyes bloomed with blood thirst. "Yes, of course. You are the only one who can scare her into telling the actual truth. Just make sure to tell me every gory detail when you're done, would you?"

"You want the woman alive at the end, don't you?" Abraxas waited for a response, but the King never replied.

Zander wandered down the hall, off balance from the wine he'd drunk. He never gave his dragon an answer.

One of these days, someone would really put an arrow through that man's throat. The King was a spoiled brat with no real understanding of consequences, and Abraxas couldn't wait until the day he was free of this lineage's clutches. Even if that meant he was passed to another dynasty of kings, no one could be worse than this man or his father.

He stalked through the halls, past all the Umbral Knights who turned their heads as one to watch him pass. None of them trusted him, but that was the magic inside them. Zander's father had them cursed so that they would protect the King at all costs. No matter who the person was that attacked him.

That was, after all, how Zander's mother had died. She'd gotten tired of the abuse, the anger, the lies. She'd only thought to slap Zander's father, but the Knights hadn't seen it like that. A direct attack was still an attack.

Abraxas stopped in front of the black gates of the dungeon. He blew a long, steadying breath out of his lungs and met the gaze of the nearest Knight. "The King has declared that I will interrogate the new prisoner."

The Knight nodded to two others, who immediately stood at attention, ready to enter the dungeon with him.

"I am going alone. The woman will be more frightened if it's just me."

The metal soldiers were clearly confused. They looked at each other, and then at the one who had originally summoned them to attention. Sometimes Abraxas wondered if there were actual thoughts behind some of them. The smoke inside their bodies had an intent right now, and that intent didn't trust Abraxas for a second.

Still, the Knight relented.

The dragon had never given anyone reason to think that he would endanger the King. In fact, they all were aware of the hold their king had over him. They knew of the eggs. They knew of the madness that hung over Abraxas every time he moved. If he put one clawed foot out of line, then everything he valued in this life would be lost.

Giving the Knights a single nod, he walked into the darkness of the dungeon and felt as though a noose had tightened around his neck. He hadn't thought this far ahead in his plan. He'd wanted to be the one to speak with her, partly for his own curiosity and partly because he knew someone else would fabricate a story that would end in him eating her.

The castle's inhabitants loved to watch the dragon feast.

Some of the prisoners stood at his approach, only to immediately hide as they recognized who it was. They'd all seen him in his dragon form. None of them wanted to test the beast who had killed so many of their kind.

She waited for him in one of the farthest cells, crumpled on the floor like someone had thrown a flower into the dirt. Her blonde hair coiled around her shoulders, loosed today from its bindings. And her dress, that beautiful bubbling dress, had become ripped and stained.

"They didn't treat you well," he snarled. "As if you really are a criminal."

She looked up at the sound of his voice, obviously startled to find him here. And did her breath catch in her throat? Did she lean forward like she wanted to come to him?

No, that was all in his head. They didn't know each other, and she had every reason not to trust him.

Lorelei licked her chapped lips and asked, "What are you doing in the dungeons, Abraxas?"

"Interrogating you."

He searched for the chair that he knew should be around here somewhere. The King visited the dungeons for entertainment when someone was being tortured for information. But Zander refused to stand for long, and there were always stools around here.

The cushioned item he found was rather out of place. In such a dark, dank room, there shouldn't be something so luxurious as a silk pillow full of goose down, and yet, here it was. Waiting for someone to be comfortable while the rest of the inhabitants suffered.

He sank down onto it with no small amount of anger.

Lorelei watched him move with a look of pure disgust on her face. He deserved that, he supposed. He did work for the man who had locked her up and he had done nothing to prevent it from happening. Not that she likely even thought he was there during the entire... situation.

He'd left, hadn't he? She wouldn't blame him for a situation where he'd been missing.

Damn it, now he had to lie again. How was he going to make it sound as though he hadn't been there, but that he'd seen everything in exact detail?

Lorelei saved him, thankfully. Her voice filled the silence like a cool drink of water after a long hunt. "When I was little, my mother used to say that the only thing I had to fear were those who were more powerful than me. She said sometimes, it's up to people like you and I to make a difference when those with power refuse to do so."

"Your mother sounds like a wise woman."

"She was." But she didn't smile, and he already knew this story wouldn't end well. "She gave her life for that belief. To the very end, she believed everyone should have a chance to live, no matter where they came from or who they were."

The prisoner in the cell next to her stirred. The man had seen better days. His horned head was covered in moss and the flesh on his body had sagged with age and malnutrition. But he lifted his head and directed his attention to the young woman speaking in her cage. As if Lorelei's words were important.

Abraxas nodded. "What your mother wanted was honorable, but I don't think you're ever going to see such a life with a king like this."

Her expression fierce, Lorelei nodded. "That's exactly the problem, isn't it?"

"You can't confess that you are part of the rebellion to me," he begged. A cold sweat broke out over his entire body, and he knew this moment would change his life forever. "I will have to tell the King and he will have you killed in front of all the other brides."

"What if you didn't tell him?" She met his gaze with a ferocity of a warrior who had seen many battles. A warrior of old. "What if you listened to what I had to say? What if you heard from the other side? From the magical creatures who have bent the knee and swayed their back while hoping people would leave them alone?"

The moss covered prisoner dragged himself closer to her cell. Abraxas watched with no small mixture of horror as the man reached through the bars, hand limp on the floor with his palm facing up. His nails were thick, like the roots of a tree.

"Why tell me any of this?" he asked, his voice thick with emotion. "You must know this is a risk."

She met his gaze head on. "I cannot be alone anymore, Abraxas. I have realized that this task I have been given will be impossible unless I have someone who will help me. And I believe you are not as cold as everyone seems to think."

He wasn't.

He burned. His entire soul was set aflame because she saw him as a person rather than a nightmare or a weapon. She'd taken the time to get to know the man underneath the scales, and he had suddenly been reminded of what it was like to live and not just to serve.

"You're asking me to go against everything I have ever known." It was a lie. He would only risk his entire lineage, but she didn't know that. Not yet.

"I'm not asking you to do anything other than let me out, Abraxas. I'm asking you to see that there are forces in effect that are greater than you or I." She smiled softly and reached behind her.

Somehow, through all her struggles against the Umbral Knights, the rose he had given her survived. She twirled it in her fingers and a single petal fell into her lap. The blood red drop was too close to her reality if he didn't listen to her. If he didn't lie for her.

"I hadn't planned on ever letting him kill you," he whispered.

"Then listen to me. Don't judge what I'm about to say, and hear my words." Lorelei watched his every move, calculating as always. "Can you do that?"

He nodded.

She opened her mouth, closed it, licked her lips, and obviously fought against herself. She didn't want to tell him what was in her head, but she knew that she had to. If he could have taken this battle for her, then he would have. But some part of his soul shouted that he needed to stay silent. That he needed to listen for the sake of them all.

"I am not Lorelei of Tenebrous," she began. "My true name is Lorelei of Silverfell. I am half elf."

The words struck him to the very core. He remembered the Silverfell elves. He had seen them dancing in the moonlight when he was but a child, nothing more than a dragonling with soft scales and a head he struggled to keep up. But he had never forgotten their lithe bodies running through the beams of silver light as they gathered their magic from the moon and stars.

"My mother was in the rebellion. She lost her life in an attempt to bring about a new age where magical creatures and mortals could live side by side. We aren't asking for the King to fall in line, nor do we wish to enslave the humans. The rebellion wants to live beside them. Equals." She shook her head. "It sounds like I was part of it too, but I wasn't. They blackmailed me into coming here and killing the King."

"Kill the King?" he repeated. The words echoed through the dungeon as each prisoner repeated the sound. More of them stood and reached for the bars, listening intently to the conversation now.

"Yes." She straightened her spine and suddenly, he saw a hero in front of him. A woman who would become immortal, as stories about her were told throughout the centuries. "The only way to free Umbra from this tyranny is to start over again. I am no assassin. But I intend to kill him. And if you want to stop that from happening, then you should give me up to him now."

He should.

He had no choice.

Abraxas couldn't threaten the livelihood of his entire kind for some half thought out plan with a woman who had never assassinated anyone in her life. He needed to tell the King, eat this woman alive, and then move on with his life.

But another part of him whispered this might be the chance he was waiting for. This woman in front of him glowed with the magic of the moon under her skin. She was more than just a woman. More than a creature of light and shadow who had appeared out of nowhere to awaken the man inside of him.

She had a purpose. And if she succeeded, then he would be free of the King. Free of this lineage that enslaved and conquered.

Would the eggs remain locked in that box for eternity, though?

It was a risk. Too much of a risk, really, and he shouldn't even consider it. But he did.

He considered it long and hard while watching her expression shift. She knew the thoughts in his head, and she must have understood his hesitation because she had the same hesitations when she'd been blackmailed into doing this.

Lorelei shifted forward. She touched her hand to the moss covered man's, and then held the rose out for Abraxas to take. "We have to try, Abraxas. If we sit and do nothing, then change will never come. We will be beaten. Broken. Used up until there is no magic left in this world. And I do not want to live in a world without magic."

He swallowed hard. The rose shuddered in the air in front of him, and then his gaze slid to the prisoner whose hand she held.

The man lifted his head and smiled up at Lorelei. His expression was shaky at best, but it was one of happiness. "You look like your mother," he said in a gravelly voice. "She would have been so proud. A Silverfell elf in the castle. This is the closest we've ever been."

Lorelei squeezed his hand, and her eyes glistened with tears. The drops sparkled like they contained the very stars in the sky. She whispered, "Let the sun rise, my friend."

She then looked at Abraxas, and every prisoner in their cells seemed to hold their breath.

They were waiting for his decision. They all waited to know what their true fate would be, and she had no idea she was asking a dragon to help her.

He shouldn't. Abraxas could hear the words playing over and over in his head. He had more to worry about than this woman on her knees. His people cried out from their graves to do whatever it took to preserve the last lines of the dragons.

But his heart... Oh, his heart wanted to be free again. His heart wanted to soar through the clouds without a chain around his neck and a king tugging at the end of it.

Abraxas closed his eyes and let long buried memories play behind them. Of an age when dragons had filled the skies with a hundred colors and roars that sounded like thunder. An age when men hadn't filled the air with arrows and spears that cut through wings.

Unbidden, he heard himself say, "Let the sun rise."

As one, in a whisper so no one outside these walls would hear, all the prisoners in the dungeon repeated the words.

"Let the sun rise."

And when he opened his eyes, Lorelei smiled at him. "Welcome to the rebellion," she said. "It's good to see you have a soul, after all."

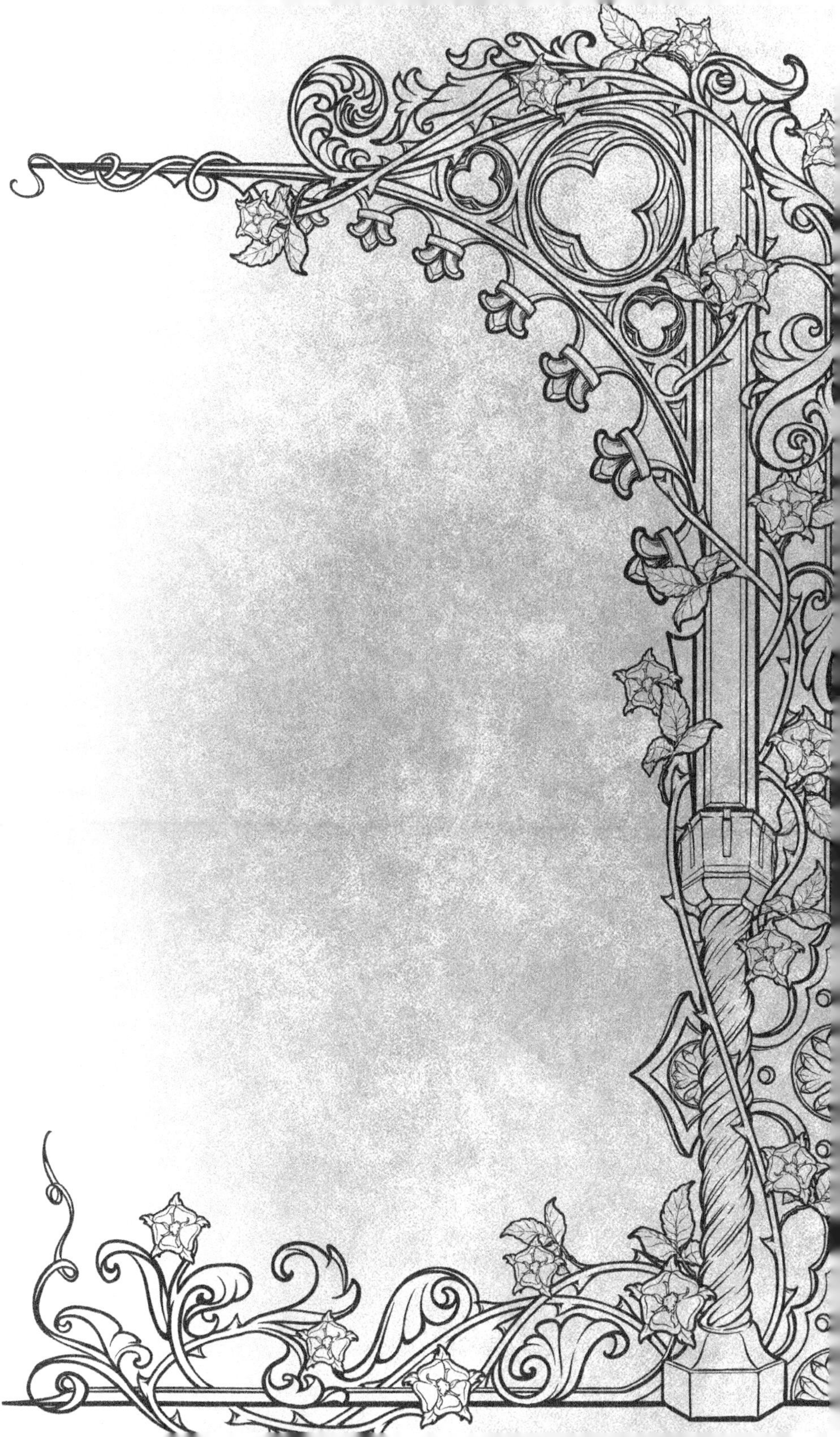

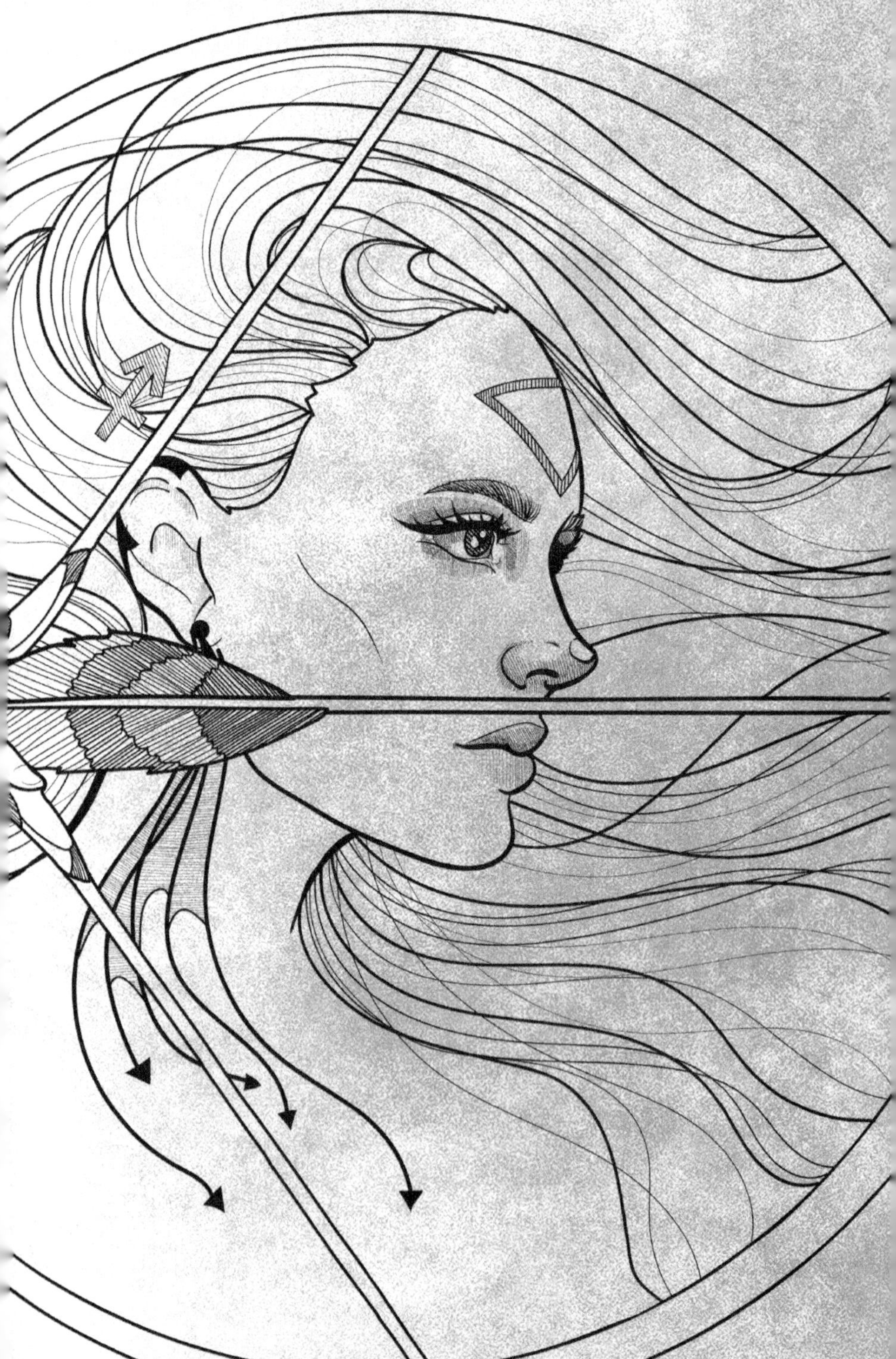

CHAPTER 18

An Umbral Knight released Lorelei from her cell the next day. The creature didn't talk or tell her why. It also didn't let her say goodbye to the countless magical creatures that stood in their cells, watching her leave with hope in their eyes.

She tried very hard not to cry when they dragged her out of the dungeon. Not in relief, but because she knew some of those prisoners wouldn't make it to see themselves released from that place. They would spend the rest of their remaining days in the darkness, hoping that she would succeed.

Lorelei had more reason than ever to kill the King.

Margaret had no right to send her to this place without telling her what to expect. She hadn't thought to find creatures like herself, or people who meant so much to her in such a short amount of time. Suddenly, it wasn't just the hope that she would survive the Umbral Knights. Now, Lorelei had to free others. She had to protect the sole friend she'd made here. And worse, she now had the personal guard of the King working with her.

Her mother would have been so proud. But Lorelei had never wanted to make her mother proud.

The Umbral Knight stalked beside her all the way to her puke colored door. He stopped in front of it, arms crossed over his chest. The helmet on his head belayed zero emotion.

She pointed at a few doors down the hall. "Why have some doors been painted white?"

Predictably, the Umbral Knight didn't respond. But it sent a shiver down Lorelei's spine that some of the doors weren't the same. She'd only been in the dungeon for a few days.

She walked into her bedroom, hoping this wasn't an afterthought to place her in the same room. Or worse, that the other women had suffered simply because they had stuck up for her.

Lorelei snorted as she closed the door behind her. No one was going to stand up for her. The other women didn't like her.

She turned around, already pulling at her nasty dress and hoping to get some of the grime off her body. They hadn't sent up a bath, so she could only hope that the water in a bowl on her vanity would suffice to clean herself.

"Pixie?" she called out. "Are you still here?"

The little creature didn't respond, and she hoped that meant it had gone back to its family. Or found somewhere else to hide while the Umbral Knights decided what to do with her.

A faint sound shushed in her closet. Almost as though someone had sneezed, or the fabric of a dress had moved on its own. Lorelei froze, hands behind her back, still clutching the ties of her dress.

Pixie wasn't big enough to make that noise. And that could only mean there was a person in her closet.

Carefully, she walked over to the nightstand beside her bed and opened the drawer. No one had gone through her things. The knife she'd placed inside the drawer was still there, and that made this all much easier. She pulled it out and made her way to the closet.

One, two, three. She wrenched the door open and brandished the knife over her head.

"Wait! Wait, it's me!" Beauty cowered against the back wall of her closet.

Lorelei quickly dropped her knife with a sigh. "What are you doing hiding in my closet?"

The moment the danger had passed, Beauty dropped her arms. "I didn't want the Knights to see me. They aren't letting any of the brides see each other at all. It's a horrible thing, but we're all managing the best we can. Usually we can sneak into each other's rooms and help."

"Help do what?" Lorelei reached past Beauty and grabbed a silk dressing gown.

Borovoi had made even that a little too pretty for putting it on her dirty skin. The interior of the dressing gown had been hand painted with bright sun patterns. How lovely, and appropriate for the conversations she'd just had with Abraxas and the others.

"Well, help you get settled back in. At least in this case. No one wanted to come other than me, but the Knights let us know you were returning." Beauty maneuvered her way out of the closet, and she somehow managed not to knock a single thing down. "You look like you could use the help, so I suspect my instincts about you were correct."

Her instincts about Lorelei were entirely wrong. She was not a kindhearted person who would help the other brides as Beauty was doing now. Lore planned to kill the man they all wanted to marry.

Lore needed to clear her thoughts or Beauty would see what she was thinking. And the last thing she needed was yet another person knowing her plan. When had she gotten so chatty?

"Help me out of this dress, then," she said with a sharp inhalation. "I'd kill for a bath, but I don't think that's going to happen any time soon. When do they provide us with a tub?"

"Um." Beauty tried her best not to smile, but didn't manage to cover her grin. "You know what? Get yourself out of the dress and I'll make all your wishes come true. How's that?"

Lore had no idea what the girl meant. Wishes come true? Had she lost her mind?

No matter, Beauty wasn't her servant. She had gotten herself into this dress and she supposed she could get herself out of it. Lore looked down at the lovely fabric and winced.

"Sorry," she muttered before she tore it straight down the middle.

If he'd been here, Borovoi likely would have screamed. The fabric was only holding on by a thread anyway, and she didn't think it was right to let it stay ruined. She might as well ruin it even more.

"Don't you touch that dressing gown!" Beauty shouted, although her voice was muffled. "You're far too dirty and you'll ruin the silk. I know you don't care about that, but I think whoever designed the dress certainly would."

Was the girl working with Borovoi to make sure that Lore didn't destroy any more of his creations?

"Where are you?" she muttered, turning around and realizing that the girl had somehow opened up a door Lore hadn't realized existed. Between her wardrobe and the wall, an opening now led into an enormous bathroom.

Where had that come from?

Lore wandered toward the room and stared in awe at the hand tiled floor made entirely out of opal chips. It shifted and changed colors when she looked at it from different angles. The walls were painted white and there were no windows, considering the room was in the center part of their wing. But glowing white flowers hung from the ceiling, an obvious enchantment, and cast a lovely gleam on the steaming bath set into the floor. The tub was so large that it could easily fit five people.

Beauty stood beside it, glass bottles in her hand and a frown on her face. "Now are you more of a rose person or perhaps lemongrass?"

"Neither," she replied. "I don't need a scent."

"Everyone needs a scent. And after all you've been through, I think you've earned yourself a bubble bath." Beauty put them both to the side and picked up another bottle with bright green liquid in it. "I think mint is more your style. What do you think?"

She really couldn't care less. "I'll leave it up to your expert opinion."

Lorelei sank into the warm water that filled the tub with a sigh. She leaned her head back on the edge and inhaled the steam that filled her lungs with a sense of warmth that she hadn't had in days.

What was it about a bath that immediately relaxed a person? It was like she could finally let go of all the stress in her body.

The faint trickling sound of perfume filling the water let her know that Beauty had decided on the mint. No one could think it was anything else. But the bright scent helped clear her mind.

"Was it terrible?" Beauty asked.

Lorelei opened her eyes and watched as her new friend pulled up her own skirts and sank her feet into the warm water of the bath. Beauty sat on the lip of the tub, clearly not intending to rush Lore at all.

When was the last time someone had cared enough to want her to be comfortable after a stressful day? Lore told herself not to cry, but it was damn hard when someone showed that they weren't a monster like so many other people here.

"It wasn't so bad," she whispered. "I've been in worse situations than a castle dungeon."

"Really?" All the color drained from Beauty's face. "I don't know if I could survive it. Not knowing what the King was going to do with you. Being in the cell with all those terrifying magical creatures."

"They aren't so terrifying." Lore didn't want Beauty to think her kind was dangerous, but she also knew that so many mortals found magic to be the worst substance on earth. "How many of them have you met in your life?"

"How many what?"

"Magical creatures," Lore chuckled. "You claim they are terrifying, but how would you know if you haven't met any of them?"

Thoughts danced behind Beauty's eyes and across her face like an open book. Maybe she hadn't ever thought of it like that, but so few humans had. They grew up being told that magical creatures were to be feared, and therefore, that meant they were dangerous. Most of them had never conceptualized that someone, at some point, had decided that creatures like Lore were bad. But that they had never decided to feel fear themselves.

"Well, I suppose I've never met a single one." Beauty shrugged.

"Unless they were in hiding and I didn't know what they were, of course."

"As someone who has met many magical creatures and spent a large portion of my life among them, I can tell you with utmost certainty that they are not terrifying." She lifted her arm and reached for the bottle of soap Beauty had placed next to her. "Most of them want to be left alone to their own devices. Unfortunately, as mortals grow in numbers, that means a lot of their lands are lost."

"Oh. That's quite sad."

"It is." She dunked her head under the water before Beauty could see her expression. Lore was too tired to hide her real feelings right now. She didn't want the young woman to see just how impacted she was by their conversation.

But, as she came up for air and slicked her hair back from her face, she noticed that Beauty's eyes had widened and her mouth had dropped open.

Lore hadn't ever let her guard down so easily. Maybe it was the couple of days in the dungeon that had made her so lax. Or perhaps she liked Beauty so much that she'd forgotten to hide. Whatever it was, she had moved her hair away from her ears and that was it. The gig was up.

Beauty reached out a shaking hand and touched the tip of Lorelei's ear. "So that's why you feel for them more than the others."

She had never been so terrified in her entire life. This young woman, this young mortal woman, now held her life in her hands. All Beauty had to do was tell a single Umbral Knight and everything would crumble around Lorelei's shoulders.

"I can't have anyone know," she whispered. "I'm not even a full elf."

"I don't think anyone would mind." Beauty paused, then sighed. "I suppose that's a lie, isn't it? They would mind, and they'd use it to their advantage. You've got the King's attention now. Even when he met with me, all he talked about was the woman who'd saved him. I don't think he remembered he put you in the dungeon, though."

That sounded like the King. Lore wouldn't be surprised if he had changed the story in his head so that she'd saved his life because she loved him, and he'd put her in a rose-filled room rather than a dirty dungeon.

"I really can't have anyone knowing, Beauty. He'll feed me to the dragon and then everything will be over." She couldn't tell the other woman about the murderous reason she was here. Even though she had started to trust Beauty, it was too much for her to know. She was too young to handle that kind of knowledge.

Besides, she'd already told one person. That was enough.

"Well," Beauty tilted her head to the side and chuckled. "At least you know there's one person here who isn't going to automatically give up any magical creature she finds."

Much to Lore's surprise, Beauty reached into her pocket and pulled out the tiny, glowing pixie. The little one chirped in happiness, then sat down on the edge of the bath and dangled her legs over the edge. Even though she didn't reach the water.

"You knew about the pixie?" she asked in awe.

"No, I didn't. But when I first came to your room after the Umbral Knights dragged you away, this one crawled out from under the bed before she realized who I was." Beauty smiled down at the small pixie, and that was the moment Lore realized.

This woman had the kindest heart. She wasn't faking it or lying. There was so much kindness in her being that it overflowed and overwhelmed sometimes. But it was real.

How many people had Lore met who were actually real?

"You're too kind for this place," she muttered, then sank down until the water touched her chin. "They're going to eat you alive."

"Maybe. But then I never would have met you." Beauty crossed her hands in her lap and bit her lip. "Do you know who I was before all this? My father was just a dressmaker. He worked on fabric and outfits, but he didn't make a lot of money. I was slated to become a ladies' maid and never have a family of my own. Which suited me well enough because I… well… Men…" She cleared her throat. "This is my chance to be something. Or someone. Or… know someone important."

"You're important all on your own."

"Oh, don't try to make me feel better about all of it. I know the King won't pick me, and I don't know why I stepped in front of the arrow. It wasn't for attention or anything like that. Honestly, I don't think I like him enough to sacrifice myself for him, or any man." Beauty shrugged. "It was the right thing to do. Regardless of the person. But anyway, he's not going to pick me looking like this. You, however, I think you could become the new Queen of Umbra."

"So that's why you're friends with me?" Lorelei asked, her lips twitching.

"Hush." Beauty leaned down and flicked water into her face. "I'm friends with you because I owe you my life. You saved me, remember? A couple times now."

"Ah, of course. That's the only reason." Lorelei shook her head and tried to let go of the remaining tension in her chest. "Are you staying the night, then?"

"I thought the three of us could have a slumber party. And after everything you've been through, I thought you might not want to be alone tonight."

She didn't. Because tomorrow would be even harder. But tonight she would wrap herself in the laughter of newfound friends.

Tomorrow, she would set about making a plan to kill the King.

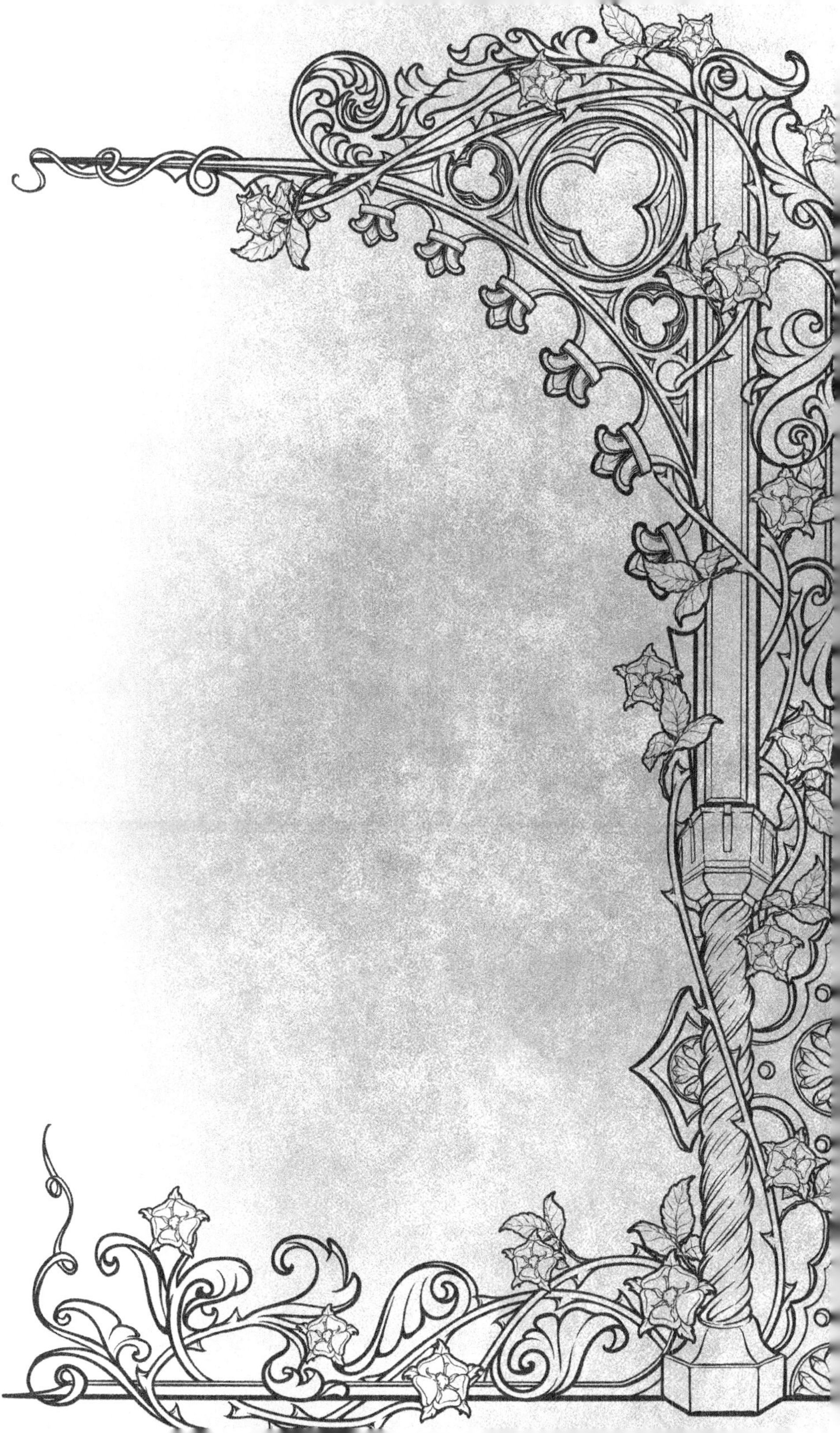

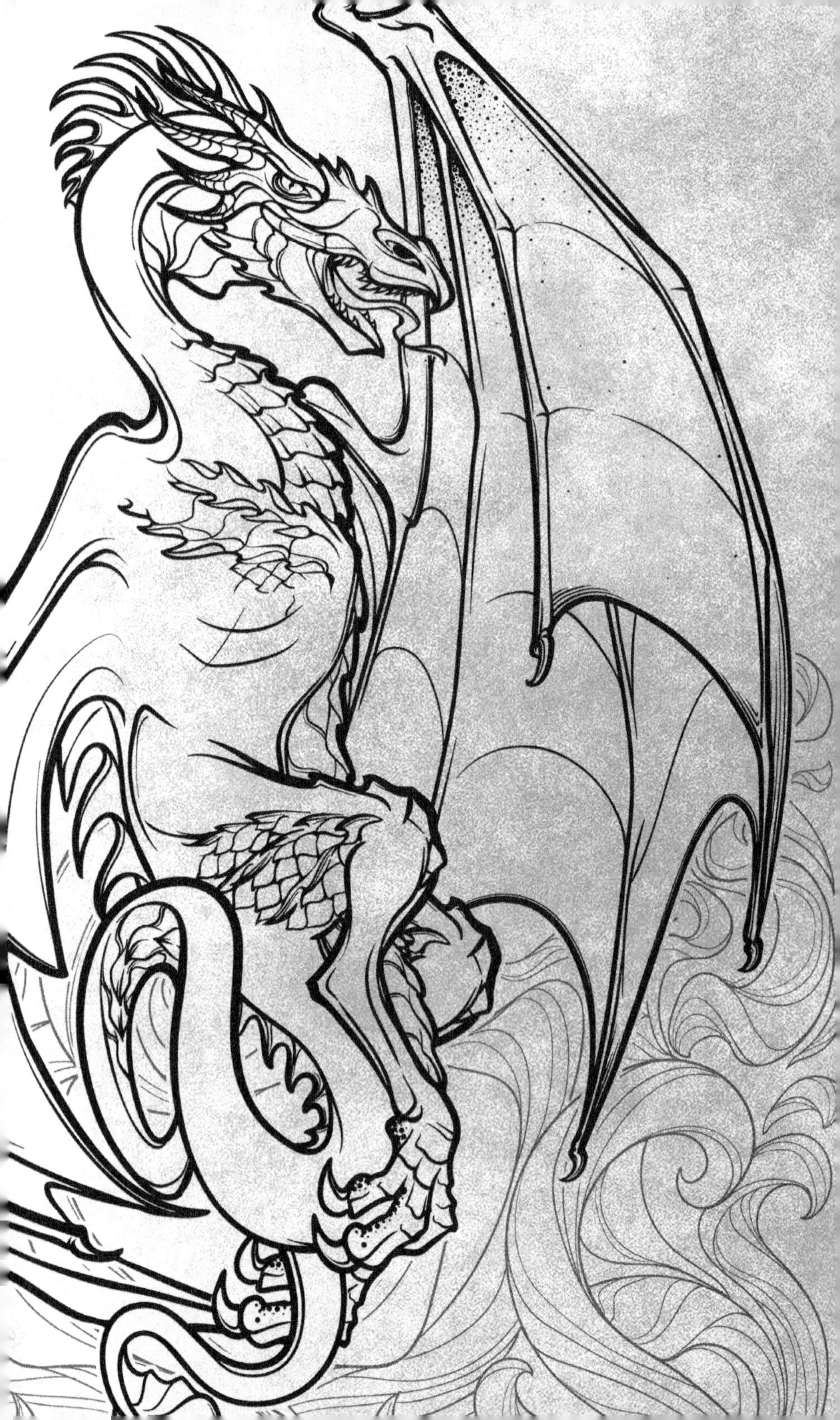

Chapter 19

She was an elf.

Abraxas couldn't stop thinking about that. She was a damned elf, and he hadn't even noticed it.

Of course she was. He hadn't thought to check her ears when Zander had chosen her to be one of his brides, but that wasn't something any of them had thought of. No magical creature would be quite so courageous as to walk into the castle without at least trying to hide what they were.

She had, he supposed. She'd kept her hair over her ears and no one had been any wiser.

How had he missed it?

He twisted his serpentine body around the pile of gold that he'd gathered around himself and mulled over what to do next. He knew she was trying to kill the King. She'd told him that much. And she was part of the rebellion, a group he hadn't heard of until lately and yet now he wanted to know more about. How long had they been working to kill the King? Longer than he'd been protecting Zander? That seemed unlikely.

But maybe this had all been happening under his nose. Maybe the great Abraxas, the crimson dragon, had missed key details that a group of people were trying to kill the man he protected.

He wouldn't let her kill the King until he knew how to take those eggs away from Zander. Her speech in the dungeons had wiggled underneath his skin and, yes, he'd fallen for it. But in the days that passed, he knew he couldn't let her do anything until the Umbral Kingdom at least had an heir.

Now, there were plenty of women around to beget an heir. Mortal women were fragile, however, and a pregnant woman didn't mean that she or the child would survive. If the King died without a wife, however, then the throne would likely go to his first bastard son. The Umbral Knights were bound to a bloodline, not to the throne. They'd help the child take over the kingdom if no one called them off.

Which stood to reason that all he needed was to convince Zander to take one of the women to bed, perhaps multiple of them, to ensure a child was actually born. Then he had to convince Lorelei and the rebellion to wait at least nine months, and then the eggs were safe. He could take them and disappear to rebuild the kingdom that the dragons had once controlled.

It was a shaky plan at best. He knew that.

"Are you even listening to me?" Zander snapped. "Abraxas, it's like your head is elsewhere and I really need you to focus."

He didn't want to focus on a king who rambled about nothing. Still, he shifted his long neck so he could stare blankly at the mortal man pacing on the cliff. "Another plan, Zander? The last one didn't work out so well."

"The last one worked perfectly. We know who the young woman is that's most likely to save me in the event of an attack. And that woman is quite beautiful, if I do say so myself." Zander kicked a pile of gold coins beside him. "The problem is that she was too good at fighting. Her reflexes rival that of the Umbral Knights, and I want to know how."

"I already told you. She trained with her father, who used to be a knight in your father's army. He was a renowned warrior who had no sons. She had an unusual upbringing, that much is certain, but she does not work for the rebellion."

Abraxas was quite pleased with the lie he'd cooked up. After all, it was the most believable story that he had managed yet. A young woman, down on her luck. A father who had served the previous king with more dedication and luck than any other. The story would tear at the hearts of most, but the King cared little for others.

"Yes, yes," Zander muttered. "That's right. You said that she had trained with the best. And you're certain you got the truth out of her?"

For effect, he opened his mouth so his shining teeth were on blunt display. Smoke coiled up from his chest and erupted from his nostrils and between his teeth. "Yes, I'm certain."

"Oh, enough with that." Zander waved a hand in front of his face as though the smoke smelled. "If you're so certain she can be trusted, then I suppose there's no reason to assume she cannot. Then the only other option is to continue the plan as I have suggested."

"I fail to see how a hunt will prove anything about any young woman on it." Abraxas hated it when Zander hunted, anyway. It was always such fanfare that no one ever caught a single thing. They made too much noise, and Abraxas hated to hunt without capturing his prey.

"Because I need to know my bride will not be boring, Abraxas. Who wants to be married to a woman who sits and embroiders all day? I want to take her on adventures! I want a woman who can hunt by my side!" He jabbed his fists in the air like he fought off an invisible foe. "Don't you agree?"

"I do not know what kind of bride you want, sire."

Zander sighed. "Yes, you're horribly boring like that. Would you just agree with what I'm saying? The ladies are going to love it. I will remain safe and sound under your watchful eye, and the rest of us will do our best not to be gored by a boar. How does that sound?"

"Fitting enough."

"Good." Zander shook his head, then rolled his eyes for good measure. "You have to make everything difficult, Abraxas! Can't you just enjoy the fun we're all going to have? Everything has to be such a chore with you."

He watched the King leave with no small amount of distaste burning in his mouth. Abraxas didn't want to hunt. He wanted to speak with a certain young woman who had consumed his thoughts.

Why couldn't he do both?

He slithered over the gold, ignoring the sound of clinking metal, and allowed the powers inside him to drift back into a mortal form. Crouching with his hands in the gold, he watched the last lingering scales disappear from the smooth skin of his hand.

He'd never get used to that. No matter how many times he changed from dragon to man, it always felt like he was losing a part of himself. As though he had to give something up to become mortal again.

Straightening, he left the dragon's cavern and hoped that Zander didn't have more to say to him. At least the King had left the cavern stairwell and wasn't lingering in the shadows to spy on his greatest pet.

The hallways were strangely silent. No women filled the corridors, giggling as he walked past them. No servants, even.

Had the King forgotten to tell him that they were all meeting? Or was something happening that he hadn't been invited to?

Abraxas tried to control the anger that bubbled in his chest. Yes, he understood that Zander might want to entertain without his personal guard looming over him. But the entire point of having a personal guard was that he would be there to protect the King. At all times.

Giggles floated down the hall and he heard Zander's voice calling out, "I'm going to find you, my flowers!"

What in the world was going on in this castle today?

A finger tapped his shoulder, and he turned with an arched brow. Whoever touched him was daring. But the lightning that sizzled down his back already warned him who it was.

Lorelei stood behind him, her dress a mass of pale, opal flowers that cascaded over her shoulders and down her hips. She was so lovely, like an elf who had wandered out of the forest in a dream.

He opened his mouth, then froze when she put her finger to her lips.

She slipped down the opposite hall and he followed her like she was a siren and he was a sailor. He couldn't deny her anything at this moment when the scent of mint and mulberry floated through the air behind her. She was a lovely nymph in a forest of boring creatures who had never once piqued his interest.

Until her. Until this wonderful creature had walked into his life and he refused to let her out of his sight today.

Abraxas waited until they were at the servant's exit before he whispered, "Why are we being so quiet?"

"The King wanted to play a game of hide and seek," she breathed, her hand on the door. "All the potential brides are hiding. I didn't want another bride to find us, or worse, have the King catch us and think we were... Having a moment together."

Weren't they? Having a moment, that was.

He didn't think she meant a tryst in the shadows, but at the mischievous look in her eyes, perhaps she had meant just that. The King would turn green with envy if he caught Abraxas and the prettiest potential bride.

She slipped out of the door with a laugh bubbling after her. Abraxas raced out of the castle with a single thought in his mind.

He'd never heard someone sound so happy.

He'd never been so happy.

Together, they snuck away from the King's games and the other women she was competing against. Instead, they had the afternoon with each other. An afternoon where he didn't have to worry about Zander's foolish plans or opinions.

Lorelei led him all the way to a small grove of birches on the very edge of the gardens. He thought it very likely that the gardeners had simply forgotten these existed. They were a lingering memory of the grand forest that used to be here for everyone to hunt and fish in. Until the King had come and decided this was where he wanted to build his giant castle.

He hummed low under his breath as she wrapped her arms around one of the trees, breathing hard from their flight. "Just where do you think you're going? The King will find you if you try to run."

"Oh, I don't intend to run. You know I have work to do here." She grinned and the wild tangle of her hair fell across her face.

He couldn't help himself. Couldn't stop himself. Abraxas reached forward and tucked the strands of hair behind her ears. The movement revealed delicate points, a clear sign of what she was. A sign she struggled to hide every day of her life.

"There you are," he murmured. "I hardly slept at night wondering if you had pointed ears and I had just never noticed them."

"Very few do. I've gotten rather good at hiding them." She was obviously uncomfortable with his staring at said ears, but he couldn't stop. Not now that he had seen her for what she really was.

"An elf," Abraxas said with a laugh. "I never thought someone would be so brave that they would walk into the castle as a magical creature. Did you know I was consumed with fear for you all night?"

"No one knows what I am but you. I put my hair over my ears." She stared up at him with those giant, seascape eyes, and he didn't know what overcame him.

For the very first time in his life, someone looked at him. Just him. This woman didn't want to know what the dragon wanted. She didn't want to use his brute strength. Even though she'd been sent to the castle with murderous intent, she never asked for his help other than his silence.

The honor that took… the courage…

One moment, he felt this overwhelming sensation of happiness. And the next, he had swooped down and pressed his lips to hers.

She was soft. Softer than anything he'd ever felt in his life. Lorelei froze underneath him for a moment before she suddenly turned into a spark that leapt from a flame. She launched into his arms and her kiss threatened to brand his very soul.

Abraxas wrapped an arm around her waist and the other around her back. He drew her against his chest, his soul weakening as she melted against him. He hadn't expected this. He hadn't thought to kiss her or distract her from her purpose.

But she'd stood in that birch grove like the elves he remembered. She was something like a memory that stepped in front of him, or a ghost from an age he desperately missed.

Abraxas wrenched his lips from hers, breathing hard and shaking his head in denial. "I was not supposed to... You have distracted me so much. There are things I have to do as well. Duties. Responsibilities."

She pressed her hand to his mouth and shook her head. "Not today, Abraxas. Today, let us be two people who found each other in the woods. Let us hide from the thoughts that lurk in the back of our mind. For an afternoon, that's all I'm begging of you."

And so he spent the afternoon with her. Kissing, certainly, but also laughing. She told him stories that the elves used to tell children, and she luxuriated in the sound of his mirth.

It was a facade. An afternoon of fictitious happiness and hope. But he enjoyed it while he could.

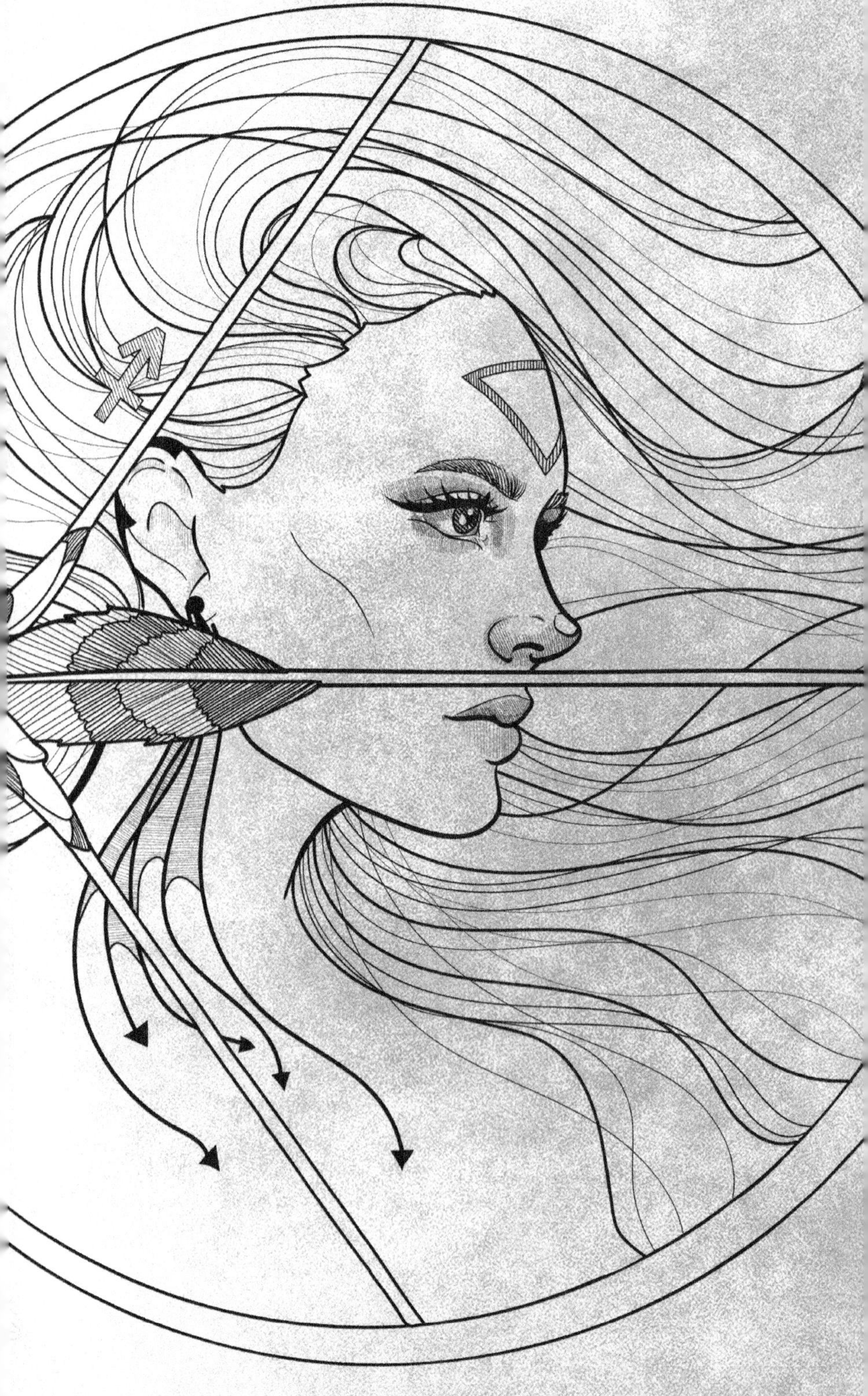

Chapter 20

She shouldn't have kissed him. It complicated things.

But as Lore tightened the leather bindings over her chest, she knew it was the right thing to do. The personal guard of the King was a liability. He had only agreed to help her under tenuous circumstances, and she knew a reluctant man when she saw one.

The last thing she needed was an idiot mortal changing his mind and deciding that the King gave him more than the rebellion could offer. The best way to control a man was through the power of desire. If she could hold his attention long enough, then he would keep his mouth shut and the King would die at the end of all this.

She looked at herself in the mirror and met her own gaze. The billowing white gown had slits up to her thighs on either side of her legs.

They were supposed to allow her movement while hunting, but of course, that was foolish. A dress was a stupid thing to wear while hunting. The leather chest plate held onto her body with only a few ties, and if a boar attacked her, then it would go right through the chest plate. Easily.

The King didn't care if they were safe, though. All he cared about was that they looked pretty. And she did. She looked like a warrior woman out of a storybook. Some figurehead of a fairytale who led her people into battle.

"And then tragically dies," she muttered before sweeping out of her room and down the hall.

Predictably, she was the first one ready and spent a long time waiting in the hallway with the Umbral Knights staring at her. It gave Lore too much time to think about the poor man, who now thought she was likely head over heels for him.

The thing was, she did like Abraxas. He was funny and light-hearted and surprisingly thoughtful for someone who worked in the castle. He made her want to know more about him, and she hadn't anticipated that. She hadn't expected meeting Beauty either, so all of this was getting awfully complicated for someone who had been sent on an assassination mission.

Unfortunately, she couldn't change any of it. She had to get the men in this castle under her thumb one way or another, and the only way she knew how to do that was through their own weakness.

Damn it, she still couldn't control the guilt that turned her cheeks bright red.

Beauty stumbled out of her pale pink door, struggling with the straps for her chest. They didn't quite fit.

Lore planned to kill that horrible housekeeper when she saw her next. "Agatha obviously had something to do with this," she growled as she walked up to her new friend.

"She said there weren't a lot of dresses in my size, let alone leather armor." Beauty shrugged, but the tears in her eyes betrayed her false bravery. "She said if I wanted to stay safe on the hunt, then I should probably figure out how to put the armor on."

Giving it a look over, Lore found a few inches that could give on some of the straps. It wasn't a lot, but it was enough. She pulled, tugged, and shifted, jerking the girl this way and that before she patted the buckles into place. "It's not the best, I'll admit. Should keep you alive, though."

"I can breathe now, at least." Beauty inhaled a deep, long breath, then let it out through her teeth. "I was worried I'd faint on the horse and get trampled by the rest of them."

A stunning beauty swept by them, her shining dark hair neatly braided in twin ropes. She was the girl who'd originally warned Lore off from the King, back in the first forest meeting. "And we would trample you if only to ensure the King never picks such an ugly bride."

Lore lunged forward without a thought. That little brat of a child had no idea what it felt like to be ugly, but that could easily be remedied. She knew how badly a broken nose hurt, and how horrible it was to fix.

She didn't get very far.

Beauty clutched her arm and tugged her back, surprisingly strong for someone so short. "It's not worth it, Lore. They all tease each other like that. She didn't mean anything by it."

Still, Lore eyed the other woman, who clearly thought her face would get her farther than anyone else in this competition. "I think she meant everything by it, Beauty. I think she wants to hurt anyone she can."

"Maybe. She'd step on the rest of us if it meant getting the King to look at her. Unfortunately, she's never caught his eye no matter how pretty she is." Beauty squared her shoulders and grinned. "But I have. And that must make her feel horrible about herself when every success in her entire life has been based on how pretty she is."

Lore wanted to remind Beauty that the King hadn't actually noticed her. After all, she had been the one to point Beauty out to the man. No one should be proud of catching his eye, especially considering what a horrible man he was.

But she didn't want to ruin the moment. Beauty had stood up for herself, and that was a success.

Lore looped an arm around Beauty's shoulders and waltzed them toward the head of the pack. "That's exactly it, my dear. Now, have you ever been hunting before?"

"Never."

"Stay close to me, then. I'll make sure a boar doesn't catch you. Or worse, a stag that's angry we'd hunt it."

Beauty's eyes widened as they all followed the Umbral Knight down the hall. "I didn't think stags were that mean?"

"They've got bigger bodies, faster reflexes, and they all have horns larger than you or I am tall! Of course you have to worry about stags." She winked. "Besides, they are by far the most beautiful creatures in the forest, and hunting them is a privilege. They know that."

She remembered a time when only the elves could hunt the stags. The King's father had put an end to all that with his own hunting parties. He'd all but killed their entire species, like he wanted to do to the magical creatures as well. No one could ever take away the memory of the silver stags and their glimmering coats, however. How they had raced through the oak trees with moonlight catching on the tips of their antlers and sparkling in the distance.

Lore had been too young to hunt them back then. She hadn't been properly trained, and by the time she was, no one but the King's men could hunt the stags. Not without risking their lives.

The group of potential brides gathered in the courtyard. Servants had already prepared horses for them to ride into the hunt, each great beast laden with bells and silver fabric. Lore had no idea why they were dressed like that. Yet another confusing part of the King's entertainment.

Beauty tugged on her arm and pointed to a large draft horse with a dappled white and grey hide. "Do you think I could ride that one if I asked? It's so beautiful."

"I think we'll be able to ride whatever creatures we want. But you don't want to be on a draft horse." She pointed to a leaner creature, mixed breed with short legs and a stocky frame. "Those are the real hunting horses. They run through the forest faster than you could imagine."

Untamed beasts were the ones that called out to her. She had never wanted to ride something that was only useful for its looks.

Lore could already feel her blood rising. The hunt called out to her, as it always did to elves. She'd ride with the best of his hunters, crack the reins, and let the moonlight fall from her skin into her steed. The horse would feel the forest calling to it, and as one, they would complete the hunt with the best kill of the day.

The King's grand entrance interrupted her thoughts. He wore an equally outrageous white suit with armor molded to make it look like he had muscles. Never once did the leader of the Umbral Kingdom look like he had a hair out of place. She wondered if the wind from the hunt might blow at least a single strand free from his oiled head.

Abraxas walked behind him. Carefully, always a few steps behind the King even when their leader slowed down. It was the practiced gait of a man who had worked a long time to ensure he never once stepped out of line.

She wished their circumstances were different. If only she could find the time to be with him without fearing that he might tell the King what she was. Why she was here.

She needed him to help her. That much was true. But when he caught her eye from across the courtyard and the tops of his cheekbones turned bright red, Lore wished she could convince herself that feeling was truthful. Honorable. That she'd actually made him feel as though she were important to him.

Not that she'd deceived him into believing her feelings were passionate and sincere. The lie stung in her chest, burning all the way to her heart until she knew without question that she would regret yesterday.

Of course she would. Abraxas was a good man. A handsome man. He had captivated her soul, and she had lied.

You're an assassin, she told herself. You were not sent here to make friends, or to fall under the spell of a foolish mortal.

Lore straightened her back and let her lips quirk into a little half smile. Anything that would make him think she was mildly embarrassed to see him, too. At least then he'd believe she felt something. That their afternoon in the gardens, hidden away from the rest of the world, was more than just a tool for her to finish this.

She was in so deep now she couldn't stop. Stopping would only get her in even more trouble than she already found herself.

The King stopped next to a midnight dark horse that shook its head as soon as he touched it. "My flowers! Each of you is more lovely than I have ever seen you. Thank you for joining me on the hunt."

So many of the young women preened around her. They were all dressed in exactly the same outfits. Lore refused to believe they thought any one of them looked better than the others. They were a sea of the same woman, and yet, they all seemed to think he was talking about them as an individual.

The King eyed a few of the women standing closest to him, then smiled at them so brightly that the women fanned themselves. "As you know, we're going on a hunt today. I have many plans for my future bride, and one of them is that we will live a life of adventure."

One of the girl's next to her leaned over to her friend. "That sounds a lot better than getting married to the local butcher."

"Adventure?" the other hissed. "We have no idea what he considers adventure, Lily. What if that means we'll be riding into his next war? Best to keep our heads down with this one."

The King wasn't starting another war any time soon, she wanted to correct them. He couldn't afford to lose any more of his army and the Umbral Knights weren't very good in a warlike setting. If they were released from their armor, then the smoke disappeared forever.

Still, she was glad at least some of the young women here had good heads on their shoulders.

"But! Do not let that strike fear into your hearts, my flowers." The King struck his chest hard. "For I am here to protect you. It is my wish that a few of the more... prominent women ride beside me. Though you are all stunning in your own way, I will admit, a few of you have caught my eye more than the others."

There it was.

Lore would have been surprised if he hadn't already picked out his favorites. If she had more time to focus on the other brides, she might have seen the front runners herself. But realistically, she'd been struggling to get any time alone with the King. He was more interested in putting her in his dungeon than having her to his rooms for wine and cheese.

The King called out the names of a few women. One of them was the brunette who'd insulted Beauty, shockingly. She hadn't really thought the woman would get chosen, but there she was. Right at the top of his list. Even Beauty was called, and Lore had the satisfying moment of seeing the nasty woman's eyes narrow in distaste. Good for her friend, though she still hoped Beauty ended up with a kinder man in the end. Someone who would actually love her.

"And Lorelei of Tenebrous!" the King shouted. "That will be the end of it all, my dears. I promise, you'll all get your time with me soon."

Had he said her name?

Oh, well. That was good, but she hadn't prepared herself for this. The King thought she was part of the rebellion and the last time she'd seen him, he had revealed the darker side of himself.

She took her time walking to the front with all the other women. A servant handed her the reins to a tame looking horse with deep chestnut eyes and withers that said it would rather be in a meadow than on a hunt.

The King paused beside her and said under his breath, "I am not one for apologies, Lady of Tenebrous. I was wrong about you, however, and that was inexcusable. If you'll allow me to make it up to you on this hunt, I would appreciate a few moments alone."

Perfect.

She plastered a fake smile on her face and tried to force herself to blush. "I would like nothing more, my King."

He walked away from her, but she noticed that Abraxas paused beside her as well. The shadow of the King already furrowed his brow in worry, and she knew that was because of her. He knew what she was thinking.

Now was the time. He couldn't change her mind.

The moment the King and his guard were gone, the servant next to her strapped on a bow and set of arrows to her saddle. It wasn't a lot, and she'd prefer a knife, but it was a start. An arrow could still pierce a man's heart if she used enough force to hide it in his chest cavity. Then she'd have to run.

Lore patted the horse's flanks. "You and I are going on an adventure today," she whispered. "I hope you're up for it."

The King mounted his dark steed and all the brides followed his lead. He had the strangest army in the world at his beck and call right now, and Lore couldn't help but look out over the sea of at least thirty women. So many were left, and yet, he'd already chosen his favorites.

Today would be the day the King died. She would put an arrow through his heart, and another through his throat for good measure. The kingdom would fall into turmoil, but she would escape.

The King lifted his voice again and called out, "I will repeat myself only once, my flowers! A hunt is dangerous, but you have no reason to fear. For we have the most formidable creature on our side! A dragon!"

Abraxas stiffened, but the brides let out shocked gasps. They were ready to see the beast up close again.

Her stomach churned. She didn't want to see the monstrous beast who'd killed her mother, even though she knew she had no choice but to endure.

Yet, the beast didn't fly over their heads.

As if living in a dream, she watched the King frown and look at Abraxas. His lips moved, and she swore he said, "Well? Get on with it."

Abraxas looked over his shoulder at her apologetically and a blast of air struck her in the face. The women beside her gasped, lifting their arms to cover their faces. But she didn't. She stared in horror as the man she thought she knew turned into the dragon she hated with every ounce of her soul.

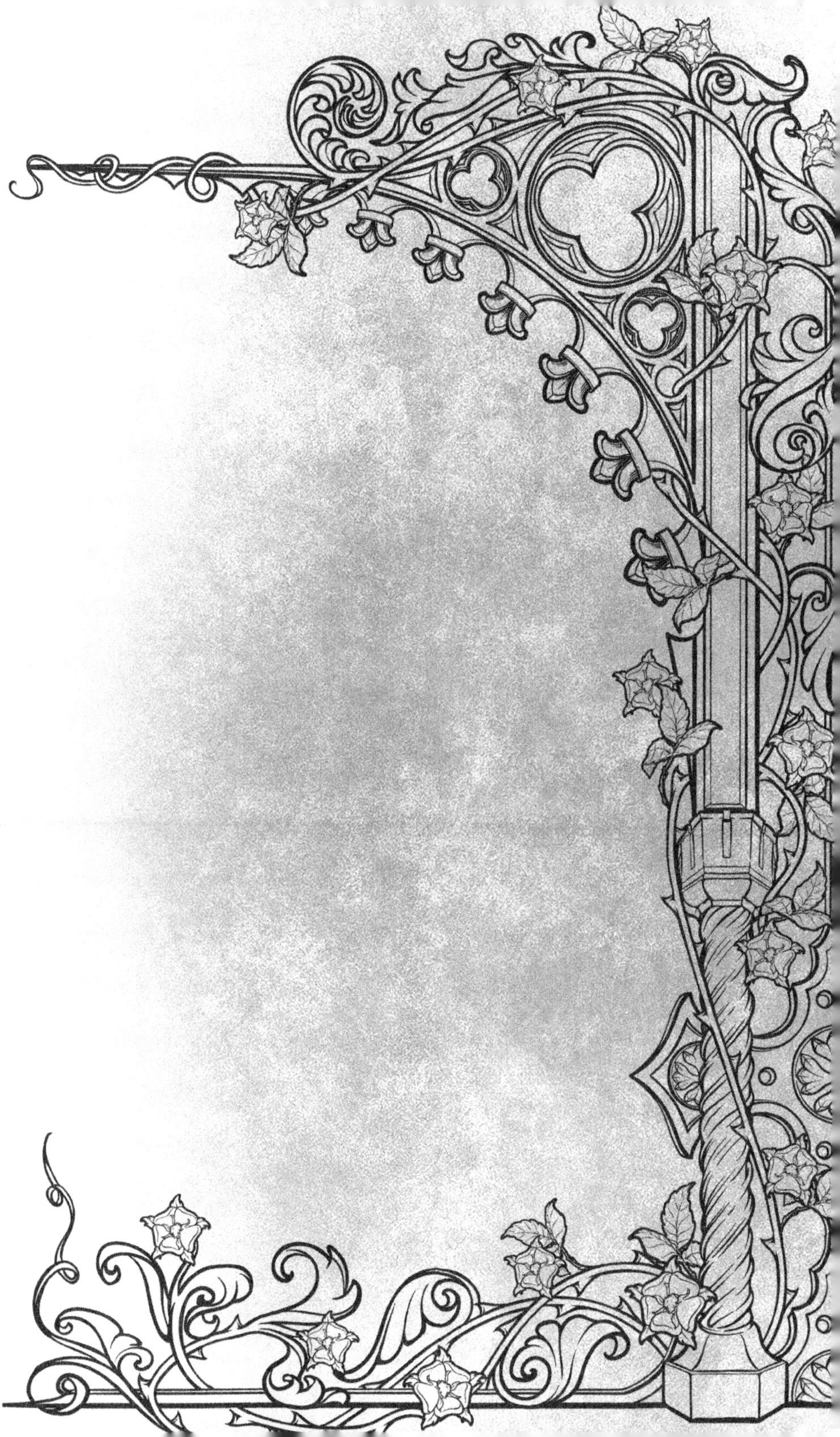

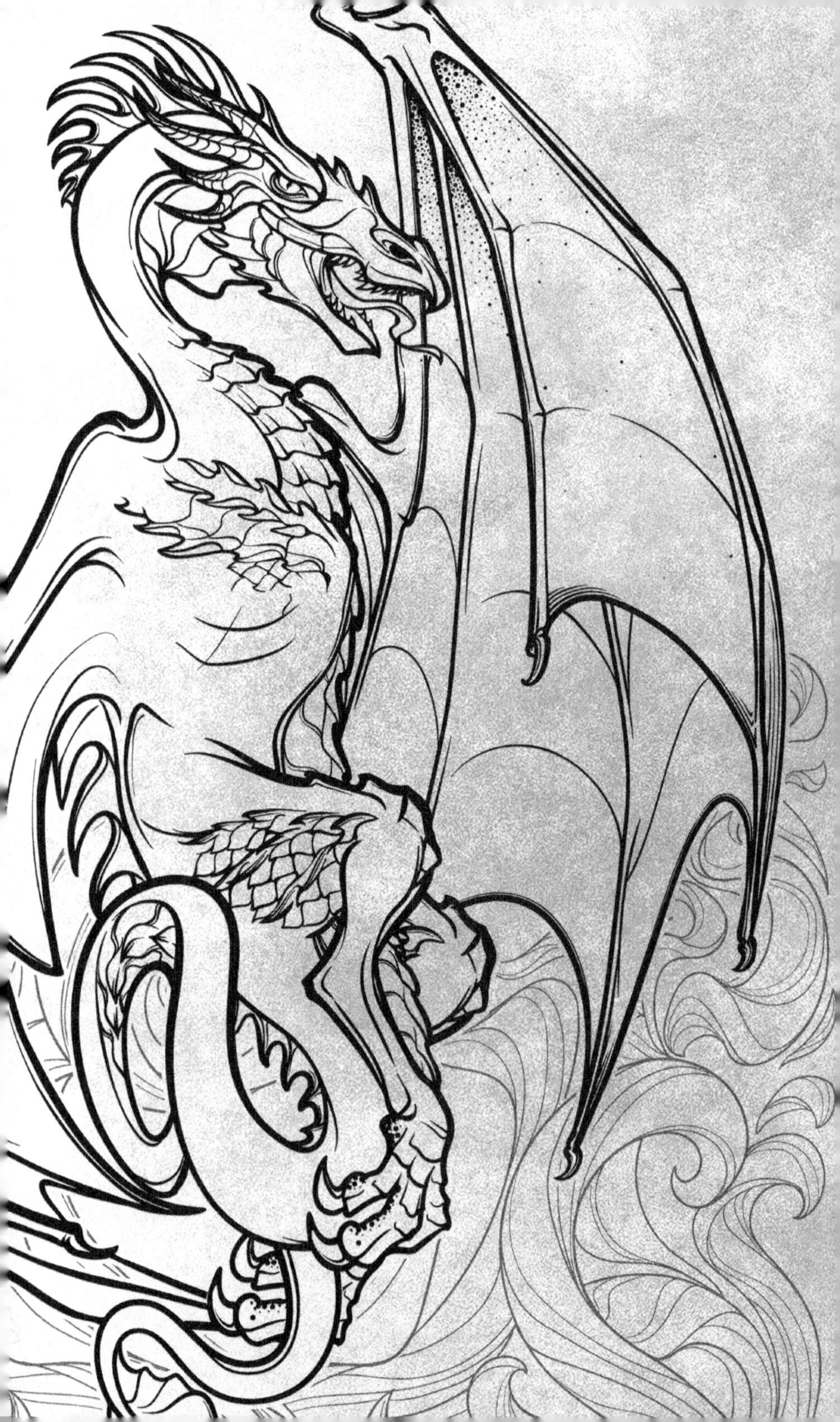

Chapter 21

He'd known this was the plan. Abraxas was meant to turn into a dragon before all the potential brides, so they could see that he was the monster. Zander had heard a rumor that some of the brides considered his personal guard to be rather handsome, and that was the end of all that.

No one could be more handsome than their king, and if they thought he was, then that had to change.

He didn't want Lorelei to see him like this, though. He hadn't expected their afternoon to affect him so thoroughly and yet; it had. She'd made a lasting impression, and he'd planned on telling her the truth sooner rather than later. The King, however, had rushed that.

The change rolled over him, blasting dust out of the courtyard and into small dervishes that terrified the horses. He watched Lorelei the whole time. She was the only woman in the entire group that never once covered her eyes or averted her gaze.

She watched him intently with an emotion that bordered on hate.

He hadn't expected that.

Abraxas had seen many reactions to his change in form. Fear. Horror. Sadness. But no one had ever hated him so much as this woman.

What had he done? He'd only been himself, and the thought that she couldn't accept that made him angry. Angrier than he'd ever been in his life. She was an elf, and he'd accepted that without looking at her like she was a monster. Yet here she was, giving him a much different glare that made him feel as though he were wrong for being what he was.

He'd thought she was against all that. Apparently, he'd been wrong.

Zander tossed his arms up and laughed with glee. "You see, my flowers? You should never be afraid in this castle when my beast protects you!"

Beast. Even now, the King had to throw insults just to make himself feel bigger than the dragon who stood among them. Abraxas shook his heavy head, getting used to this body as his mind stretched to fill the cavity of scales. Yet... Those eyes still followed his every move.

Lorelei wasn't going to let him off the hook. He already could tell that she was too angry to speak. Her hands tightened on the reins and her back was so stiff, he feared she'd pull a muscle. And she watched him with a gaze that was far too intense.

"We're hunting boar today, my flowers! The first one to bring the beast down will win a private dinner with me!" Zander struck his mount on the sides, hard, and they raced from the courtyard.

The other horses pursued the black steed, who had led the herd since they were all very young. The brides didn't stand a chance at killing a boar before Zander. He would be in the front the entire time, and Abraxas would fly overhead. Any boar in the forest would end up running straight toward the horses to get away from the dragon.

He waited until all the horses were far from the courtyard before he flapped his wings. The leathery appendages snapped in the wind, cracking hard multiple times before he finally took off into the air.

The wind might be too strong today. He had to fight with every heavy wing beat to get enough speed to keep up with the smaller horses, even though they were running through the forest. The King had created a path long ago through the woods, none of the steeds would lose their footing.

He followed them for what felt like hours. Soaring through the sky and dodging clouds so he could still see the entire group of women and his king. They moved quickly, the King continually shouting a direction. A few of the women fell behind, then more of them. Soon, there were only six horses keeping up with Zander. The same women he'd chosen as his favorites, with Lorelei in the lead.

Abraxas knew her horse. That creature had stayed in the pasture for most of its life and had little enjoyment of running or even being outside its pen. Abraxas thought it was a sweetheart, but obviously not the kind of horse anyone wanted to ride. It was a pet, not a biddable beast.

Yet, Lorelei had somehow whipped the creature into keeping up with the King's horse who had been the fastest in the herd for years. And it looked like the little horse Lorelei rode was enjoying itself.

How had she done that? What magic spell had she cast that wouldn't make the King see what she had done?

Foolish woman.

He watched a while longer, but it didn't take long until it was just the

King and two women. Lorelei and a beautiful woman who had clearly come from the richest family in Tenebrous. Not that their wealth could stand up to any other city in Umbra. But the King wheeled his horse away from the path and the two women followed until they reached a clearing.

Abraxas already knew what Zander had planned. He would steal some time with the two women alone, and Lorelei would take this as her chance to kill him.

What she didn't know was that the Umbral Knights circled that clearing. They stood at the ready to protect their king, for Zander was no fool. He wanted to make sure he was protected, especially considering his dragon would take some time to land.

He couldn't let her try to kill the King when so many eyes were watching her. Even if she succeeded, she would never get out of the clearing alive.

Abraxas did something he hadn't done for centuries. He changed mid air back into a mortal, over a part of the forest that they had already ridden through. His mortal form had just barely taken over the dragon by the time he hit the trees, and he landed hard on the ground. He rolled, protecting his head and neck, before he finally stopped in a heap at the base of a tree.

He'd have bruises in the morning, but that was worth it if he saved her.

Abraxas ran down the trail faster than any mortal man could have. Fear and anxiety fueled him, pushing him ever faster and farther than he'd sprinted. And yet, even at that speed, he reached the clearing just in time to see the King and the other woman starting their walk away from Lorelei.

She stood with her horse, clearly preparing herself for what she had to do. Abraxas had assumed she would wait until she had her own alone time with the King.

He was wrong.

Lorelei pulled out her bow and two arrows from the quiver. She notched them both at the same time, one on top of the other. And he didn't know what she thought to do with that. He'd never seen an elf hit two targets at the same time, but he knew he couldn't give her the chance to go through with her plan. It was too dangerous.

And it was the wrong time.

Launching out of the forest, he wrapped an arm around her waist and twisted her at the last second. Twin arrows loosed from her bow into the forest, hopefully not striking any of the Umbral Knights. Not that it mattered. They would come back in another suit, anyway.

He used his body to force her out of the clearing and back into the woods. Lorelei twisted and punched at his arms, but she didn't make a sound.

Smart girl. At least she wouldn't alert the King that something was wrong.

Abraxas made sure to put as much space as he could between himself and the clearing. But when they reached a small creek that split through the forest, he couldn't contain her any longer. Lorelei twisted out of his arms, fell onto the ground, and then scrambled back onto her feet with all the grace of her ancestors.

She whirled around, hair flying about her face. "What are you doing, you scaly bastard? That was my chance!"

"Your chance for what? To get yourself killed?" He gestured around them. "There are Umbral Knights everywhere, Lorelei. Do you really think the King would be alone with either of you this soon? He's a villain, not a fool."

"I don't care if they see me shoot him. It has to be done and one dead elf won't change too much." She stalked toward him, clearly intending to shove past him and back to the forest. "Get out of my way, Abraxas. I'm going to kill him."

"No, you aren't." He put a hand on her chest and shoved her back. "You are going to stay right here until the hunt is over with, and then we'll figure out a way to get you alone with the King. But you are not going to risk yourself in the process."

"Everything I do here is a risk," she snarled. "I'm the woman trying to kill the King, Abraxas. I will lose my head one way or another, but I will not fail."

"You aren't thinking straight."

"No dragon will tell me what to do." Her eyes flashed with that same emotion. That hatred that burned too deep for him to understand.

And it killed him. He hated it that she had decided he was a horrible creature because his other form had scales and wings. Nausea rose swiftly. Did she think there were creatures more worthy of freedom than others? Was she just as cruel a monster as Zander?

"You hate me," he murmured. "Don't you?"

"I didn't know what you were before, but I do now." Her eyes flashed again, this time with obvious emotion. "Get your hand off me."

He hadn't moved his hand from her chest? Damn it, he realized that now. He could feel her breath heaving underneath his palm where he touched her ribs.

Abraxas reluctantly removed his hand, but he didn't want to. Even angry with her, even knowing that she wanted to take his head off his shoulders, he wanted to touch her.

"Why?" he asked. "I'm not letting you go until you explain this to me. Everything was fine yesterday."

"I didn't know you were the dragon yesterday." She took a step back, her feet splashing through the stream until she was ankle deep in the icy water. "I hadn't even guessed the dragon might be a shapeshifter, but I should have known."

"And what does it matter if I'm a dragon? I didn't look at you like you were lesser when you told me you were an elf." And he had more reason to, although he didn't add that.

The unsaid words floated between them. Many creatures looked down on the elves. Even before the previous king had forced them all to bend a knee, they had not been the favorite of the magical creatures. Elves were beautiful. Their magic was entertaining to watch. But both of those things made them too popular with humans. If any of the creatures could have walked among the mortals, it was the elves.

She tossed her hair away from her face and glared at him. "I don't care what you are, Abraxas. I care that you are the dragon who killed my mother. You are the dragon who has forced all of my people and Tenebrous to be slaves to a king that will never see any of us as people. You are the reason why we're all fighting so hard, Abraxas. Without you, the King would be dead already."

It was true. All of it was true, but one thing struck him harder than the rest.

"Your mother?" he repeated. "I killed your mother?"

"She was part of the original rebellion, when the kingship turned over to the young son." Every word was spat at him like a poisonous dart. "She stood with the elves and she fought against this king until they were captured. The King wanted to make an example of them, so he turned them all over to you."

He didn't remember that time. It was so long ago. Her mother might have been one of the many who had been killed by the dragon in the beginning, but he wanted to remember the woman's face. He desperately wished that the faces of the dead hadn't blurred as hundreds had fallen.

"Did she die by fire?" he asked, suddenly needing to know the answer to his own fear. "Or teeth?"

"What does it matter?"

"It matters." Oh, it only mattered to his soul, but it mattered. More than he wanted to admit.

Lorelei glared at him ever harder, but she squared her shoulders and faced the horrors of her past. "I stood in the crowd and watched them tie my mother to a pyre. You came down from the sky like some kind of demon out of mortal nightmares. You looked my mother in the eye and she didn't flinch when you breathed fire over her. There was nothing left for me to claim. No bones. No jewelry. Not even a scrap of clothing. You made sure there was nothing left of her but ash and dust."

The words rolled over him and came with a sense of relief. The cool feeling of peace eased through his soul, and the anxiety drained as though her words were the crack in the urn of his body.

"Good," he replied with a heavy sigh. "Good. Then she died an honorable death."

There was no greater insult than for a dragon to eat someone. It meant they were only worthy as food, and he had done that for the King a few times. Each of those deaths haunted him far more than the others.

If he had killed her mother with flames, then her soul rested well. She'd earned that death and she would have remembered the old ways. He hoped.

Her face turned bone white. "Good? You think it's a good thing that you killed my mother?"

He shook his head, trying to find the words that would explain. "No! No, Lorelei, listen to me. Dragons have a different way of dealing with traitors. If I had eaten your mother, then that would mean her soul had wandered. To be cleansed in fire is to wash away all of her sins. She went into her afterlife as a hero."

"A hero? Who cares if she died a hero? She's still dead!" Lorelei lifted her hands, palms out and shaking. "I don't want to hear any more of this, Abraxas. I can't. Your excuses are empty and they mean nothing."

She walked away from him. Trudging through the forest and away from his sight. He couldn't let her go. She couldn't kill the King like this, she'd make a mistake.

Abraxas took off after her. "Lorelei, you can't!"

"I'm not doing anything stupid, Abraxas!" she shouted over her shoulder. "The timing is wrong now, anyway. Leave me alone!"

He couldn't keep up with an elf in the woods. He tried, though.

Abraxas ran through the trees until he lost sight of the lithe body that glimmered with moonlight underneath her skin.

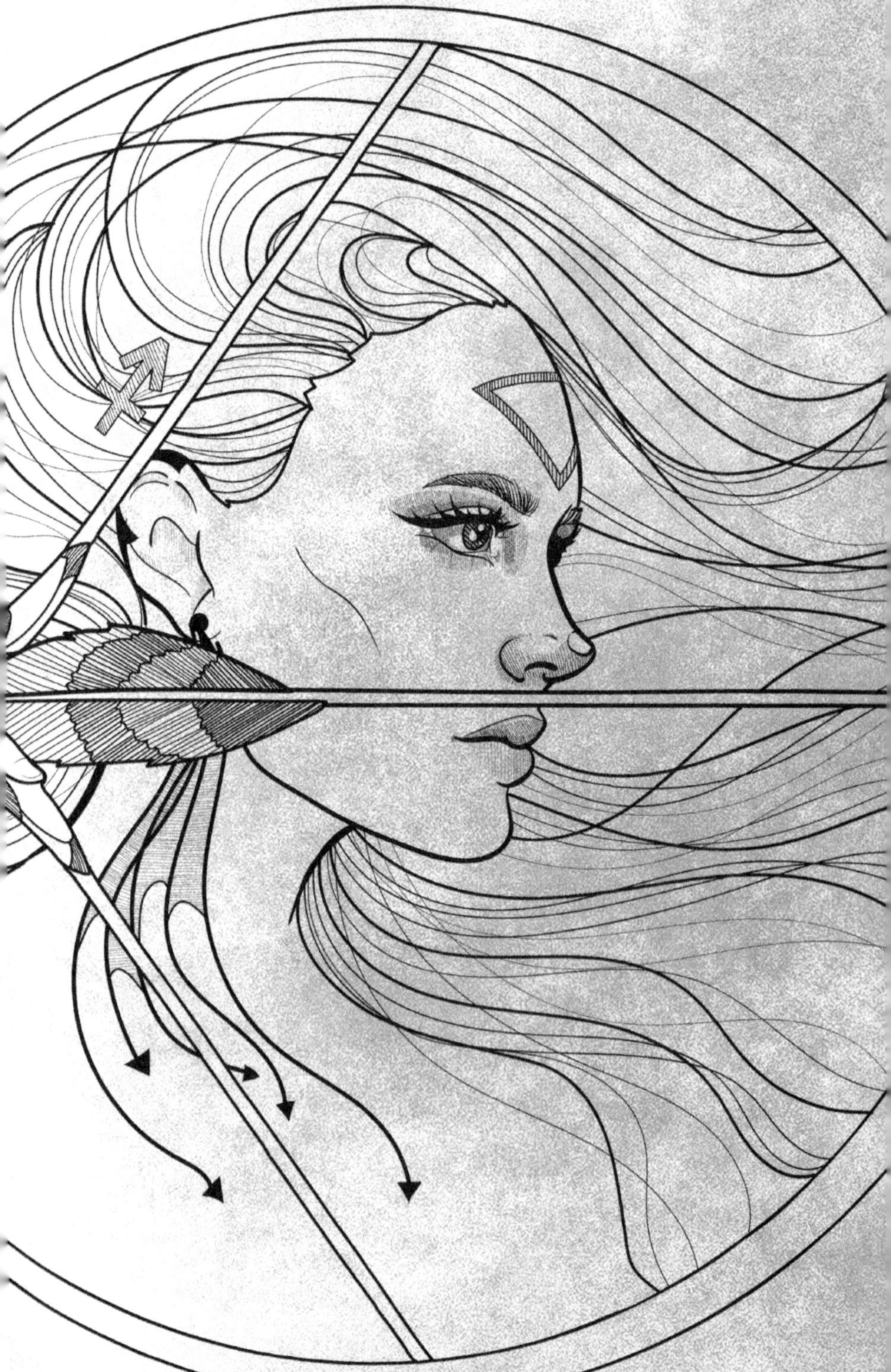

Chapter 22

Lore couldn't think through the anger that coursed through her veins. He dared to say it was a good death? That her mother had been given an honorable end when she hadn't needed to die at all?

She understood the problem with dragons now. They only saw the world in black and white. His actions couldn't have possibly been wrong, because he was the all mighty dragon who everyone should bow down to and appreciate that he'd even given them a second of his time.

She slapped a branch out of her way and continued marching through the forest. She didn't even know where she was going. The castle remained behind her, and she would have to return at some point. The King would think she'd run off, and then the Umbral Knights would be after her, regardless of her reasoning.

If only she had loosed that arrow into his back while he walked away from her and this would all be over. She might be dead. The Knights wouldn't have let her get away that easily. But it would be over with.

And she was ready for this to all be over.

At some point, she realized the trees had turned her around. Trees had at least some differences about them. But these trees were exactly the same as moments ago, right down to their gnarled roots.

She slowed, then stopped. Lore turned around in a circle as she gathered all the information about the trees surrounding her. They were the same ones as ten minutes ago. She was certain of it.

Which meant someone had cast a spell on her so she couldn't keep moving.

The King? Perhaps. She wouldn't be surprised to find out he'd placed an enchantment on the castle so none of the brides could leave. But this magic had a familiar flavor to it that she couldn't shake off. The magic clung to her like shadows, and the forest bent too easily for this to be anything other than a creature she'd already met.

"Borovoi!" she called out. "I would know your magic anywhere, leshy. Come out and talk to me rather than trapping me."

"Then stop trying to run," Borovoi replied. His words echoed through the trees themselves. "I've been keeping you from leaving your duties behind, but you're rather exhausting to watch, little girl."

"I think I've survived long enough to not be called that any longer," she snarled.

The trees gathered together to her right. She spun in time to see them form a single, twisted trunk. They coiled around each other like a snake before they split open down the center, just as the tree had done to spit her into the King's party.

FIRE HEART

From the shadows of the gash, two figures stepped out. One pale man with tangled long locks and a woman dressed entirely in leather.

Lore could handle the leshy. Borovoi might be a meddling old man, but he was logical. He understood that the King was very dangerous and would be very difficult to kill, no matter how hard she tried. Lore had experience, too, but that would mean nothing to the woman standing beside Borovoi.

Margaret crossed her arms over her chest, then looked Lore up and down. "Just what do you think you're doing?"

Chest heaving, Lore refused to give in. "Getting away from the dragon, who apparently is the same man I've been trying to rope into this whole plan. Why didn't you tell me the dragon could change his form? He's mortal, Margaret, and he walks with the King."

"I thought everyone knew the dragon was the King's personal guard."

"No one knows that he's a man!" Lore threw her hands up in the air, exasperated that this woman would ever say such a thing. "You have got to be kidding me, Margaret. The dragon can change into a human form. He's the one that follows the King's every step. You sent me into battle against the strongest of our own kind with no warning."

"You said you were working with him," Margaret corrected. "If you got the dragon under your thumb, then we're closer to killing the King than you want to admit."

Lore's jaw dropped open. She didn't want to even consider working with Abraxas again. She'd kissed the man who had killed her mother. She'd thought that man was funny, intelligent, and thought she might actually like him.

Of all people, she'd thought Margaret would understand that. Her mother and Margaret had been friends long ago. They had run through the forests together before the King of mortal men had ruined this world. Her death should have hit Margaret hard.

Obviously, it hadn't. Margaret would stop at nothing to complete this mission. Even offer up her best friend's daughter to the killer who had ruined the family she'd once been a part of.

"I can't do this," Lore muttered. "I can't look him in the eye or work with him when I know what he's done. My soul screams at me to get vengeance for the mother who should have lived. For the thousands of souls who have met their premature end because he follows the King's bidding like a dog."

Margaret slashed her hand through the air, silencing Lore's words. "Be silent, you spoiled little brat. How dare you even question this mission simply because you are uncomfortable!"

Seeing his opportunity to step in between the two rabid elves, Borovoi walked into both of their lines of sight. "Lore, what if the dragon doesn't want to work with the King either? I find it hard to believe that one of our own would help someone like that boy. The dragon is old. He's seen countless kingdoms start and fall. He's not a pet. He's ancient."

"And yet, he allows the King to treat him like a well trained animal," she snarled.

"Then what does the King have to hold over his head?" Borovoi waved his hand in the air, and an image appeared like mist over his open fingers. An image of a scaled belly passing over the treetops. "They didn't hunt us in the old days. There used to be a hundred dragons all over Umbra. Where did they all go?"

"I don't care."

Sure, there might have been a small amount of curiosity that sparked inside her. Dragons weren't abundantly available for people to ask questions of, and it was strange that he worked with the King. This horrible child who had held them all captive must hold something to convince the dragon to be biddable.

But no. She didn't want to waste her time trying to figure out what that thing was. She could spend the rest of her life trying to figure that out, or to justify Abraxas's loyalty. In the end, it wouldn't change a thing. The dragon had still done horrible deeds in the King's name. He'd still killed her mother.

Borovoi saw these thoughts play across her face. He grinned and pointed at her. "You want to know just as much as I do, elf."

"I don't want to know anything. I want to get this all over and done with, and the dragon stopped me today. The hunt was the perfect excuse to get the King on his own and I could have blamed the wound on a boar that I didn't kill while trying to save his life. It was all exactly as I needed it to be. He's a liability to the mission."

Lore knew she shouldn't have said anything at all. She knew that expression on Margaret's face, and it was one that meant she would be unhappy for a while. Margaret was about to throw her to the wolves and hope that her insane new plan worked.

"No," Lore interrupted the woman's thoughts. "Whatever it is that you just cooked up in your head, I'm not doing it."

"You don't have a choice, Lore. You're going to finish this, because you have to. You haven't come all this way to stop now, have you?" Margaret lifted a challenging brow.

"Don't put me in any more danger, Margaret. Killing the King is a hard enough task. Now you're going to ask me to do something else, and I don't appreciate it." Lorelei tried her best to sound like a wise woman. She wanted the assassin in front of her to take her seriously.

But she also knew that if Margaret changed the mission, then she would do whatever the older elf wanted her to do. Because she had done everything possible already and it hadn't worked. She needed help.

And if she really looked inside her own heart, she wanted to kill the murderous tyrant who had ruined this kingdom. She wanted all this to end so she could free those creatures in the dungeons. So she could give them all the life they deserved.

Margaret knew when she gave in, long before Lore had known she would give in. "That's my girl," she muttered. "Listen to me. This dragon could be more useful than any of us imagined. Borovoi has a point, he's only following the King because that evil man has something over him. If we take the dragon away, then we leave him more vulnerable. You're the first person who might be able to do that."

"I thought you wanted me to kill the King."

"I want you to do both," Margaret snapped. "Take his life, and then bring me that dragon. You think the King will fall and that all the other pieces are ready to align right into the vacancy? The entire kingdom is going to crumble the moment you put an arrow through that villain's neck. Which means we're going to need all the help we can get in the coming months."

It didn't escape Lore's notice that Margaret was absolutely certain that she would succeed. The realization shouldn't have made her proud, but it did. The other elf's opinion mattered a great deal, and at least she knew she hadn't let Margaret down so far.

But this plan... It was madness.

Lore swallowed hard. "I already cut ties with the dragon. He knows he killed my mother, and that I want nothing to do with him."

"People change. You were understandably angry, and he can't take that away from you. But you will go back to him, Lorelei. Convince him that you still need him, and that you were cruel for no reason." Margaret waved a hand. Leaves fell from the oak trees behind her and landed on her shoulders in a brightly colored shower of green. "Dragon or not, men are easy. They are not confusing beasts, Lore. You know that as well as I do."

Borovoi seemed to bristle at the tone, but then even he shrugged.

She squeezed her eyes shut and took a slow, even breath. "You want me to seduce a king and a dragon?"

"You will do whatever it takes, girl. Grab this kingdom by the throat and make it bend a knee to your will." Margaret eyed her with a piercing gaze. "Can you do that?"

No.

She was just Lorelei of Silverfell. A young elf who had barely seen the old days before they had all ended. She didn't know how to act around people and so far, she'd only had one chance to kill a king and she had wasted it.

She was no closer to her goal than she had been at the beginning of all this mess. The only people she had on her side were a mortal girl, a pixie who was still hiding, and potentially a dragon who thought she hated him.

This wasn't a mission. It was suicide.

She opened her mouth to tell Margaret that, but the elf clapped her hands. The sound sent a shock wave through the forest and everything fell silent. As though even the trees were holding their breath and waiting for what she would say. "Good. Then you will do this all for me, Lorelei. You will complete your mission and then I will name you a hero."

"I don't want to be a hero," she whispered as they both walked back to the split in the tree. "I just want to be me."

Margaret disappeared, but Borovoi stopped to look at her one last time. "Miss Lorelei, have you ever considered that maybe those two people are one and the same? The woman you want to be, and the hero you don't."

He left the clearing as well, and Lore found she had forgotten to breathe. Her head throbbed with his words that echoed over and over in her head.

Maybe those two people were the same.

Was she the hero? She didn't want to be. Heroes never ended up happy in any story. But the people who did end up happy were the ones who weren't involved at all. They were the side characters in the background. The farmer whose field was originally destroyed, but then made better. The mermaid who drowned the sailors but was left alone when no one could find her underwater grotto.

That's who Lore wanted to be. The forgotten character who remained in the background for all eternity.

The trees shook over her head. Leaves fell through the air, but these weren't green at all. They were yellow and egg-shaped, with pointed tips and serrated edges.

Birch leaves. Just like the ones she'd grown up with and played in while her mother watched with a smile on her face. Birch leaves that had always reminded her of where she came from and who she was.

Lore tucked a single yellowed leaf behind her ear and nodded firmly.

So be it. If fate wanted her to be a hero, then a hero she would be.

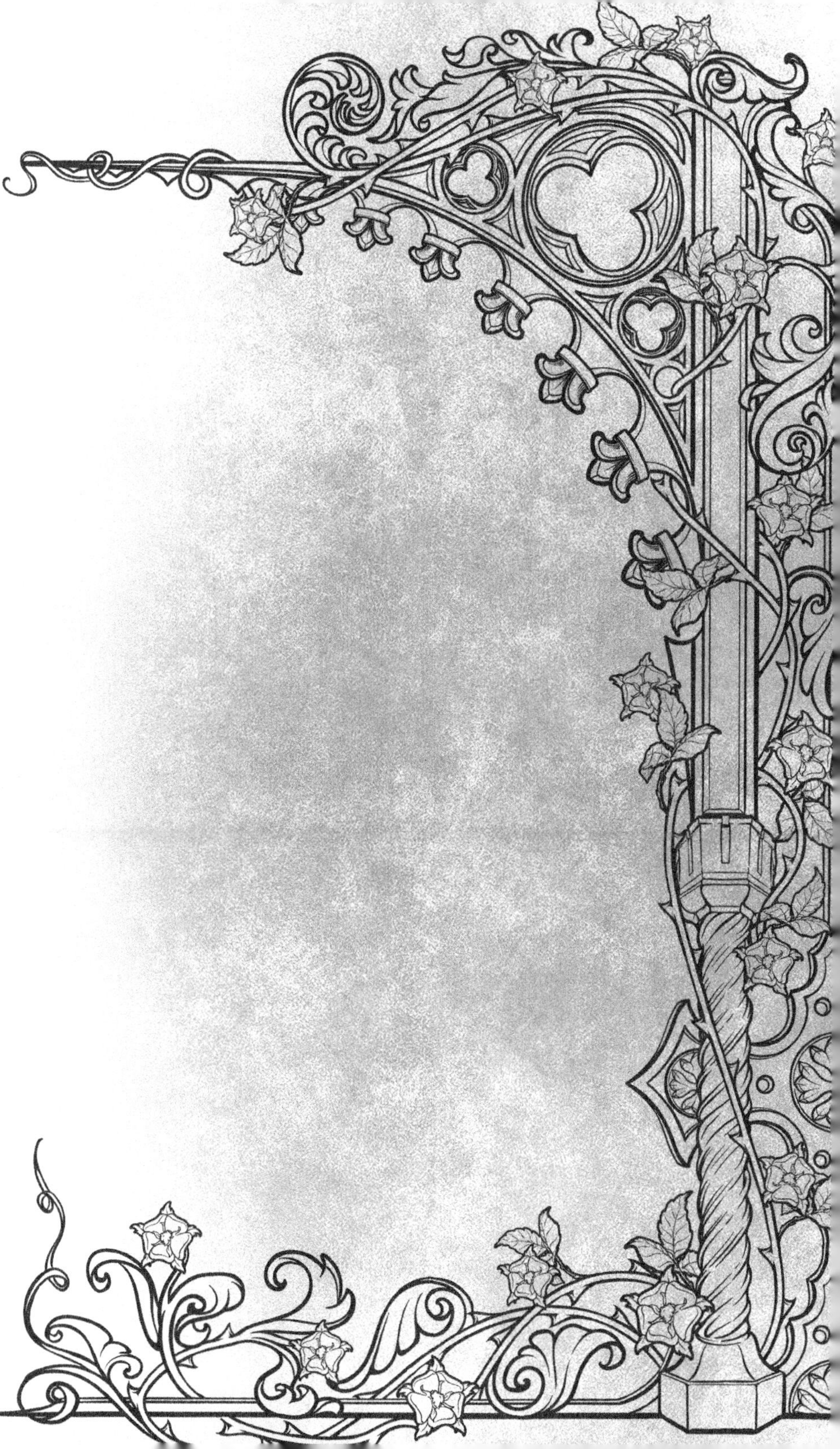

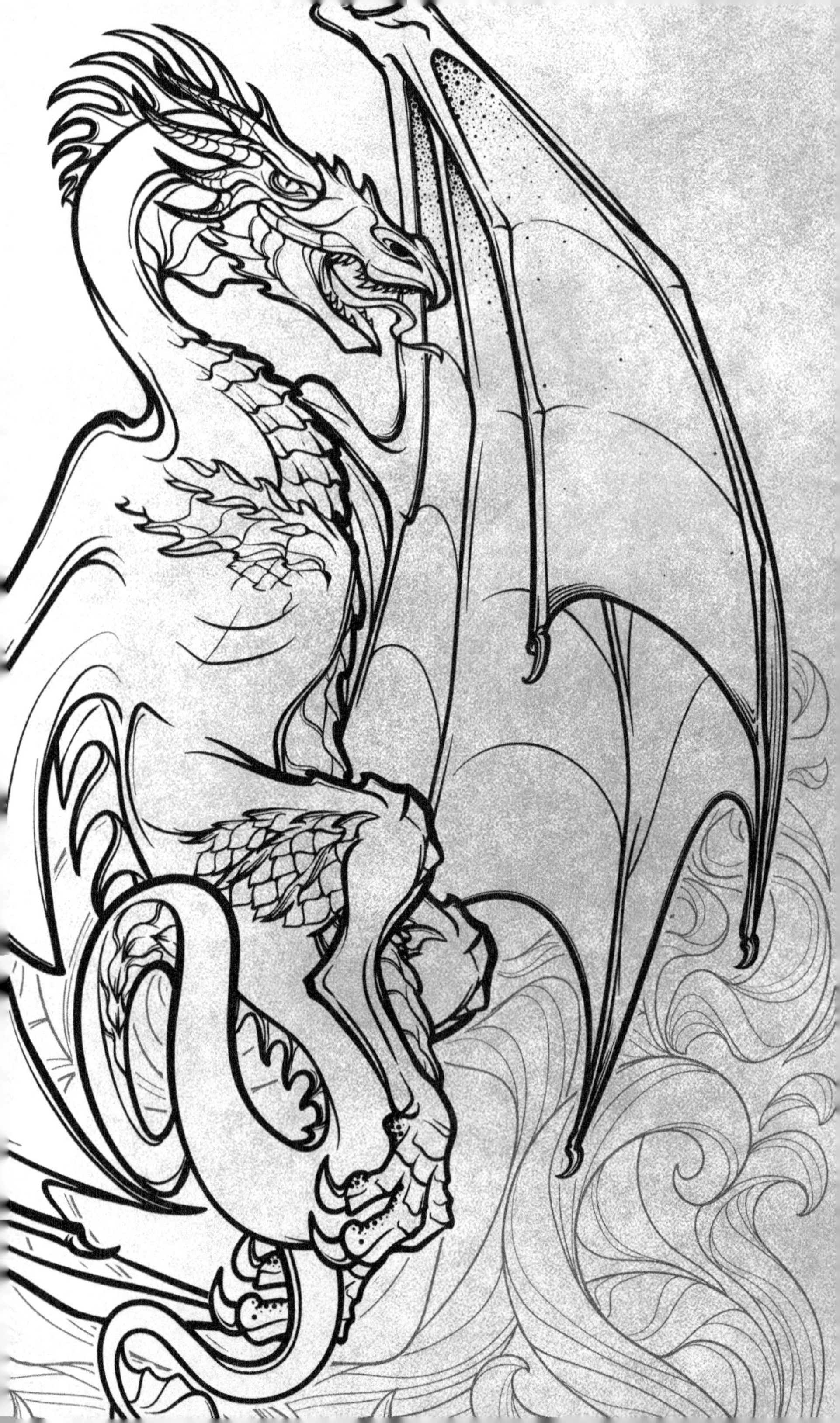

Chapter 23

"What do you mean she got away?" Zander screamed. His cry echoed throughout the dragon's cavern.

Abraxas had yet to return to his dragon form. Instead, he stood on the last ledge of stone before the cave that opened up into a pit of gold coins and jewelry.

"She wanted to go through the forest and return to the castle on her own," he muttered while counting each gold piece in front of him. "She said the journey wouldn't take long, but that she had enjoyed the hunt. I already told you how she made her apologies."

"You know that makes little sense. Even you couldn't come up with a lie that poor." Zander walked up behind him and shoved his shoulder. "Tell me exactly what happened, Abraxas. No lies this time."

He already knew what the King feared. Zander thought that Abraxas had found one of the brides to be entertaining and that he wanted to take one as his own. He was right, of course. Abraxas would sooner die than see her in the hands of this horrible king.

But he also couldn't let Zander know that. The fate of Lorelei rested on his shoulders now. Along with the fate of the entire dragon species.

He hadn't felt like this in a long time. An overwhelming maw of anxiety and fear waited at his feet for him to take the plunge into the darkness that would swallow him up for months to come. It would be so easy to retreat. To dive headfirst into that dark place that refused to allow him to leave.

In some strange way, it was comforting to let the anxiety take control of his life. The control was what he lacked, after all, and at least if he were hibernating in his cavern, then nothing bad could happen again.

Zander shoved his shoulder a second time. "Are you even listening to me? What is this habit that you keep getting into? I'm your king! You have to listen to every word I say, and you know the consequences if you don't."

He'd lose everything. Yes, he understood.

And he lived with the mountain of guilt that came from working with Zander. The guilt of his own extinct kind. The guilt of an innocent woman's soul who only wanted to save this kingdom from a child who wore a crown on his head. How much more could he take?

"I understand," he muttered, his voice pitched low and his heart racing in his chest. "I know what threats you wave before me, King of Umbra."

"Good, then you understand the gravity of the situation."

"Certainly, my king. If I do not follow your every whim, I truly will be the very last of the dragons." And that thought terrified him more than anything else.

Abraxas had clung to the hope that someday he would see another dragon. He longed for the flash of scales in the sky, like starlight, but so much brighter. He dreamt of a roar that shattered the clouds like thunder. Even now, the thought of seeing someone who was exactly like him made tears prick in his eyes.

He wanted that more than anything. And he would stop at nothing to get it.

"The last of your kind," the King repeated. "That must weigh on you. The rest of the kingdom believes you really are that, but you and I are the only ones who know just how tied to me you are. Without me, all your hopes and dreams crumble. Don't they?"

He licked his teeth, feeling the canines lengthen as he desired nothing more than to turn back into the dragon and crunch the King's bones between his teeth. "I fail to see why you're bringing this up, Zander."

"Maybe I want others to see what I know. Maybe it would be better if the entire kingdom knew why you were at my beck and call." A fanatic light grew inside the King.

Abraxas thought it was a stupid idea. There were plenty of bleeding hearts in Umbra who would hear of his plight and want to help him. But the King clearly didn't see it that way. He thought that if the kingdom knew he held the dragon under his thumb with good reason, and the entirety of the dragon species, then they would think him even more powerful.

Zander had never seen very far into the future. He'd always thought the world revolved around him and his decisions. It would be his greatest mistake to release this information to the world.

The dragon would not stop him.

Abraxas turned around, towering over the King while he breathed out a low growl. "I fail to see what game you think you're playing, Zander."

"I think you fear the others, knowing that you're so thoroughly tied to me. You don't want anyone to know your greatest mistake is in falling under the control of mortal men." Zander grinned, as if he'd discovered a secret he wasn't supposed to know. "Is it embarrassing to be my slave, dragon?"

"Embarrassing?" The word slave burned through his mind. Not for any reason that Zander might think, but because it was such an insult for a dragon to be called that.

He was no slave.

He stayed because of his honor and duty to his kind. At any point, he could fly away from this horrible castle and this childish king. Abraxas could choose to be the last dragon and live out his long life in the mountains where no one would find him.

He was a good man at his core. That is why he stayed. That was why he allowed the King to run his mouth and not be killed.

With a sharp toothed grin, he let a long snarl erupt from between his teeth. "You know nothing about me, Zander. Don't think you are capable of understanding a creature who has lived ten of your lifetimes."

"I think I understand you very well." Zander lifted his hand and the gold coins beside them shifted.

The circular coins clinked against each other as the mountain of wealth rolled, shifted, and revealed the box that contained the eggs. The enchanted box that changed the entire world for Abraxas.

He couldn't even get close to it. That was part of the problem. He would give his right arm if he could hold one of the eggs. Even just to touch them to make sure the magic of his people still lingered underneath the cold crust of the shell. Something. Anything to ease the fear that the eggs had died, not that they were dormant.

Zander walked up to the box and opened it. The twin eggs that lay within were so stunning. They could have bought a kingdom if he ever dared to part with them.

The anger at the death of the other dragon bubbled back to life. Abraxas had buried it deep, hoping that he could forget the traumatic event so he could save the other two. But the dragon in his chest wanted to destroy this king for what he'd done.

"Look at them," Zander said under his breath. "I remember the first time my father showed me these eggs. Do you remember?"

"Of course." How could he forget? The boy had been little more than a child then, and he'd looked at the eggs as though they were toys that he'd been given as a gift.

"I thought they were the most beautiful things I'd ever set my eyes on. Little did I know how much I would adore the feminine form when I got older," Zander chuckled. "But these eggs still have a certain charm to them. A hope that lingers underneath the gemstone shell. Wouldn't you agree?"

"I do."

"What is that hope, Abraxas? Even I feel it when I look at them." Zander touched a finger to the sapphire egg, then stroked the emerald one. "They make me feel strong every time they are visible. And I don't think that's because they are the reason why I control you."

"That hope comes from the realization that you hold in your hands the power to destroy or begin a species of creatures that once ruled this realm." His words turned into a deep growl filled with strength and pride. "It is a hope that burns in all of us from the lives we lived before.

Our souls remember what it looked like when dragons flew through the clouds. When we could look to the sky and see a flock of dragons as they migrated to their winter hunting grounds. And those souls wish for that time to come again."

His words rang through the cavern like an omen. Even the King could have felt the tragic wonder of what their history used to be.

The time of dragons had ended centuries ago. Mortal kingdoms had risen and fallen in the time since Abraxas had last seen all the dragons in a flock. Their numbers dwindled from a plague. Then they fractured among themselves. Until it was just his clan left. Then the mortal king had come, and now, it was only him and the eggs.

How long had he been alone? How long had he suffered, hoping and praying that he'd get the chance to wake those eggs so that he could see a scaled face one more time?

He was too old now. Too old to do what he had to do and too weak to kill this king. Too weak to find someone who might break the enchantment on that box without the King's interference.

Zander sighed. "Ah, is that what it is? The hope that someday I will release these creatures upon the world? Maybe if I could train them to become like you. What do you think about that, Abraxas? Shall I have three dragons on a leash?"

If he tried, then Abraxas would kill him. He'd rather see those tiny dragons die in the eggs than endure the same life he had suffered through.

The King's eyes saw through his thoughts too easily. Zander chuckled and shook his head. "No, I think not. I can see that anger in your eyes, you know. It's like looking at a dragon rather than a man, even in this form."

Abraxas snarled in response.

"Just like that," the King replied. "That's exactly how I thought you would respond."

He wanted to leave this place. He imagined turning into a dragon and forcing Zander out of his cave. But he couldn't, and that frustration was slowly eating him alive. If only…

If only. That was where the thought ended every time he tried to think about it. Abraxas could torment himself with what his future could be, or he could realize that he lived here. Now. And it would never change, no matter how hard he tried.

Zander slowly closed the lid of the enchanted box, then patted the top. "I sent a large group of the brides home. They were no fun during the hunt, and they continued to fall behind. They clearly are not the women I am looking for in a partner. But I have decided I now wish to have a brave wife as well. A wife who would be comfortable holding a dragon in the palm of her hand."

The swift change of subject nearly gave Abraxas whiplash. He struggled to keep up with the King's intent in this conversation. "I suppose a brave wife is something that all men desire."

"But I am not all men. I am a king and she will have to suffer through more than wandering through this life as a princess or a queen. Life is difficult enough as it is." Zander laughed. "And to think, I had thought this would be easy to pick from a set of beautiful women."

"You have only seen the women from Tenebrous," he reminded the King. "You've never thought to look to the Highlands or the Lowlands for a bride."

"That's because I don't want a woman who won't appreciate that I plucked her from poverty and gave her a life like this." Zander threw his arms wide. "But my next plan will ensure that only the best of the women remain. Only the few who deserve to be here."

A pit knotted in Abraxas's stomach. He'd heard this before from the King, and now there were only going to be a few women left.

Would he send Lorelei home? No one knew where the elf had gone. Even Agatha sent her maids through the entire castle, but they could find no trace of the young woman.

"What of the girl?" he asked, risking sharing how much the elf intrigued him. "The one who slipped through the forest?"

Zander waved a hand in the air. "It doesn't matter. She's proven herself to be a rather impressive young woman, even though I hate to admit that to anyone. She can stay."

Relief flooded over him. His ears rang from it, so hard that he almost didn't hear what the King said next.

"I want them to steal an egg from you," Zander continued. "I think that would be the most entertaining challenge to watch yet. Even though no one will succeed, of course. But we'll have to see who gets close enough. You will, of course, do your best to stop them."

Abraxas surely hadn't heard the King right. No one could touch the box but the King. If one of those women even tried, the magic in it would kill them. It had almost killed him, and he was a hundred times larger.

He shook his head and took a step away from the box. "You know what will happen if you do that. You could kill one of them, Zander."

"If they die, they die." Zander shrugged. "There's so many of them, anyway. But I want to see if any of them can get to the box. It's a good test to see how capable they are. Besides, if they can trick you, then they're someone to watch. It'll be fun, Abraxas, don't ruin this all with your worrying."

He wasn't trying to ruin it. He feared for the lives of these innocent young women that the King simply did not care for in the slightest.

Zander had little pity when it came to those he thought could provide him with a little fun.

It made Abraxas sick.

"Fine," he muttered. "If this is what you want, then this is what we will do."

"It's what I want. And I know we're going to do it. I already sent news to the ladies." Zander preened in happiness. "Now, I'm going to leave the box here for the ladies to find, but they're going to come into the mouth of the cave at the bottom of the cliffs. What do you think?"

"I think you're asking them to do the impossible."

"Yes, I am." Zander clapped his hands, but then opened the box one more time. He grinned down at the eggs, then let it slam shut too fast. Too hard. "After all, rumors are the best way to get people to start talking, you know! The first one who realizes there are dragon eggs here will tell everyone. You have an hour alone with them, Abraxas. Then I expect you to be ready to stop my brides from stealing what is yours. You're able to do that, aren't you?"

The King didn't wait for his response. Instead, Zander wandered from the cave with too much confidence. Too much bravado.

Abraxas sank down onto his knees in front of the eggs. "I'm sorry," he whispered. "I'm so sorry, my children."

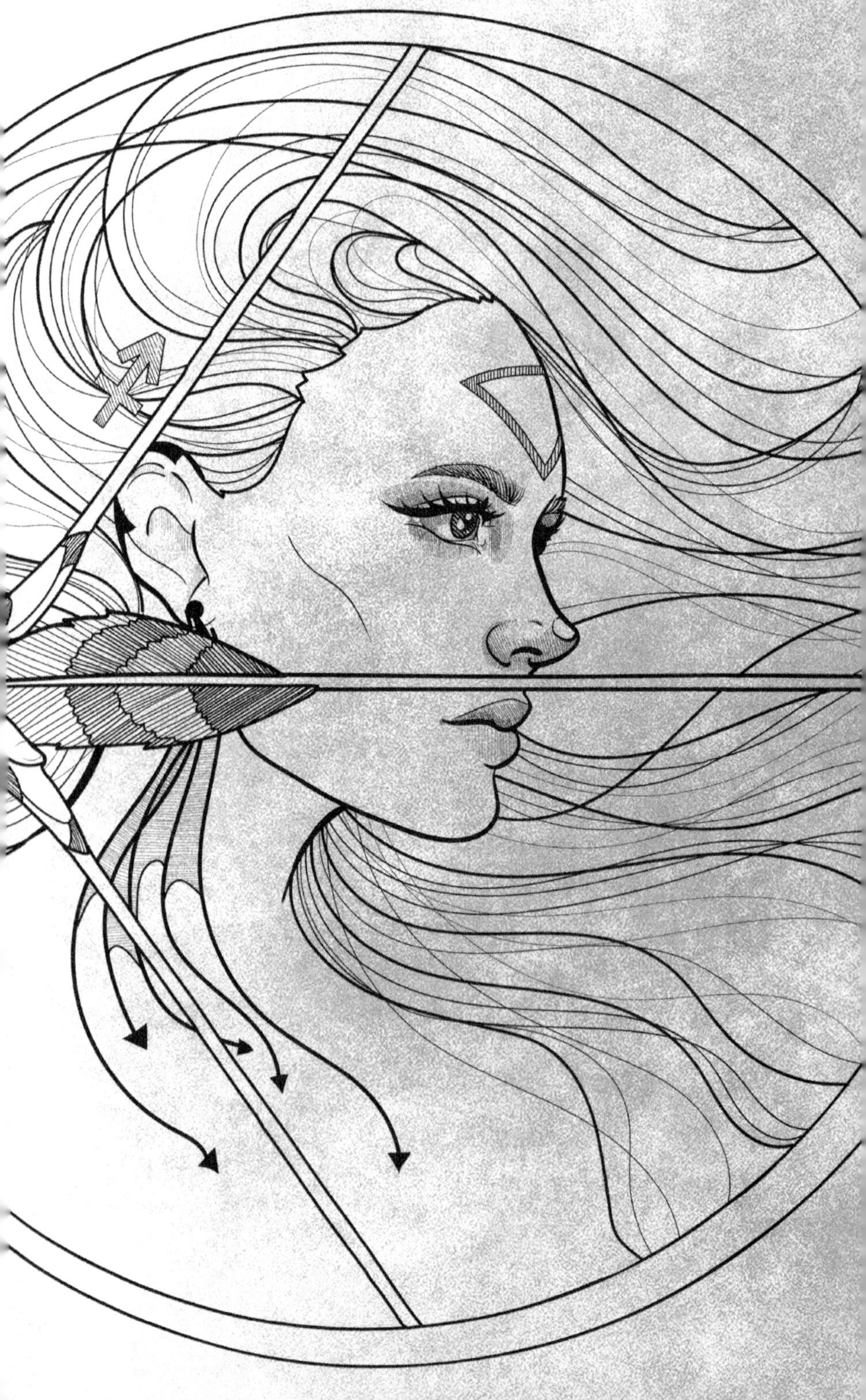

Chapter 24

"The dragon has one thing in his hoard that I want you to bring back more than anything else," the King called out to his brides. "It is the only thing that my heart desires, but I want to see what you choose to return with. There are a great many treasures in his trove. But I must warn you, he will not make this easy on any of you. The dragon will do everything he can to stop you from taking a single thing from the cave."

The whispers started already. Some women clustered together in groups. Each one of them already had trusted individuals who would help each other. There were only fifteen of them left now. They were bound to form friendships.

Lore straightened her shoulders and clasped her hands behind her back. If the King wanted her to steal from the dragon, then she would. It would give her a chance to converse with the foolish man, anyway.

She shouldn't even consider this. The dragon would turn into a man and focus on her while all these other women stole from him. And she remembered the stories about dragons who lost bits of their hoard.

Beauty leaned over to her and whispered out of the side of her mouth, "Don't dragons kill people for stealing from them?"

"One has to assume that this is a different circumstance," Lore responded, although she wasn't very confident in her words. "I assume he has warned the dragon we are coming to his cave and trying to steal from him."

"And if he hasn't warned the creature?"

Lore didn't know what to say. The dragon could kill them all if he wanted to. It would be so easy for him to breathe fire upon the entire lot of brides that entered his cavern, and then this whole thing ended in flame.

The King would shrug. He didn't care if they all died in this insane attempt to entertain himself. He'd find more young women from other towns until someone captured his attention for more than a few heartbeats.

How Lore herself remained here was a miracle. She hadn't returned until the middle of the night and Agatha had sent a message to the King explaining the situation. Obviously Lore had dallied with a young man or someone other than the King.

Lore didn't know what the King's response was, but it had made Agatha's face pinch even more. She hadn't thought that was possible.

"You have a few hours to prepare, my flowers!" the King shouted.

Why was he shouting, anyway? They were all in the same room. A small sitting room, really, with no reason for him to yell. They could hear him just fine, but instead, he was a grand showman, gesturing wildly with his arms and crying out for everyone to hear him.

She didn't like this man. He went out of his way to be a git.

But she had a little time, and that meant she got to wear her own clothing. Clothing that would let her sink into the shadows and find herself a path that the others wouldn't see. The tension in her shoulders eased with the thought of donning her own armor, her own clothing that she'd worn for ages. It would be a bit like coming back to herself after a long adventure.

Beauty clutched Lorelei's arm as she tried to move away. "I have no idea how to steal from a dragon," the young woman muttered. "I don't even know how to climb a cliff."

Damn it.

Lore couldn't leave this little thing on her own or the dragon would eat her. And as much as Lore didn't care who fell in this journey... She didn't want Beauty to die.

"Come on," she said with a long sigh. Lore tucked Beauty underneath her arm and guided her toward the pink painted room. "We're going to prepare together, then. Stay close to me, and I'll make sure you find a treasure to bring back to the King."

"Thank goodness. I think I might die if you don't help me with this one."

Like all the other challenges, but Lore didn't mind. She did like Beauty. A lot.

"All right. First thing you need to know about stealing from any magical creature is that you don't want to be seen," she started as soon as the door closed behind them. "What do you have?"

Beauty blinked at her. "What do you mean?"

"What clothing do you have that will give you some way to hide from the dragon if he looks at you?"

"Um..." Beauty bit her lip, looked at the wardrobe, and then back to Lore. "I might need to get back to you on that. You go get ready, and then meet me back here?"

She supposed they both needed to hurry, and it made sense for Lore to get ready at the same time as Beauty. "All right, but be ready by the time I get back! Remember, the whole idea is to hide."

As if that was going to be easy. The dragon saw everything. That was part of what made dragons so difficult to fight. Their eyes were like that of an eagle or a hawk. Hiding from a creature like that was next to impossible.

Thankfully, Lore had prepared for this. Or at least for having to hide.

She knew the exact outfit she wanted to wear, and she knew Goliath would pack it because it was his favorite of her looks. The dark leather leggings slid over her limbs like a second skin. Countless buckles and straps roped down her legs, ready for knives, darts, and arrows to slide into their holders. The leather corset allowed her to move swiftly, and the long dark sleeves underneath kept her arms mobile.

Lore twisted her hair up on top of her head, the blonde strands slick to her skull. The best part about this outfit was that it had come from her mother. The elves of Silverfell knew how to disappear into the shadows when they needed to. And they knew when to glimmer like moonlight to entice their enemies closer. But this elven garb would keep her safe. She was certain of that.

Thankfully, very few people remembered what a real elf looked like.

Lore looked at herself in the mirror and sighed. Her ears were too visible. She couldn't keep her hair up like this. So she spent too long trying to figure out the best way to keep her hair out of her face, but also hold down the pointed tips of her ears.

Finally, she settled on a much lower twist at the base of her neck. Though it would get in the way if she had to look up for a long period. It was the best she could do.

With one last glance in the mirror to make sure everything was in place, Lore firmly nodded. This would do. She could steal from the dragon and she could find her way through whatever hoard he had mustered in this place.

If he looked at her, or if he decided they needed another conversation about herself and her mother, Lore would deal with it. She wasn't some fainting young woman who couldn't face the tragedy of her own past. Even if that meant looking her mother's killer in the eye and not attempting to do the same to him.

"You have a job to do," she told her reflection. "You are going to kill the King, and with him, you will release the dragon into the rebellion's control. The kingdom will be better for it."

The guilt trip didn't help. Some part of her mind still wanted to run from all this and disappear. Too bad that was definitely off the table.

Time to plunder a dragon's hoard. She never thought she'd do this.

Lore ducked her head out of the room, watching for a moment when the Umbral Knights looked a different way so she could dart across the hall and down to the pale pink room. She didn't knock or hesitate. She opened Beauty's door and stepped in, closing it behind her so there wasn't even the click of a latch.

"There," she sighed. "Are you ready, Beauty?"

Lore did not expect to turn around and find a blindingly horrible coin standing behind her. Or not a coin, although the dress made Beauty even more round than she already was.

The metallic fabric was ridiculously painful to look at. A single beam of sunlight could blind someone if they weren't careful. The full skirt had a built in hoop that billowed out from the bodice, right underneath her breasts. It made the entire dress... well. Round. Beauty looked miserable standing in the middle of the room with her arms held out at her sides.

"What in the world are you wearing?" Lore asked, trying not to laugh.

"You said something I could easily hide in! The dragon must have a ton of gold coins, so I thought if I was in the middle of it and hunkered down, like this, then he wouldn't see me." Beauty sank into the skirt.

Literally.

She bent down and the skirt just swallowed her up. It rose to her shoulders, past her neck, until just her head could be seen over the top of that horrible, horrible fabric.

Lore couldn't help herself. She burst into laughter so loudly that it hurt her stomach. She pressed a hand to her sides and sank onto her own knees. "What... What... Where did you get a dress like that?" she gasped.

"My father," Beauty replied. The poor thing was miserable and looked a bit like she might be sick. "He said it would even out my complexion, but it just made me look more fat!"

Oh, that was horrible. It didn't... actually, yes. It made her look as round as a ball.

Lore struggled to stand and then staggered over to the young woman. "Let me help you get up. This dress is horrible, and I hope you get to use it as camouflage so you never have to wear it again. Maybe the dragon will burn it for you."

"It would be ever so kind if he would." Beauty let Lore haul her up to her feet. "You're quite strong for a woman, you know?"

"I'm really not that much stronger than the average person, Beauty." She'd leave it at that, but she knew what the young woman was implying.

Someone, at some point in her life, had told her she was too heavy to be lifted. Beauty implied that an elf must be stronger than the average mortal if Lore could help her friend stand.

She wasn't any stronger. And anyone who claimed that Beauty was difficult to lift clearly needed to get their head on straight. Or perhaps they needed to get away from their desks and pick up items heavier than a pen.

Thundering footsteps echoed down the hall, heralding the arrival of the Umbral Knights who prepared to bring the brides to their next trial.

She nodded at Beauty. "You're ready for this, you know. I promise you that. Just stay close to me, find whatever you think the King might like, and then get out of the lair. Is that understood?"

"Whatever the King wants will be buried deep inside the dragon's hoard," Beauty replied. Her expression turned fierce and prepared. "I'm ready to do whatever it takes to find what he said he wanted above all else. I understand it will be dangerous."

Lore groaned. "I don't know what it is about that man that makes you so determined! He has nothing in the dragon's hoard he wants, Beauty. This is all a game to see what we'll find. He'll make up some lie about how one of us found what he wanted, but there were no hints, no clues. He doesn't care what we get, only that we played his stupid little game."

The door slammed open and the Umbral Knight on the other side reached out his metal clad hand. If he noticed that there were two brides in the room, then he didn't seem surprised. If there was a way to tell if an Umbral Knight was surprised.

"Time to go," Lore said. She reached out her hand for Beauty's. "Remember what I said. I can only look after you for so long."

"Why does it sound like you're going to leave me to retreat on my own?" Beauty asked, her eyes narrowing. "You're planning something, too."

"I'm not." Lore marched after the Umbral Knight and dragged the young woman with her. But, as they joined the others, she bent down and whispered in Beauty's ear, "I'm more curious about the dragon himself. I'll let you know what I find."

"You shouldn't meddle with creatures more powerful than yourself," Beauty scolded.

"Perhaps not. But I need to speak with the beast, and I think it will be utterly important that I hear what he has to say." Sure, that sounded likely. At least now it appeared Lore intended to meet the dragon, not that she already knew the beast.

She had to talk with Abraxas at some point, and she needed him on her side. Margaret was right about one thing. Losing the dragon's regard could easily mean he returned his allegiance to the King and told the man what she was.

Lore couldn't afford that happening. She had to do whatever it took to get inside the dragon's lair, and bring Abraxas back underneath her spell.

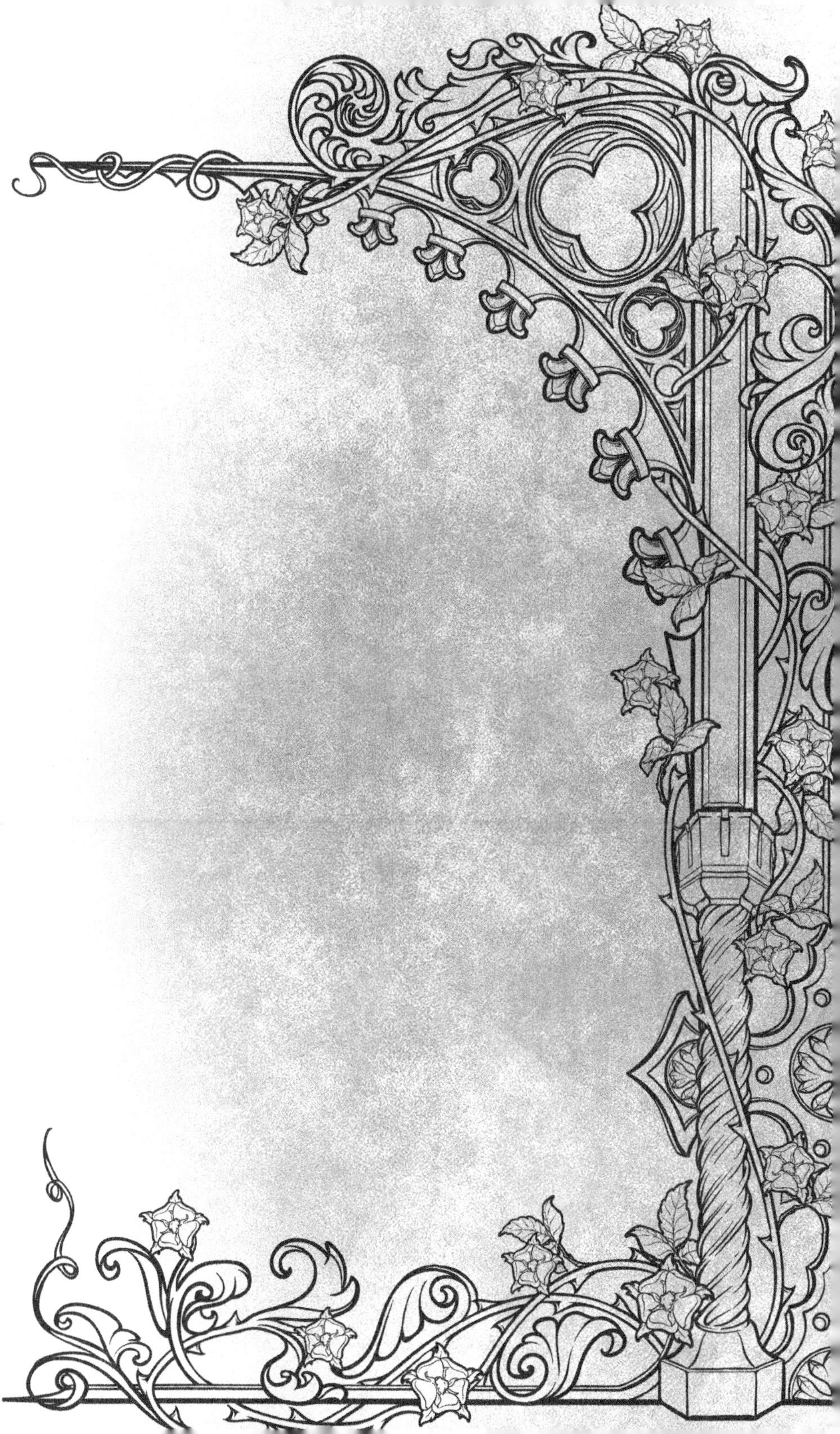

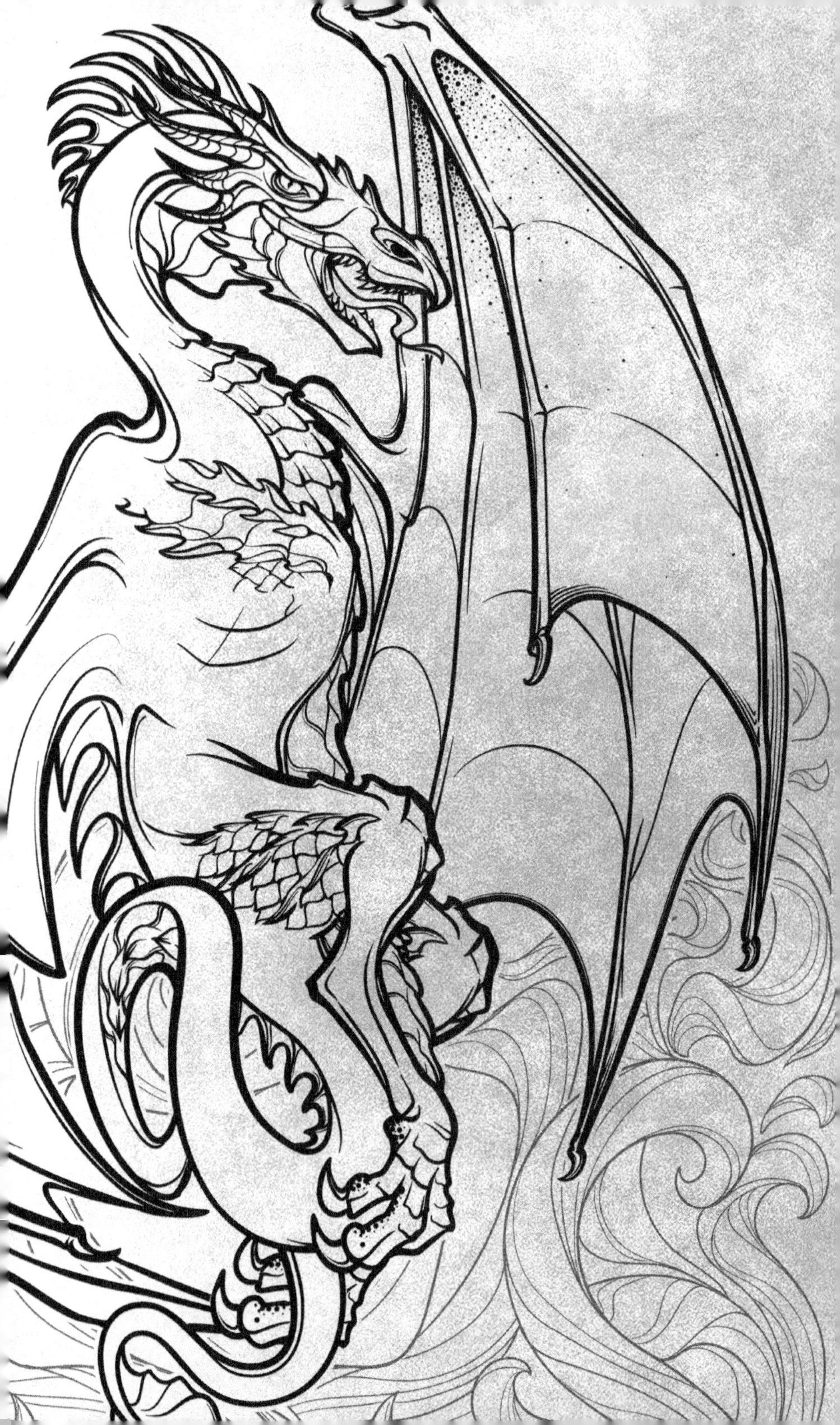

Chapter 25

Abraxas went along with the King's plan only because he had to. He stood in front of those eggs for countless hours, even though the King had only given him one. But they were so close that he could still sense their dragon souls wiggling underneath the crystals.

Innocents. They slept and lay dormant until the world was ready for them, and that was how it worked with dragons. The eggs wouldn't hatch until an elder dragon told them they were ready.

The sapphire egg was female. He could feel her heart deep inside the egg. That beautiful mind already radiated with kindness and a ferocity that would destroy this city once she hatched. The emerald egg was male. He had a sense of honor to him that rivaled Abraxas, and a beautiful determination to grow and learn. They would be a fearsome pair once they hatched, although he still didn't know if they could save dragon kind.

Their children would be the last, potentially. But at least the world had a chance to see dragons one last time. And three generations was a long time to find others. He'd have time to find more eggs that could hatch and prepare them for a second coming.

A bell tolled, and he knew that was the last chance for him to turn back into a dragon. Abraxas sighed. He could have spent a century staring at the little ones as they gently twitched inside their eggs. He could see them through the wood, their glow so bright it burned his eyes. But he had to perform his duties or they would never hatch at all.

With a blast of magic that rocked through the cave, he stretched his wings wide and let out a roar so loud one coin mountain tumbled and fell.

Let the brides come. They thought they could easily steal from him, and the King wanted a story for later tonight. Abraxas would give him hours of screams.

They started in the lower part of the cave, just as the King claimed they would. The first ones were brave, but that bravado would get them nowhere. He heard them a mile away and coiled himself around a larger pile. The first girl, a young woman with dark hair who still had her baby cheeks, picked up a single coin. Her movements were hesitant, as they should be.

She should fear what the dragon would do. Because he didn't plan on being kind.

His tail slithered through the coils behind the young girl and then slammed down on the mountain behind her. She screamed and tried to run from the tumbling coins, but they caught up with her. She was swept out of the cave and into the waters below before she had a chance to even look at what caused the avalanche.

Another potential bride lifted a helmet in her hand. He'd gotten that a long time ago from a warrior who thought he could rob Abraxas. Obviously, the man had ended up here. The last time he'd looked at it, the helmet still had the man's skull in it.

He remembered that at the same time the young woman discovered there was indeed a mortal skull inside the metal. She looked into the holes where the eyes once were, screamed, and dropped the helmet. He supposed that one would run soon enough.

Abraxas shifted his long neck and drew his head out of the shadows, looming above her. All it took was a single drop of saliva to fall onto the coins in front of her. She didn't even look up. The young woman let out another scream and ran from the cavern.

And so it went. Many of the young ladies were afraid to see his shadow. They ran away from his lair without even trying to find something to steal. A few of them were a little more brave. Particularly the young brunette who had captured the King's attention early on. She had won him in the forest, after all, but he still didn't think she held a candle to Lorelei's beauty.

She was sneakier than the others, though. It took him a while to track her down, as she'd used the commotion from another young woman to slip past him. It was hard to find all the rats when he had to take another one out of a trap.

The brunette had beaten him, fair and square. He found himself curious what she would find in his hoard and think the King wanted. It wasn't like the eggs were all that hidden. They were at the highest point of the coins, so high up that only a crazed person would dare the climb.

The brunette already knew what she wanted. He found her digging through the coins and jewelry, tossing bits and pieces aside until she lifted a crown that was so encrusted with gemstones that it looked ridiculous. But that was her plan all along, it seemed. She let out a hissed, "Yes," before plopping onto her bottom and sliding down the mountain of coins.

He supposed that was good enough for her. A crown. The King had a hundred crowns that he could trade whenever he wanted. Why would he desire another one? Especially from the hoard of a dragon from whom he could take anything he wanted whenever he wanted. But if that was what the young woman thought...

Dumb. Abraxas reminded himself. So many of them were ridiculously young and foolish, and they saw nothing wrong with living so shallowly.

He turned his attention to one of the last young women who were still in the cavern. Little Beauty, with her heart of gold and laughter that lit up a room. He'd noticed her the moment she walked into the cave, sparkling like a coin to add to his collection. The dress was hideous, but it was quite amusing to watch her shuffle a few steps and then slouch down until the entire gown enveloped her body. If this had really been his hoard, he might have let her live simply because she was such a delight to watch.

Abraxas slithered down his mountain of coins and used his wing to block her passage. Same as before, she crouched down like a bullfrog and froze.

"I can see you," he said. His deep voice rumbled through the cavern. "Beauty, the dress isn't hiding you at all."

She sighed and came out of her frog-like pose. "I really thought it would work. I blend in with the coins!"

"You do indeed. And you shine like one, too." He rested his head on the pile of gold beside her and blinked. "You aren't afraid of me?"

Beauty smoothed her hands down the brightly colored skirts and shook her head. "Not really. I've met many people in my time here, and I can't imagine that you're as terrifying as everyone says. The King sent us here to gather up something from your hoard, and I thought... Well, if anyone knows what the King might like, then it's you."

Did he? Not really. Zander was just as confusing to Abraxas as he was to everyone else. But he wanted to help this little girl who refused to show fear, even in the presence of the dragon.

"Hmm," he hummed out the sound long and low. "The King is not a very complicated man. He likes wealth and shows of his own power."

"But he must like something other than that. Everyone has something they enjoy that's outside of the norm. The King is exactly who I expected him to be, but if you've known him since he was a child, what did he like back then?" She blinked up at him with those gigantic eyes and he realized of all the brides, this was the one all the girls should have been worried about.

She was a thinker. Beauty could wiggle her way underneath Zander's skin without him even realizing it.

"When he was a boy, he used to like puzzle toys," he replied with a narrowed gaze. "There may be some around here. They would be a little dented from use."

"But I could get it for him and ask if he would mind fixing it. In my experience, people who like those kinds of toys are also the kind who like to know how they work." Beauty straightened her shoulders and nodded. "May I have permission to find such a thing?"

"Permission?" He was so surprised that he reared his head back, forgetting such a movement might startle her. "The King sent you here to steal from me, little mortal."

"I know that. But stealing is exceedingly rude and I feel the right thing to do is to ask." She tucked her hand into the voluminous skirts and shrugged. "So if you don't mind, might I take a broken toy from your hoard?"

Abraxas blinked, but then slowly nodded. "You may, Beauty of Tenebrous. You are more than welcome to whatever you find in my hoard. You may even take something for yourself if you are so inclined."

"I have no need for wealth or pretty things." She smiled. "But thank you."

Curiouser and curiouser. She didn't want wealth, and she didn't want power or jewelry or money.

Abraxas narrowed his eyes on the young woman, who suddenly seemed rather suspicious. "Then why are you here, Beauty? You're not afraid of a dragon, you're not interested in coins or jewels. There has to be a reason why you are here and suddenly, I don't think it's for the King."

She met his gaze without flinching. "I think you should probably be more concerned about the woman scaling the mountain of coins behind you, instead of keeping your attention on the daughter of a dressmaker with the wrong name."

Who should he be focused on?

Abraxas turned his enormous head around, only to find that while he was so focused on Beauty, Lorelei had made her way halfway up the largest pile of coins. She was going right for the eggs, the damned woman. Her eyes saw everything, and he knew without a doubt that she would try to steal one of them.

His heart stopped. His stomach dropped out of his body and all the air in his lungs ceased to be. She could die. She could die doing that and then all the light would go out.

How dare she take that risk?

"Excuse me," he snarled.

"Good luck!" Beauty called out while she dropped onto her hands and knees, swallowed up by the fabric as she searched for her own treasure.

He beat his wings, propelling his reptilian body through the cavern so he could get to Lorelei faster. Sure, he knocked over a few of the coin mountains in the meantime, but he would gather them all up again later. His ridiculous elf had decided to take her own life in her hands. He couldn't knock down that mountain now without killing her underneath a landslide of gold, so the best he could do was hover behind her like some kind of overgrown chicken.

"What are you doing?" he snarled. His voice was much larger in this form, and he'd expected it to startle her. Instead, she sank her feet into the coins even deeper and continued pulling herself up inch by hard fought inch.

"I'm getting to the box," she grumbled. "Isn't that the whole point of this?"

"You and I both know the King has no intention of giving anyone a prize. This was a test to see what people would bring." He arched his neck, trying to see if he could lean forward and grab the back of her with his teeth. But if he did that, he feared he would bite right through her entire body, and then she would be dead and he'd be the reason why she was dead.

He couldn't grab her like he wanted to. And these damned wings didn't make for very good hands.

"I know that," she snapped in response. Lorelei released her grip with one hand and leaned back to look at him. "But he left the box up there for a reason, didn't he? You're over here thinking you can guard anything, but then you went all puppy dog with Beauty and gave me the chance that I needed."

"Were you two working together?" He was in danger if they were.

"No, of course not. She's just adorable and you're a sucker." She blew out a breath at the hair that fell in front of her face. "Now, would you stop distracting me? I have to get up here so I can jump onto that ledge."

"You will do no such thing. You'll fall to your death and I will not watch that happen."

He could already see it now. She would tumble, the scream cut short by a dull thud as she landed on metal and shards of earth.

Lorelei rolled her eyes and continued her climb. "Right. So you're fine watching my mother die, but me? That's an entirely different story. Couldn't stand to watch another elf die."

There it was. He should have known this would come up, even if he hadn't been so certain she'd return after fleeing into the forest.

Abraxas knew he needed to handle this situation with care and purpose. He could not afford for her to think he was the monster, because she meant something to him. He found himself captivated by her wit and her determination. How she gave up so much to save others. This was a woman he wanted to know more about. He wanted to delve into her mind and... well. He liked her.

Abraxas hadn't liked anyone for a very long time.

Clearing his throat, he tried his best. "Your mother was an entirely unique situation. There are circumstances unknown to you that have led me to this point. I understand your anger at me, and that anger is justified. But my hope is that—"

He didn't get to finish his speech.

Lorelei reached the top of the mountain and moved her body with effortless grace. She gathered all her power into her thighs, launched off the gold, and reached for the stone. He swung his wing underneath her in a final attempt at saving her, even though he knew she'd bounce off the membrane.

Her fingers connected with the jagged stone edge. She grunted, swinging too much, but then got her momentum under control.

He held his breath the entire time, certain that she was about to die. But Lorelei was far too impressive for that. Dying was never an option for her, not when she wanted to get to the top of this mountain and find out what was inside the box.

Damn, she was impressive.

Lorelei scrambled to the top of the cliff and then sat down on the edge. Legs dangling over open air, she leaned her elbows onto her knees and looked him over. "I prefer you as the man."

"Many do."

She nodded. "Just so that we're clear. I don't like you as the dragon."

"Understood."

"Good. Now I need you to listen to me. I'm sorry for how I acted when I found out what you were. That was cruel and callous of me. I know better." She cleared her throat, obviously struggling to find the right words. "I need you to know that I don't want to hurt you. Or anyone else. And that I'd appreciate it if you continued to be my friend."

"Your... friend?" he repeated, his breath caught in his throat. Why did those words hurt? He didn't... he didn't want to be her friend.

"I thought we were friends." Her eyes widened a little too much. "Are we not?"

Abraxas thought his heart might break. But if that was what she wanted, a friend, then he'd take it. "Ah, yes. Yes, Lorelei. We're friends."

She smiled, but it didn't reach her eyes. "Even though I was... wrong?"

"You weren't wrong," he replied, lowering his voice so it was soft. "I killed your mother, Lorelei. You should hate me."

She stared into his dragon eyes and shook her head. "I don't hate you."

And if that wasn't all he'd needed to hear. Abraxas felt his chest swell, hoping she might still see something other than this scaly beast. "Good. I would be quite upset if you hated me, and that's a new feeling for me."

"Any reason it would bother you so much?"

She was fishing. And he supposed in a strange way, he was as well. Abraxas didn't know what she thought of him now, but he still remembered their afternoon and the taste of her on his tongue. He wouldn't get that thought out of his mind for a while yet.

Ah well, if she wanted him to say it, then he would. "I like you, Lorelei of Silverfell. You have a better hold on being a good person, I think, and I'd like to know how you do that."

"Be a good person?"

"Yes."

"I don't." She stood up, feet dangerously close to the edge, and shrugged. "It's all a matter of perspective, Abraxas. You think I'm a good person, but I'm just surviving."

"You do it well," he replied.

Except then she went ahead and did everything she shouldn't. Lorelei turned, sprinted toward the box, and grabbed it with both hands.

His roar of outrage and fear shook stalactites free from the ceiling.

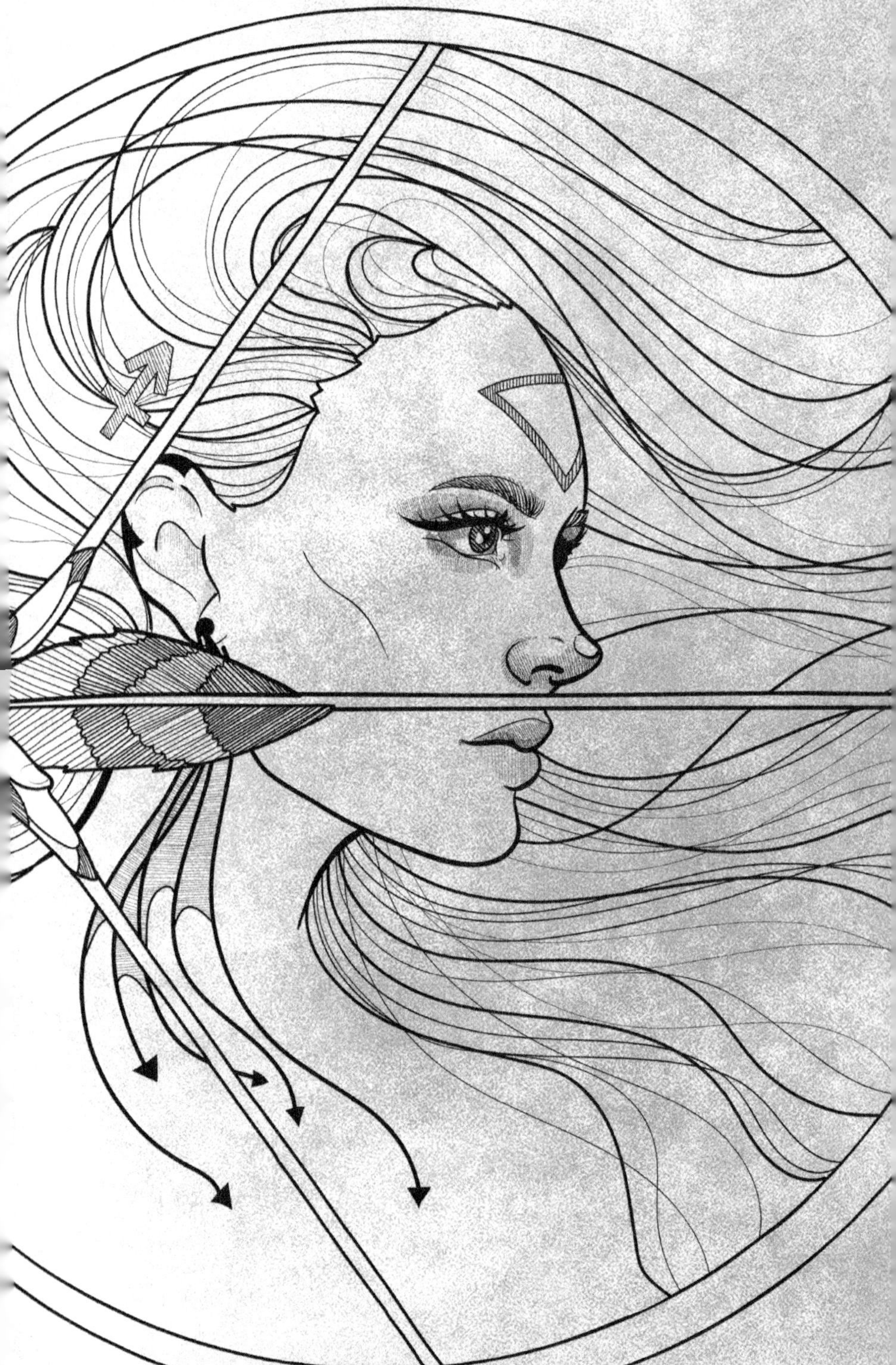

CHAPTER 26

Lore had taken one look at the box and knew the King was hiding something. Not because it was right at the top of the mountain. She'd already noticed the stairs hidden in the stone. Sneaky, but the King obviously came down into the cavern whenever he wanted.

And it wasn't the box itself. The faint scratches on the side of the wood meant there were many years of people opening and closing that box. Lore always appreciated history attached to an object like that.

No, she knew the box was important from the magic radiating off it. Someone had put a very powerful spell on it to make sure its secrets were kept quiet and impossible to discover. She intended to find out what the King was hiding, and why he had sent so many of his potential brides into this place. He risked their lives stealing from a dragon. For what?

Abraxas would try to stop her. He was supposed to do that, she assumed, but also the magic surrounding the box was insanely strong. She hadn't felt a spell like that in ages, so it was probably from the time of the King's father. Not the current king. Few magicians remained who were so mighty, and even then, it was unlikely they could conjure up a spell like that.

She sprinted toward the box, arms pumping through the air, and then leapt for it. If Abraxas thought he could knock her back with a wing, then he'd have to hit the box too. And she didn't think he'd want to do that.

Her hands slapped either side of the box and the dragon's roar pierced through her skull. His anger sparked through the air like lightning, but she couldn't stop now. She'd already done the thing he didn't want her to do.

Curiosity had her thumbs moving and gently lifting the lid.

Magic punched her in the chest like she'd been struck with five arrows at the same time. They hit her so hard that she flew backward. Her shoulders and spine hit the ground before her legs. Dust puffed up around her and she tried to inhale, but couldn't at all.

The magic clung to her, scrabbling at her skin. It grabbed onto her shoulder and sliced down her ribs to her hip as though it wielded a blade. She let out a soft wheeze with the last air in her lungs, but her mind wasn't on the pain.

That box had contained two eggs.

Two perfectly preserved dragon eggs that glowed even in the dim cave light. A sapphire egg with diamond shaped scales covering it. And an emerald egg with rounded scales that looked so real she wondered if it was actually stone.

She arched her back as the magic sawed deeper into her skin. Lore dug her heels into the ground and regretted every moment where she thought she could touch that box. She knew what magicians did with their magic. She knew how dangerous they were.

But she couldn't regret seeing the eggs. They were the last lingering hope that someday, the magical creatures would return to the life they had lost. There were still dragons out there. Still the possibility that someday she would see more than the one who had tormented them for years.

She stared up at the ceiling as another sawing motion of magic tore through her body. Her physical form jerked again, but her mind was elsewhere. At least this made the pain easier to manage. The magic waned, and Lore thought perhaps she might survive this. Perhaps she wouldn't die.

Stones skittered on the other side of her, tiny pieces of the ground coming up as someone slid onto their knees beside her. The person lifted her entire weight rather easily, shifting her into their lap so she could finally see the hard angles of the face peering down at her. His hair covered one side of his sharpened cheekbones, hanging over her like a curtain of night.

"Breathe," Abraxas said. "You need to breathe, Lorelei."

As if his words were a command, she sucked air into her lungs. Finally. Even the damp, warm air of the cave was a blessing as she inhaled again. But with that breath came a rush of sensation. The pain of the wound from her shoulder to hip. The ache where her back had hit the ground, and her skull felt a little rattled as well.

Abraxas sighed and touched a hand to her shoulder. Once his fingers were in her sight again, she could see they were slick with dark red blood. His eyes widened and for a moment, his hand shook.

Was he frightened? A dragon shouldn't care about the sight of blood. He'd seen countless wounds and unnumbered deaths in his lifetime.

But apparently the sight of her in his lap, nearly cleaved in half by magic, was enough to make his hands shake.

"I'm going to do something that you can tell no one about," he muttered. "But it will hurt."

"Will it help me live?" she asked.

"Yes."

"Then go ahead and do it." She was no stranger to pain. If it meant that she would see another day, then he could do whatever he wanted to her.

Abraxas pressed his palm against her shoulder and she felt his skin heat. As if he had fire inside of him, or wielded it in his palm. Her skin singed, then burned together as he stopped the bleeding by searing her flesh.

Lore bit her lip, back arching once again into the pain. But this time, at least, she knew it would not end in her death.

"I'm sorry," he said, wincing as he peeled away her leather clothing so he could see more of her flesh and stop the bleeding. "I didn't know that it would do this to you. I thought... Well, the last time I touched the box, it didn't make me bleed."

"The last time?" She stared at him with hope in her eyes. "Please, distract me."

He nodded. "The box was enchanted a long time ago. I'm sure you know that. But when I tried to touch it, the pain was internal. It took me nearly a week to recover, and I still have scars on my wings from laying on the gold for so long that some of the coins had embedded in the membranes."

Magic strong enough to take down a dragon? It shouldn't exist. She'd only heard of it once before, and even then, the magician had been sent to his death long before this mortal king had lived.

"Why?" she gasped.

But she already knew.

He stilled, his palm cooling for a moment before he resumed his work. "Now you know," he growled. "Now you understand why I have done what I have done for a hundred years."

"The eggs?" She had to know. She had to know if they were real or if she had imagined them. "They're really in there?"

"When his father first found them, there were four." His lips twisted with a sorrow that made her entire soul scream. "Now there are only two."

Two eggs.

Two beings who would become the hope of the entire kingdom if they succeeded in their plan.

She didn't know what fate had placed in her lap, but here was another layer proving that she had to get rid of this king once and for all. What person was so heartless that they would trap two innocent souls like that? Two dragon souls who could have changed the entire fabric of the world if they hatched?

Lore coughed, her lungs still aching from the fall and seizing every time he shifted his hands. "How?"

"His father found them before I did." Abraxas shrugged. The heat of his palm moved down to her ribs, and when she winced, he cupped her torso with his free hand. As though he wanted to comfort her, even though she had thought him incapable of that. "We were both searching for the eggs, all rumors at that point. But he found them and was quicker to enchant the box than I was to find him."

"Why can't you kill him?" That's what she would have done. Remove the person who had harmed her so.

Abraxas snorted. "The King is the only one who can open the box. You've seen what happens when you or I try to open it. If the King dies, the box will remain locked for all eternity."

"Dragon fire?"

"I've tried that. I've tried other magicians, and I've even buried it in molten gold. Nothing changes the magic enchanting that box. No matter what I do, how hard I try, or who I get involved, only the King can get me those eggs." His hands turned to claws against her skin before they returned to the mortal hands that slowly healed her wounds. "He will stop at nothing to control me. Just before the brides arrived, he'd killed one of the other eggs. A dragon who would have become like me. A crimson dragon who could have protected the other two."

She knew nothing about dragons. She hadn't realized their coloring meant anything at all.

His hand reached her hip and though she was still in a significant amount of pain, she knew this was something she could heal from. It would take days, perhaps months, but she would get out of bed tomorrow and pretend that she was all right.

Abraxas let the magic drain from his hand, and then lifted it to her face. His fingers were still warm. Almost too warm for comfort, but she didn't mind when he stroked her cheek, following the lines of her face all the way to her jaw. "You should never have come here," he murmured. "You're so unlike the others. He would eat you alive if he could."

"Too bad it's difficult to do that. Even a dragon couldn't stop me from stealing." She coughed again as her lungs seized another time. "A crimson dragon? That's what you are?"

His lips twisted into an awkward smile. "Yes. There are many colors, each with specific traits that come with them. Crimson dragons are the keepers of the dragon realm. We protect those who matter to us."

"Ah. That's why the King made you his guard dog, then?"

"No." He touched a finger to the tip of her nose. "I don't care for the King. I don't care for his line or for anyone he has bid me to protect. Not until you."

The words rang in her ears, even though there was nothing left in the cavern but silence. He cared for her? How?

She had been nothing but horrible to him. Though she had lied and cheated to get him on her side, she supposed. Even though he'd killed her mother, she was rather fond of him as well.

It was the quiet moments like this that made her realize how kind he was. He didn't want to hurt her. He didn't want to hurt anyone.

The eggs were the last of his people. What would she have done if the last of the elves relied on her? Anything. Even though she wasn't close with any of her kind, nor did she have any interest in speaking with them, the idea of being the last one ate her alive.

As it must have eaten him alive for centuries.

"It was wrong of me to not understand that there must have been something controlling you," she whispered. The words hurt to say. She hated to admit she was wrong. But this was important. "I apologize for that. I shouldn't have judged you so quickly without even attempting to know what the truth of the matter was."

He leaned down, dark eyes searching hers for something she couldn't guess at. "And I cannot tell you how sorry I am that your mother was caught in the middle of all this. If I could have saved her, I would have."

Somehow, she doubted that. But it didn't matter now. Her mother was gone, and the dragon had done it. They could move forward together, or she could murder Abraxas for what he hadn't wanted to do.

Lore wished she was a bit more like the woman she had been before all this. She wanted to turn her nose up at him. To let the anger and rage of losing a parent overwhelm her.

But she couldn't. Not when she knew he'd been protecting something so precious. Not when she knew the King had a chain around his neck and a whip in his hands.

"He killed the other dragons?" she asked. Even saying the words hurt.

"The other two eggs, yes. I watched his father crack one open and feast upon the yolk. But now they are fully formed inside those eggs. They are waiting to be hatched, and watching this king plunge a dagger into the heart of..." His voice wavered. "I have struggled. There are few options for someone like me, and I will admit, I've done terrible things in the hopes that I will not be the last."

She couldn't blame him for that. Not really. Not when the rest of them feared they would end up in the same place as him.

Didn't all the magical creatures fear they would also be the last of their kind? That he was the prime example of what happened to magical creatures when they fell under the eye of the King?

Lore looped an arm around his neck and drew him down against her. She hugged him tight, trying to squeeze him so tightly his sadness and grief disappeared. "I'm sorry for what they did to you," she whispered against his pulse. "I'm so sorry."

"You were my first hope that someone might stop him," he replied. "Please tell me you haven't given up yet."

"I haven't." And now, she couldn't.

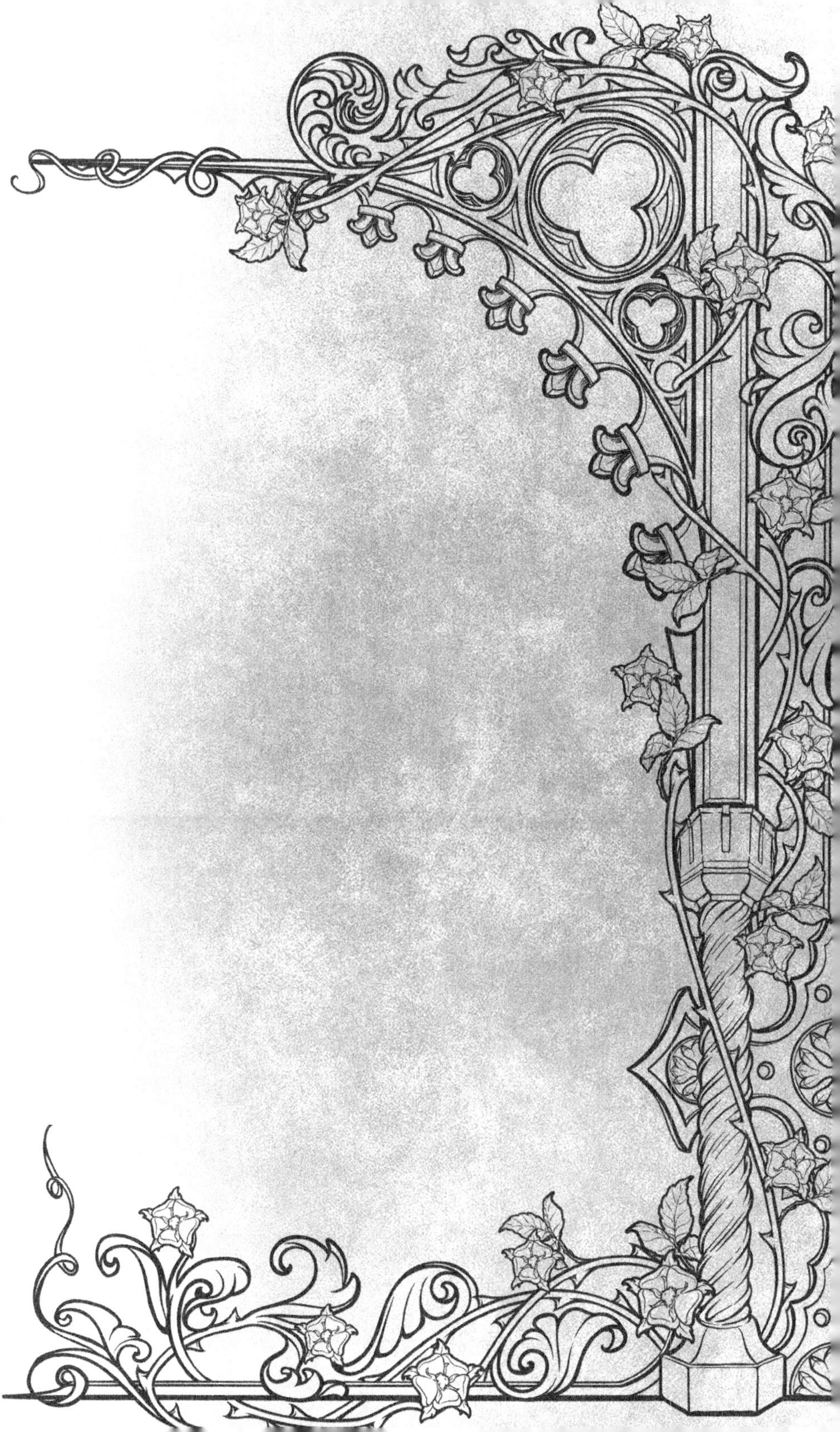

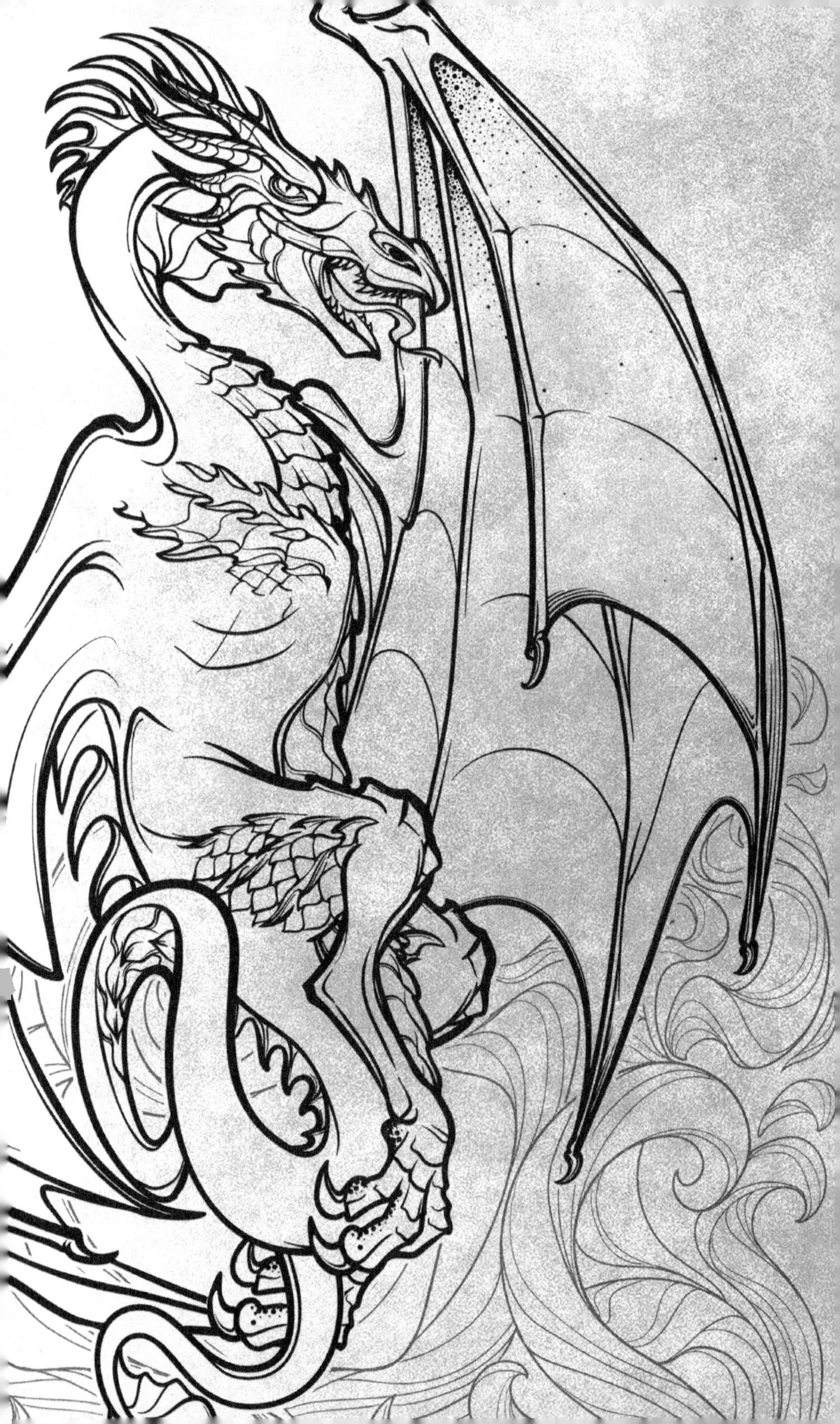

Chapter 27

"So I am sad to admit, there will only be three of you left when all is said and done." The King's voice echoed throughout the Great Hall where the fifteen brides had gathered with their stolen items from the dragon's hoard.

Abraxas stood behind Zander and searched the crowd of young women for the only person who mattered. Lorelei had left his cave in horrible condition. She said elves healed quickly, but... Well, she wasn't an elf, was she? The mortal part of her might not heal as well, and if that was the case, then she would be in considerable pain.

She stood in the back, her gown hiding most of her wounds. The blood red dress spilled over her shoulder like liquid, hugging every part of her body but covering her from her shoulders all the way to her toes.

The other shoulder remained bare, but it was the uninjured one, so no one would know what happened.

Although, now that he looked at her, that lovely pale skin was tempting. He wanted to press his lips to her pulse there, just to see what she would do. If she would taste like cold dewdrops on spring leaves.

She'd hugged him. He had told her the most embarrassing detail of his life, and the reason why a mortal man had enslaved him, and she'd hugged him. No one had ever cared about him that much in his entire life, dragons included, and he didn't know what to do with that.

He was ancient, even compared to her. He'd lived countless mortal lifetimes and yet... no one had made him feel like she did. With her, he wasn't a dragon or a legend or even the mythical figure of a story. He was just Abraxas, the man who had killed her mother but was desperately trying to make amends for that horrific deed.

The women in the group before them groaned. Each one of them started talking and asking questions of the King. A few even begged, likely the exact reaction that Zander was looking for. They wanted to stay with him. How could he let them go when they were so close to him now? Surely he wouldn't send them away to their families when they loved it here. They loved him. Didn't he feel the same?

Zander lifted a hand and chuckled as they all fell silent. "My darling flowers. The weeks you have been here are the best weeks of my life. I will remember them and you always. But only one woman can become my wife."

A few young women threw dirty looks at the others. Those were the girls everyone needed to watch out for, and he refused to take his eyes off them. They were the ones that would hurt the others if they were allowed to. And he refused to let Lorelei get hurt any more while he was on watch.

Zander clapped his hands together. "Well! I understand you're all disappointed, so let's get on with this. What did you bring me, my flowers?"

The aggressive brunette stepped forward first. She even shouldered a few of the other women out of the way so she could get to the front of the line. With a cocked hip and a smile that was far too confident, she handed Zander the gem encrusted crown.

The King nodded, turning it over in his hands and grinning. "Why did you bring me a crown, my flower?"

"Because of all the kings in this realm, you deserve not just the most beautiful crown. You deserve a crown that was once held by a dragon. A crown with history and power so that all will know you are the most powerful king we have ever had. And will ever have." She sank onto her knees in front of him, her bodice shoving her breasts up so high they almost touched her chin. "It would be my honor to remain. Not only to see you and be in your presence for a little while longer, but to worship you as only the most powerful of all kings should be worshipped."

The words were pretty, and Abraxas didn't think Zander would fall for them. But he was wrong.

Zander preened under her words and care. He obviously had gotten a little too interested in the brunette because he didn't hesitate for a second.

The King leaned forward, put his finger underneath her chin, and turned her face up to his. "You knew I was going to pick you long before you found this crown."

"I couldn't have known, but I had hopes that you would see my worth." She was bold, this one. The woman took his hand, turned it over, and pressed a kiss to Zander's fingers. Lingering a little too long. Was that her tongue flicking out?

Obviously, this young one was here to play as confidently as she could. The only problem was that Abraxas wasn't even certain who she was. Yes, she was beautiful, and she'd made her case well known. But who was she?

As the woman walked away, he leaned down and whispered, "What is that one's name?"

"I have no idea." Zander grinned, eyes on the young woman's bottom. "But I intend to find out. Remember to ask Agatha for me, will you? When I have my private time with her, I want to make sure she's... well, biddable."

And if that wasn't the most disgusting thing he'd heard all day.

Abraxas nodded and then leaned away from the King. As far away as possible.

The other women approached, but most of them hadn't gotten anywhere near the real treasures. Many had coins. A few had single gemstones or crystals that they thought were beautiful. Most of them made up a story about how they were brave, but the dragon knew how strong they were and he targeted them first.

It took every fiber of his strength not to roll his eyes when they told stories like that. As if he would ever worry about the actions of a mortal woman.

Lorelei walked up to the King and all the talking in the room silenced. It was like they all knew she had made it. That she'd gotten to that lofty peak where the King had left something important, and they all wanted to know what it was.

Even Zander leaned forward in anticipation. "Well, if it isn't the most surprising of my flowers. You, my dear, always seem to do everything that I wouldn't expect a woman to do. What did you find in my dragon's hoard?"

Don't look at me, he thought. If you look at me, then he'll know. He'll know everything.

She didn't. He thanked all the gods he could think of in the relief that she didn't look at Abraxas. Instead, she winced as she knelt before the King, and kept her eyes on the floor.

Zander shifted forward. Almost as though he knew she'd seen the eggs. Why else would she move like she'd just returned from battle? Zander was no fool. He wanted to see her pull a dragon egg from behind her and then listen to the shocked gasps.

Lorelei reached into her bodice and pulled out a single gold coin. It shimmered in the light, cleaner than the rest, but still just a coin.

The King slumped back on his throne and waved a disappointed hand. "A coin? Really? All the others brought me the same thing, and you're supposed to be the one who surprises me. You cut an arrow out of the air but you couldn't find a single interesting thing in the dragon's hoard?"

"It's a coin from when your father was king," her voice rang out. "This coin is older than you and I put together, and was the only coin in the hoard that I could find which still held your father's image."

Now that... that was rare.

Zander had Abraxas melt the entire gold pile and all the coins in it when his father finally died. He didn't want anyone to remember the previous king, because he was so certain they would think he was lesser compared to his father. He was, of course. But no one would tell him that when there was nothing left of the previous king to remember.

Even he didn't think a coin like that still existed.

With a shaky hand, Zander reached for her offering and held it between his fingers. He turned it over and stared into the eyes of his father. "I didn't think I would ever see a coin like this again."

"Neither did I." She stood far too slowly for Abraxas's liking. "But I want you to know that it was there. And that if anyone could find something so precious, it would be me. You want a wife who is adventurous and capable? Then you found someone you could find nowhere else. If you want to remember history, then the woman who stands before you is one who does not forget."

Abraxas knew she'd overstepped, but Zander seemed to grow even more intrigued with her as every word fell from her lips.

He nodded frantically with the words until he cleared his throat and replied, "Yes. I believe you will be a good second choice, Lorelei. You have been a thorn in my side since you arrived, I'll admit. But every time you come into the room, I know something interesting is about to happen."

"It is an honor to know you would describe me as such," she murmured, backing away.

One left. Damn it, Abraxas should feel relieved this was almost over with, but he couldn't stop the angry feeling in his gut that the King would dare to choose Lorelei. Yes, he understood that they needed the King to pick her. She had to be physically around him to do whatever it took to force the King to bend a knee.

But he didn't want Zander to touch her. Not ever. Not when Abraxas himself wanted to find out what this feeling was in his chest. He wanted to discover what it would feel like to be around her without a thousand questions and suspicious intentions. He couldn't do that if she was still on the list to marry the King.

Zander was a dead man walking, however. He needed to remember that.

A few other women walked up to the throne, but the bored

expression on Zander's face never changed. Not once, until Beauty stepped up to him.

She didn't sink to her knees like the others. Instead, she stood holding something between her hands, with a blush spreading across her features.

"What do you have for me?" Zander asked, his cheek cushioned on his hand. He was bored.

"I thought to find you something great and magnificent from the dragon's hoard, but I saw this and I thought… Well, I thought if anyone might enjoy it, then it would be you." She opened her hands and revealed a tiny toy bird with broken wings. The mechanical pieces of the toy had once been a marvel. Now, they were crushed by the weight of years. "I saw this toy, and I thought that you were the only person intelligent enough to fix it. And that maybe you might want to let another child play with something so delicate. Something that surely an artist placed time and energy into making. Perhaps your own child."

Abraxas watched Zander with curious eyes. He remembered the boy having a grand time building such things when the previous king had ignored him. The light in his eyes, the one that always revealed he was interested, sparked.

He took the toy bird from Beauty with reverent hands. "I can fix this. I'm certain of it. But how did you know I could?"

Beauty leaned closer to him, almost until their heads touched as they stared down at the broken toy. "Great minds recognize each other, don't you think? A toy this small might make others think it's broken, but I think it's just waiting to be fixed."

The scene was almost touching. Beauty could likely fix the King if he let her. Abraxas knew how a gentle touch could calm a fragmented mind like Zander's. But he'd never know if she softened the villain.

The doors to the Great Hall slammed open, and a servant staggered inside. The man had been getting ready to be one of the few guards who wasn't an Umbral Knight, judging by his clothing. The arrow in this throat, however, was not part of his uniform. He staggered to a halt, touched a hand to the wooden shaft, and then fell onto his knees.

Blood spilled out of the wound and the women closest to the man screamed. Abraxas hated that sound. He stalked toward the man at the same time that Lorelei took off for the door.

He wanted to shout at her that if she tried to run after the assassin, it would only look like she was working with that person. Instead, she slammed her entire weight against the Great Hall's entrance and shut the door with a quick snap that echoed through the room.

Abraxas watched her, noting her wide eyes and horrified expression. She didn't intend for this to happen. She hadn't known that the Great Hall or anyone was being attacked.

Which meant this wasn't from the rebellion. This wasn't... planned?

He knelt down beside the dying man and wrenched the arrow out of his throat. There was the smallest piece of parchment wrapped around the shaft of the arrow.

Peeling it off, he cursed under his breath.

Of course, it was the rebellion. Who else could it be?

Abraxas now faced a dilemma he hadn't expected. Unfortunately, he had to read the letter because the King had seen him unravel it. He couldn't pretend someone else was attacking them. No other group was so foolish that they'd send a warning into a building full of Umbral Knights.

"Well?" Zander called out. "What does the note say, Abraxas?"

He met Lorelei's gaze and hoped she saw the apology in his eyes. "Let the sun rise."

FIRE HEART

As if they were waiting for his words, the rebellion rained hellfire upon the castle. They loosed a hundred arrows that whistled through the air and screamed as they fell through the open ceiling and windows. One bride fell with an arrow in her chest, and the King didn't even move. He sat there on his damned throne, wearing a dumbfounded expression while obviously certain that he couldn't get hurt. No one would try to kill him. Why would they?

Abraxas had no choice. He would rather die himself than see more of these innocents slaughtered because of an idiot king who refused to move.

He loosened the power of the dragon and let his form shift. The dragon's shape was too big for this room, and he took up most of the space. But his wings stretched over everyone. His neck and back could withstand the onslaught of hundreds of arrows that rained down upon them like hail.

"Knights!" the King screamed. "To me!"

Abraxas didn't care if Zander called upon his tin soldiers. All he cared about was saving a single life today. A single life of a single elf who had changed everything.

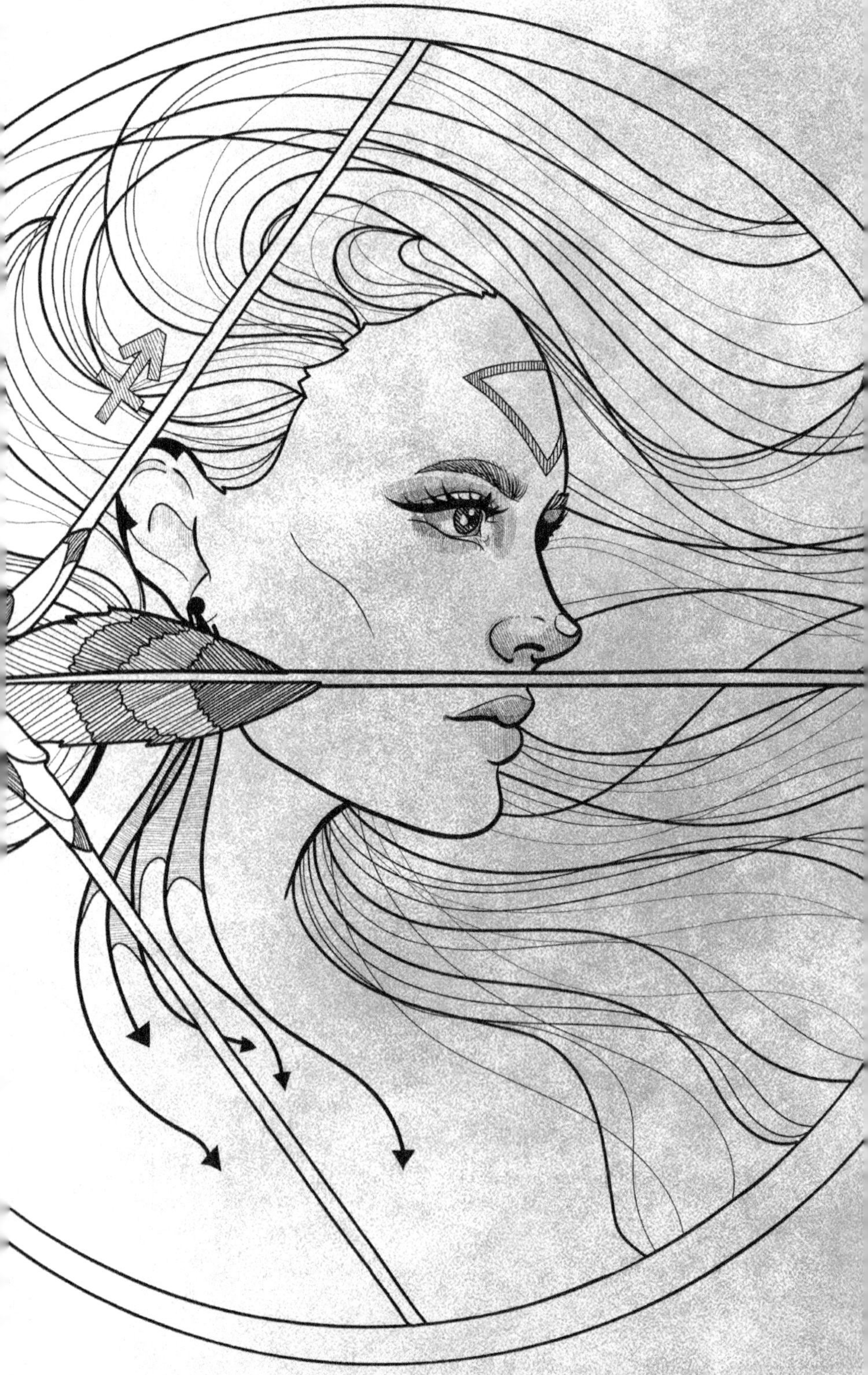

CHAPTER 28

Everything dissolved into chaos. Strangely, Lorelei remembered this. She remembered fighting to control her own fear and desire to run, even though she hadn't been in battle herself for many years. Or had she ever? The souls of her ancestors filled her chest and whispered what to do, how to run, how to hide.

But she couldn't. Not when the dragon spread his wings even wider as more arrows sliced through windows and broke through the glass ceiling above them.

Another bride screamed. Lorelei ran past a young woman who bled from a triangle-shaped shard of glass that had stuck straight through her skull. The woman stumbled to the side, let out a horrible death gurgle, and then fell onto her hands and knees.

This would be a night the entire kingdom would never forget.

Let the sun rise.

Why hadn't they told her they were attacking the King? Why hadn't they let her prepare?

Lore ducked behind a statue as more arrows rained down. Less this time. Perhaps the Umbral Knights had already moved in on the forces of archers who had thought they might have a chance. Regardless, had she taken too long? She knew nothing of Margaret's plans or how quickly the rebellion had planned to move. She could only assume that this was all meant to be part of it.

Perhaps they thought to drive all the brides and the King into a single room. Perhaps they were giving her an opportunity to kill him in close quarters, but... It didn't feel like it. This felt sloppy. Uncompleted. More like a band of people who had branched off without Margaret's permission.

"Beauty," she gasped. Where was her friend?

She leaned around the statue but couldn't find the lovely figure who had made this entire ordeal a little better. Hopefully Beauty had learned the talent of running from dangerous situations, rather than trying to get involved as much as she had before.

Lore's eyes locked on the King. He stood beneath the dragon's wings, screaming at the Umbral Knights to do something. But there was something in his posture that made her fists curl with anger.

He wasn't trying to hide. There wasn't an ounce of fear in his body or the set of his shoulders. The King confidently stood among a rain of arrows as though he knew not a single one would touch him. He didn't care that there were dead women laying all around him, nor did he care all that much that the dragon was wounded.

All he cared about was that this attack had ruined his fun. His moment. His shining achievement where he finally picked the last three of his brides. He'd wanted this to be a spectacle and now, it was that for a reason other than him.

Lore wished she had her hands on a bow. She'd put an arrow through his throat now and hope that finally taught him a lesson.

Ten Umbral Knights marched into the great hall, and the King turned on the dragon. "You're supposed to do something!" he shouted, and then kicked Abraxas in the face. "Instead, you're just lying over everything like a damned blanket!"

She heard the crackle before her mind remembered what it was. In any mortal battle, the ball would have been soaked in oil and tar. A flaming nightmare sent through the air to destroy whatever it could. But these weapons were made of magical creatures. The ball was dipped in poison and set aflame with elven magic. Old magic.

She wanted to scream in rage. The rebellion knew what they were doing with a weapon like that. It wouldn't hurt most of the people in the room because it wouldn't touch them.

It was a weapon targeted at a dragon.

The ball of poison struck Abraxas in the center of his back, right between his wings. For a second, he looked back at it as though he were confused by the pain. He had felt little pain in his life. Dragons were notoriously strong and... and...

Lore pressed her hands to her mouth as he sagged. Abraxas set his head back on the floor, his wings shuddering as he struggled to keep them raised so that he still protected the room and those still alive within it.

"Get up!" the King shouted. "You're a dragon, damn it! You shouldn't be so weak!"

The doors slammed open again and a wall of Umbral Knights rushed in. Some of them lifted shields above their heads and created a barrier for the King to step under. The evil, horrible, nasty man only sent one last glance back to his dragon before sighing in disappointment. Then he walked out of the room. He just left.

The brides were ushered out of the room with the Umbral Knights as well, but not her. Lore was still hidden behind the statue and no one knew she had remained behind. They opened the doors, left the great hall, and all that remained was a dreadful silence.

No more arrows came through the sky. Abraxas let his wings droop. They hung awkwardly off the walls, like a bat that had fallen out of the sky and landed hard on the ground. He let his giant eyes close and the long sigh that rippled through his sides was one of pain. So much pain.

She skittered across the floor, still halfway concerned there would be another rain shower of pointed arrows that searched for her heart. But no more attacks came. She was safe. They had made it.

But not without a few losses.

A long time ago, the idea of standing next to the dragon who killed her mother would have made her stomach roll. She'd have been searching for the right way to kill him. A way to plunge a dagger or a sword into that eye that was almost as large as her.

How strange it was to realize things had changed. She had changed.

Lore fell onto her knees beside his giant head and put her hand on his scaled cheek. "Abraxas? Please tell me you're still alive. Open your eyes, darling. I know how to fix this."

Elf magic could only be undone by other elves, although she'd never tried to do it before. It would probably be difficult, and it might take whatever power she'd gathered from the moon, but... He was worth it.

When had that happened? When had she looked at him and decided he was worth saving, not hating?

Abraxas opened his eye, and she stared into the slitted golden orb. He didn't look convinced she could do anything.

Lore almost argued with him, but then she saw his wing shudder. Inch by agonizing inch, he dragged the leathery membrane across the floor until it shielded her from above. Just in case. Because he was always trying to make sure that someone wasn't killing her, even when he had known little about her.

She smoothed her hand in a wide arc over his cheek again. "You're worth saving, Abraxas. But I can't heal you like this. You're too big. I know it will be worse when you change back. I know the pain will get worse, but let me heal you like you healed me."

His entire body trembled and the magic that shifted him from dragon to man was weak. She'd gotten used to the blast of power that should have shoved her back across the floor. Instead, this was a gentle breeze that blew her hair only slightly before a man lay on the cold stone floor in front of her.

"There you are," she whispered.

He'd looked better. Naked as the day he was born, she should have been feasting her eyes on the wide swaths of muscles laid out before her. But all she saw were the marks on his arms, the bruises covering his chest and back, and the long legs that he curled in on himself as the poison made everything ten times worse in this form.

Lore worked quickly. She couldn't drag him. Abraxas was too large a man for that. But she could ease his head into her lap.

Her fingers trailed through the long dark length of his hair, untangling knots as she went. Magic bubbled underneath her skin. It shimmered like a diamond, just like the night when they had first met in the forest. The night when she had let herself truly be an elf for the first time in centuries.

Abraxas rolled his head in her lap, staring up at her with those golden eyes. "Ah, I missed you, Lady of Starlight."

She couldn't help the smile that eased over her lips. "You shouldn't call me that."

"It's what we called Silverfell elves ages ago," he winced. The muscles of his chest rippled as pain must have danced from the top of his head to the tips of his toes. "It's an honorable term, Lorelei."

She ghosted her fingers over his lips, letting magic spill from her fingers and onto his tongue. "My friends call me Lore."

"Lore," he repeated, whispering the word against her fingertips. "Lore, that suits you far better."

He was hurt. In pain. She should focus on the healing, but the moon magic poured out of her body unbidden, as though it already knew what to do. And instead of focusing on that, she was staring at his lips. At those plush, lovely lips that she'd kissed already, but never because she truly wanted to.

Until now.

He must have felt that same electric pull. Even in as much pain as he was in, Abraxas still wore a darkened expression that made her entire body clench. He lifted a bloodied hand and pressed it to the side of her face. "It's better already."

"Is it?"

"Mhm." He drew her down, just a bit lower. Not much, but enough that if she wanted to kiss him... she could.

She could lean farther down. Already her hair fell like a curtain around them. She couldn't see the arrows or the dead bodies on the floor. All she could see was him and the sharp angles of his face. The too long nose that somehow made him even more handsome. He had a faint scar above his right eyebrow, and his eyes weren't entirely yellow. There were the tiniest freckles of dark among the light.

"You tried to save us all," she whispered. "Why would you do that?"

"Because there was no one else to do it."

"I didn't think I would come to this castle and find a good man underneath all those scales." She trailed her fingers down his chin, tilting his head back into her lap. "I thought you would be some evil, dastardly beast who enjoyed hurting people."

"I am not."

"No, you are not." Lore hated that he was different from what she'd expected. At this point, she almost wanted him to be a horrible person because that would be so much easier than admitting to herself that he was... Kind. Sweet. Interesting in a way that no other man had ever interested her.

"Why did you have to be so sweet?" she asked, her lips a hair's breadth away from his.

His breath was metallic and the air around him tasted like poison. "I'm not, Lore. I promise you, I'm not."

Maybe he wasn't. Maybe he was the nightmarish creature who stalked her home in the night and made children cry in their sleep. Maybe she should fear him and all that he had done. She should run, screaming from this room, and hide under the covers of her bed.

Somehow, she didn't think that was the truth.

She closed the space between them and kissed him. Soft at first. She didn't want to hurt him anymore than he was already hurting. But then

Abraxas came alive in her grip. He wrapped his hand around the nape of her neck and pulled her into him until she couldn't breathe. Couldn't think. Couldn't do anything but kiss him and hope that this never ended.

They were two lost souls in this castle, and she couldn't believe that she had found herself in him. And yet, here he was. The impossible man who had haunted her dreams.

She should hate him. She should despise him for everything that he had done and more.

But she didn't.

She couldn't.

When they finally drew back for breath, he squeezed her neck just slightly, as though he didn't want her to draw away from him. "You are stunning," Abraxas whispered. "And I'm sorry if anyone ever made it seem like you weren't."

"You and I have suffered the same life, I believe." She smoothed her thumb over his cheek. "How are you feeling?"

"Almost entirely better." Abraxas chuckled. "I think I can sit up now."

"Oh, right."

She gave him room to breathe. To sit back up and arrange himself in whatever was the most comfortable way for him. Although, now that she'd thought about it...

"You usually seem to change back into your mortal form with clothes on." She eyed him with a slightly unimpressed look. "What changed?"

Abraxas scratched the back of his neck, a little sheepishly. "I can only imagine that it was the pain. The change is a bit more magic than most people recognize, and I just... well. I thought I was doing it right at the time, but I suppose I was not."

"Good," she whispered. "I mean, not good. I suppose it's good that you're better now, though. I just... Well. You're..."

Now that she was looking at him, she didn't know what to say. She hadn't thought he would be so... so... Everything. His overly large body translated into wide shoulders, stunning pectorals, and a muscular "V" shape that drew her eyes where she shouldn't look but wanted to.

She could spend hours on that body. Hours enjoying every inch of his caramel skin and getting to know all the places he liked touched. That should have scared her far more than the kiss, but it didn't. Not even remotely.

"Lore..." His eyes had gotten dark again. The pupils were almost entirely blown out as he watched her every move.

"Abraxas."

He chuckled at her tone. "If I had known that a half elf would walk into my life and turn everything upside down, I would never have left my cavern."

Another voice interrupted them, echoing through the chamber. "Elf?"

Lorelei froze. She glanced over at the door, only to see the brunette who the King had picked first. The woman's eyes went wide, then narrowed with glee. "Knights!" she screamed. "There's an elf in the castle!"

That was all it took.

All it took for the thundering sound of metal boots to strike the ground and race toward her. Any second now, they would pick her up by the arms and toss her back into the dungeon she'd already seen.

Abraxas snarled. She felt his power rolling in him so easily now. Like a blast of heat that warned he was about to return to his dragon form.

"No," she said, grabbing onto his arm. "Abraxas, you can't."

"They will not lay a single finger on you." He spat the words at her, and she already saw his fingers curling into claws.

But that wouldn't do. He couldn't withstand more pain, more torment, simply because someone had heard them. Though Lore knew she was giving up everything, it was the only option here.

"One of us has to stay," she whispered. "One of us has to be here. Get a message to the rebellion, to someone. Okay? Stay alive for me."

He reached for her, pulling her tight against his side and pressing his mouth to her hair. His hand pressed against her ribcage as though he were trying to feel her breath. Her heartbeat. And her own breath caught at the size of his hands, so big. So comforting.

"I can't get you out of this one, Lore," he breathed. "The best I can do is fly us both out of this place. Right here. Right now."

"And what would that do?" She smiled against his shoulder. "I knew this could be my fate. But I also know that you are still here. You can finish this, Abraxas."

He pressed one last kiss to her head before she felt metal hands tugging her out of his arms. And she knew, ah how horribly she knew, this would be the end of them.

The last dragon stood in the middle of the Great Hall, hands clenched at his sides, and watched her get dragged away from him.

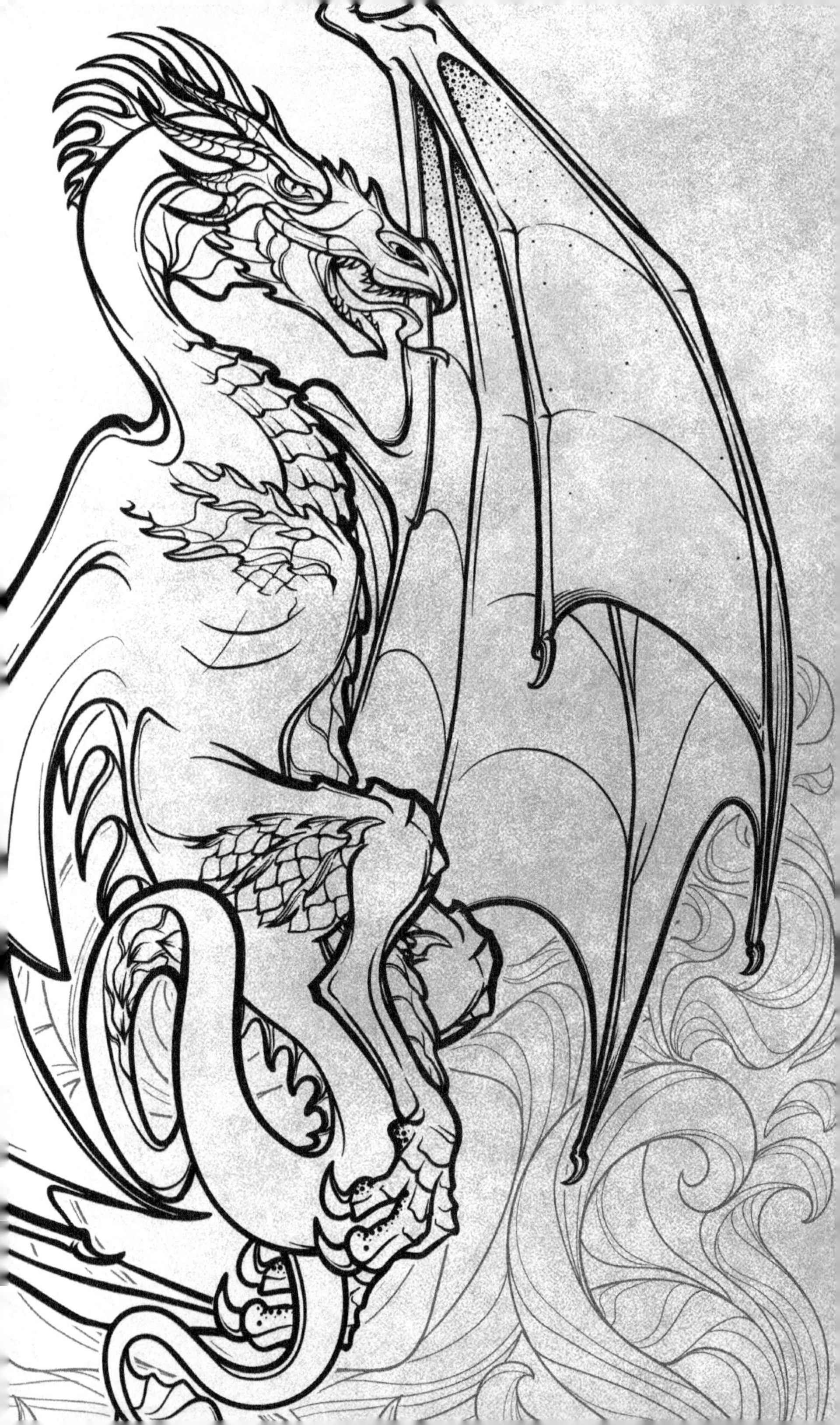

CHAPTER 29

He could do nothing. His hands were tied. But as he watched the Umbral Knights drag Lorelei away, Abraxas realized two very important things.

First, the King had to die. Yes, that meant Abraxas would lose the dragon eggs, and that he would have to spend the rest of his life searching for a magician or warlock who was strong enough to break the enchantment. That might never happen at all. But he couldn't continue to selfishly choose himself and his kind over the rest of the creatures in this kingdom.

Second, losing that woman to the horrible treatment of the guards was like losing a part of himself. She had become an extension of his own body. A severed limb that he felt had always been there. Attached to him in some way, although he hadn't found her until just recently.

If he didn't heal himself faster, then he would lose her. Forever.

Abraxas had lied when he'd said he felt better. He could stand on his own and function, but there was something wrong with his dragon still. His back ached where the poison had hit him, and he recognized the magic from the old days.

He needed time in his gold. He needed the opportunity to soak himself in fire and heat until his scales recovered from the wounds that flayed through his skin and back.

If he couldn't fly, then he couldn't get them where they needed to go. And he intended to save her.

The flames in his chest burned hotter again, glowing through his mortal skin like a light inside him. Whatever tin soldier touched her, he would crush them beneath his claws. That scheming bitch of a bride would crunch between his teeth while he chewed her bones. Savoring every bite. And lastly, he would make sure that the King died in the most dishonorable way possible.

He wouldn't even kill him as a dragon. He would give the man a slow, undeniable death with a sword and knives. And if Lore wanted her piece of him, then he would hold the villain down while she took her own pound of flesh off the King.

It was the least he could do for the woman who had shown him out of the darkness and back into the light.

He stalked from the Great Hall and down to the corridor that would lead into his cavern. If anyone saw him marching naked through the halls, then he didn't notice. Instead, he thundered all the way to his only safe place in the castle and launched into his dragon form. The magic was weak. Weaker than it had ever been in his life, but he changed and crawled onto the nearest mound of gold.

He opened his mouth and let fire pour out. Even that was almost too thin to melt the gold, damn it. He needed more. More heat, more gold, more everything so that he could get her out of that dungeon.

The coins eventually gave in. They liquified before his eyes, the image of the King on their backs melted. He couldn't wait until that was the reality, and the King really had disappeared into nothing.

Abraxas dug himself deeper into the molten gold, letting it cover the wound on his back and the holes in his wings. That would help. He could heal in a few hours if he stayed like this, all but holding himself together by the very end of a thread. He needed to sleep. Hibernation healed far more than just gold for dragons, but that would come when they were gone. When Lore could look after him while he slept.

The sound of metal footsteps down the hall to the cavern echoed, and he knew this wouldn't end well. He wouldn't get to rest or sleep, or even linger in his pool of gold for very long.

"Dragon!" Zander screamed. "You've been lying to me!"

He knew the shout of a child who had a broken toy that he had wanted to still play with. And Abraxas could only guess at what the young, nameless brunette had told him.

She'd found them in the Great Hall, wrapped in each other's arms while Abraxas had been entirely nude. They'd looked like they had known each other, as though they regularly had moments where they were curled together, whispering secrets while all the others were gone. The image conjured in his mind reeked of betrayal.

For that was the truth. He had betrayed the King. And he'd done it with a woman who was the scourge of the earth, at least in Zander's mind. He'd not only gone against the King's wish for the dragon to only remain as one of Zander's playthings. He'd done it with an elf.

Zander stomped toward him, barely even acknowledging that Abraxas had a pool of gold all around him and over his wings. "That little witch was an elf? And you know her?"

"I don't know what you're talking about," he replied. But he didn't even try to hide the sarcasm in his voice or the way his entire body rattled with rage. "There are no witches in the castle, my king."

"Oh. Oh, your king?" Zander laughed, though the sound was entirely without mirth. "We both know that's a lie, old friend. You threw out any loyalty the moment that walking wet dream entered the castle. And I can't blame you. She has legs longer than most horses I've seen, and lips that beg to be wrapped around a cock. But you have never been interested in women, so I have to imagine this is all about me."

How dare he?

Lore's name was too good to even be on his tongue, let alone mixed with those foul, loathsome words. Abraxas reared out of the gold, flecks raining down from his outstretched wings and pinging on the stone as they hardened in the air. "Hold your tongue, King, or I will rip it from your mouth."

Zander took a large step back, closer to his wall of metal soldiers who could at least provide a barrier. But he replied with sarcasm and disapproval, striking a hand to his chest and muttered, "So that's how it is. You think you're in love with the girl, is that it? You think because one magical creature walked into this castle and decided you were good enough for her to stick her tongue in, that you suddenly manifested feelings?"

He moved his neck like a snake, slithering over the stone until he loomed above the King. "One last warning, Zander. I would not advise speaking ill of her again."

"Or what?" Zander lifted his hand and made the same movement as always. The movement that shot the box of eggs out of the gold until it hovered right beside the King. "Or you lose all your hopes for the future? You know what I'll do to these. I like the idea of having more than one dragon at my beck and call, but I really don't care either way."

"You kill the eggs, and then you destroy any chance at controlling me at all." Abraxas bared his teeth and felt the hungry drool of the hunt slip down his chin. "I am hungry, Zander. I haven't hunted for centuries after being dedicated to both you and your father. Destroy the eggs, and you release me upon your kingdom. I will feast. I will gorge myself on your people until there is nothing left."

He'd never stood up for himself before. Never did what it took to make Zander see that he was controlling a very dangerous creature who could so easily kill him.

His teeth hovered close enough to snap. He could eat the King now, get this all over with, and destroy everything that Zander's father had fought so hard to build. But the eggs. Oh, how they called to him. Even as the King opened the box, he knew that tiny sapphire girl was more precious than all the stars in the sky.

His soul tore right down the middle. One half of him hoping, wishing, dreaming that he could have a daughter to call out to as they soared through the clouds. Their trumpeting calls would fill the entire kingdom with the hope of a new age.

But the other half of his soul whispered that the woman of his dreams languished in a cell somewhere. That perhaps the King had already tortured her. Flayed her skin from her spine so that he could see her bend a knee. As all the magical creatures should to this nightmare of a king.

His hesitation was his downfall.

The King threw something at him. A rope, perhaps. A chain. It didn't matter what it was, because the band closed around his neck and tightened until he couldn't breathe. He writhed backwards, falling into the pool of gold as he struggled to free himself.

Zander stepped up to the edge of the cliff and stared down at him with apathy in his gaze. "My father gave that to me before he died. Said I always had to be watchful of how a dragon could deceive. And that if you ever stepped out of line, the same magician who made that box provided this. I hope it hurts, Abraxas."

It did.

Blindingly so. He wheezed, sucking in the smallest amount of air, just enough to keep him alive but never enough to ease the choking.

Zander tsked. "You could have worked with me, Abraxas. We could have taken this entire world by storm and you wouldn't have needed to fear a single thing. You'd be the dragon everyone thought ruled the kingdom. I don't care. Whatever you wanted would be yours. Instead, you proved me wrong. That dragons are untrustworthy, just like my father said. Now, I'm going to deal with that little elf you are so infatuated with. I wonder if elves grow their fingernails back faster than humans?"

He watched the King leave, desperately trying to throw himself back at the cliff to grab onto the human who thought he had everything under control. Unfortunately, Zander did. Abraxas couldn't move at all, not without all the air in his lungs disappearing. The best he could do was lie in the gold and stay alive.

The weak, keening cry he let out was one only a dragon made for its mate. A cry that said someone had died. That a dragon was in mourning.

He didn't know how long he lay there. Alone, boiling in gold that slowly cooled. The metal would solidify around his body soon. It would trap him in his own hoard, and maybe that was for the best.

Lore was dead by now. His tail lashed behind him, but even that movement was weak. He had to focus on breathing. On staying alive. And he wasn't doing a good job of it.

Hands touched his nose, patting his nostrils as though they were trying to see if he was still breathing.

Abraxas cracked open an eye and couldn't have been more surprised to see Beauty standing in front of him. But... not. Not Beauty and yet, it had to be.

She'd swept her hair back from her face in a tight bun and wore leather clothing that looked suspiciously like armor. Was she even wearing leather pants? Like a warrior, not like the little cream puff who had made him laugh at how kind she was.

"Oh good, you're still alive." She patted his nose again, all business, as she peered around his head. "What did he do to you?"

The chain around his throat was so tight he could barely speak. But he tried his best and whispered, "Enchanted... neck... same as.... box."

She frowned and marched across the cooled gold to his neck. What did she think she was doing? Beauty was just a little girl from Tenebrous. She'd never seen magic like this. He couldn't imagine, at least.

But as she walked, she started talking. And everything fell into place.

"I know this might be hard to believe, but I'm not who I've said I was." She patted his neck while she walked down his body, actively letting him know where she was. "Look, the rebellion isn't stupid. They knew Lore would have a hard time in this place by herself, and I was here just as a... watchful eye. We'll say. Someone who was a backup plan in case anything went wrong. Like you."

Like him?

He wheezed in a deep breath, but then froze when she touched the magical band around his neck. "Ah. Well, this isn't as complicated a spell as he thought. Let me just... meddle."

Meddle? Absolutely not. No one was going to tamper with the magic that made it impossible for him to breathe. He tried to shift his neck, but was trapped in the gold. And then she pulled out what looked like a wand from her pocket and the tension around his throat eased.

Not disappeared, but eased enough for him to take in a deep lungful of air and snarl, "You work for the rebellion, too?"

"Of course I work for the rebellion," she replied. "I have since I was a little girl. My father was one of the first mortals to get involved, because he saw the rightful place of the magical creatures here. Don't move for a second."

The wand zapped him like he'd been struck by lightning. Snarling, he tensed as the band tightened again, then loosened. Almost like a snake was wrapped around his throat and fought against her.

"Sorry," she muttered. "It's not as easy as I thought."

Of course it wasn't! If the magician who had made that box had enchanted this rope, then it would not be as simple as flicking her wrist and muttering a few magical words.

Beauty continued on as if he wasn't in pain. "Look, I'm sorry I had to lie to you all. It was better if no one knew. In case the King caught anyone or... well. In case what happened actually happened. You threw a tear into things, did you know that?"

"I did," he grumbled.

"But she likes you. Really likes you if those stolen looks were anything to note." Beauty waved the wand one last time and let out a loud, "Aha!"

The band tumbled from his neck as though she'd unlocked it. The little human gathered up the band, shoved that into her pocket as well, and then marched in front of him. "You can't attack the King right now."

"I'd like to see you try to stop me."

"No, really. There are things in the works that you don't know, and that I can't tell you for reasons I refuse to explain." She held up a hand when he tried to argue. "No, Abraxas. I will not tell you a single word more. However, I want you to find Lorelei. Give her hope to stay alive. All that romantic stuff, or whatever it is you want to say. We need her alive, not dead. If that means you have to sneak into that dungeon with her and keep healing her, do it. She's integral to the plan."

"Why?" he snarled, the fires in his throat already heating the gold around him.

"You'll see." She winked, hopped off the gold mountain, and raced toward the entrance to his cavern. "You're part of the plan, too!"

Damned rebellion. He never should have gotten involved.

But, as Abraxas warmed the gold around himself and shook his massive body free, he felt a renewed sense of hope. If this worked, maybe he could get her back.

If she was still alive.

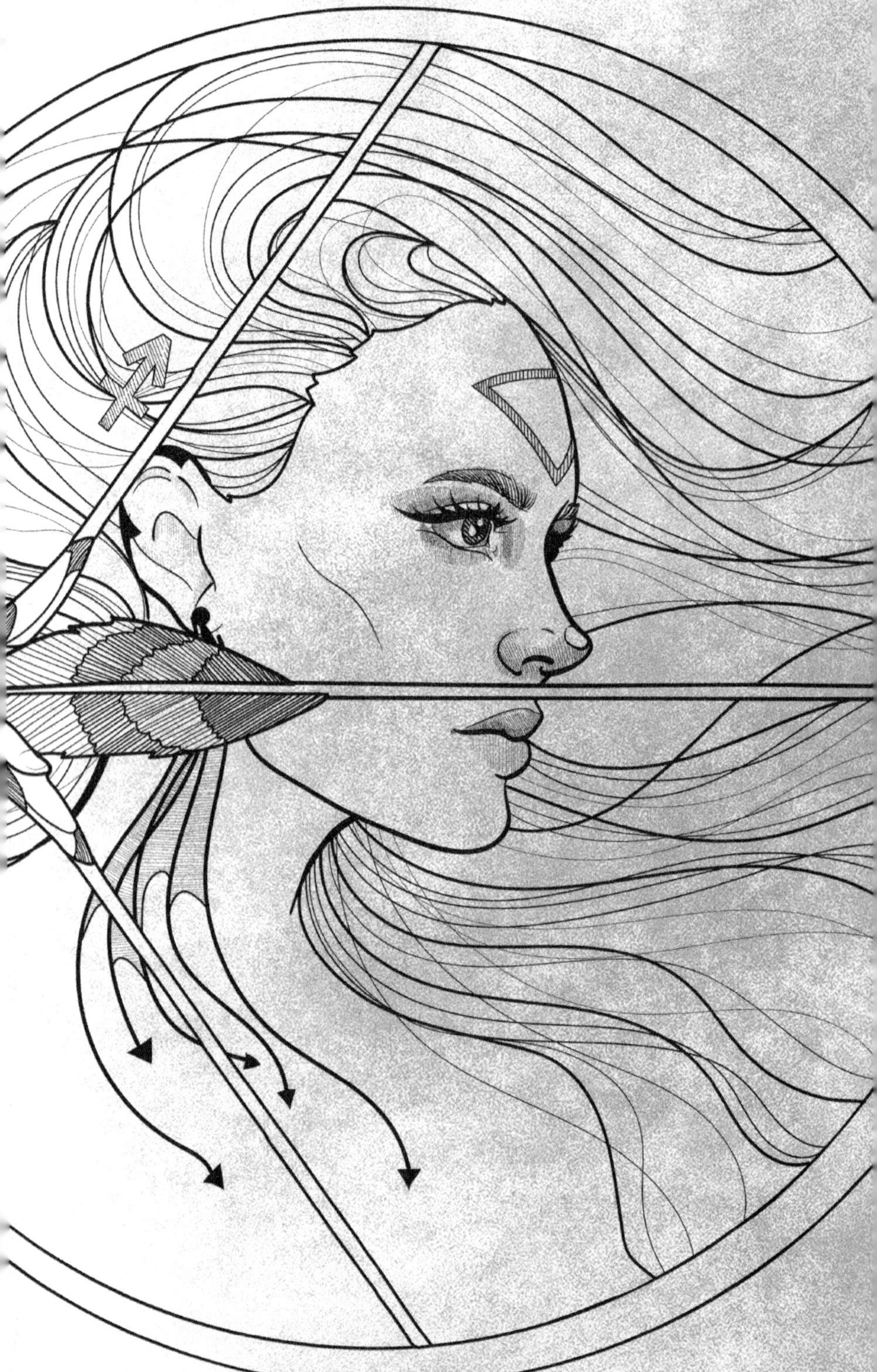

Chapter 30

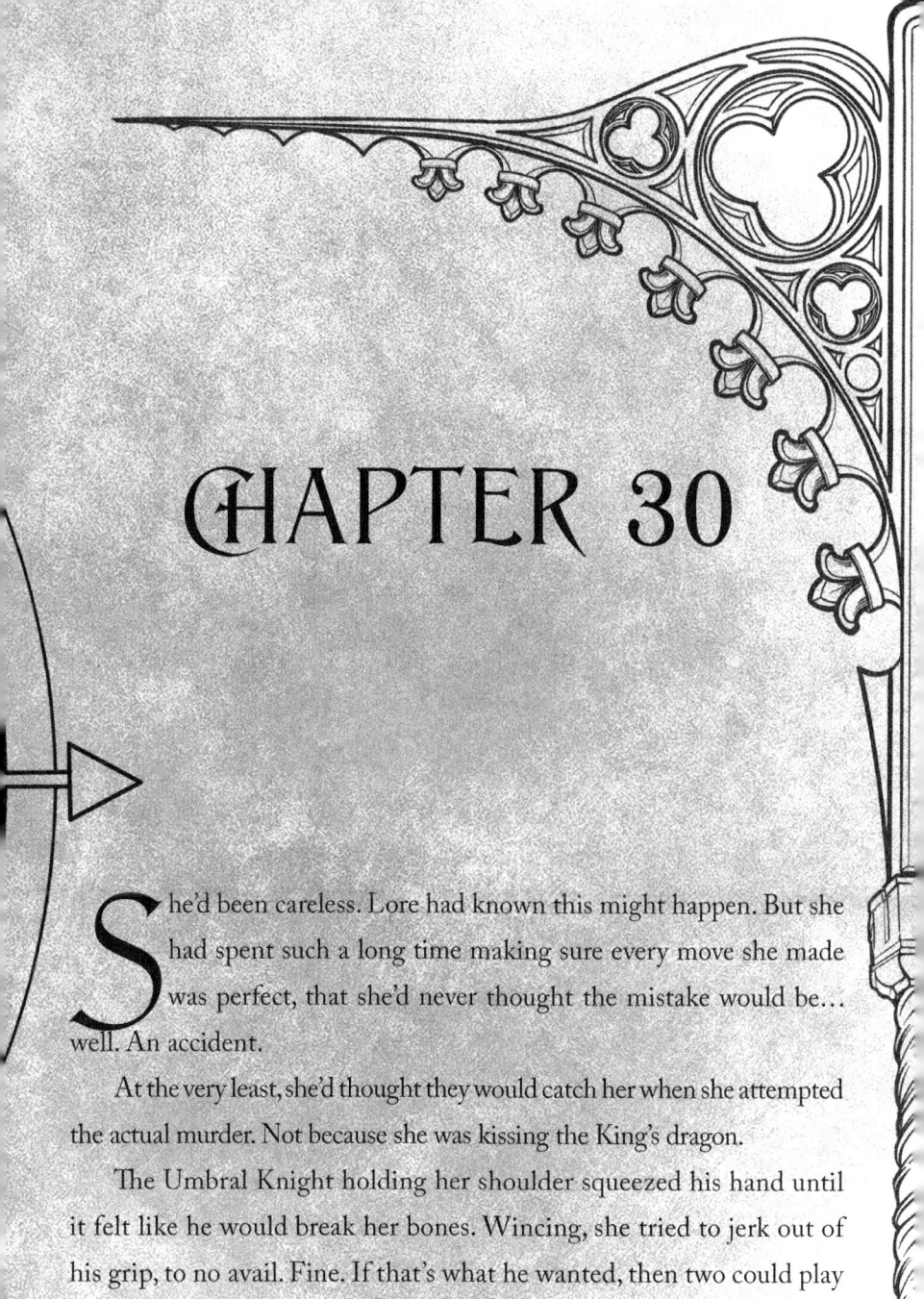

She'd been careless. Lore had known this might happen. But she had spent such a long time making sure every move she made was perfect, that she'd never thought the mistake would be… well. An accident.

At the very least, she'd thought they would catch her when she attempted the actual murder. Not because she was kissing the King's dragon.

The Umbral Knight holding her shoulder squeezed his hand until it felt like he would break her bones. Wincing, she tried to jerk out of his grip, to no avail. Fine. If that's what he wanted, then two could play that game.

They rounded a corner of a hall and that gave her enough of a chance. Lore kicked out her foot, shoving all her weight into the Umbral Knight as she sprinted up the wall. The momentum spun her behind him and cracked the metal hand off his armor. Smoke poured out of it, leaving the tin frame empty of what had made it run. Of course, there were still the other nine Umbral Knights to deal with.

Each of their helmets turned to look at her, then back at each other. Almost as though they couldn't believe what they had just seen.

When their attention returned to the elf, who should have been in their hands, she shrugged. "Sorry boys. Guess I'm a little more than you're used to handling."

At least they didn't do what she had expected. Which was rushing at her one by one. Instead, they stood shoulder to shoulder and pushed her down the hall. They'd created a wall of metal and smoke that should have been impossible to bypass. But she wasn't a normal young woman, and elves were tricky.

Lore looked up at a small beam of wood that held the flags of the castle on it. Good enough. She sprinted forward, planted her foot on the chest of a Knight, and launched herself into the air. Her fingers grabbed onto the sharp wood, splinters digging into the palms of her hands. Only enough to dangle precariously over their heads while the Knights tried to reach for her. They couldn't jump, though, and that gave her the advantage.

She swung her legs up and over them, then landed in a crouch behind the idiot soldiers. They really were only good for brute force or people who hadn't spent their entire life evading them.

Lore didn't waste time looking back. They'd run after her once she started moving and she'd only get so many steps ahead of them.

Arms pumping, she sprinted down the hall. Where? She did not know. Maybe in the direction of the dragon's cavern, but that wouldn't get her very far, either. Lore had to finish this. She had to find the King and... and...

She slammed into a hard chest, bouncing back and hitting the wall, spine first. Breath knocked from her lungs. She stared at the King who had apparently been making his way to see her.

"Ah," he said with a feral grin. "Just who I was looking for."

"Who? Me?" She pointed to herself while standing straight and shaking out her arms. "I don't think you should be excited to see me."

"You're an assassin sent by the rebellion, I assume." The King held his arms out at his sides, fingers spread wide. "We should have met like this sooner, Lorelei. I'm afraid I misjudged you. No longer."

"You watched me cut an arrow from the sky and you still thought I was a normal mortal woman," she snarled. "I think all the blame is on you for not seeing what was right in front of you."

The King's smile never wavered, although he took a step to the right, blocking her path. "Sure, you could say that. I should have seen through your little ruse sooner than I did. But you were supposed to be here to marry me and you are rather beautiful. You can't blame a man for falling under the beguiling looks of an elf."

"I absolutely can." Lore's eyes darted left and right, trying to find any kind of weapon she could use. "You have a lot to answer for, Umbral King."

"Oh, please. We're past that." He flinched toward her, laughing when she jolted back. "Call me Zander."

She didn't know which one of them moved first. But she ducked underneath his flying fist and pounded her own underneath his ribs. He let out a loud 'oof' as the air was forcibly expelled from his lungs. She pivoted, ducking underneath his arm and dragging his bicep with her, locking his arm behind his back.

"I don't need a weapon to kill you." Lore pulled hard on his arm, her back against his. The tendon made a horrible popping sound as he strained to keep his arm in its socket.

"Don't you?" He sounded slightly out of breath, but that could have been from the pain. "You're so confident that your skills as an elf will help you here, but you forget the wars always ended with mortal men winning. Do you know why?"

She dug her heels into the floor and pulled hard. "Why's that?"

"We weigh more."

He heaved his arm and sent her flying with it. Lorelei gulped down the shout of anger and fear as her back struck the wall again. She fell onto the floor, hands slapping the stone and vision reeling.

A boot came out of nowhere and connected with her face. She felt her nose crack under the strike, then her teeth clacked together as he stomped again. Stars burst in her vision until she couldn't see him, couldn't tell which way was up and which way was down.

The King grabbed onto her red dress and hauled her back up, holding her by two fists on either side of her chest. "You creatures always have this ridiculous sense of self worth. As if anyone would care if you were gone."

He threw her again. Lore barely had time to brace before gravity brought her back down onto the hard floor. Her back screamed in pain, but this time she crawled a few feet before he grabbed her by the back of the head.

Hair fisted in his meaty hands, the King lifted her so she could stare him in the eyes. "A single elf in the royal castle. That was their plan? Did you think I had never trained? That my father wasn't a warrior like yourself?"

"No," she croaked before he slammed her head into the floor.

Lore didn't get up when he released her hair. Her head screamed in pain and her teeth hurt from being knocked around. She felt blood drool from her mouth. She needed to fight and not let it all end like this, but... her limbs refused to work even as her mind screamed at her to rise to battle

He pressed his boot into her back, holding her down on the floor with a slight chuckle. "Look at me, elf."

She couldn't. Wouldn't.

"I said, look at me." The King pressed harder until her ribs screamed and her heart thudded quickly in warning that he was going to squish her. Like the bug he thought her kind was.

So she tilted her head and peered up at him through eyes already swollen.

Zander, the Umbral King, watched her with his head tilted to the side. He'd already pulled a white handkerchief out of his pocket and wiped his hands clean of her blood. The stains bloomed like roses underneath his touch. "When I first took the throne, I thought maybe I could talk to your people. Listen to your concerns. And when I did, I realized all your troubles were petty and small. Your lands were gone. No one listened to your opinions. You were here first."

He pulled one hand free from the white fabric and pinched his fingers together like a duck's bill, mouthing words in a mocking gesture. "We want our ancestral lands back. You can't build there. The fairies believe that site is sacred. Blah, blah, blah. Your vision is so limited that you would stop progress simply because you want to preserve history when history is still being written."

A wall of Umbral Knights appeared behind him. More than the original ten that had been sent to drag her to the dungeon.

The King ground his foot against her back one more time before lifting his weight off her. Lore heaved in a lungful of air, fighting to stay conscious.

"Anyway," he continued, as though he hadn't just beaten her within an inch of her life. "I realized then and there that my father was right about you lot. All you want is to stay in the same place forever, and I want to move forward. You're standing in my way."

The Umbral Knights pulled her up by the shoulders, forcing her to stand in front of the King.

Even limp as she was, Lore still spat a mouthful of blood at his feet. "History makes us who we are. If you forget the past, then you become the past."

"Fancy words for a dead woman." He waved a hand, and the Umbral Knights dragged her back down the hall. Toward the dungeon.

Toward her doom.

Lorelei didn't drag her feet this time. She had tried her best to escape, as any honorable warrior would do, and she had failed. Namely because she'd underestimated her opponent, and she was surprised.

The King was supposed to be a figurehead of luxury and sloth. He'd given none of the rebellion the impression that he also knew how to fight, or that there was a single drop of strength in the man.

They'd all been wrong. They had all been fooled into thinking their jobs would be easy to kill this man.

Perhaps Margaret had known. The elven warrior couldn't have not seen the hard edge in the King's eye. The edge that Lorelei had taken as a man who was spoiled and unkind, but not a man who knew how to battle. Margaret should have known. She had seen more warriors and battle than any other elf Lore knew.

And if Margaret had known the King could fight, then she had sent

Lore into battle without the proper tools. Without the knowledge she needed to stay safe and alive.

The King had beaten her so easily. The Umbral Knights brought her to those darkened doors, but she hardly noticed that they'd arrived. Instead, she lingered in the dark recesses of her own mind. She'd been beaten.

Her feet dragged on the stone floor as they shoved her toward the same cell they'd placed her in before. Belatedly, she realized that someone had occupied the cell since she'd been there. Blood stained the floor in the corner and no one had attempted to clean it up.

The Umbral Knights threw her into the cell and locked the door quickly, as if even the magic inside them was terrified she'd try another escape.

If she wasn't in so much pain, she might have warned them that she was finished with her escape attempts. Finished with her theatrics as well.

Lore knew when she'd lost. She knew when there was nothing more for her to do but sit and wait.

Elves were good at that. Her mother had trained her long ago to sit in the middle of a meadow and watch a flower unfurl until the very end of the night. As though the waiting was part of them.

Lore never understood what she was waiting for, but the older she got, the more she thought it wasn't that she was waiting for something to happen or someone to come. She was merely waiting for the next heartbeat to pass. In essence, she was waiting for herself.

She folded her body in the center of the cell, tucking her knees up to her chest and resting her chin on the bony parts of them. No one would come for her here. No one had come for the others, so why would she think she was any different?

A gnarled hand slid through the bars. His nails had grown longer since she'd last been in this dungeon. But the soft smile on his face, the one that said he still believed in her, that hadn't budged.

"It's all right," he murmured, his deep voice echoing through the dungeon. "You aren't the first to try, lass."

"I'm the first to have been sent by the rebellion," she replied. "I'm the first to get so close and to fail so spectacularly, all because a stupid girl heard something that she shouldn't. Careless, all of it. I was so careless, and I was so close."

"It's not about the completion of the job, but the message you sent. Your story will travel throughout Umbra. To the far reaches of Lux Brumalis to the southern shore of Solis Occasum. The heroic attempt of a single elf to kill the King will soar over the Stygian Peaks and sink into the Fields of Somber. You did what no one else has attempted for years."

A few other prisoners shuffled to the front of their cages. They grasped the bars in their fingers and she saw a hunger in their eyes that hadn't been there before. They wanted to be released. They wanted to fight, and they hadn't wanted that in a very long time.

She met their gazes, one by one. "But none of that story will leave this place. No one will ever know what I did because the King will never speak a word of it. He'll kill anyone who tries."

The prisoner directly across from her moved out of the shadows. He had once been a leshy like Borovoi, one of the last of his kind. She'd thought they were all gone, but apparently, she'd been wrong about a lot of things.

The pale wraith stretched his closed fist forward and, in what could be the last of his magic, he uncurled his fingers in a flourish. A single moth opened and closed its wings. Words decorated the pale, velvet soft appendages. Lore saw her own name written on them before it took flight. She watched as it floated up toward the ceiling, clung to a crack in the stone, and wiggled free.

"Let the sun rise," the leshy said, then disappeared into the darkness once more.

Lore wished she felt the power of the phrase still. She wished she could believe in the message that it held.

But she still stared into the shadows and whispered, "Let the sun rise."

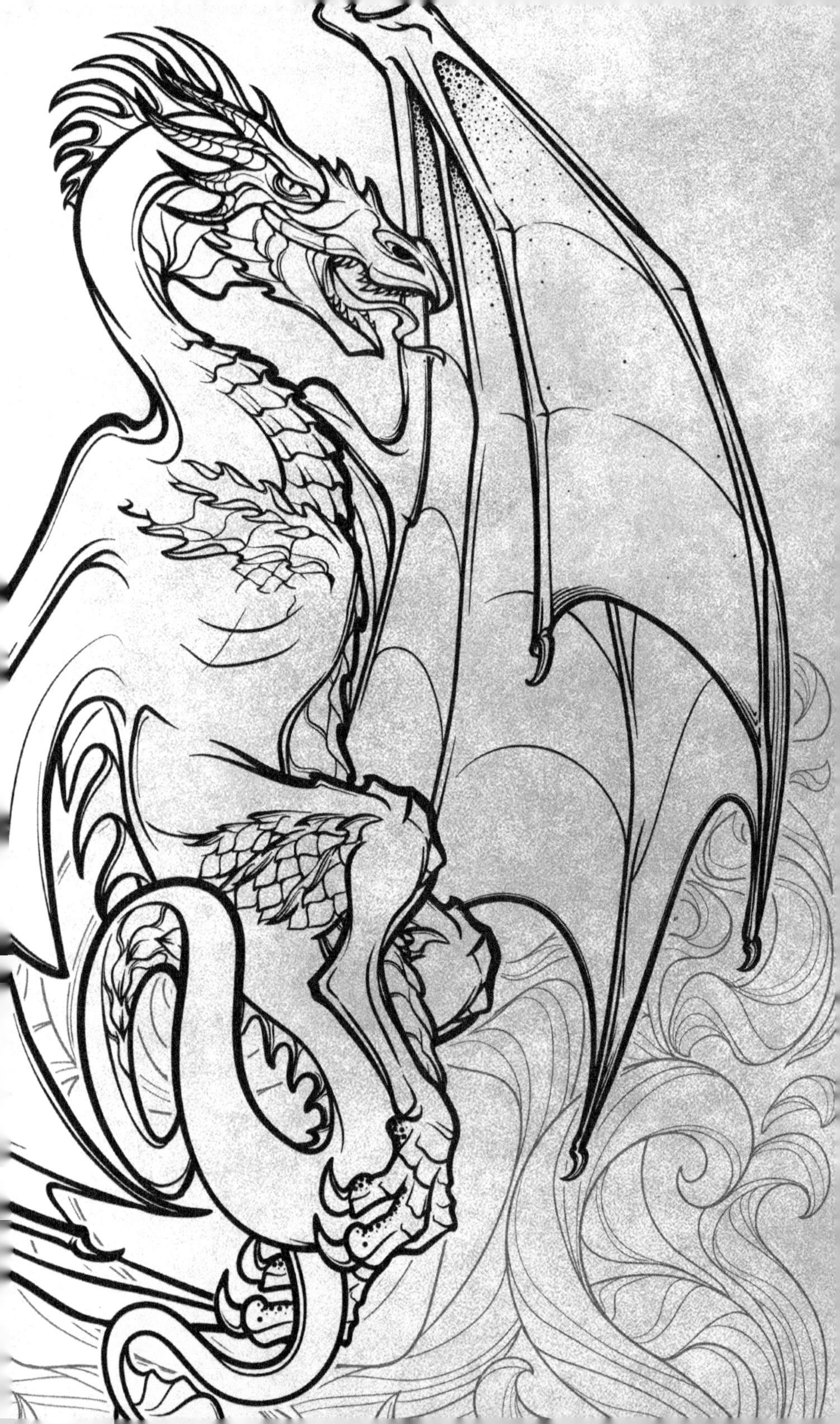

Chapter 31

Abraxas had never tried to sneak through the castle before. The realization baffled him, considering how little he trusted the King and all the people who served him. But Abraxas had never been in a situation where it was dangerous for him to be seen.

He was the King's dragon. Who would dare attack him?

Now, he didn't want to find out. The Umbral Knights were an extension of the King. The power that animated them would likely report to Zander that the dragon was no longer in his cave. And though he was a powerful being and very large, the Umbral Knights were many. They knew how to attack a dragon; he was certain of that. They'd been made to keep their king safe, after all.

Zander's father hadn't been foolish. He'd seen the writing on the wall that eventually Abraxas might decide this journey wasn't worth the pain and suffering. The King could die. Abraxas would die with him, but not immediately.

So he pressed his back against the shadows in the corridors and watched the Umbral Knights pass. He tried his very best to not capture their attention and shockingly, he managed.

A quiet thrum in his chest urged him to tell Lorelei how he'd learned from her. She was more suited to this kind of work. Sneaking throughout the castle and hiding in every nook and cranny. His body was built for heavier stuff. While she was a dagger in the night, he was a blunt hammer ready to bash skulls.

Apparently, she'd taught him how to be more than that. And it showed.

The dungeon was so close he could smell the rank air billowing out of the door. As he watched from his hiding place, the King exited the black doors. Zander wiped his hands on a bloody cloth and muttered something to an Umbral Knight who trailed after him.

The doors were still open. The creaking hinges would give him away if he tried to open it, so now was his only chance. He needed to distract the Knights guarding it, however, or the doors would close and then his plan would get very messy very quickly.

He glanced around, but the only object at hand was a candlestick a maid must have left on the windowsill. But, as he reached for it, his hand paused. A bright light glimmered on the other side of the window. A sparkling, tiny woman who tapped on the glass to get his attention.

He frowned, narrowing his eyes and trying to understand what he was looking at. Was that a pixie? They were supposed to be far away from the castle, or the King would put them in a tiny bottle.

Then it dawned on him that a long while ago, Lore had let out one of those pixies. And apparently, the little creature had stuck around.

Abraxas opened the latch of the window and cracked it open just enough for the pixie to enter the room. She landed on his hand, her entire body still burning with light. He'd never seen someone so delicate. Her wings had the tiniest hint of veins where the light darkened at the edges.

She frantically pointed at the Knights and then herself.

"Are you going to help me, little one?" He stared down at the brave creature in his hand. "I need to get to her, even if she's in the dungeons."

Again, the pixie pointed to the Knights.

"Distract them, and I'll sneak into the dungeons." Abraxas gave her a quick nod, but then held his opposite hand above her head to prevent her from flying off. "But I haven't thought about how to get out of the dungeon yet. Any guesses?"

If he saw through the glow correctly, she gave him a look that said how unimpressed she was. Darting around his hand, the pixie headed off toward the Knights.

It didn't take much. They saw a free flying pixie in the castle and they knew what to do. Both of the Knights in front of the dungeon took off after her, their armor clanking noisily as they tried their best to snap their metal gloves around her like a cage.

He lurched out of the shadows and tried to run to the dungeon. Quietly, he reminded himself. But he was a big man and quiet wasn't his specialty. He was lucky the pixie had showed up when she did, or he'd never have slid into the dungeon without being caught.

Abraxas made his way down the coiling stairwell, hand on the wall, heart thundering in his chest. What would he find in the darkness here? Obviously plenty of the other prisoners, but he hoped that she was still alive. That he wasn't too late.

His soul screamed at the mere idea that he might find her dead on the dirty stone floor. She was too precious to him already. Abraxas wasn't all that sure he'd survive finding her like that.

The other prisoners shifted, some of them staring at him with hatred in their eyes. He couldn't blame them. He'd been the one to put many of these creatures into those cells, and no begging or kind words would ever make them forgive him.

Abraxas didn't search for their forgiveness, though. He was only here for one reason, and one alone.

The last cell held the elf that made his heart skip a beat and then resume its ragged thumping. She sat cross legged in the center of the cell, her face already swollen and bruised, but alive. She was alive.

He stopped in front of her cell, completely and utterly undone. The sight of her like this?

He wanted to destroy this entire castle. He would rip it down stone by stone if that's what he had to do to find whatever bastard had dared lay a finger on her. To touch her. Already fire burned in his chest and his nails elongated into wicked claws. He wanted to burst into his dragon form and raze this entire building to the ground.

But first... First, he had to make sure she was okay.

"Lore?" he breathed, wrapping his fingers around the bars of her cell. "Lore, please tell me you're alive."

She opened a single swollen eyelid. The other had stuck together with dried blood. The whites of her eye were red and bloodshot. Her fingernails were dirty with earth and what he suspected was someone else's blood. But she still smiled when she saw him, and that nearly sent him to his knees.

"Abraxas. Didn't I tell you not to get involved with all this? The King will kill you too if he sees you in here."

"Fuck the King," he snarled. "Did he do this to you?"

The laugh that spilled from her lips was dark and horrible. "In a way. Yes, he was the one to lay his hands on me, but it was the rebellion who sent me here. It was a lifetime of hatred from mortals that locked me in this cell. It was a decade of pain and solitude that put me on Margaret's list to begin with. How many people hurt me, Abraxas? A hundred? A thousand? So many mortals who hate us, and want to see us dead."

He slid down, sitting on the floor outside her cell with his face pressed against the bars. "You can't think like that."

"Why not?"

"Your decisions didn't lead you to this place. Countless innocents didn't send you to your doom. This is all from the machinations of one evil man who passed that poisonous hate down to his son." Abraxas truly believed that. He couldn't allow himself to think for even a moment that the people of this kingdom were the real problem. They were honest and true. He had seen it before.

Or at least, he thought he had. Long ago, when the dragons had still flown through the skies.

"You've never lived in the city, Abraxas. You've never seen what I have." She shifted, working hard to pull her legs from the cross legged position, though she had to pull her legs free with her hands. "Listen to me. The rebellion is not what it once was. Why else would they send me here? Alone? And then to attack the castle while I was still in it..."

"There's more here than either of us know." He reached his arm through the bars, keeping his hand outstretched for her to take. "I wish I could tell you everything, and maybe you could help me piece it together. I wish you had seen what I did. But Lore... Lore, please. Just stay with me."

For a second, he thought she would give up. Her lost expression was one he'd seen before on the faces of prisoners who remained in this place. It was the face of a woman who had forgotten why she had come here. She didn't care about the meaning anymore. All she felt was the pain.

Abraxas gestured with his hand, hoping she would trust him. "Lore. You're letting him get inside your head. This is exactly what he wants. He wants you to feel weak and to think that no one else in this world is going to want you or listen to you. But I'm telling you now, Lady of Starlight, that is not true."

The King was a master at mincing his words so that people would believe whatever he said. Was that what had happened in this cell? Though she was still alive, his gut twisted with the fear that it might be too late.

But Lore sighed and dragged herself across the floor. Inch by inch, until she tucked her tiny fingers against the wide strength of his palm. "You're just as good at getting in my head, dragon."

"Good," he replied. Relief tinged his words with too much emotion, but he didn't care. "Good, I think we both need that."

She looked up at him with those blue sea eyes and his heart shattered into a million pieces. Lore watched him as though he had the answers, and could fix all the broken things in her life, but he didn't know how. He didn't know how to be that hero who broke her out of this cell and carried her away to a far off land. To a place where no one would hunt her or her people.

That place no longer existed.

"I don't know where the keys are," he whispered.

"The King keeps them on his person, right next to his heart." She shook her head, but he saw the tears in her eyes. "He said he didn't trust anyone with them. Not even an Umbral Knight."

"And his plan for you?" Abraxas had a sick guess at what the King wanted to do. But he had to hear her say the words. He needed to know the man he'd served had really fallen so far.

Lore's throat bobbed in a thick swallow. "He plans to sacrifice me at the wedding. He's going to announce his new bride, and then he's going to show the entire kingdom what happens when a creature tries to rise against him. The idea of a martyr in his kingdom is not one he's willing to entertain, so he wants to be sure the message is truly sent out. He claims that message will be crystal clear when my head hits the ground."

His stomach dropped. Of course, that was Zander's plan. The boy didn't know how to end any fight other than with anger and pain. Zander's father had always wanted to hurt people, and thus, the boy had become the spitting image of that evil man.

He searched for the words that would make this right. He tried his damnedest to think of something that would ease her torment and fear. But he couldn't. He only knew that she shivered like a leaf, her hand clutching his as though it were her lifeline.

Abraxas put his shoulder against hers through the bars, holding her up with their hands intertwined between them. "Has anyone ever told you about the Castle of the Lost?"

The question was so strange, so unusual and unexpected, that it knocked her right out of the fear. Lore stirred, her brows drawn down in a deep frown. "Are you going to tell me a children's story?"

"So you have heard of it." Abraxas felt his chest squeeze with deep pleasure. "It's not a children's story. It was the home of the dragons years ago, long before you were born. I have only seen it once, but it was the great nesting grounds where all dragons were born. Long, long ago."

He didn't know if this would help distract her, but he had to do something.

Abraxas looked at her, at the lost expression on her face, and he felt as though he had failed somehow. As though he would never be the same if he couldn't put back the broken pieces she desperately needed mended.

He reached with his free hand and tucked a matted strand of her hair behind her ear. Fingers ghosting over a cut on her cheekbone. "I remember it was green. An oasis had created everything around the nesting grounds. A deep well of water that spilled out like emeralds dotted with sapphire flowers. The female dragons would come from all around Umbra and they would lay eggs that looked like gemstones. Each one was more beautiful than the last. And the sun..." He smoothed his fingers over her forehead, easing down her eyes until they naturally closed. "You could always feel the sun on your face."

She took a deep, calming breath. Her eyes moved underneath her closed lids, as though she could see what he spoke of.

He could do this. He could paint a picture that transported her from a dungeon into an ancient realm. "I remember the feeling of the wind on my face from their wings as they cooled the eggs. The sound of their humming deep in their dragon throats as they sang to their babies. And the feeling of hope that came with every moment I watched them in their nests."

"I remember the cool touch of the moon," she whispered, a single tear dripping down her cheek. "Running through the woods beside my mother. Our legs felt longer in those moments when the moon sent her rays to give us strength. To chill the heat from the sun."

Abraxas cupped her jaw and turned her head to his. He ever so gently touched his forehead to hers. His emotions rioted, warring from wanting to kill the King for all this harm and sadness that she had ever suffered.

She reached between the bars and mirrored him. Her hand clutched his jaw, her fingers still shaking and so thin. So delicate. Her tears spilled out then, falling onto his cheeks until he could taste salt on his tongue.

And his heart squeezed. He never wanted to see her hurt. Never again.

He took a deep breath, chest swelling with some unnamed emotion that felt so important. Life changing. As though if he didn't say the words that pressed against his tongue, then nothing would ever be the same again.

Or maybe it was that he dreaded his life remaining the same.

"Oh good," Beauty's voice sliced through their quiet moment. "You're both here."

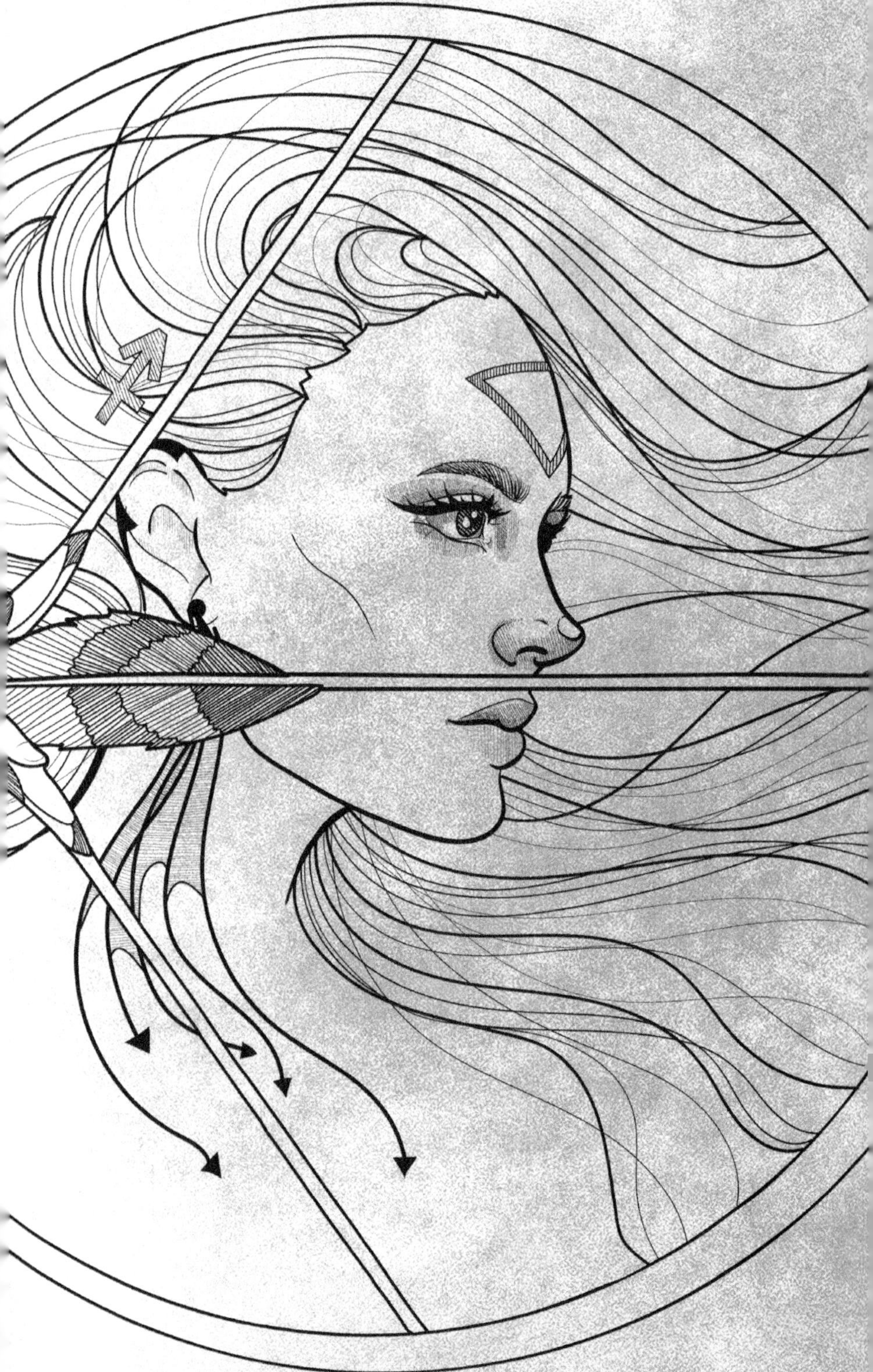

Chapter 32

She wanted to kiss him.

Damn it, Lore wanted to kiss the dragon who had killed her mother, and she didn't feel even an ounce of guilt over that. The entire time she'd sat in the dark, listening to the other prisoners' quiet conversations, she had wanted Abraxas to come. She'd wanted to see him one last time after the King described in detail what it would feel like to die. She'd wanted to see Abraxas's stupid face and scold him again for not seeing the world the way she did.

Mostly, she just wanted to be around him. The peace that came from him standing next to her eased her mind. So much so that Lore didn't even know what to call this.

She was a half elf. Forgotten by both sides of the coin and not wanted by either. But he made her feel like she was wanted by someone.

When he'd arrived, it was as if her heart had started beating again. Sure, she was going to die soon. And yes, they had only known each other for a short amount of time. None of that mattered.

He was here.

She could hold on to his stupidly sharp jaw and stare into his yellow eyes and wish and hope and pray that their life was different.

He told her about his homeland and it was right on the tip of Lore's tongue to place them into that scene. She wanted to stand in that emerald grass and smile at him. She wanted to dream of him in a moonlight clearing while the silver light danced over the muscles of his arms and shoulders.

"Oh good. You're both here."

The words struck her over the skull as though someone had attacked her. The thoughts in her head, the ones about him and her and a future that was without mortals, were foolish. They were the dreams of a child who had yet to see what real life was.

And she couldn't wander down that path. Not easily, anyway. Not without losing her heart in the process.

Lore wrenched herself from Abraxas's grip and stared in shock down the dungeon hall. Beauty stood there, although not the Beauty she knew so well. The young woman was dressed as though she were going to war. That outfit was the exact one Lore had been looking for when they went to steal from the dragon's hoard, but... That couldn't be Beauty.

She untangled her fingers from the dragon's and slowly shoved herself upright. The process was long and arduous, though Lore refused to sit while she had this conversation with the young woman in front of her.

"You don't look like yourself," Lore growled. "Why's that?"

At least Beauty winced. She knew how much trouble she was in. "Lorelei, please don't get mad at me. It's not like I wanted to deceive you."

It all came crashing down around her shoulders.

Margaret. The rebellion. Beauty not being in the Great Hall when the arrows fell.

"You work for her," she mumbled. "You work for them."

"I do. I always have. But you have to listen to me. This was all to keep you alive. Margaret didn't want to send you into the castle on your own, but if one of us was caught, then we couldn't know..." Beauty ran her fingers through her hair and blew out a breath. "You couldn't know I existed. Otherwise, everything might have fallen apart. Your mission was entirely more dangerous than mine, and you could be more easily found out."

Lore replied as though her tongue had swollen in her mouth. "Margaret knew I would fail."

"She didn't know. She hoped this wouldn't happen, but you aren't the first, Lore. You couldn't have imagined you would be the first they sent to kill the King. He knows the tricks, and all the old ways." Beauty took a step forward, reaching out her hands as though she wanted to touch Lore, but then letting them fall back to her sides. "No one wanted to see you fail."

"But everyone would sacrifice me if I did." The truth hurt worse than she thought it would. Of course, she knew the rebellion wouldn't stop if she got caught. That was the entire plan the whole time.

But she had thought—

She had hoped—

Lore straightened her spine and her shoulders. With a quick nod, she pushed herself back into the present. She had to let go of all that. No one had ever been there for her, not a single moment of her life. She could get through this as well.

Except a hand snaked through the bars one more time, and broad fingers twined with hers. Surprised, she glanced over at Abraxas to see he had stiffened with her. Every inch of the dragon vibrated, as though he were ready to kill anyone she pointed him at. Anyone who dared to hurt her.

"Maybe not everyone," she whispered, still staring into those burning eyes.

"Not everyone," he repeated.

This was troublesome. More than she had bargained for when she'd agreed to sell her soul to Margaret, but she supposed... Well. If she had more time to think about this development, she might not mind it. Not all that much, at least.

Beauty sighed. "Lorelei, I can understand why you feel that way, but you know Margaret even better than I do. Do you think she didn't have a plan in case you got caught?"

"Of course she did. But you're right, I do know her very well. Too well." Lore wrenched her gaze away from Abraxas so she could look Beauty dead in the eye. "And I know her well enough to understand that she had hoped it would all go this way. She wanted me to fail."

"She gave you all the time she could."

"You believe that if you want to. But we both know it's a lie." Lore nodded though, at least relenting so Beauty could go on. "What is it, then? What magical idea did she come up with that would save my head from hitting the ground without my body attached to it?"

Beauty hesitated, and that was the moment Lore knew she wouldn't like this plan any more than the original. It would still put her in a lot more danger than she wanted to be in. She could still die.

But she supposed it was better than waiting for her death in the dungeon.

"Out with it," Lore said when Beauty still didn't talk. "It can't be all that bad."

"It's not bad, it's just..." Beauty hesitated again.

"A mad one?" she supplied. "All Margaret's plans end up that way. It's impossible for her to think through a situation without making it worse. That's the way of the elves, I suppose. Complicated plans that must be endured by all those who are sucked into their webs."

Beauty's leather pocket wrinkled, and the pixie shoved her head out of it. With a slight squeak, the little woman illuminated the gray edges of the dungeon. She spun around in the air so quickly that she cast a light on all the prisoners, as though daylight had entered the room.

And Lorelei stared at the prisoners, who raised their arms against the sudden brightness. They were all emaciated, broken, and bruised. Not a single one of them could fight for themselves.

She knew what the pixie was trying to say. She knew how important it was that she at least try to help them, even though it felt like she was pulling herself apart to do so.

Beauty cleared her throat, eyes darting between the figures while clearly trying her best to not outright stare at them. "Margaret thinks between the three of us, we might be able to catch the King off guard. He's still considering me to be his bride, why I will never understand. But he won't choose me. I'll get close enough to steal the keys, and then I can pass those to Abraxas."

The man in question startled, as though he hadn't been prepared to be a part of this.

"You'll let Lore out," Beauty continued, nodding at the cell. "She will sneak past the Umbral Knights and you will then return to the field where he will announce his bride and Lore's death. You're the distraction, Abraxas. We need you to create some sort of scene that will keep the King busy long enough for Lore to get into position."

"I can do that." His deep voice sent a shiver down Lore's spine. "But I can't do it for very long. The Knights have weapons that can pierce through my armored scales."

"Then Lore will have to be quick," Beauty replied. "It's up to you to kill him. If that's a task you can finish."

She would like nothing more than to spill his blood. She wanted to see the red river fountain from his neck and soak into the earth of this land. It was almost as if Lore could feel that Umbra desired to devour the soul of the King. The very dirt itself wanted to feel his life force drain.

"I can," she replied.

"In that state?" Beauty looked her up and down, then glared at Abraxas. "You were supposed to heal her."

He snarled, the deep sound rumbling in his chest. "I'm a dragon, little girl, not a healer. If she bled, I could stop that. But I cannot magically make her better."

"If I had access to the moon, I could do it myself," Lore interrupted.

They stared at her with matching shocked expressions. Though Abraxas snapped himself out of it first. "That's right," he muttered. "Silverfell elves were different."

"Not different." She rolled her eyes and stared up at the ceiling. "We used what we were given."

She could feel him staring at her. As though Abraxas was trying to bore a hole through her head if she didn't look at him. What did the dragon think he was doing? He knew she was a Silverfell elf. A rarity, it seemed, although she didn't know why.

Finally, she gave in and looked back at him. The heat in his eyes, the way a muscle ticked in his jaw, it was too much.

"What?" she snapped. "Why are you looking at me like that?"

Like he wanted to break anyone who dared touch her. She didn't need that. She knew how to break a man with her fists and how to end a life with a blade. Abraxas didn't need to help protect her, nor did he need to get involved.

Though it was nice. The idea that someone wanted to help her.

"The moon can help heal you?" he asked, his voice deep.

"Yes."

He looked past her then, to the wall of stone that tunneled deep underneath the castle. Or so she thought.

Abraxas nodded, as if that settled it, and then returned his attention to Beauty, who watched him with a rather stunned expression on her face. Even the pixie didn't know what had just happened. Her glimmering light dimmed as her attention focused on what the dragon's plan was.

When no one talked, Abraxas nodded again. "I'll make sure she heals, then. And I don't need the key."

"But..." Beauty shook her head. "What are you talking about, dragon?"

"You asked me to heal her, and I said I would. So I will." He gently squeezed Lore's fingers. "I'll make sure she's ready for the moment you need her to be. She'll kill Zander."

His confidence in her burned right through any remaining discomfort or fear. He thought she could do this, and Lore knew without question that she could.

She would walk through whatever fires remained in front of her. And then she would end this.

All of it.

Beauty watched the expressions play over her face before she let out a long breath. Apparently, she'd been holding it while waiting to hear what Lore would say. "Good, good. That makes everything so much easier. After Abraxas makes his distraction, get to the dais. We'll give you the path of least resistance, but... this is our one chance, Lore."

"That's fine. It ends here." She could do this.

"Then Margaret said you're going to want this." Beauty reached behind her and apparently there was a weapon pouch attached to that leather corset because she pulled out a wicked black blade.

The waved metal had been hammered into textured strikes so as it sank into the flesh, it ripped and tore. Once pulled out of any wound, that knife would shred muscle, fat, even bone. It was a weapon made for nothing other than death.

"A grimdag?" She shook her head and released Abraxas's hand. Lore took a step away from that horrible blade. "I won't take that."

"Margaret said you would know what to do with it." Beauty seemed to understand that it was dangerous to touch that knife. She put it on the floor and kicked it over to the edge of the cell. "She also said you'd know what it meant."

Lore shook her head again. "I don't want that. Give me another knife. Any other knife."

"What is a grimdag?" Abraxas asked.

She didn't want to say. She didn't want them to know what horrible things the elves could make, like that terrible dagger lying on the floor.

But she had to. They had to understand.

She swallowed hard. "There were other elves, some that no longer live. A small group of them dug deep into the earth. They called themselves the Ashen Deep and made those blades. The grimdags are magical weapons. To kill with that is to bind a soul into the dagger for all eternity." She lifted a shaking hand to her mouth. "It's torture. Forever."

Abraxas knelt down and picked up the dagger. She didn't know what thoughts could run through his head, but he didn't hesitate. He held the blade out for her to take. Wordless.

"Aren't you afraid of what that knife can do?" she whispered, the words ragged and harsh.

"I only fear what is in my own head," he replied. Were the lines around his mouth formed from pity? "You have to do this, Lore. It would be an honor to rip him limb from limb for you. For what he has done. But you have earned the right to end this. All of it."

And wasn't that so lovely that her feral dragon wanted to give her a gift of blood and pain? Because Abraxas must know what he offered. A chance to no longer fear the night and the shadows. To end the suffering in her memories of a king beating her within an inch of her life.

She didn't want to touch that cursed weapon, but she also knew that now was the only chance she'd get. Otherwise, Zander would haunt her every step.

Her hands reached out, fingers shaking, and she closed her fingers on the blade's hilt.

Memories played through her thoughts. Of a dark skinned elf bent over an anvil, heavy hands holding a hammer that sewed a curse into the metal with every strike. She saw the faces of every person this knife had killed, mortals, men, women, even children. So many people.

The weight of that responsibility weighed on her shoulders. And when she opened her eyes again, Beauty was gone. All that remained was a dragon in front of her, waiting for her to open her eyes again.

Abraxas reached through the bars once more and wrapped his hand around hers. Around the blade. "I need you to live, Lorelei of Silverfell."

Her true name danced through her. A lick of power followed, as though him using the term gave her energy like the moon.

"Why?" she asked.

"Lady of Starlight," he murmured, then stepped so close she could count the gold flecks in his eyes. "My fire heart. Live for me, and I will lay a kingdom at your feet."

Before she could say anything else, he disappeared. Racing from the dungeon without a second glance.

A kingdom? She didn't want a kingdom.

But as she stared at the dagger in her shaking hand, she wondered if that's what she was fighting for.

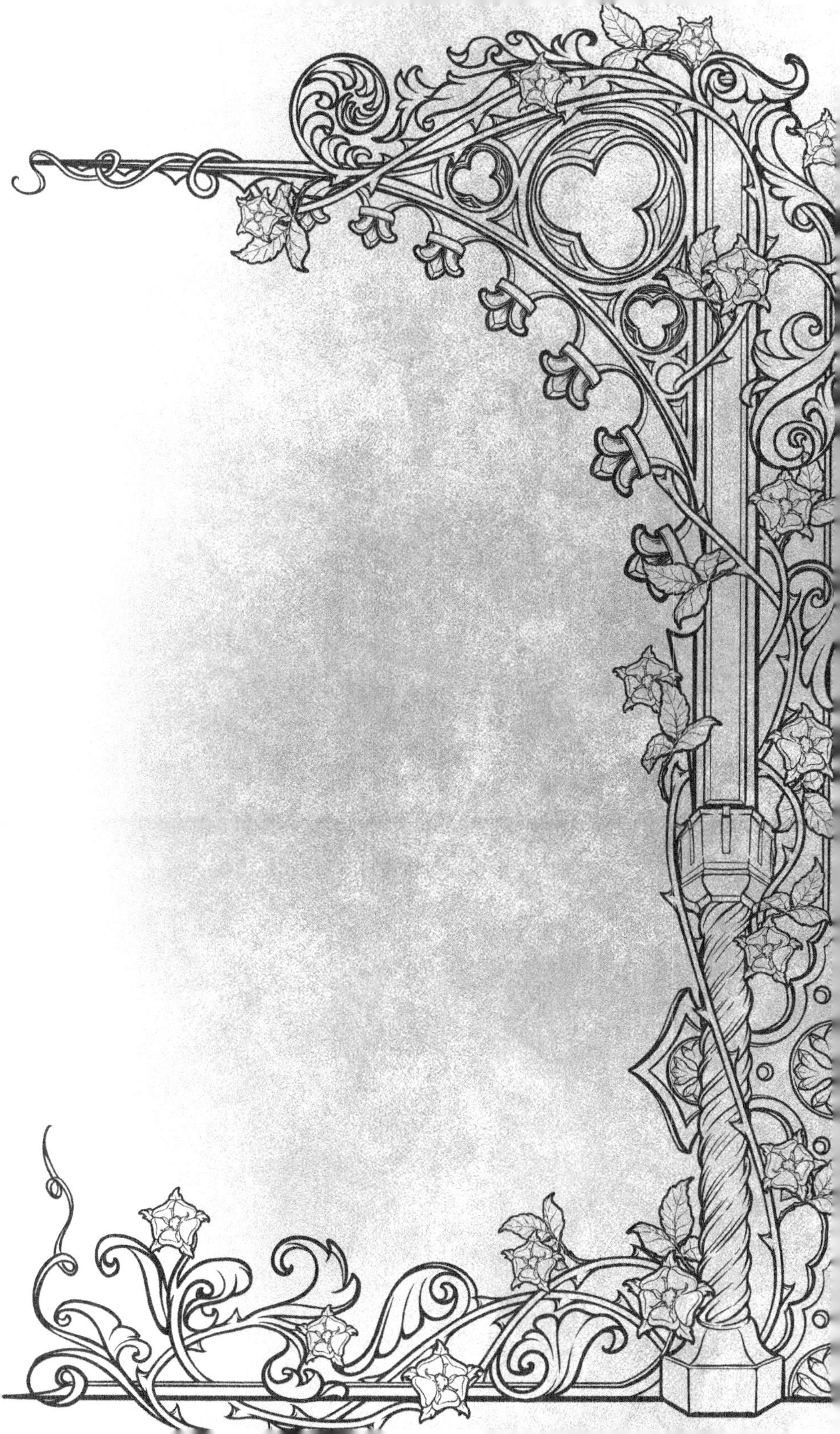

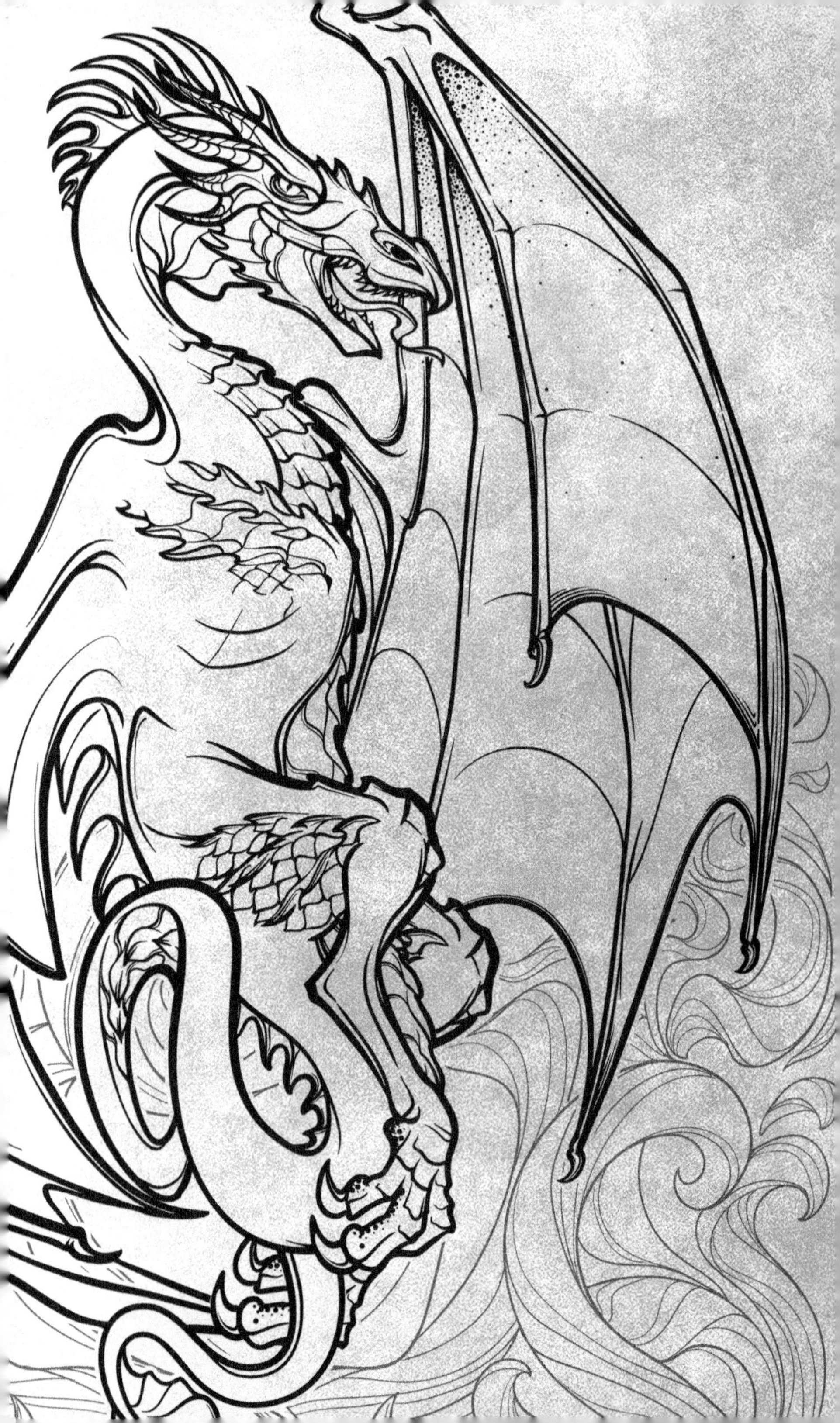

CHAPTER 33

His entire body felt... wrong. Abraxas stared down at his hands while he sat on the edge of his cliff. The melted gold waited far below him. He already knew what to do. He'd dug a tunnel down to Lore's cell and broke through the wall. She'd escape that way when she had to, and hopefully had healed enough to climb that precarious tunnel.

Now he had to wait.

The King would announce his bride. Lore would kill the King. Everything would be fine.

Except... it wasn't.

One glaring problem remained at the base of his melted gold mountain. A problem he could now see poking through the edges of the far corner. The wooden box containing the eggs would remain there for a very long time now. He didn't know when or how he would find someone to open it.

Sighing, Abraxas slid into his dragon form and glided through the air. It took only a few heartbeats for him to land beside the box, and he could almost feel the sadness of the eggs inside.

As if they knew, somehow, that he would not let them hatch any time soon. Perhaps they did. Dragons were knowing creatures like that.

He opened his mouth and let out a fountain of fire that melted the remaining gold clinging to the box. And then they were alone. Again. Just him and the two babies who should have been born by now. Who should have been with him so he could talk with them, hear their opinions and weigh their choices against his own.

Abraxas set his head down beside the box, forlornly sighing as he tried to see straight through the wooden edges. "I'm sorry. I have always made choices with you in mind, but it's not fair if I... If I abandon them all like this."

His words fell on silence at first, but then he swore he could see their outline through the box. As though the eggs were glowing with the powers of the dragons inside them.

"The dragons were always protectors first. We always sought out the other magical creatures and did what we could to keep them alive. We were there for them in the old days. I don't know when that stopped." But the urge had never left. At least not for him.

Abraxas wanted to wrap himself around these suffering souls so no one could ever hurt them again. Sure, he'd ignored that desire for a long time. He'd thought it was a passing fancy every time he brought a creature to the dungeon and told himself he didn't care.

Lore had changed all that.

She was the key that had unlocked his soul and suddenly, he remembered. He remembered the laughter of the dwarves telling their dirty jokes. He remembered smiling at the centaurs while they raced through the fields. He missed the age of magic and hated this new age of man.

"I will not stop trying to hatch you," he murmured. "I swear on my life and all the power in my body that I will find a way for you to join me in the air. We will have our days in the sun, you and I. Soaring through the clouds and sharing memories of a time long past. Give me the time to solve this mystery, to right these wrongs."

The eggs glowed even brighter. He knew deep down in his soul that these dragon children remembered their previous lives. They knew what he had to do, and they understood his choice, even if it meant they had to wait even longer.

He could only hope that was the truth. The journey he would need to take to find another warlock or magician would be long and arduous.

But perhaps if a young elf came with him, for her keen eyes, of course, then perhaps the journey wouldn't be so bad.

Sighing, he nudged the box with his nose and endured the zing of magic that sliced across his snout. "I really am sorry though," he whispered. "If I could have both of you right now, I would. But... This is the right thing to do."

Still, he didn't want to do it. A part of him hated that he was giving up on these innocent souls so easily. As though he hadn't fought his entire life to keep them safe, to bring them back. Now that he'd seen so much of the other side, though, he understood why the other magical creatures had hated him.

He tapped the box one more time with his nose, the zing of pain reminding him that no matter the path he chose, it was always going to hurt. He'd never get out of this without it hurting, and that seared across his very soul.

Abraxas stretched his wings wide and let his neck reach up to the ceiling of the cave. The deep roar that erupted from his throat was chased by fire that rained down upon him and the box. The metal lock turned bright red with heat, but it never melted. Nothing could melt it.

The call was one of rage and ruin. He let all of his anger and sadness and hatred for this place and its people pour into the sound. Let the people gathered for the King's announcement hear him. Let them tremble in fear as they realized the dragon was coming for them all.

The distraction the rebellion needed had to be one that no one could ignore. They wanted to see what a dragon could really do, and he was happy to provide them with that. After all, it had been a very long time since he'd let loose.

Abraxas beat his wings against the air and rose. The exit to the cave was large enough for him to fly through, and he sliced through the waterfall like a knife parting through a curtain. His wings felt stronger, somehow. Almost as though the idea of finally terrifying this mortal king had given his soul the power it needed to get through what would happen next.

Beauty's last words rang in his ears, the ones she'd said when she waited for him in the hall.

"If she fails, you have to burn it all down. Kill the King and everyone there."

He'd agreed, but only because there were no other words he could say to her. Of course, he agreed, knowing that he would never be able to kill the elf who had stolen his heart. He already felt the beating thrum of the mate bond in his chest. One he wouldn't ignore.

He couldn't kill Lore, no matter how much the rebellion wanted him to. If she was in the courtyard and failed, then he would do whatever it took to get her out of there alive. If that meant the King survived, then... he did.

Abraxas almost hoped that was how the plan went. The eggs would remain alive, Lore wouldn't die, he would flee with her and they'd return stronger. Together.

If only he could change the plan to that. If only his own desired outcome would fall into place, and then the rebellion wouldn't believe he'd betrayed them.

The wind rippled across his throat and around the still healing wounds on his back. The holes in his wings were barely closed, and he'd admit he was a little shaky as he flew. But he didn't think the King would want to attack him first. Not yet, at least. There was a show to be had with a dragon who had stepped out of line. This would all become another display of power. Another point in Zander's life when he could pretend that he was the good one after all.

He flew around the back of the castle and listened intently. Already the King was shouting at the audience, who listened to every single one of his words with rapt attention.

"In my attempts to find a bride, I found even more deceit! My friends. My family. There is an imposter among the brides who were sent to the castle and I will have you all know, an elf thought she could kill me!" Zander laughed and the sound was horribly cruel. "She thought she could sneak into my home, in secret, and slit my throat in my bed!"

The crowd gasped, as they should with a story like that.

"But we found her! I battled with her myself and I would have you know that the magical creatures are weak! They are nothing compared to our might. They will fall underneath my heel just as they did my father's."

Except they wouldn't. His shadow fell over the crowd, long and wide. They all cheered when they recognized the dark shape, because the dragon had always worked with the King. They thought that the dragon would battle the magical creatures with them. Surely, he would destroy their opponents with ease.

And yet, when he landed in the back of the courtyard, he glared at the King. He didn't settle next to their leader, nor did he seem to protect Zander at all. Instead, they stared at a dragon whose stomach was already bloated with fire and rage.

Zander stood on a podium with that nameless brunette who had already stepped back. She should fear the dragon more than most, he supposed. After all, she was the reason Lore was in that cell.

They'd decorated the podium with white arches overhead and wisteria falling down in purple coils around their heads. It was beautiful, a setting that would have made any woman fall over in happiness. A wedding.

The crowd of people in front of the King were dressed in their best clothing. The sun beat down on their heads, however, and drops of sweat already slid down a few temples. They would soon know what heat really felt like.

His plan was to startle everyone here. He wanted them to cry out for mercy, and not just because he stood near them. No one but the King had ever heard him speak. Abraxas knew revealing that would make Zander angry, but there was more to this than the King would anticipate.

"Mortal king," he rumbled, his words echoing across the courtyard and silencing all the humans who had cheered for him. "You will not lay a finger on that elf's head."

The silence that came after his words was deafening. Wide eyes stared first at him, then back to their king, who had placed his hand on his sword. As though that would save him. Protect him. Give him any shield or safety from the rage of a dragon.

Zander was no fool. He knew this moment would define him for the rest of his legacy, whether he lived or died. He needed the people to see him as strong and capable. As the King who faced down a dragon without fear.

But Abraxas smelled the stench of his fear.

"That's right," Abraxas grumbled, the fire burning ever hotter in his chest. "Fear me, Zander. You know why I'm here."

"I do." The King didn't disappoint. His voice raised as he called out to the crowd of people who watched them. "The greatest betrayal is one that I never saw coming. You were supposed to protect me, dragon. You were supposed to be the only person I could trust and then you fell to the whims of pleasure and the call of a pretty woman."

He was going to use this moment to condemn Lore even further. The King would make her out to be some harlot that had seduced a dragon.

Abraxas wouldn't stand for that. "She didn't seduce me, as you wish everyone to believe. You want to spread your lies and hatred so you can justify killing an innocent girl."

"Innocent? She wanted to kill me!"

"She wanted to free her people from your clutches. She wanted to set the magical creatures in this kingdom free so they weren't hunted down and thrown into a dungeon to rot." Abraxas roared the last words. "You used me as a weapon for too long, mortal king. I will not stand by any longer and watch my people die."

Zander's eyes narrowed and Abraxas knew he'd said too much. He'd given the King something that he could use, and that was...

No.

Damn it, he should have kept his mouth shut.

"Your people?" Zander repeated, cocking his head to the side as though the very words confused him. "Your people are dead, dragon. They died a long time ago, falling to the blade and the sword and magic that knocked them from the sky. Other than the two dragon eggs I have in my possession, or have you forgotten that? I'll allow you to speak your mind. I'm not so cruel that I wouldn't allow you to say your peace. But... Abraxas. If you continue like this, you already know what will happen."

A flash of a dying dragon played in front of his vision. He remembered that horrible scream and the cry of a tiny beast who had never gotten a chance to spread its wings and fly.

He would not falter. He couldn't.

Lore needed him to keep the King distracted and if Zander wanted to play all his cards like that, then he would. It would take a while for the King to summon those eggs. They had to travel a long way before the box would reach his hands.

Now, he prayed that Lore was fast. Because Zander had already lifted his hands and made the twisting motion that summoned the magician's box.

Abraxas reared back and spread his wings wide. They wanted a scene, the rebellion said. They wanted people to run screaming from the beast.

He was happy to oblige.

Opening his mouth wide, he roared into the fire that spread from his jaws. People screamed. He knew they would as soon as they saw the power that he contained. But the King didn't move. He remained right on that podium, hand still on his sword.

Did the boy really think he could battle a dragon?

When Abraxas finished, he remained reared up with his wings spread out wide around himself. He knew what picture he painted. Leathery wings and fangs that dripped with drool. Every wet slap against the ground sizzled and boiled with the heat from his chest.

Zander glared at him with so much hatred, Abraxas wondered how he hadn't seen it before. Such a potent emotion wasn't from the small amount of rebellion Abraxas had shown thus far. No. That hatred had grown for ages, and the dragon had ignored that it brewed in the chest of this child.

"You're going to battle me over a woman?" Zander snarled.

"You always wanted me to find one," he replied. "Wasn't that what you said? Come join you. Linger in the bedroom with yet another soft body. You never stopped talking about them, Zander."

"I wanted you to find someone for yourself. For a passing dalliance so you wouldn't be such a fucking prick all the time." Zander lifted his hand from his blade and pointed to the nearest Umbral Knight. "Kill him," he snarled. "I want that dragon's head on the ground in front of me. I can make another."

He couldn't, but Abraxas would not tell him that. Instead, he braced himself for the arrows and the magical weapons that the Umbral Knights would use against him.

Hurry Lore, he thought. I have little time left.

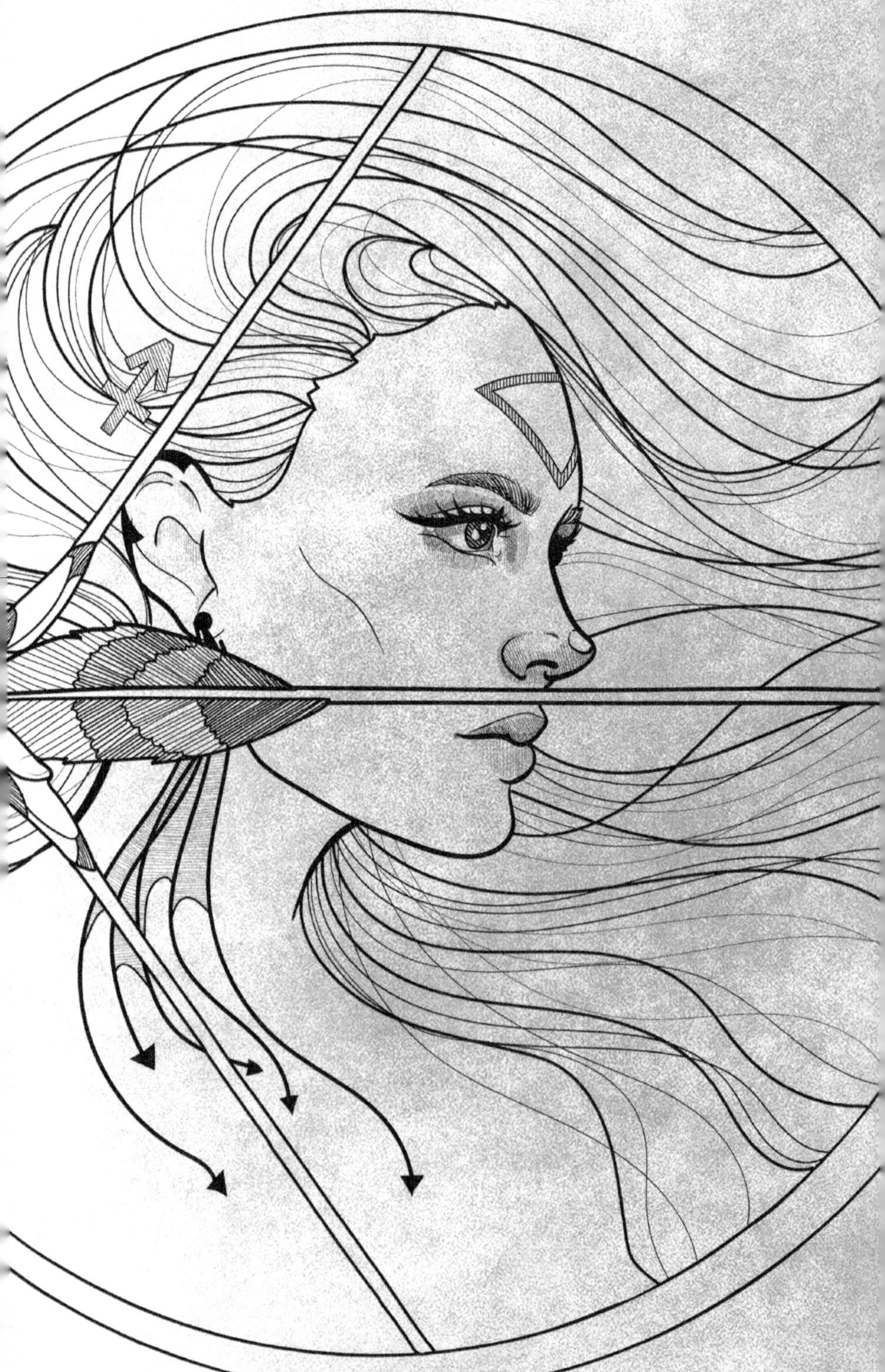

CHAPTER 34

The moonlight had filled her with more magic than she'd ever gathered. Lore didn't know if the maiden in the sky knew she needed all the help she could get, or if there was someone in the dungeon helping her. Either way, she felt almost bloated with power.

Abraxas had advised her to leave the cell closed. At least then she wouldn't let the Umbral Knights know too early that she'd escaped. So she waited until the sun just peeked out over the horizon before she climbed into the hole he'd dug.

How had a dragon done something like this? She couldn't imagine it had been easy without hands. But he'd somehow tunneled deep into the earth, enough so that the moonlight could fill her cell with welcome beams.

The hole was steep. She sank her hands into the wet earth and grasped onto the roots of plants to pull herself up and out of the strange hole in the ground. Mud clung to her skin, dotted her hair and face with debris, but it didn't matter.

Good looks weren't required for murder, after all.

Her hands crested the top of the hole and that was when she felt the knife. It pulsed against her spine where she'd tucked it into the back of her torn dress. The power nearly caused her to lose her grip and fall back into the damn dungeon. The blade sensed that death was near, and it wanted her to know how excited it was to sink into another person's flesh. To devour yet another soul that would feed it for centuries.

She shivered. Goosebumps popped out down her arms and legs even as she looked around to make sure no one saw her exit the dragon's massive tunnel. No one stood around the castle, but she'd expected that. After all, they were preparing for a feast and a royal wedding. There was much to be done.

Those poor maids were probably running about like chickens with their heads cut off. Agatha would run them ragged, that's for sure. And, of course, the Umbral Knights would cluster around their king. Preparing in the best way they could to ensure that no one got close enough for an assassination attempt.

Although, she'd already seen them fail to prevent an arrow from striking their king.

Frowning, Lore rolled to the castle wall and pressed her back against the stone. Was that assassination attempt all for show? Beauty would have known if there was someone attacking, if she worked for the rebellion. And Beauty had stepped in front of that arrow.

It made little sense. None of this worked into a path that made her mind think all this was the rebellion. Some of it was just dumb luck.

She glanced up at the ramparts and saw a few of the Umbral Knights had already stationed themselves at the top. She'd have to take those Knights out first, and then she could get a better vantage point on the wedding.

Ugh, even the word made her stomach roll. Wedding. He was going to marry that bitch of a brunette, and then he would summon the Knights as if killing a woman on your wedding day was honorable. As if that was a good show for people to see while blessing a holy union.

She hated the man. She hated him with every fiber of her soul, and that hatred flowed into the damned blade at her back. The grimdag soaked in her emotions and grew in power. It wanted to feel blood on its blade so badly, she almost could hear its voice in her head.

"Take what you want," it whispered in her mind with a voice like a crackling fire. "Take the pain and the anger and turn them upon someone else. They will fall under our blade and they will taste your pain as they fall. Let me do this for you."

She knew why the clan of elves had died making these weapons. The magic they imbued into what they made was evil. This magic had come out of so many years of pain and heartbreak. They had made this knowing that the elves were going to die.

That fear had turned their powers into something lethal, but that would turn against them at every chance it could. The grimdag didn't care who it killed or who stood in its way.

She couldn't listen to that nightmarish weapon. If she did, then perhaps she would kill more than just the King. She'd walk through the crowd of people at his wedding, the ones who would have watched her die without a single shred of pity, and she would slice their throats. Like some kind of avenging being who wanted them to see what it felt like to really hurt.

"Yes," the grimdag whispered in her mind. "Feed your hatred, girl. Let it flow through you until you see the reality of our world is bitter and cruel."

It wasn't, though. Not all of it. She remembered Goliath with his radiant smile and how he always bought tankards of ale for any mortals that saw him. Not a single one of them had reported him to the Umbral Knights. They'd always grinned, then pressed a finger to their mouth. His secret was safe. He was safe because the light of his soul spread out through the inn and they knew they could trust him.

She'd believed her entire life that the mortals were capable of being more than just life ruiners. That they had a purpose here, just like she did. That's why she'd never joined up with the rebellion.

She couldn't let that change. Like Abraxas said, she was stronger than this hatred.

Swallowing hard, she turned the blade's attention to the creatures above their heads. "Do the Umbral Knights have souls?"

The question seemed to confuse the weapon at her back. It paused, seeking out the scent of a soul above their heads. That horrible voice grated through her mind once again. "Not really. Something like a soul, but made through magic and not as tasty."

"Could you still eat it?"

It thought about her question thoroughly before answering. "Yes."

"Then I want to give you a feast, grimdag. No mortals other than the King, but I wish for you to devour the souls of those monstrous creations. Set them free or feast upon them, I don't care. They aren't really people."

At least, she hoped they weren't. The Umbral Knights had always seemed other to her. They weren't capable of thought or dreams. They didn't even react when they were ejected from their armor, as though it were merely a surprise to them, but one that they suffered through because they had to. She'd never seen a hint of emotion in their actions or reactions.

These were the things she told herself while she climbed the castle. The exterior had seen better days, and apparently the current king didn't think it was important to fix the tiny crevices or cracks that allowed a person to clamber up the sides of the stone walls. It was yet another flaw that he was incapable of understanding. Someone had to have told him that he needed to fix this?

Lore sank her fingers into the cracks and ignored the ineptitude of their king. This was all part of her plan. She would move forward with this, no matter the costs.

She would feel the disappointment later. She'd feel the guilt of taking a life when there was time for that. Until she was alone and could scream into a pillow. If she survived, that was.

Her fingers curled over the top of the first rampart and she stilled. It wasn't hard to figure out where the Umbral Knights were. Their armor always shifted and clanked, their footsteps harsh against the stone ground.

Lore waited until one was close to her, then launched over the edge of the rampart. It took all of three seconds. She landed in a crouch at the creature's feet, and then her hand wrapped around the grimdag.

The dagger knew where it wanted to go. It whipped her arm around, sinking the blade into the weak spot at the back of the Knight's knee. It dug deep through the armor until the magic of the blade touched the smoke inside the metal.

For the very first time, Lore thought she saw surprise on an Umbral Knight. It tilted the helmet down to look at her, and then it was just an empty suit of armor. Frozen in place because nothing inside it helped to animate the suit.

She froze as well. Lore stared at what she'd done and realized she didn't know how to feel remorse for a creature like this. Should she look at this empty metal contraption and wonder about the black smoke that had... what? Given it life? It wasn't alive.

None of the Knights were really living. They followed orders, and she had now freed them from that.

She didn't have time for this pity. More footsteps echoed behind her.

Pivoting, she swept her leg out while remaining in a crouch. The Knight wasn't expecting there to be someone on the ramparts, and it tripped over her leg and fell right in front of her.

The grimdag flashed in the light and pierced through the eye hole of the Knight's helmet. Sinking deep where an eye would have been, the dagger drank deeply of the dark smoke until this suit stilled.

Lore stood with the dagger held out in front of her. There would be more. She would fight until the very last breath to get to the King's wedding, but it would be a hard pressed battle. Except...

There were no more Knights around her.

"Two?" she whispered. "Why are there only two?"

Why weren't there more?

The roar of a dragon shook the air, and then she realized that Abraxas had created more of a distraction than he'd given himself credit for. He had made such a scene that all the Umbral Knights had raced from their posts to help the King. And that could only mean that they thought that Zander was in grave danger of dying.

Hadn't Abraxas said there were weapons that could kill a dragon? Worry fisted in her stomach and she ran down the ramparts, down the first set of stairs and all the way to the end that bordered the courtyard.

She saw his wings before she could see down into the courtyard. They stretched high, nearly as big as the castle itself. He was so large, but that only made him an easier target for the Umbral Knights that pointed giant crossbows at his heart.

She couldn't let them fire those. Lore burst into movement, pumping her arms and legs faster than she ever had before. The grimdag in her hand crowed with glee as it touched the first Knight. It had barely finished drinking before she whirled on the next, the one that cranked the wheel that would release the first arrow into Abraxas's side.

Another arrow fired from above her head and caught the last Knight at this stand. She looked up to see Beauty leaning precariously out a window with a crossbow in her own hand.

Beauty gestured wildly for Lore to keep moving, but... She couldn't. Her eyes found Abraxas and she could think of nothing other than the holes in his wings that leaked bright red blood. He threw his head back again, roaring with such rage and anger that her chest rattled with the force of it.

She wanted to help him. She couldn't let him die here while she tried to kill the King. Sure, it was important, but wasn't he more important than all that? Wasn't he worth saving?

A hand clapped on her shoulder and threw her forward. Lore caught herself on the edge of the stone wall before that same hand whirled her around.

Margaret hissed, "You have the grimdag, girl. Move or all of this will be for nothing."

Then the other elf whirled around and pinned a Knight between the two daggers in her hands. Margaret wrenched the blades from side to side, sawing through the Knight's helmet until it popped off and all the smoke poured out of the armor.

Her time had run out. The rebellion was here, and they would get her to the King if it was the last thing they did. But in doing so, she feared she might lose the one person who had given her back her soul.

Squeezing her eyes shut for a moment, Lore stilled the rapid beating of her heart. She took long, deep breaths. Her mind needed to be clear about what happened next. She needed to be focused and calm, just as her mother had trained her to be all those years ago.

One foot in front of the other, she turned herself from the sight of the wounded, screaming dragon. She propelled her body toward the podium where only the King could be. And when she saw him, she let all the rage come back out.

The grimdag sang in her hand. The dark sound was a funeral dirge of a King whom no one would miss. A King whose soul would taste like ash and dust.

She sprinted toward the edge of the castle walls. She ran like she'd never run before, because a dragon's pained cry echoed in her mind.

Lore reached the end of the tower. Her bare, bloody feet hit the edge, and she leapt into the air. She lifted the dagger over her head, the sun catching on the edge and sending a sparkle of light down on the King.

The woman saw her first. The brunette dropped to the ground before the King even noticed that Lore's approach was inevitable. He turned his head up to see her at the last second, and it was as though time had stopped. Their eyes met. His widened, and hers narrowed with determination.

Lore brought the knife down on his throat with a wild slice of her arm, then landed on the ground just beyond his reach. Her arms outstretched, blade in her hand, she made an easy target if he'd survived her attack.

But she turned her head to look and saw a bright line just below his jaw. It was smooth and clean, like he wore a ribbon of red around his throat. Until the blood poured out.

The King clutched the wound and made a horrible, gurgling sound. The Umbral Knights swarmed him immediately. They drew their king from the podium but didn't retreat to the castle. No, they gathered around him like a swarm of locusts and fled the castle with Zander in their arms.

The rebellion didn't rush after him. They stood on the ramparts and watched in utter silence. It was so fast. Everything had happened so quickly, and Lore still crouched on the dais trying to catch her breath.

The wing of a dragon stretched in front of her, shielding her from the eyes of the crowd and the rebellion above. She looked up into the giant yellow eye and the first tears of guilt fell down her cheeks.

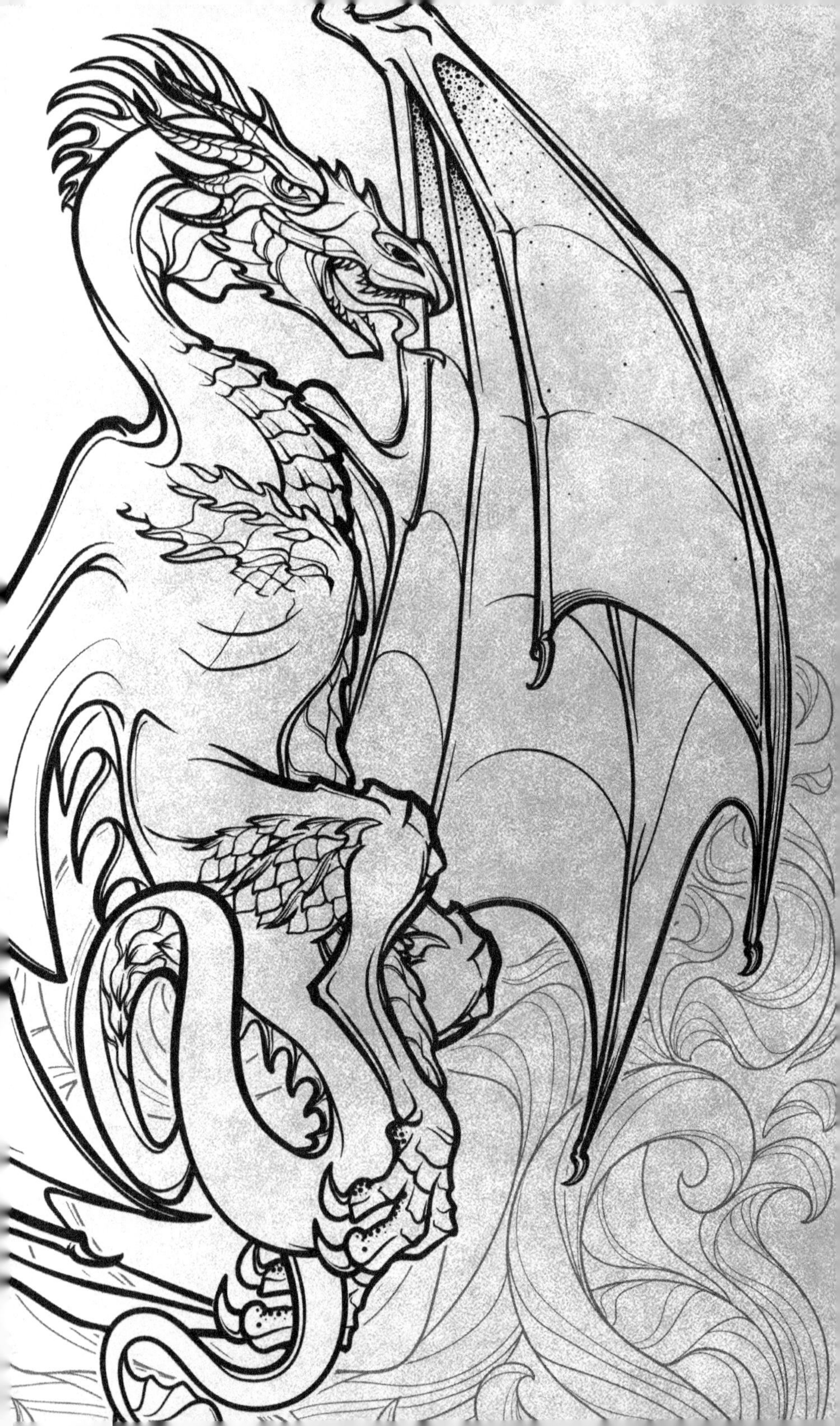

CHAPTER 35

She'd done it. Abraxas couldn't believe that she'd actually done it. Actually, he could. She'd impressed him every single day that he'd known her, but somehow, seeing her leap through the air with a dagger above her head had been beyond everything he'd imagined.

Lore was more than just a killer. She was a woman who slowly fell apart in front of him as she dropped the grimdag from her hands. And for the very first time in his life, Abraxas didn't feel like it was better to be in his dragon form. He'd never once chosen to be a mortal because it could fix a problem.

But right now, he would bring the castle to rubble if it meant he could hold her in his arms. If he could drag her against his chest and promise her that nothing bad would happen to her again. That he would take care of her. He swore it on his life and those of the eggs still buried in the gold beneath the castle.

A deep rumble shook his throat, not one of anger or rage, but of concern as he leaned over her. Abraxas checked to be sure his wing still hid her from the hundred of eyes that stared. The crowd hadn't yet made it to the exit of the courtyard, and many of them remained to see what would happen next. They'd all seen the elf who had sliced open the King's throat. They knew that their world was about to crumble before them.

He couldn't care less about their world. Their kingdom. Their people.

"Lorelei," he murmured, trying to keep his voice low so no one could hear them speak. "Are you all right?"

She sniffed hard, belaying the grief that poured through her body before she looked up at him. And he was almost broken from the sight.

Red rings surrounded her eyes, while deep purple furrows grooved underneath from lack of sleep and surviving the dungeon. Bruises and dirt covered her lovely face and he... He couldn't stand to see her like this. Not when he knew how vibrant she usually was. Lore was a pillar of strength, not this broken woman who had endured so much.

The membrane of his wing rippled as a woman slid underneath. The tall elf reminded him of the elves he'd met long ago. There were countless like her. The numbers of their warriors had been more in the past, though. This elf moved like she'd stepped out of history and hadn't lived a single day of her life in Tenebrous.

"Pull yourself together, Lorelei," she hissed. "The people are going to see you and you will need to be more than this."

"Easy, elf," he snarled. "Give her time."

"Time for what? To sink underneath the waves of guilt and convince herself that she was a killer only because I pointed her in the right direction? Never." The elf looked him up and down, clearly unimpressed with the dragon she found before her. "She has to be a figurehead of the rebellion now. She's more than just Lorelei of Tenebrous or Silverfell. All the magical creatures will want to see her. To know that she is strong. And the humans will need to fear her, or they will think an army can attack us."

"You're asking too much of a woman who just killed her king." Abraxas wanted to breathe fire on the little gnat in front of him and get it over with.

Lorelei would come with him, he'd already decided. They would go to the old forests, past the Stygian Peaks and into the whisperpines. She would stand beneath the moon every single night until she felt more like herself. Until she was strong enough to face the memories head on while he guided her through the woods.

Together, they would heal.

Together, they would start a new journey where they found a magician who could sink his magic into that box. And then they would focus on bringing about a new age of elves and dragons.

Apparently, that was not the plan the rebellion had for her.

The tall elf flattened her lips and grabbed Lorelei forcefully by the shoulders. She even ignored the low rumble from Abraxas as he warned her not to touch what wasn't hers.

"Lorelei," she said, shaking Lore's shoulders. "Pull yourself together. Now."

Lore let out one more hiccup before nodding firmly. "I am. I am together."

"You are not. I will not stand this any longer, and neither would your mother. You are a Silverfell elf. You do not cry at the loss of a villainous soul. The time of victory is now, not mourning." The tall elf shook her one last time before releasing her. "They are expecting you to say something."

"I can't."

"You can, and you will. Your duty is to give them a reason to believe there will be more. A single elf did not kill the King. Our hatred of him, our pain and anguish and suffering, that was what led to the King's death. Now is the time to give them a spark to light the fires."

So that was the rebellion's plan. After all this, they wanted someone to lead the charge so that more would join their ranks.

Abraxas knew Lore had come to the same conclusion as he did. She looked up into his eyes and he saw the sadness there. He saw her suffering and the way she wanted to leave this place. But also the knowledge that she couldn't. Not yet.

Lore reached out a hand and touched his nearest warm scale. "Abraxas, let them see me."

"Are you sure?" He angled his head so he could watch every movement. Every flick of her eyes and every shuddering breath she inhaled. "We don't have to do this."

"Because you'll fly me off into the sunset?" A soft smile graced her face before she sighed. "Our life cannot be that, Abraxas. You know there is no escaping the path we've been thrust upon."

"You are Lorelei of Silverfell, and I am a dragon." He bent his head low and gently nudged her with the tip of his nose. "Nothing and no one tells us what to do."

And if the look in her eyes didn't rip his heart out of his chest, he didn't know what it did. She grinned at him with all the trust of a woman who knew he would destroy the entire world to see her smile. That was the first time she'd ever given him that look, and now Abraxas knew he'd stop at nothing to see it again.

"Move your wing. It's time for me to let the world know that magical creatures are not dead. And that we are not going anywhere." Her palm eased over his nose as she said the words.

He hesitated for a brief moment, but then he moved his wing.

She walked out of the shadow of the dragon and stood before all the mortal nobles who trembled before her. The sun outlined her silhouette, catching in the glimmering gold of her hair. Bright blue eyes, still filled with tears, watched the mortals as they slowly approached her. She was covered in dirt and grime. Her dress ripped at the shoulder and sagging over her chest, while the rest of it had turned into a moth-eaten rag hanging off her muscular form.

She stood strong before them. Shoulders back, jaw set, eyes staring out at the rolling hills of Umbra on the other side of the castle. This was not a weak woman who had endured a lifetime of hardship.

This was a queen.

Lore licked her lips, standing in front of these mortals as a woman who had gone through hell and back.

"The King was right," she started, her words too loud in the silence. "I am an elf. And perhaps I came here expecting to kill him. But you have to understand, we have been dying for so long."

One of the men in the crowd lifted his fist and cried out, "For good reason! You murdered our king!"

A few others murmured their agreement, although they mostly looked at Abraxas in fear. The looming dragon over the young elf would make sure no one harmed her. Even if they were foolish enough to try.

"I don't expect you to understand," Lore replied. "You haven't looked at your children and wondered if they would live through the winter.

You haven't hidden your features your entire life, so that someone didn't try to harm you. You haven't lived through the moment where someone noticed you were different and then had to hold your breath, wondering if they were going to call for the Umbral Knights. Every night you put your head on your pillow, you don't sleep with nightmares of clanking armor and a sudden piercing pain through your heart."

Surprisingly, no one in the crowd said anything after that. They listened to her, and maybe that was the image of this broken woman still standing in front of them. Her swollen eyes and the cuts on her jaw were easy to see. And yet she was alive.

"For years, we have been tucked away from your sight. Forced to live in the shadows and in hiding, hoping that no one found us. But we are still here." She whispered the last words, as though she was still frightened of saying them. "We never left."

Margaret stepped up beside Lore and put her hand on her shoulder. With that movement, all the others in the rebellion stepped up to the edge of the ramparts as one. They stared down at all the mortals who looked up at them with fear in their eyes. As they used to in the old days.

"We did not want to fight," Lore said, this time with more power than before. "We did not want to battle or kill your king. But we spent a generation begging for you to see us and to help. No one did. You left us to drown and now you are angry that we survived."

Eyes widened. Hands touched hearts in the crowd. Abraxas could smell their fear and the hot stench of their guilt.

The brunette woman, the one he'd honestly forgotten about, stumbled in front of the crowd. She held her hands up, pleading with the other mortals. "Listen to me! She's lying. She's always lied. Killing the King was her plan from the beginning, and I caught them. I was the one who found her and the dragon entangled in each other's arms, and the King was going to marry me! I will lead you all in the right direction—"

The tall elf snapped her fingers and two of the rebellion archers climbed down the walls. They grabbed the young woman underneath her arms and dragged her away. Although she kicked and screamed the entire time.

Lore watched the young woman fight with dark, stormy eyes. Apparently, there would be words between those two. Soon, but not just yet.

"The battles are only just beginning," Lore continued. Her words were tired, already exhausted from the fighting that she would be forced to partake in. "I need you all to return to your homes, to every corner of Umbra, and you will tell this story. You will tell everyone of the elf who killed the King. You will whisper into the shadows so that the magical creatures will come here. To me. To the rebellion. They will be safe here."

"Safe?" a woman shouted from the depths of the crowd. "This is our castle! The King's successor will take his place."

And just like that, sharpness returned to Lore's words. Her eyes narrowed and her shout sliced through the crowd like an arrow. "Not anymore. This is our castle now. The home of the magical creatures who lived here for centuries before you thought you could walk upon our graves. Let it be known, mortal. The castle of Umbra is ours."

A cheer erupted from the ramparts. All the rebellion members threw their hands in the air, jabbing at the sky with their weapons as they shouted their approval.

The mortals trembled before his half elf and Abraxas had never been more proud than in this moment.

His little fire heart had grown wings.

Once the cheer stilled, Lore nodded at the rebellion members, who stood beside the gates. They slowly opened the courtyard so all the mortals could leave, but not without one last word from the elf who had killed the King.

"Ready yourselves," she called out to the retreating nobles. "The magical creatures of this realm are preparing to cut out the poison. If you are part of that venom, we will slice you from the body of our land. We will let the sun rise!"

The rebellion repeated her words, chanting, "Let the sun rise!"

He could only imagine the fear those mortals felt as they fled the castle. They would go home and tell her story. Then, they would likely return here with armies to battle for the right to their beloved castle.

Lore was correct. The battles had only just begun, and they would get infinitely worse before they got better. But for now, they could all relax. They could rejoice that the first, and arguably most difficult, victory had been won.

When the last mortal disappeared, he let his power drift away. Returning to the mortal form he had once hated so that he could finally pull her into his arms.

By the time he was a man again, Abraxas found Margaret deep in whispered conversation with Lore.

"Listen to me," the woman hissed. "That was not a clean kill. There is no way to know for certain that we have finished this. You will stay inside the castle with me until I figure out where we go from here."

"I have no interest in staying here," Lore replied. "I want to go back to my little apartment and back to the life I left."

"You want to steal again? You want to go back to that dirty hovel and live in poverty?" Margaret laughed, but the sound was cruel. "You know

I won't let you do that."

Abraxas could sense the fight in Lore long before she raised her fists. If he let these two elves continue arguing, then he would never get a few moments alone with the young woman who had so captured his attention.

And he found he was tired of quarreling. They'd already done so much of that.

Stepping in between them, he cleared his throat. "If I might offer another option?"

Margaret blinked at him. "Excuse me? What are you even doing here, dragon?"

He ignored her question and turned to Lore. "If you would stay here for a while, Lore, there is much I would like to discuss with you. I have... questions."

"Questions?" she asked, her eyes a little too big. "What kind of questions?"

"Ones that need answering." He should keep his hands to himself, but he couldn't. Abraxas reached out and cupped her jaw, feeling the rough edges of her wounds against his calloused hands. "I think you're the only one that can answer them."

Oh, if she kept staring at him like that, then he'd never be able to leave this place. He'd fall onto his knees in front of her and place kisses to every wound, every bruise, every single spot on her body that needed his attention.

And then he'd start all over again.

She cleared her throat, cheeks blushing a pretty red color. "Perhaps I can stay for a little while. I don't really know where to go anymore, I suppose."

"Good," he whispered. Abraxas leaned down slightly, just enough to inhale her scent. "I had hoped you might agree."

Margaret sighed, and the sound interrupted their moment. "Just get her clean, dragon. There's much we have to do and we don't have time for her to second guess all this. Tomorrow. We'll all talk tomorrow."

He replied with nothing more than a grunt. How was he supposed to rip his gaze from this lovely young woman who had captured his heart?

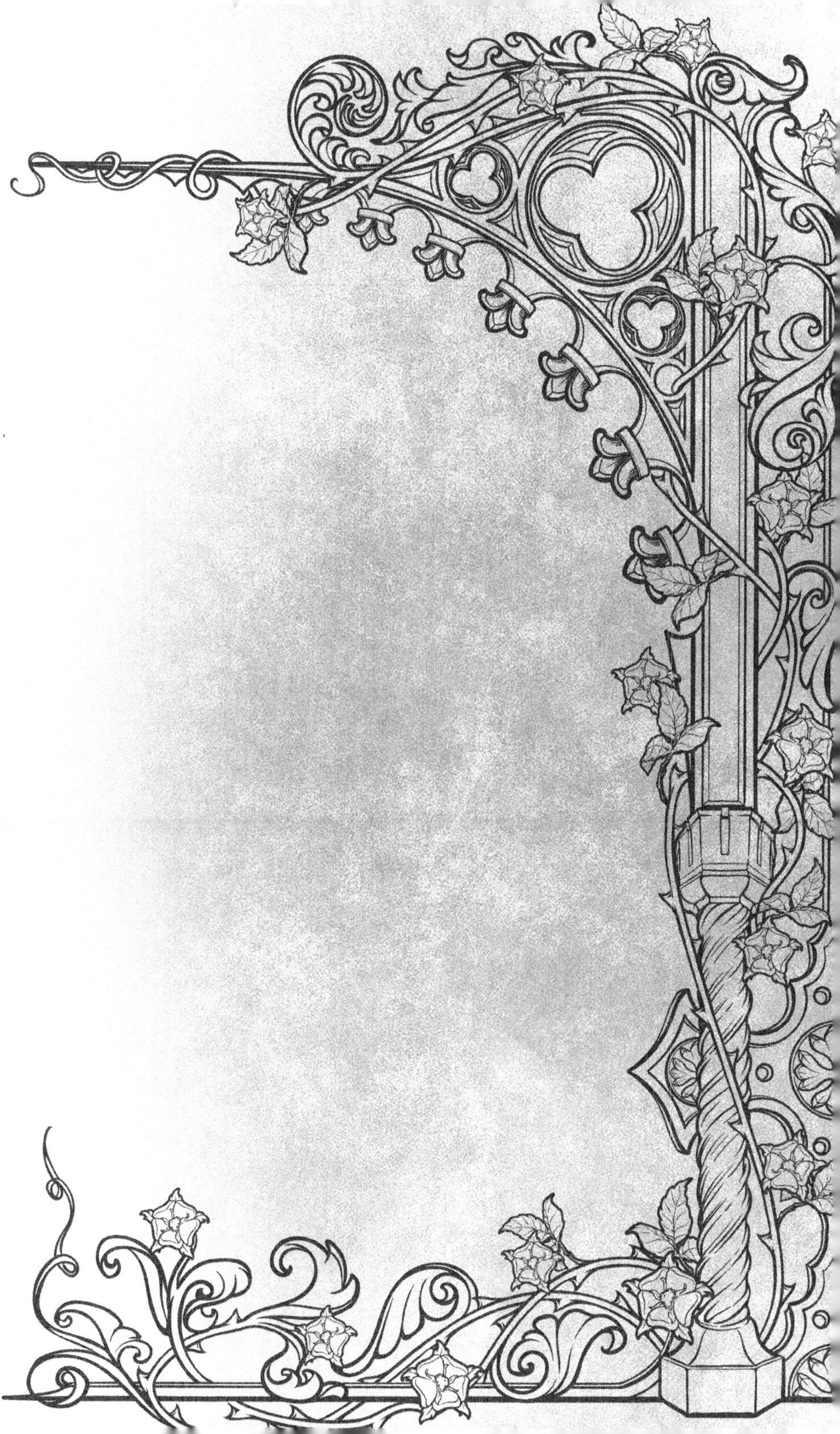

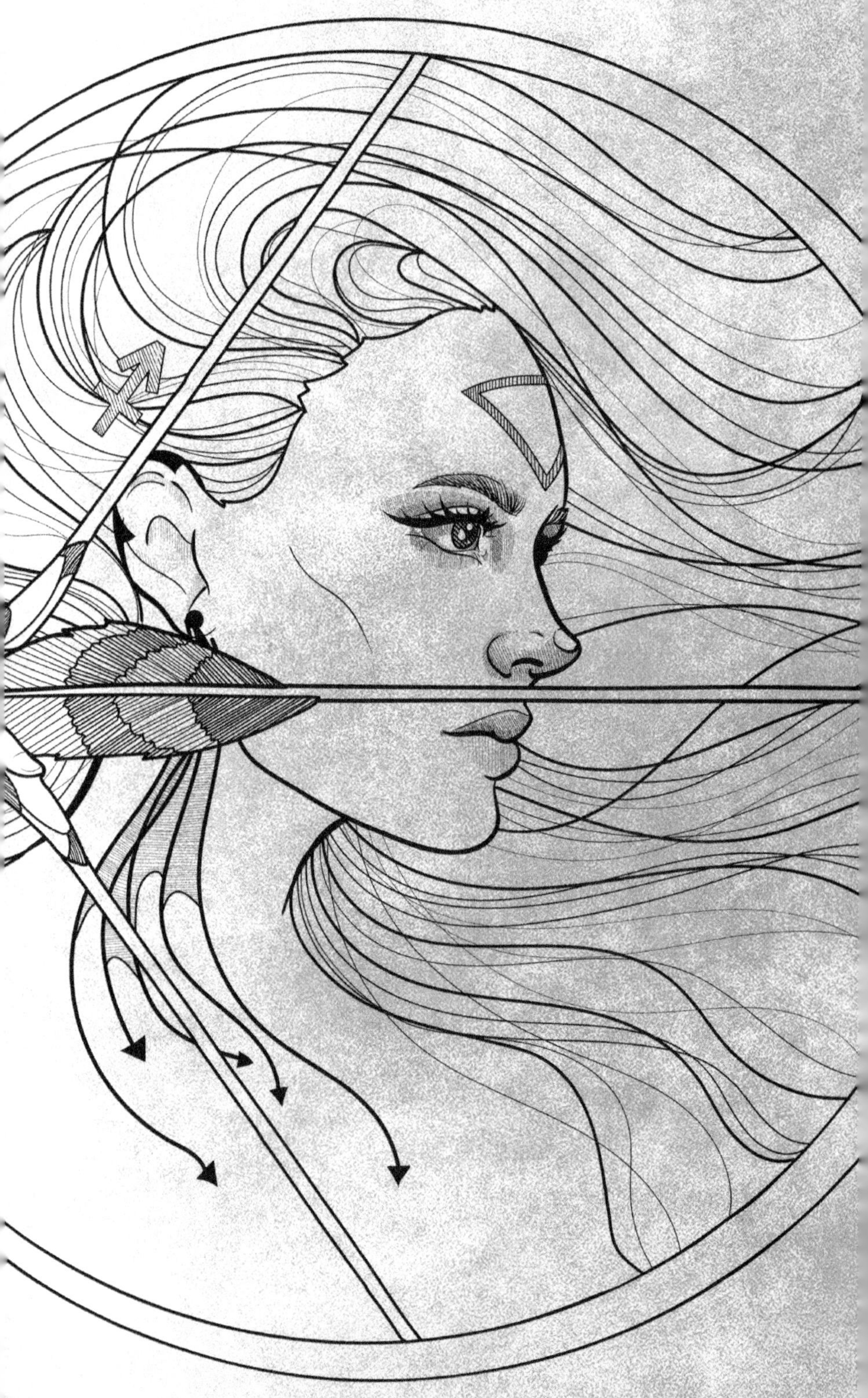

Chapter 36

Lore trailed after Abraxas out of the courtyard under the promise that he would bring her back to the castle soon. But first, he wanted to make sure that she was in one piece and no, Margaret could not send anyone with her. He was a dragon, and if anyone attacked them, he would eat them.

Margaret argued hard. But eventually, even the leader of the rebellion knew that she had met her match. Abraxas would not bend. He would not yield, and she would have to let them go.

Thankfully, Lore didn't have to say a word. And she feared what would have happened if she said anything, because she had a feeling she might have simply screamed.

One foot in front of the other. That's all she had to do.

They were about a ten-minute walk outside of the castle when Abraxas turned to her. He held his hands out at his sides, stretching them toward her as though he were going to touch her face, but then letting them drop to his sides again.

He battled something. She could tell that. He opened his mouth, closed it, then shuffled his feet in a step closer to her.

"What?" she asked, her voice filled with exhaustion. "What is it?"

He let out a long groan before grumbling, "I hope you forgive me for this."

He lunged forward, almost too fast for her to see, and scooped her up into his arms. Abraxas buried his face in the side of her neck, holding onto her with a shaking grip. His lips pressed to her pulse. Not in a kiss, but as though he wanted to feel that she was alive against his mouth.

Oh, this man. This sweet, kind dragon who had been used by the worst of people.

He'd given up so much to help her. More than she ever had any right to ask.

Lore wrapped her arms around his neck and let him hold all her weight. "I'm sorry," she whispered in his ear. "I'm so sorry for what you had to do."

"You shouldn't have wielded the blade. It should have been me," he said at the same time.

Guilt bounced between them both, rolling into anxiety that pressed against her neck. She couldn't breathe through it. Through the realization that she'd killed again, and that the knife was torturing the King right now. That she'd forced this dragon to give up his chances of ever having other dragons in the world just so they could get rid of a corrupt ruler.

Now there would never be dragons in this realm again.

A choked sob caught in her mouth. She tried hard not to let him know she was crying, but...

"Oh, Lore," he whispered.

His hands slid down her back, and he palmed the back of her thighs. Abraxas guided her to wrap her legs around his waist and then he took off for the forest. Slow, measured steps brought them deep into the heart of the woods. Until she could hear nothing other than the soft chirp of birds and the sound of his breath.

Sunlight turned the forest into gold and emerald. Mossy outcroppings grew up the surrounding trees, and then Abraxas sank to his knees in the moss.

He just held her. Their hearts slowed, beating together until the guilt eased from her soul. She drew back from his embrace, still seated on his thighs while his arms held her steady around her back.

"I'm sorry," she repeated. "You shouldn't have had to make that decision for me. I thought... I thought you wouldn't..."

Abraxas touched a tear that ran down her cheek, following it from her eye all the way to her jaw. "You thought I wouldn't save you?"

"You had good reason not to."

"Lore..." Her name on his tongue was a whispered hymn. "You have etched your name on my soul. What kind of world would this be if you were not in it? Lady of Starlight. My Fire Heart."

"What does that mean?" she asked.

"Fire heart? It is the way a dragon names a person who was born in the wrong skin." He tucked a strand of hair behind her ear, fingers lingering in the tangles. "You are half elf, but with the soul of a dragon. I knew that the first moment I saw you."

"The first time we met?" Lore smiled at the memory. "You didn't like me in the woods."

"I did. I liked you too much." He frowned, tiny wrinkles appearing between his eyes. "You nearly suffocated me with maddening hunger. The mere sight of you ruined me, Lore. I didn't know how to be or live, and that is not something I am accustomed to."

How was she supposed to respond to that? How did one honor a dragon in such a way?

"I..." Lore swallowed hard, wishing she knew how to say pretty words. How to explain that he made her heart feel like it would burst just by looking at him. "I..."

Abraxas grinned, and the expression was blinding. "Lore, you're glowing."

She gasped and looked down at her arms. She was indeed glowing. Her skin lit up like a thousand stars had exploded in her veins.

Hesitantly, she smiled at him. "I am."

"For me?" he asked, but he should have already known the answer to that.

Oh, she didn't want him to think otherwise. Lore wasn't a woman of words, though. She'd never been able to explain how she was feeling or why she was feeling.

She slid her hands into his hair at the back of his neck. With a soft sound, Lore pressed her lips to his. His hands flexed at her waist, tucking into the indent where her ribs met hips. And this was... more. More than any kiss they'd ever shared before.

She could tell the instant everything changed. His hands gripped her a little too tight. The hitch in his breath as his chest swelled. Where she had been the one to kiss him first, now everything changed. He heated underneath the palms of her hands until it was almost uncomfortable to touch him.

His large hand shifted up her ribcage, tracing the outline of her body, gently lingering over bruises that eased beneath his fingers.

He kissed her like a starving man. One who had prayed in the darkness for a last meal and she was what he desired most.

Teeth nipping at her bottom lip, he begged her to open up to him. To let him devour her as only a dragon could. She should be afraid. She should fear him unraveling all the dark parts of her soul, but she... didn't.

Instead, she bit back. Lore caught his lip between her teeth, biting a little too hard. He made a guttural sound deep in the back of his throat, hands spasming against her sides.

This.

This was what she had been waiting for.

She drew back for breath, but then couldn't stop looking at him. Her dragon.

He might not be the most handsome man in the world. He had scars and a history that could never be forgiven. But he was real, and he cared for her.

That was terrifying. And lovely. And horrible. And wonderful. All at the same time.

"What is it?" he asked. "Why are you looking at me like that?"

"I just... I don't know what this means. For us. For..." Lore struggled to find the right thing to say. "What do you want from me, Abraxas?"

"I hope the same thing you want. Lore, for a dragon..."

She wished she knew what he was going to finish that sentence with. Branches behind them snapped and cracked, then Beauty burst into the mossy glen. Breathing hard, eyes wild.

She stilled the moment she saw them tangled in each other's arms.

Cheeks bright red, she spun around until her back was to them and stared up at the sky. "I'm sorry. I'm so sorry to interrupt. I know you've both earned a few moments to yourselves. Gods know we all could use a few moments with the ones we love."

Love?

No, that wasn't right. That wasn't what this was, or Lore absolutely would have known. It was too much to say a word like that.

But Abraxas's eyes burned ever hotter. As though Beauty had said what he wanted to say, and now that the words were free, it made his feelings even stronger. She stared into his eyes and swallowed hard. Was this...

What had he been about to say?

Beauty continued, as though she didn't realize the two people behind her were breathing hard for a much different reason. "The King is alive. Margaret sent a raven after the Umbral Knights and they managed to keep him alive. Somehow. Black magic, maybe? We aren't sure."

The words burned through whatever feeling she had for Abraxas. Lore's breath caught in her throat and she repeated the words slowly. As though they couldn't be real.

"The King is alive?"

FIRE HEART

The story continues in Bright Heart, preorder today!

ACKNOWLEDGEMENTS

This book wouldn't be what it is right now without the help of a few special people who really put in more hours than they needed to. Nic, Bego, and Denise, you three were rockstars. When I needed you to jump in on a weekend even to help beta read and edit this book, you were all more than happy to do so. I don't know where I'd be without you ladies, but I know it wouldn't be where I am right now.

And then there's my prince charming, my pain in the ass, and my wonderful fiance who regularly gives me the inspiration to write all these incredible stories. Because of you, I know how to write a romance that makes people swoon. That's all you, baby. I love you lots and lots, forever and always.

To my family, thank you for enduring my neverending conversations about books, people that aren't real, and stories that have nothing to do with real life. Love you mom and dad, you two... you made me who I am today. And I'm forever thankful.

ABOUT THE AUTHOR

Emma Hamm is a small town girl on a blueberry field in Maine. She writes stories that remind her of home, of fairytales, and of myths and legends that make her mind wander.

She can be found by the fireplace with a cup of tea and her two Maine Coon cats dipping their paws into the water without her knowing.

For more updates, join my newsletter!
www.emmahamm.com